Frank P. Seudo

WHAT IF...

FLAT EARTHERS WERE RIGHT?

Independently Published

WHAT IF... FLAT EARTHERS WERE RIGHT?

First independently published by Frank P. Seudo in Hong Kong in 2022

579288afe77dffc725130b00801796105fd5fdbf761a0834fd8a7f0f0fe05704

This is a work of fiction. Names, characters, places, and incidents are the products of the author's imagination or are used fictitiously. Any resemblance to actual events, locales, or persons, living or dead, is entirely coincidental and hilariously unfortunate. The opinions expressed by the characters and the narrator should not be confused with the author's.

International Standard Book Number. 978-988-76548-0-3

10838143d09f61ebb8eb84d8597c12d1aae421a4275c4b0027deb160036986da

Chapter 1

Thursday is the worst.

Just as he gulped down the third instant coffee since dinner, the PMD (an acronym that in NASA could stand for (1) Productivity Monitoring Device, which received tremendous support from management before launch, triggered an even more overwhelming outrage upon rollout, got taken offline on its very launch day and subsequently licensed out to the Wall Street banks for keeping tabs on their staff; (2) Please More Damn, an organization-wide initiative aimed to promote empathy with co-workers; or simply (3) the job title of Project Management Director, which was applicable in this case) repeated his favorite refrain for the nth time this evening.

Smith Robin, who had quitted his job as a senior business consultant and joined NASA three months ago, always not so secretly wished this phrase would catch on and become a thing. He dreamed that it would someday become his legacy and the history book of Corporate America would forever remember him as the visionary who coined the phrases "Dream big and talk bigger," "Thursday is the worst" and "Fake it then you won't have to make it." And yet, it never caught on, to both his dismay and surprise. His surprise was not entirely unfounded, considering that people do have an inexplicable tendency to set deadlines for assignments, settlements, enrollments, installments, shipments, payments, repayments, accounting treatments and accounting adjustments on the last working day of a week, while having a much more explicable tendency to *not* plan their working week ahead and therefore have to pull an all-nighter the day before. If the Friday in question happens to be the last day of the month and the month in question the last month of the quarter, then truthfulness of "Thursday is the worst" will be raised to the power of four. And this was precisely the situation that Smith found himself in. Five hours sixteen minutes before the submission deadline of the quarterly budget plan to whoever would read it.

Since he always prided himself a big-picture guy with a detailed oriented mindset, Smith had developed a high-level idea of to whom the budget would be submitted. *Some kind of federal agency that is paid by the federal budget to review budgets, I suppose.* In other words, he had no idea. But this was the least of his concern at the moment. His biggest concern was to get his boss to sign off version 13.2 of his draft plan.

Thursday is the worst, he repeated to himself, for the nth + 1 time.

As if to wake him up from self-pity, the notification bar on Smith's desktop reminded him that the tollgate meeting with Miranda Lin was in fifteen minutes. Smith quickly did a last-minute touch-up on his slides to highlight changes he had made since the last morning huddle and double-checked that he had addressed all Miranda's comments from the Wednesday touch-base call.

That should kill it.

Having physically patted himself on the back, he sent over the presentation deck, put on a nice shirt (yes, he was shirtless until now), dialed in, and greeted his boss over the webcam.

"Give me another minute, I'm still going through it," said Miranda before Smith had a chance for chit-chat.

Miranda Lin was many things: the youngest Director of NASA, a bureaucratic nightmare, the hell gate for allowances, a fan fiction writer in the vampire romance genre. She also happened to be a speed reader tested at eight hundred words per minute. It didn't take her long to skim through the budget plan and start doling out her feedback.

"That was some pretty good work, Smith. You have basically addressed all my comments from our last call—"

Oh no, thought Smith, *it's not good. She is sandwiching me, again.*

The ten years he had spent in management consulting had equipped Smith with a very acute sense of detecting subtext, bullshit, lies and a variety of speech shenanigans such as the word sandwich, the recipe for which was two slices of patronizing sugarcoat and a big chuck of critical feedback.

"... except for one."

For both dramatic effect and practical purpose, Miranda quickly drew a deep breath before howling.

"WHICH PART OF 'I CAN'T SELL THIS UP' DO YOU NOT UNDERSTAND!?"

Miranda's voice echoed throughout the office of PMO (an acronym that could, again, stand for multiple things in NASA, including (1) Pluto Memorial Officer, a duty assumed by a randomly selected staff member from the Public Communication Department, whose sole mandate was to organize social events on the Pluto Demoted Day, (2) Perspective Manipulation Overhead, an expense item abusively used by Rounding Operations to justify otherwise questionable outlays, or simply (3) Project Management Office).

Yelling at a colleague certainly was against the policies and guidelines of PMD (standing for Please More Damn in this context), but Miranda found it the only way to get her message across.

After taking a quick scan at the office to make sure no one was around to witness his humiliation, Smith began to explain himself.

"Ma'am, this budget plan is totally in line with the guiding principles of federal budgeting, supports all of our strategic initiatives, and its year-to-year growth rate won't attract too many questions in Q&A." Smith stopped doing his weird hand gesture and did a few clicks with his mouse. "Just now I shared with you on screen a mapping between our budget plan and the three-year strategy roadmap. As you can see—"

"Yes, I certainly can see, but this is not the problem I have with your plan."

Oh my god, thought Smith, *please don't do the ask-everyone-in-the-room-what-is-the-problem thing. It is so demeaning and annoying. Everything I guess it right, they just re-phrase the problem statement to make it look like I don't understand the problem, although in this case, I really don't understand the problem.*

"The problem is you are cutting too big a slice for the Round Ops, and it will make us look bad in the next G12 conference."

G12 referred to the twelve countries that had independent capability to put satellites on orbit, namely China, France, India, Iran, Israel, Japan, New Zealand, Russia, South Korea, the United Kingdom, the United States and Ukraine. Despite the reportedly successful launch of *Kwangmyŏngsŏng-3 Unit 2* in 2012, North Korea never became part of the G12 because the satellite was in fact shot down before attaining orbit and since then the Japanese satellite *Yamato Go* had been feeding signals to the command center in Pyongyang on *Kwangmyŏngsŏng-3 Unit 2*'s behalf. To this day, it is still unclear if North Korea ever figured out what truly happened to its enchanted *Kwangmyŏngsŏng-3 Unit 2* and its successors, which all met the same fate.

Bringing up G12 finally struck Smith why his budget plan was at an impasse. It was all about optics. How much did China spend on Round Ops last quarter? Less than five million dollars. How about Russia? Just two million dollars. But according to his budget, the U.S. would be spending eight hundred million dollars to "round off" the Earth in the next three months alone. Admittedly, it still accounted for less than 4% of the NASA budget, but when compared to other G12 member states it would seem like the U.S. had a problem in keeping its people in line.

"Ma'am, I got it," said Smith slowly, resuming his weird hand gestures. "But we do have a need to reserve more resources for our Rounding Operations task force, or else it would eat into the pool of small-scale project spending."

"And you think I was not aware of that?" retorted Miranda, who couldn't help but get all worked up again. "This afternoon alone I had to approve two unplanned spending items for Round Ops. First for this kid in Florida who is going to measure Earth's curvature by shooting laser beam across a river. To 'bend' his results, our guys will need to instantly boil – and cover it up afterwards – the midsection of the river such that the steam will distort the laser's path. And then there is this lady in Texas who just bought a gyroscope to prove that there is *no* angular rotation of Earth. For flat's sake, I had to send a Round Ops team down there and pull an Ocean's Twelve on her house. You know, literally jacking up her house and rotating it fifteen degrees per hour. They are still doing it now as we speak. And when their team lead asked me an hour ago when they can go home, I don't know what to tell him. We can only pray that she will give up on proving the Earth is flat and goes on to pretend she never did this little experiment."

"True, the flat Earth movement has indeed got some momentum recently and increased the demand for Round Ops' services," said Smith, conscious that he was simply stating the obvious and didn't add any value. It was because only a small part of his brain at that time was directing his vocal organs to churn out those words. The majority of Smith's brain cells were now racing to find a solution to the dilemma between the political need to keep Round Ops spending in check and the threat posed by the flatees, a derogative term initially red-flagged but eventually approved by NASA's HR for colloquially referring to the flat Earth believers.

If there is anything – really, anything at all – Smith had learnt from the hundreds of hours he had spent in meetings, workshops, conferences and strategic off-sites, it is that the best way to solve a problem is always do one of the following: delay or be vague. Delay is undoubtedly a popular approach, hence the wide array of business language to its effect, such as "Let's park this item for further deliberation," "Why don't we take this offline," "Remind me to circle back to this," and "My secretary will pencil another block on your calendars for it." Unfortunately, with less than five hours before the deadline, Smith could clearly see that being vague was the only way out.

It felt like an eternity, but in fact less than a second went by since Smith last spoke. Nevertheless, it was more than enough for him to find the right words to say what he had to say.

"Let's re-structure our value propositions by consolidating the projected expenditure under initiatives that are tangentially related but with similar core competency. That way, we can re-vitalize the marketability of our ask, piggy-back on the goodwill from previous success, and incentivize the stakeholders to get on board. Moving forward, when we socialize it among the G12, as long as we only paint them a thirty-thousand-foot view and not take a deep dive, we will be coming out on top. Sounds like a quick win?" (Translation: rename the budget items and do not bring up Round Ops in the G12 conference.)

As an accomplished scholar who had won NASA Spelling Bee twice, Miranda was of course familiar with techniques used for identifying falsehood, tautology and sophistry, but what Smith said was something else. It didn't quite seem right, but at the same time Miranda was hard pressed to pinpoint what was wrong about it.

After stealing a quick peek at her watch, Miranda made a decision and unmuted her microphone to speak.

"Why don't we take a short break and re-group in fifteen minutes?"

* * *

A street across Miranda's humble house in Maryland, agent A set a timer for fifteen minutes and took off his earphones. He exchanged a look with agent B and quietly slid his digital watch and transcript to her. Without saying a word, he rose from his chair, walked past the window where one could see Miranda's dimly lit study, and crash-landed on the couch.

Chapter 2

Fun fact #1: Almost 99% of the private jets on the planet Earth only fly across the Northern Hemisphere over their entire lifespan. All of their airspeed indicators (ASIs) have been modified by Round Ops to overstate their airspeed by 25%. That is, whenever the ASI tells you the plane is flying at 800 km/h (or 497 mph for those who refuse to catch up with the rest of the world), it is lying to your face when actually travelling at 640 km/h (or 397.7 mph). Similarly, the remaining 1% all unwittingly have their ASIs modified to downplay their speed by exactly 30%. As a result, the flight times of travelling across the Northern and Southern Hemispheres are in proportion and do not betray the fact that landmass in the Southern Hemisphere are much more scattered apart than they are shown in a conventional map (and vice versa for Northern Hemisphere).

Fun fact #2: Winston Kanshū, the youngest winner of Japan Academy Award for Best Director at the age of thirty, once commissioned an actual atomic bomb to be built for shooting the atomic bombing of Hiroshima. Despite his success in securing enough funding from domestic investors, the project was eventually turned down because the western film distributors deemed it "culturally insensitive."

Fun fact #3: Kane Shotto Studio, founded by Winston Kanshū, reportedly has purchased from Walt Disney Pictures the rights to adapt the computer-animated film Planes *into a live-action movie. The movie is rumored to be the first of a trilogy depicting a business jet's quest for vengeance on Al-Qaeda. The Japanese American director has refused to comment on the rumor but confirmed that the series would be filmed using no green screen at all.*

"But, Sensei – how do I put this politely in English – it doesn't make any sense," said Ohi Toyoshi.

"First, you didn't make it sound nice at all," said Winston. "Second, I would expect more support from my personal assistant. You know I could have hired that provocatively dressed lady ten years ago instead of you."

"I am, I am supportive."

"But I am not sensing a lot of supportiveness around here," Winston said offhandedly, while using both hands to draw the shape of an Ohi Toyoshi in air.

"Sensei, when making your first English movie *Run, Forrest Run*, you unleashed a pit bull on the lead to capture the fugitive's genuine emotion. Was I the only one who did *not* refuse to come to work that day?"

"... yes, and I remember how you committed perjury for me when I stood on trial for animal abuse and pre-mediated murder."

"When you were making *Modern Tennō: from Crib to Throne* and insisted on filming the scene of Naruhito's birth with a pregnant woman in labor, was I the only one who supported your decision?"

"Yes, so were you when we had to do a re-shoot nine months later. I will never, ever forget those sixteen hours," said Winston, closing his eyes to recall the twenty-minute one shot that earned his first major film award.

"Neither will I. Nor the camera operators. And, when you made the documentary *The Queen of Competitive Eating*, did I do so much as to bring her water when Kui 'Deep Dog' Shinbou was choking to death during her routine? No, I even stopped everyone on-site from screaming for help in order not to ruin the live sound recording."

"This one doesn't count. It was obviously not her first near-death experience, and we had a duty to educate the audience on the occupation hazard of competitive eaters. Plus, at the end she came out OK. I heard she has happily retired and is using her unique skillset as a performer now."

"True, true, true, that's true," admitted Ohi sincerely. "But didn't I have earned enough credit for being your true supporter through hell and high water? I literally broke you out from hell when you were done shooting the *Prison Break* reboot."

"That reminded me: The crew and I would need to be back in by fall for shooting the second season."

"No problem, Sensei. The friends we made last season will no doubt continue to serve as the supporting characters," said Ohi with no pun intended.

"By the way, what were we talking about?" wondered Winston, who figuratively got lost in thought. "Oh... you were saying how supportive you are. I got it. I really do. I just don't understand why you can't get on board with this."

"We just landed at Narita, and it doesn't make sense for us to immediately turn back to Singapore just to find out why the plane went *faster* than expected. We will miss out on the premiere of *Kyoto Jungle*."

"Which is fine. I don't want to have the PETA people throwing paint on me anyway."

"Still, spending another day airborne seems unnecessary. There is obviously something wrong with this plane you asked the props master to put together. Or it may be the pilot," muttered Ohi and immediately took a quick peek at the cockpit door to make sure the pilot was not hearing any of these.

"No way, Chandler has been flying for fifteen years and swore he was flying at normal speed throughout the trip."

"Then it must be the plane. Maybe the speedometer is broken and misled Mr. Chandler how fast we were. Otherwise, we would not have landed almost ninety minutes earlier than scheduled. And if Sensei you still have any concern with the plane's quality, maybe we can re-visit our option of buying a jet off the shelf rather than assembling one in house."

"I am not above that option. It is just that no aerospace manufacturers are able *and* willing to build us a business jet that can do twenty different facial expressions with movable nose and flight deck. You would think that technology has been invented already," said Winston in frustration. He then picked up the phone to cockpit and was told that the plane was refueled and ready for another test flight.

"There is no point to further argue about go-or-no-go. We will be taking off in a minute, and Chandler told me the speed sensor and transmission gear were both checked out," Winston said nonchalantly, while opening his luggage to take out his laptop. "Why don't you take a nap while I do some logging for the scenes we shot this week?"

Chapter 3

According to certain edition of the *Cambridge Dictionary*, "wait" is a verb that means "to allow time to go by, especially while staying in one place without doing very much, until someone comes, until something that you are expecting happens or until you can do something."

According to Smith Robin, "wait" and its derivatives were all nouns. They all meant (1) an optimist's way of doing something while doing absolutely nothing, and/or (2) a secular attempt to entice divine interference.

Having gone through three failed marriages and three equally successful divorces before his 33rd birthday, Smith Robin was the embodiment of optimism. However, he was not going to just wait while the NASA Director mulled over his buzzwords.

Waiting is not an action. Did I ever wait till Friday night to watch the new comic book movie? No, I read spoilers. Did I wait for the plaster cast to harden when my hip got comminuted fracture? No way, I discharged myself and gave a tearful testimony that won the custody of Casey. And did I patiently wait for my bed-ridden mother to pass away so that I can inherit her

Porsche?

Smith slowly turned to the family photo on his desk and reminisced about the last time he and his mother took a trip to Bordeaux.

Hell no! I dropped out of grad school, found a job in consulting and took good care of her till she fully recovered. What else would I have done?

Smith put down the photo and faced his desktop again.

Again and again, the universe has told me that NOT waiting delivered results. And this is what I am going to do.

His fingers danced on the keyboard like raindrops. Raindrops that could spell and knew all the shortcut keys of MS Office. Raindrops that checked all the right boxes on several bureaucratically necessary but otherwise pointless documents. Raindrops that industrially experimented with various entry animations in PowerPoint.

About ten minutes later, the video panel of *ML* came back to live on Smith's monitor. It showed Miranda in a study room featuring a bonsai, waterfall and double rainbow.

"In the interest of time, I suppose we have to go with the quick patch you suggested," said Miranda resignedly, "but we still need more substance."

As one of the most commonly used words in modern workplace, the word "substance" bears virtually nothing of what it is supposed to mean, thanks to its uniquely high degree of vagueness. Its lack of substance enables the word to mean anything from "a holistic impact analysis encompassing all extraneous and inherent factors that can exert influence on the agenda in question," to "technical specification, roll-out plan, fallback strategy, and implementation roadmap of the solutions in pipeline," to "talking points that can explain to the layman audience why they can convince themselves they have perfectly understood the proposition and therefore feel safe to provide buy-in without actually understanding any of it or feeling stupid."

However, Smith knew exactly what Miranda meant with it.

"Ma'am," said Smith after clearing his throat, "you want a long-term solution to take care of the flatees and their social movement,

I presume?"

"No, I want a double cheeseburger with mustard, honey, mayonnaise and no veges whatsoever in it plus a black milk boba," said Miranda as if she meant it. *"Of course I want a long-term plan!"*

Smith was not bothered by the yelling at all as he already muted the speaker when Miranda was still specifying her sauces of choice. Steadily, he shared on screen the one-pager he just pulled together during the break. A slide with nothing but five empty arc-shape textboxes arranged in a circle.

"What could be a better way to unravel the flat Earth movement than attacking them from within?" As always, Smith began his pitch with a question.

"Assassination of the most out-spoken flatees and the people they love."

"Yes, this was my first idea, but all our best men in murder cover-up have jumped to work for North Korea and Russia for higher pay and lower tax rates."

"Brainwashing the flat Earth priests and turned them into our puppets."

"Yes, but IT said the technology can only be used by CIA and they are not allowed to operate on the American soil."

"Putting a horse head on the flatees' beds every morning until they start believing the Earth is round."

"No!" Smith exclaimed in disapproval. "That would leave too much evidence behind and may not get the message properly across. By the way, thank you for jumping in, but I was just asking a rhetoric question. Please reserve your input for the Q&A at the end."

"My bad," Miranda made a quick apology, "and sorry for my yelling and sarcastic comments earlier."

"Don't worry, ma'am. It didn't even cross my mind," said Smith softly, "that the comment about cheese burger was in any way not a genuine ask."

After assuring his boss that no written complaint would be filed to the HR for the two counts of PMD policy violation, Smith clicked on the slide to resume his presentation. Slowly but not annoyingly, text began to appear in the text boxes through the Grow & Turn animation.

"Allow me to introduce the five-step approach to countering flat Earth – R.D.G.A.R.," said Smith, and pronounced the acronym like he was doing a short shout at the end of performing a Karate kick, "which stands for reconnaissance, discovery, gaining access, attack, and reporting."

Miranda would like to ask if this five-step diagram was a rip-off from the first Google search result for "security penetration testing," but managed to suppress her intellectual curiosity and exercise the active listening skill she had learned from the conflict management workshop last week.

Meanwhile, Smith eloquently explained how he planned to plant a mole among the flatees, discover their vulnerabilities, earn their trust, undermine their messages and efforts to uncover the globe conspiracy, and, with all said and done at the end, deliver a detailed report chronicling the events for senior management signoff. As a seasoned speaker, Smith could go completely auto-pilot when delivering a scripted presentation and had a kind of out-of-body experience where he could see and hear himself talking from a third-party point of view. During the experience, sometimes he would even find himself rehearsing the talking points for Q&A and sometimes, as in this case, he would be congratulating himself on the presentation.

Phew. This is over. In less than four hours, the budget plan will be submitted and then I can have another relaxing ten weeks before the next quarterly prep kicks in. Maybe I should take Janice to a trip. Maybe I should propose to her during the trip. I recall the third strike threw her ring to my face when the judge declared I was not financially capable to pay another woman alimony. And Chuck said he would give me a return-customer discount should I over order another wedding cake. I should totally do it. I can even—

"I only have one question."

Miranda's voice brought Smith back from contemplating his next triumph of hope over experience. This time, Miranda didn't interrupt the presentation; unbeknown to Smith, his auto-pilot already thanked and invited questions from the audience.

"Sure, I am all ears."

"Who would be executing this strategy?"

Smith almost failed to suppress his grin. *That is the best you have got? I thought you were going to ask me for a pro forma cash flow statement or if I have come up with a mission statement, which I already did: to deliver a uniform world view, repair the social fabric of America and round off the Earth once and for all.*

"This will certainly involve multi-disciplinary efforts, like Pub Comm, Sci-Edu, NSD," replied Smith and secretly congratulated himself on already having the paper work ready, "but since the objective is to neutralize the threats posed by flatees, Round Ops should be leading this project and have their men," Smith caught himself neglecting to use gender-neutral language and immediately added, "and women, on the field," Smith heard what he just said and further added, "and I didn't mean only men and women. Whatever pronoun works for them, as long as they are from Round Ops, I'm more than happy to see them lead the operation, as I have pledged to—"

"Cut it. HR isn't listening," said Miranda reassuringly. "So I take it that someone will need to submit a WPG-50 to apply for cash advance covering the Round Ops agents' per diem and out-of-pockets during the operations."

"Done, ma'am," interjected Smith and proudly flapped the said form in front of his webcam."

"And did you think of also submitting a 42J to raise the cap on cash advance in case the project overruns?"

"Also ready, just pending you signature," said Smith with a confident smile and two hands frantically flapping papers around his cheek. "I also drafted the affidavit declaring the purpose of expenses, enclosed with the project charter as supporting document."

"Excellent work. And FYI, I just received version 13.3 of your draft and will endorse it for submission. Once you send the forms over, I will see to it *you* get the resources you need for R.D.G.A.R."

"Thank you, ma'am," said Smith and began to look for the business card of Chuck.

It took him a few seconds to realize something was off.

"Um... not that we are not already there, but just so we are perfectly on the same page," Smith ventured to ask, "what did you mean by '*you* get the resources'?"

"Oh, never shy away from asking questions," said Miranda in a surprisingly warm tone, "even if it is a stupid one. Since you will be managing this operation, or project, obviously the resources will be at your disposal."

"But... I am just a project manager," said Smith without forgetting to make a fake laugh.

"That's exactly why you will be managing the project," said Miranda, still very warmly.

"Oh... I see where the confusion comes in. You see, back in the days when I was working in a consulting firm, what we sold to the clients as *project management* essentially means that I and some interns – mostly the interns – will ring up the stream leaders every week for status update, prepare a status pack with charts and tables that few people find helpful, and take minutes during the project steering committee meetings," Smith delicately recited the explanation that he used to give his clients when they refused to pay the invoice and contested that the consultants had failed to deliver the *solution implementation support* or *end-to-end project management service* agreed in scope of work.

"I see, I see. The upside is," said Miranda, wearing a rare smile on her face, "I find 'facilitating the project delivery according to the Head of NASA's instruction' in your job description and I interpret it quite liberally. So don't worry if you will be overstepping when you work with the Round Ops agents in executing the practical work. I expect tangible results before the next quarterly prep kicks in and please keep me posted with your informative charts and tables. Thank you again for the great work. Good night, and good morning."

With that said, Miranda and her unrealistic virtual background disappeared from the monitor, at which Smith's dead-looking eyes were still staring in disbelief.

She is sooo not gonna get invited to my weddings.

Chapter 4

Agent B put down the earphones and wondered if she had just

listened to a bottle episode of *The Office*. She didn't really like the R.D.G.A.R. acronym, which sounded unprofessionally lazy. She thought *They* would hate it too.

While her mind tried to come up with a better project name, her fingers danced frenetically on the keyboard, typing up the transcripts by agent A and herself.

Chapter 5

Sitting tightly in his cradle seat, Winston Kanshū was "in the zone" now. Being immersed in Britney Spears' dance music – which was one of the two prerequisites for him to get into the flow state – Winston could effortlessly edit hundreds of hours of footage in the span of one night. He could also notice otherwise imperceptible mistake or nuance. For instance, during the post-production of *Kyoto Jungle*, which depicted a post-apocalyptic Japan overrun by zombie deer, Winston noticed in a crowd chase scene that one of the food-crazed deer looked straight into the camera. Standing by his no CGI policy, he immediately ordered a reshoot. Unfortunately, the incident unduly drew the media's attention to the overtime work and underpay of deer, away from the movie's central message in promoting awareness of chronic wasting disease, more commonly known as the zombie deer disease.

Winston was almost done with editing the clips he shot last week in the West Siberian Plain. It was for advertising the Mobile Suit (MS) instant ramen that would be launched in X'mas, featuring two 1:1 life-size MS statues. One of them was the moving RX-78 borrowed from Yokohama, another a build-to-order red MS-06 Zaku II commissioned by the ramen marketer. In this thirty-second TV commercial, the two MS units would overcome their historical enmity, travel in opposite directions – one from Nadym to the south, another from Omsk to the north – and meet in the middle to share a MS instant ramen at Surgut. By the standards of Japanese commercials, there was nothing weird about this idea. Granted, the production crew received several unfriendly letters enclosed with razor blades, but those were from some homophobic locals who misconstrued this short film as promoting robotic homosexuality.

The misunderstanding was peacefully resolved when the locals were made to understand that those statues innocently symbolized Russia's annexation of Crimea.

Still, something bothered Winston. Something felt amiss.

"Wins, don't make me say it again – stop it, now."

Suddenly, Winston was snapped from the flow state. Tilting his head, Winston could barely see an imposing figure standing next to him. The figure wore a pair of classy sun-glasses and was angrily mouthing something. He just couldn't quite make out what was being said.

"OK, that's it. I am taking this off." The angry man leaned in and swiftly removed Winston's headphone.

"Chandler, what the hell?" Winston shouted in bewilderment. "You know I need this to work."

"Yeah, but not on the plane *I* work," retorted the British pilot, who had known the young director since the days they shared a room in boarding school.

"Since when you got a problem with our Queen of Pop? You know, you should be subject to disciplinary actions for blatantly violating the Britney Army Manifesto, which I clearly recall you signed. *You traitor!*"

"Noooo, you know I love Britney. I still have the *Baby One More Time* poster in my bedroom!"

"The... the same poster you used to put in our room and one day found a sticky stain on it, which I truthfully explained was a result of amazake spillage?" Winston asked with a poker face.

"Yeah."

"Oh," Winston's eyes involuntarily dashed right and left for a second before he changed the subject, "then, what's the problem here?"

"*This* is the problem," Chandler shouted and pointed at the bong in Winston's hand, still spewing out fume. Getting high was the second prerequisite for the director to get into the zone.

"You made the cabin like San Francisco. I know I said there was no regulation against smoking on a private plane, but I didn't mean you could chain smoke weed for six hours straight."

"Alright, alright," Winston said as the flowers on his Hawaiian shirt smiled at him, "no more weed in this flight. You can go back to the cockpit and do your piloting thing."

"It won't be necessary, because we already landed at Changi."

"What? I thought you said I chain smoked for *only* six hours? The last time I flew from Tokyo to Singapore it took around seven and a half."

"Here is the thing. The ASI shows we are at most four hundred and seventy, which is the normal speed for this route, but we still landed almost ninety minutes ahead of schedule," Chandler said with a shrug.

"So you were wrong when you said everything on this plane was fine?" Ohi gently interrupted, emerging from the slowly dissipating marijuana smog.

"No, I wasn't. We triple-checked it. Except for the aesthetic yet aerodynamically neutral changes your boss made to the deck head, this plane is as normal as it comes."

"Then what does it mean?" asked Ohi solemnly, who was reaching for the water pipe protruding from Winston's rucksack, but stopped cold when Winston gave me a disapproving head shake.

"Well, I suppose," the pilot paused for a moment and came up with the two most plausible explanations off the top of his head, "either the landmasses known as Japan and Singapore suddenly decided to get close and intimate, or there is something insidiously wrong with all the planes I have piloted up to this point of my life."

Normally a remark like that would be construed as sarcastic and invite more unhelpful satire from Winston, but not this time. Winston fell silent and moments later had an epiphany.

"Oh my god, I think you are onto something."

"Sensei, you look pale," Ohi asked anxiously. "Do you need another smoke?" The valet finally grabbed the bong.

Chapter 6

Just as Ohi Toyoshi was frantically looking for a lighter on the uncertifiedly modified Learjet 35 parked in the Singapore Changi Airport, a report about the jet's erratic flight route just reached the inbox of a Britta Geller ninety thousand six hundred and fifty miles away.

Since the plane travelled at an unusually high speed back-and-forth between two airports without any passenger getting on or off, the aviation authority at Japan first suspected foul play. After six hours of inquiry, clarification, escalation, intelligence sharing, jurisdiction assertion, name calling and finger pointing, the incident was finally reported to Britta, a senior analyst of NSD. (Curiously, NSD was the only unmistakable acronym popularly used in NASA, which could stand for either National Surveillance Department or No Such Department, used interchangeably in written communication without ever causing confusion.)

As one of the three thousand intelligence analysts employed by NSD in service of the Global Lie agenda, Britta was responsible for identifying, evaluating, tracking, monitoring and reporting on any risks that could uncover the true shape of Earth. She and the rest of NSD were all hired from the compliance, risk and internal audit functions in private sector. In other words, the NSD staff exclusively consisted of people with high tolerance of boredom, moderate to low career ambition and absolutely zero doubt of the value and purpose of their works.

Having just passed her probation not long ago, Britta was still learning her ropes but already knew enough to judge the delicacy of an incident report without reading it.

What the flat, thought Britta as the report from Narita came in. *Fourteen Fwd:'s and Re:'s in the email subject? This can't be a false alarm.*

The Geller family never understood what Britta did for a living – neither before nor after she joined NASA – and appreciated very little why she was constantly frustrated by what she called *a cry of wolf.* It was not uncommon for her to receive, say, a tweet from Jaden Smith doubting the Sun's temperature or a YouTube video promising evidence that orbital space tourism was a hoax. As credible as they were as red flags, every time Britta would find them posing no immediate threat after spending days on corroboration and research.

Britta tapped her glasses for melodramatic effect and clicked to open the email.

According to the report, the Learjet 35 in question underwent unusual modification in its nose and flight deck. Judging from the flight manifest, the customization was not for any aviation purpose and probably commissioned by the renowned realist filmmaker onboard. At this stage, one must assume that the filmmaker's involvement had something to do with his previous email inquiry to NASA about the availability of any "moon set" for movie making. The uncertified modification and unusual airspeed both suggested that the private jet in question had not yet been debuffed, i.e., the ASI onboard would display the correct airspeed.

Here you go, red flag number one, thought Britta and typed a few keys on her keyboard to update the Bayesian probability model.

The model was an essential tool for NSD to predict how likely someone, when given a certain piece of information, would believe the Earth was not a globe. Given the ungodly low likelihood that all the governments of technologically advanced countries, which apparently had lots of geopolitical and economic conflicts with each other, would collude to lie about something as innocent as the shape of our inhabited planet, the base rate used in the model was infinitely close to zero. To be specific, the model predicted that normally a WEIRD person (i.e., someone from a western, educated, industrialized, rich and democratic country, arbitrarily taken as a given in most sociological literatures) should expect that the chance of their planet being flat was two to the power of five thousand to one against. However, after Britta finished inputting the information of red flag number one, the odds sharply rose to one hundred to one against.

The report continued to describe how the jet was refueled as soon as it touched the land of Narita Airport and shortly afterwards departed without any passenger movements. In the report's appendix was a profiling analysis concluding that the subject flight was either hijacked by activists upset with the filmmaker's alleged animal abuse, or being used to measure the true physical distance between Japan and Singapore.

Viola, red flag number two. Britta promptly made a few keystrokes. *Oh, the odd barely moved. Well, the tech must have tweaked the information value of profiling analysis since that time they identified B.o.B. as a credible threat to the Global Lie.*

One of the most recent entries in the report stated that when the flight returned to the Changi Airport, a local mechanic observed through the jet's windows that it was full of white smoke. Terrorist attack was suspected, alarming the airport police. At the request of U.S. embassy in Singapore, the local police were instructed to stay put.

What? So it's just a typical terrorist attack? Britta could not be more disappointed. She felt like a gun owner whose home was invaded and the police arrived to arrest the unarmed intruders when she was still excitedly loading her shotguns. She was convinced that Winston Kanshū and his company were up to something. Something much more relevant than simply an American citizen (and several aliens) being held at gun point on foreign soil. She did some digging into the schedule of Kanshū, which was extremely easy given how prolific he was on Instagram, and something caught her eyes.

What? Why would anyone do something like that? It is as if he was trying to... Britta stopped in her train of thought and quickly checked out a name on Wikipedia. *Here you are, red flag number three.*

Overcome with joy, which had nothing to do with whether a compatriot was in a real terrorist situation, Britta fed the Bayesian model with the clue she just discovered on Kanshū's social media. Just before the system could churn out the revised probability estimate, Britta's desk phone rang. It displayed a caller ID that made her instinctively take a deep breath as if she was walking along the Avenue des Champs-Élysées with bags of designer clothing, stumbled over the top hat of a mime who was about to get pretty irritated but then a lot more amused, and saw that at precisely the spot where her face would land in 0.2 second there was a piece of fresh *merde de chien.*

Oh no, not again.

Chapter 7

Notwithstanding his previous tenure in the Operations Transformation function of *MacCheddar & Co.*, Smith Robin suffered no illusion as to how much value he could add to operations of any kind.

My job is like the PA system on a plane diving with both engines full of roast geese: benchmarking the altitude against industry best practices, reporting on any gaps between the as-is state and a fully functional plane, reminding everyone to follow the playbook that was thoughtfully designed and socialized when they got onboard, and most importantly re-assuring the key stakeholders that everything is being well taken care of by the professionals. I am never supposed to find myself behind the steering wheel, because that would make me actually accountable!

Distressed as he was, Smith reminded himself that he was a man of actions and the creator of a plethora of dazzling buzzwords. He gave himself a ten-minute prep talk before getting off his car.

Though he just came back from home after a short nap, he was already fully refreshed. He greeted his colleagues who were also flocking to the NASA HQ – which was, unlike the NASA field centers around the country, fully occupied with staff doing real work – did some pleasantry exchange in the elevator, pretended to care and be impressed by Karen's weekend plans, and then made a bee line to the expresso machine on his floor.

While waiting for his coffee to brew, Smith contemplated on his next steps.

OK, we are at the R of R.D.G.A.R. now, which means we should be reconnoitering. How are we going to do it?

Even in a monologue, Smith could not help but use "we" as the subject pronoun, a practice advocated by Dickson Cheddar Jr. in his best seller *10 Effective Habits in Diffusing Responsibilities*.

Smith closed his eyes for meditation, hoping that his mindfulness would guide him to answer his self-directed question.

Fun fact #4: Meditation is a tool powerful enough to prove the existence of God with no input of data whatsoever. Through meditation, René Descartes formulated his own versions of ontological argument for God's existence. One of them can be best illustrated with the language of bro talk as follows:

"Hey, bro."

"What's up?"

"I got a proof for God."

"Sweeeeeeet, what were you smoking?"

"No, man. I mean, for real. I got it all figured out."

"How so?"

"Last night I was thinking, and you know I've done a lot of thinking lately, right? Then, I got this very, very clear idea of a perfectly perfect being, perfect in all possible ways."

"All right, all right. I'm with you."

"And you know, for a being to be perfect, it has to exist."

"Sure, sure, sure, sure."

"So, a perfectly perfect being, or we can call it God, must exist."

Fun fact #5: A comedian further developed the dialogue above to prove the non-existence of God.

"Man, you are gonna be rich. You just proved this world was created by this perfectly perfect being."

"Thanks, bro. And I am sure God did it with just a snap."

"Cool. Would it be cooler if God created this world with as much handicap as possible?"

"Why not? A perfectly perfect being would be able to pull off anything with any possible handicap. That's why it is perfect in all possible ways."

"Well, you know, the greatest handicap would be to not exist."

"So you are saying an existing creator would not be as perfect as a non-existing creator?"

"Yeah."

"O mama, then I just proved the perfectly perfect being must not be existing."

Fun fact #6: The said comedian was beheaded by religious zealots shouting, "Off with the heads of those who disrespect God and call us violent!"

Deep into his thoughts, Smith had another out-of-body experience and found himself in a memory palace. A palace made of big words, big ideas, and big names of self-made men who built their powerful enterprises from nothing but a generous interest-free loan from their parents. This palace was full of drawers, labeled with letters, arranged in alphabetical order. Within those drawers were loads of case studies, facts, opinions that were mistaken as facts, and imagination that was misremembered as the actual past. When he opened the drawer labeled *SM*, he found what he was looking for.

Smith was at the same time both ashamed and ecstatic. Ashamed for taking so long to recall an idea so simple. Ecstatic because the answer was so simple that by conventional wisdom it must be true.

SME! What I need is a subject matter expert that I can leverage to find an entry point into the flatees' inner circle.

Of the seventeen thousand qualified liars employed by NASA to advance aerospace technology and mislead the public about the true shape of Earth, one name in Garamond 48pt font popped right up into his head.

Chapter 8

In 2016, the science journalist David Robert Grimes published an equation estimating how long a conspiracy could be kept as a secret. Presumably for simplicity, his model only estimated how likely an *internal* leak, which could be either accidental (e.g., Jim from the NASA Arts Department unwittingly sent an unedited version of the "Blue Marble" picture to his mistress with a euphemistic *#miss_you#blue_balls* caption) or intentional (e.g., a retired stuntwoman published her memoir *12 Years Hanged in Balance* to expose the unsafe working conditions on spacewalk sets), would result in the failure of a conspiracy. Based on three well-known examples of conspiracies, Grimes calculated that the average number of internal leaks per year that would be fatal to a conspiracy was about four in a million. Based on his model, if a conspiracy plans to celebrate its fifth anniversary, it is not advisable to involve more than 2,521 conspirators. And if it is of a scale so big that a million people are involved, then there is a 95% chance that the conspiracy will not survive for more than three years and eighteen days.

The model was, without a shred of doubt, well known among conspiracy theorists from all schools of thoughts, who appreciated Grimes' efforts in formalizing the relationships between number of conspirators and time of cover-up in plain mathematics. However, they lamented that the statistical model had failed to consider the possibility of external agents revealing the conspiracy operations, which they very, very confidently believed would substantially *reduce* the likelihood of a conspiracy collapse.

NASA was, of course, also well aware of the pathetically simple fact that the number of conspirators went hand in hand with the expected number of fatal leaks over time. That was, surely, the reason why the number of persons working for NASA drastically dropped from around four hundred and twenty thousand in 1966 to less than two hundred and twenty thousand in 1969, the very year that *Apollo 11* allegedly landed on the Moon. That being said, it did not mean that Grimes' model could accurately predict the lifespan of the Global Lie. For one, the three uncovered conspiracies that fed the science journalist's estimate (i.e., the scientific misconduct of FBI Laboratory, the unethical Tuskegee Syphilis Study, and the PRISM surveillance program that single-handedly put the *Government Agent Watching Me* meme on the map of memes) were all deliberately leaked by NASA in anticipation that someday someone somewhere somehow would attempt to estimate the probability of conspiracy failure with precisely those three examples. By doing so, NASA artificially inflated the odds of conspiracy being discovered and reinforced the public's confidence that nothing fishy could stay undetected for long.

Another reason why the Global Lie could out-live the theoretically short life expectancy had everything to do with the world-wide P-clearance Induction & Mentoring Program, which had a rather unfortunate acronym in English speaking countries.

As unequivocally suggested by its name, P clearance was a rung higher than the access authorization enjoyed by the legendary whistleblower known as "Q" on the imageboard website 4chan. P security clearance was required for conducting *real* scientific research, producing compasses, organizing Antarctica cruises, manufacturing aircrafts, constructing bridges, building oil facilities, being employed by or transferred to any NASA departments besides Public Communication, assigning or revoking P clearance, or basically doing anything that would entail knowledge of the true shape of Earth.

In the United States, the PIMP was administered by NASA. Each month, around a hundred of NASA recruits, prospective professors, and new joiners for sensitive positions in public and private sectors were invited to the NASA HQ for a five-day orientation. Following the tried and test recipes, first halve of the orientation consisted of multiple workshops and breakout sessions. The orientation facilitators first warmed the participants up with the idea that paradigm shift was a commonplace in the history of science and guided them to reflect on conventional wisdom like "20% tip is the norm," "unions are evil," "Canadians apologize too much" and "The Earth is a spinning ball." Once the facilitators felt that the participants were ready for some cultural shock, they brought out the big gun, explaining how the true shape of Earth had been a carefully guarded secret and what it meant to their career. To keep the materials packed into half a day, there was no Q&A session, so no one really got to know why *They* went to such trouble to hide the truth, how long *They* had been hiding it, or who the heck *They* were. Once the participants were enlightened, the second halve of the orientation began.

For the remaining four and a half days, the learning objective was to indoctrinate the participants with the unsurmountable importance of keeping their new found knowledge a secret. The contents were basically the same as those of the Hell House run by well-intended evangelists who correctly surmised that moral education was best provided through trauma and nightmare. While the target audience of PIMP (no pun intended) was much older than that of Hell House, their operating approaches – namely, the depiction of Hell of sinners to scare the bejesus out of the uninitiated – were exactly the same.

It was through such an educational and exciting event that Smith

Robin made the acquaintance of Britta Geller three months ago.

Chapter 9

"Britta Geller's desk, Britta Geller speaking."

"Morning, this is Smith Robin calling from PMO. You may not remember me; we had a lunch the day after our new joiner orientation," said Smith, even though he was exceedingly confident that he made a good impression on Britta during that lunch.

"It is pretty hard to forget you after that lunch, Robin."

"Please, call me Smith. I insist," Smith said gently, getting quite excited.

"I'd rather stick to the last-name basis. I insist more."

The curt remark came as quite a surprise, as Smith remembered Britta was quite cheerful. "Um... did I do something that offended you?"

"Offended? no, I would never call it that," replied Britta, switching the line to her blue-tooth and walking out of the office to make sure no one would overhear her. "Call me old fashioned, but I am just not used to being proposed on the first date. Actually, it wasn't even a date; it was a working lunch as far as I am concerned."

"What, no way I can't re... Did you really mean I proposed to you, like, asking you if you would like to spend the rest of your life with me till death or prison do us apart?"

"Yes, with exactly the same words."

"I wouldn't happen to have presented a ring..."

"You did. And what kind of person would carry a proposal ring around like .38 Police Special?"

"I got so many questions to you about the gun part, but did I also kneel down..."

"On both your knees, which was the worst part. That was the most shocking thing in my life, which is saying a lot after that five-day orientation."

"Oh... now I remembered; I must have blocked it out," said Smith like he just re-discovered fire. The reason for Smith's failure to recollect an event so cringy was not in any way related to the traumatic experience in PIMP; it was a result of his willful ignorance of drawback and failure, another useful trick he had picked up from *10 Effective Habits in Diffusing Responsibilities*. As for the failed proposal, it was just another typical example of Smith misinterpreting the social cues from the opposite sex.

"Geller, I am sorry for my unprofessional behavior and promise it won't happen again," Smith apologized, "until there is unambiguous sign that..."

"No, don't count on it," interjected Britta, "but your apology is accepted."

* * *

Smith had explained the reason for his call, how R.D.G.A.R. was not a rip-off from network security test methodology and the challenges he had in finding a vowel-beginning verb to replace "Discover" in R.D.G.A.R.

"So you need to find someone who can bring you into the flaters' camp, someone who is neither a troll nor a paranoid nutjob. Someone who is a confirmed believer in the flat Earth gig?" Britta tried to summarize the situation in her language. The prerogative term "flater" she used in describing flat Earth believers was on the ban list of NASA's Internal Communication Policy and seldom used in formal occasion. It landed on the list because it could easily cause confusion in a heated verbal exchange.

"Precisely. Does NSD happen to have someone fitting this profile on the radar?"

"You bet we do. It came in like ten minutes ago," Britta said and walked back to her cubicle to check something on her desk. "According to our model, the subject is 69% certain that the Earth is not a globe."

"That's almost as high as I got after the first orientation workshop. What exactly do they know?"

Chapter 10

"I figured out what's wrong with the footage we shot last week," said Winston.

"You mean the commercial that almost got you shot in Russia?" asked Chandler, still waving hands to dispel the gas from Winston's earlier chain smoking.

"Yup, let me show you," Winston said and returned to his cradle seat. Before long he had pulled up two video player windows side by side on his laptop.

"Look, shown on the left-hand side is the clip I shot in Nadym. The time stamp shows that it was exactly 12 p.m. local time," the director said and clicked pause on that video. "On the right-hand side you have what I filmed in Omsk on the same day. Now let me freeze it at exactly 12 p.m." The two videos were now frozen at the exact moment. Both of them showed the bird's eye view of a life-sized mecha, respectively located at the far north and south of West Siberian Plain. "Now, look closely at the shadows casted by the statues. Do you see any difference?"

Winston then turned around and looked at his companions for any sign of eureka. Chandler had barely any interest in studying the frozen images as he simply expected it was just another they-are-the-same-picture prank from Winston. Ohi, however, showed profound excitement after scrutinizing them for a while.

"I see it, Sensei, I see."

"So you see it too?"

"Yeah, plain as the sky," Ohi enthused. He took a look at Chandler, who had been silent, and continued with unconcealed contempt, "you see, Sensei was trying to use the parallel structure of the two statues, which themselves are a metaphor for Übermensch, to bring out the dichotomies of light and darkness, reality and imagination, being and not being." Ohi turned to Winston and looked for a sign of approval from his raised eyebrows. "The idea is to subliminally allure the audience to reflect on the antitheses, reconcile those superlatives, and come to terms with the underlying juxtaposition."

"Which is...?" asked Chandler, with exactly zero interest.

"Which is, the prejudice for truth and the value of untruth pioneered by Friedrich Nietzsche in *Beyond Good and Evil*."

"I see," Chandler remarked with negative interest. "How about the difference that Winston was asking about?"

"About that." Ohi pointed to the statue's shadow on the left window, and said, "Don't you see this shadow is two shades darker than the other one? Not to mention it is notably shorter.”

Seeing that the pilot was still unconvinced, Ohi gave up on talking to the lesser man and turned to face Winston again, “Is there anything I miss, boss?”

“Ohi,” Winston said in awe, “what the heck were you talking about? Those two shadows are exactly the same.”

I knew it, Chandler thought to himself.

“Those two shadows, casted at the same time by statues of identical height, located more than one thousand four hundred miles apart, are exactly the same,” Winston proclaimed. “I saw it very clearly when I was in the zone. I just couldn’t quite figure out what’s the problem with that.”

“So I was wrong about the whole thing?” Ohi said with a hint of guilt and shame.

“No, no, no, just the shadow part. You got the whole juxtaposition thing right,” Winston reassured his assistant before returning to the topic. “But when Chandler mentioned how the flight time was not in line with the distance between Japan and Singapore, I knew what was wrong with the shadows being the same.

“They shouldn’t be. Given the Earth’s curvature, the two shadows should have different length at the same time of the day. The length difference should be very obvious given they were casted on a level ground and a thousand miles apart from each other.”

“Oh my god.” Chandler finally snapped out of apathy and took a serious look at the two images. “You just pulled an Eratosthenes.”

* * *

A dozen of airport police agents had had the Learjet 35 surrounded. One of them just visually confirmed that the co-pilot was alone with his cellphone in the cockpit, presumably texting a distress signal. The control tower then instructed the co-pilot to stay calm and be prepared to lower the airstairs when given the cue. On the other hand, four of the agents quietly moved to where the airstairs would be and put on their thermal goggles. With the white smoke filling the cabin, they surmised they had a tactical advantage over the terrorists onboard and could neutralize the threats before they could react to the raid. At the leading agent’s signal, they unlocked the safety on their MP5s.

Chapter 11

For the benefit of Ohi, Chandler grabbed the laptop from Winston and opened the Wikipedia page about Eratosthenes.

"This dude," Chandler explained, "was the first human who calculated the circumference of the Earth. He first estimated the distance of two cities with the help of professional walking slaves who carefully counted the steps they took to go from point A to point B. Then he put two sticks at the two points, measured the length of shadow casted by point B's stick when it was exactly noon at *point A*, and then worked out the angle of Sun's ray. Knowing that angle and the distance between those two cities was enough for him to compute the Earth's circumference."

"And I just proved this story was total BS," Winston supplemented, "because I did the exact same thing but the two sticks, which happened to look like two cool mecha, casted shadows of the same length. Damn, I should have known this is just another plot to glorify slave owners."

"Sensei, you can't be seriously suggesting that..."

"Yes, I am," Winston said and stood up from the cradle seat. "Think about it, everything makes sense now. Our trips today show that either all maps need to be rewritten or every plane out there is measuring their speed wrong. And now this... this Eratosthenes thing I did, proves that this dude is just a slave-owning Santa Claus, who never existed, and the Earth is not round."

Like the U.S. citizens during the 45th president's tenure or the quality assurance specialists of organic fertilizer producers, Chandler and Ohi had long developed an immunity against bullshit, thanks to their prolonged exposure to the thoughts of Winston Kanshū. But what they just heard smelt like something else. It had a hint of truth in it, which worried them all the more. They took a while to think through everything Winston said, before Chandler broke the silence.

"Let's calm down for a moment. I know you are thinking of how to announce your discoveries now, but we must tread very carefully from now on. If you are wrong—"

"Which I am not," Winston interrupted.

"For argument's sake, let's say there is a hypothetical chance that you *were* wrong and there is a rational explanation behind everything we learnt today," Chandler said tensely, "then announcing this discovery would put you in the same social circle as the Scientologists, but not in a good way."

Winston took a moment to think through the hypothesis and painfully shook his head.

"On the other hand," Chandler continued, "if you are right, then we are literally dealing with a global conspiracy. Coming out with these findings will put all of us in grave danger."

"Danger? I am a world-renowned director. Do you seriously think whoever covering up this BS would just barge in through that door, tase us and put on our heads black hoods that smell like Batman's underpants after a night of crime fighting, then lock us up in an abandoned warehouse, make us watch everyone we love get gunned down, strap us on these chairs with no seats and whip our balls from below, before finally giving us a nefarious speech of why they do what they do and slitting our throats? Is it what you think would happen?"

Before Chandler could comment on this extremely specific scenario, Ohi heard a metallic clank behind him. He instinctively turned around and saw several red dots moving swiftly across the cabin's ceiling in his direction. Chandler was the second one to react. He took off his sun glasses and could barely see through the smoke that the tips of two semi-automatic weapons were pointing to his way.

Damn, I thought they were going to use tasers...

Chapter 12

Back in the days of boarding school, Chandler and Winston led such a bold lifestyle that many anthropologists are surprised by the duos never obtaining the Darwin Awards, which recognize outstanding achievements contributing to the evolution of homo sapiens. According to the Award's official website, to win the award, the contestants must "eliminate themselves in an extraordinarily idiotic manner, thereby improving our species' chances of long-term survival."

Besides constantly wagering their genitals as an expression of confidence, Chandler and Winston once in a while would bet their lives to advance scientific knowledge.

Their most daring adventure took place right after an economics class that introduced them to the two-player conflict model in game theory commonly known as the game of chicken.

From that class, they learnt that signaling – in this case, signaling the commitment to not turn the wheel under any circumstances – was essential for winning. Therefore, both Chandler and Winston convincingly advertised how the brake and wheel of their respective vehicles were sabotaged before the game. Not to be outdone, Chandler blindfolded himself and asked to have his hand tied behind the driver seat, which was something he still did from time to time after becoming a pilot. To further outdo him, Winston had himself tied up and locked in the luggage compartment. After the game, both of them swore that they had an anthropologist start the car for them and they were completely incapacitated from start to finish. Neither of them knew exactly how they somehow managed to avoid mutual assured destruction.

Therefore, when the masked gunmen showed up and shouted what he could only make out as "fish," it was the first time for Winston Kanshū to really see the face of death.

Oh... so that's what flashback before death is like, thought Winston, who gave one out of five stars to his life review.

To the left of Winston, Chandler was also wondering why the gunmen demanded fish, and swore he would abandon his bohemian lifestyle and spend the rest of his life like a career internal auditor if he could survive tonight.

Standing in front of them was Ohi, the descendent from a line of noble samurais. He was trying to remember his rusty *shinkage-ryū* techniques, one of which according to legend could take the opponent's weapon in a split second. With four gunmen in a two-by-two formation, Ohi calmly gauged his odds while controlling his pelvic floor muscles.

I can manage it. This was the same thought that occurred to Ohi and Winston simultaneously. The only difference between theirs was that Winston's was preceded by an urgent desire to delete the browsing history of his laptop.

Before Ohi could showcase his martial art techniques, Winston made a sudden movement to the laptop lying on his cradle seat, startling everyone in the cabin. The MP5s' red dot sights scrambled to converge on the Hawaiian shirt of Winston, who froze in dread. At that very moment, all he could think of was the configuration of his browser history retention period, which only led to endless regret and despair.

Worst technology mistake in my life, topping the loss of bitcoin hard drive.

The ensuing shooting, bleeding, hugging, tear shedding, flashbacking, monologuing, deceased relatives sighting never happened. Before the four police officers could pull the triggers, they all pressed their left hands to their ears as if they were obliged to signal that some important message just came in.

Chapter 13

Smith was beginning to enjoy the music on hold when Britta's voice came back online.

"Sorry, I had to jump on a call with the embassy in Singapore to stop some would-be flatters from getting shot. As much as we want them to keep their opinions to themselves, we can't just let them die."

"Sure, sure, sure," Smith said and stopped playing crossword, "for humanity, rights, morality, principles, equality, and stuff."

"Exactly."

"Any chance those were the 69% subject you were briefing me on?"

"No, they ain't," Britta said and checked the screen on her right, which was now showing the calculation result of a Bayesian probability model she ran earlier this morning. "They are not bad, 42%, which means they rationally disbelieve in a spherical Earth but still irrationally reject that a global conspiracy is perpetuated to hide something as innocuous as the figure of Earth."

"Well, I can relate to that. Before joining NASA, I used to think the government would spend more efforts to cover up things like election rigging, civilian surveillance, prisoner abuse, police brutality, or stuff like that."

"On the contrary, I straight out thought the government was not competent enough to cover them up, but here we are."

Smith felt he just shared a moment with Britta, which Britta sensed and got a bit nauseated. Before Smith could start naming their children, she dragged him back to the business.

"About the 69% subject," Britta said, "I just forwarded to you a brochure for the True Earth Summit. My colleagues picked it up from a classified source this morning."

Smith just received the email and read out loud the brochure's first page, "United by truth... blah blah blah, the Toronto Summit will be the first global dialogue since the Second Schism... blah blah blah, interpreting and anti-bugging services will be provided by the United Ways... blah blah blah, See you there. Praise the Earth." He turned to the second page, which explained the inspiration for the event mascot. Underneath the text was the cartoon illustration of a smiling brown beaver in red shirt, leaning on a vertical wood log, below which lay a broken globe.

They pulled no punches to make their point, Smith thought.

He had so many questions about this brochure that he didn't even know where to begin. Surely there would be a ton of flatees in the summit, but most of them would be just trolls.

"Turn to page ninety-five, which is page ninety-seven of the PDF file. When you are there, check out the 2 p.m. event on day three."

On page ninety-five of the brochure, or page ninety-seven of the PDF file, was the run-down of the four-day event. Following Britta's instruction, Smith found what she wanted to show him.

> *2 p.m. – 3 p.m.*
> *"Missing Link Between Modern Physics and Figure of Earth"*
> *Dr. Gina Stinson, postdoctoral fellow of California University and lecturer at MIT, will present her discovery that completely debunks the globe hypothesis. The presentation will also be live streamed on multiple channels.*

"Gina Stinson...?" Smith muttered. "Where have I seen this name before?"

Chapter 14

Gina Stinson was fun, adventurous, food-maniac, dog-loving, ready to party and loved to keep it real, according to the Tinder bio of Gina Stinson. In other words, she liked to be thought of as someone who was fun, adventurous, food-maniac, dog-loving, ready to party and loved to keep it real, a description that was roughly 50% accurate.

A more concise and faithful description of her personality was this: Gina Stinson did not like being told what to do.

When shown the world map for the first time at four, she refused to believe there was any country outside of the United States, a belief she dearly held till the age of sixteen when she took a school trip to France. Since then, she acknowledged the possibility that the commonly used maps might not be entirely inaccurate and that there could be thousands of people leaving outside of the United States of America.

When taught evolutionary biology at eight, Gina contested that Charles Darwin was obviously wrong and single-stomachly refuted "survival of the fittest" using her teacher's belly. She sternly believed in intelligent design until she was twelve, when she found out how messed up the designs of retina and recurrent laryngeal nerve were. She would later state that she joined the evolutionists' camp only out of spite.

Growing up, Gina went on to be involved in hundreds of escalator accidents, several industrial disasters, and almost one nuke launch. The root causes for them were a mystery, but some keen observers had noticed that a prominent "Do not press this button!" sign was in presence of all those incidents and written to their senators to outlaw such hazardous materials. A bill to that effect, however, was never submitted to the congress, because the law makers were worried that the legislation would upset the sign manufacturing companies.

Gina did not become a big reader until she was fourteen. That year, she was told that the final exam would cover the geological evidence of Earth being a 4.5-billion-year-old spinning globe. It was at that very moment she swore she would re-write science as mankind knew it. The rest of how she became a theoretical physicist was just history and her standard ice-breaker topic on a first date.

"... so that's the story of how I became a physicist and proved over a lunch that light refraction is not subject to the second law of thermodynamics," Gina said and took a sap of her mojito.

She initially was not sure of this restaurant picked by her date, but she began to find herself fond of it. The exotic menu, the rumba music, and the second-hand Cuban cigar. They not only convinced her that Cuba probably existed, but also made her start thinking about a second date. A second date with this man who really listened.

"Interesting, so what is a typical day of yours like?" asked the man sitting across Gina. His plate was barely touched.

"Well, my official job title is a lecturer, so most of the time I am teaching, doing preps, grading and, you know, being disturbed by over ambitious students outside of consulting hours. Besides the teaching duties, I am all about research."

Gina sensed that her date was genuinely interested in her days. *Who said romance is dead?*

"And, do you have any career plan on your mind? Like, professorship or Nobel Prize?" asked the man while leaning in.

"I wouldn't mind a million-dollar prize," said Gina jokingly and put down her drink again. "I was asked a couple of times if I want to get a tenure, reduce the teaching workloads and do more *real* research, but I was like, 'I am good. I don't need you telling me what to do with my life, Faculty Dean.'"

Her date almost choked on his drink and ruined his nice shirt.

That's why she was never put through PIMP? With the papers she has published, she should have become a full professor years ago. Her Colinear Analysis of Extremely Unmeasurable Boson Excitation in Super Asymmetric State *was a real page turner!*

"Enough about me. Why don't you tell me more about yourself?" Gina said, while taking out her phone to double-check her date's profile. "Other than 'This is Smith and I have a job, eggplant emoji.'"

"I am what people call a public speaking guru," said Smith Robin, with both hands doing a tight OK sign, "but I think of myself more as a life coach. Most of the time I am on the road, but when I am not, I do corporate trainings, give seminars at colleges, and tutor aspiring televangelists."

Unlike the majority of Tinder users, Smith was not lying to get laid. In his own language, he was simply trying to "get from D to G," which only sounds weird to the most dirty-minded thinkers.

Three weeks ago, Smith learnt of Dr. Stinson's upcoming speech in the True Earth Summit, which NSD had predicted would be a huge boost to the flat Earth's camp. After several very productive meetings with Round Ops and NSD, it was decided that the project manager of R.D.G.A.R. would be the one making contact with Dr. Stinson, due to his outstanding accomplishments.

"I only believe in numbers," said Miranda Lin, the NASA Director in one of those meetings, "and since you, of all NASA staff, score the highest number of marriages, you are the ideal candidate for honeypotting Dr. Stinson."

On the other hand, NSD would only provide remote support, while Round Ops would not yet be engaged at all, despite the properly completely WPG-50 and 42J forms.

After two weeks of texting under the pseudonym Smith Johansson, Smith finally got to meet Gina in person and throw in the bait.

"Speaking of work," Smith casually said, "I will be leaving town soon and be in Canada till the end of October."

"No way," Gina said in disbelief, "I am also going to Toronto next week to do a presentation. Any chance we can meet up again there? I could use some pointers on that presentation. My materials are a bit technical and I was wondering if I need to, um…"

"Dump it down?"

"I was actually going for 'layman friendly,'" lied Gina. "And if my message can come across half as effectively as those prosperity gospel preachers, then it would be great."

"Sure. If you don't mind sharing your slides and speech with me, I can start working on them this week," said Smith, while mentally ticking the box next to "Discovery."

Chapter 15

His digital watch indicated that his shift was just over. Before taking his leave, agent A casually looked over his shoulder to get a visual of Dr. Stinson.

A brain and a rack, he thought. *A shame that she is not my assignment.*

After taking another puff of the fake Cuban cigar, he hurriedly took off, leaving agent B behind to take care of the bills.

Chapter 16

"Knowledge comes the most unexpected place" is a slogan dreamed up by one MBA program marketer to justify why anyone should pay a hefty tuition fee for reading case studies in the business school, instead of browsing business magazines on the toilet. Although the idea was scrapped once the marketer realized how it might backfire on the tertiary education industry as a whole, it is still the best idea that humans have ever come up with since credit card convenience fee.

The greatest testament to how knowledge – and, more often than philosophers are comfortable to admit, wisdom – comes from the most unexpected place is none other than the comment section of PornHub. There, one may find World War II anecdotes, food recipes, investment tips, relationship advices, game guides, wholesome encouragements and book ideas. All thanks to a moderately understood phenomenon called post nut clarity, which has inspired phenomenal research interest across scientific as well as non-scientific communities.

The PornHub comment section is also the junction joining the paths of Smith Robin and Winston Kanshū.

"True Earth Research Workshop, Panel Discussion about the Future of Geopolitics and Antarctic Treaty in Twenty Years, Ceremony for Content Creator Awards, The Great Debate of Round Earth Fallacy," Winston read out loud an ad he just found online.

"Jeez, I am telling you, these people know their stuff. They even invited a MIT lecturer to talk about how the globe hypothesis isn't legit."

"But, Sensei, where did you find this?" Ohi turned his head around and asked, with his hands still on the wheel and the speedometer indicating that he was driving 10 mph safely above the speed limit of Japan National Route 4. He and Winston were on their way from Sendai to Tokyo, having spent the better part of a day in cat hair.

"I am afraid I am not at the liberty to discuss it," said Winston solemnly in the backseat. "My source would like its privacy."

Since the misadventure they had in the Changi Airport, Winston and Ohi had been working alone to make sense of their discoveries, while Chandler had gone into full paranoid mode. The pilot had quitted his job, abandoned his family, cut his cable subscription, rented a bunker, and started a plant house in an eastern European village. Now Winston could only unilaterally communicate with Chandler by leaving messages in the *r/crochet* forum. He was quite upset that Chandler never replied how he managed to terminate the cable subscription.

Glimpsing a plane that just flew overhead, Winston recalled the last time he spoke with Chandler, three weeks ago, in the morning they returned to Tokyo-Narita.

* * *

"Dudes, wake up, you need to see this," Chandler said to Winston and Ohi, who were exhausted after being interrogated all night by the Singaporean airport police. Staying sober throughout the examination was no easy task for the two of them, as they were more accustomed to the graphic approach adopted by Yakuza loan sharks.

"Look at this," Chandler said agitatedly while holding out his phone to the film making duo.

"Ew, why would you show me a picture of the human centipede?" Winston shouted in disgust while Ohi was trying to figure out what he was looking at.

"No," Chandler clarified, "not the wallpaper of my phone. I wanted you to look at the time. Do you know what it means?"

Winston had never been that tired, shocked and confused at the same time. The last time he felt that way was four years ago when he woke up with a girl he just met in Bangkok.

"You still don't get it? We were right on time," Chandler exclaimed and took off his sunglasses. The vein on his forehead and his wide-open bloodshot eyes made Winston wonder whether they were meeting in a room with very soft walls. The pilot added, "I flew the same route with the same speed we did yesterday, but this time we were *not* ahead of the schedule."

"So you are saying we are *not* early. We are late, comparatively speaking, but actually on time," Ohi recapped what he just heard. "Okay, it is not confusing at all."

Winston looked at Ohi the way he looked at the toilet seat that remained upright after that Bangkok girl exited the bathroom.

"*They* must have done something to the plane when we were in custody," Chandler said while pacing up and down the cabin.

"Who is *They*?" said Winston, asking the same question he asked when he pondered on that toilet seat.

"I don't know," Chandler said with his head in hands, "someone is covering this up. Someone with the resources, the know-how, and the most twisted motive to convince everyone on earth that they are living on a globe."

He suddenly stopped in his track and squatted on the cabin floor, as if he was searching for a lost car key. After a while, he resumed talking.

"Okay, it seems they are not smart enough to bug this plane. We can keep talking."

"Dude, you are over-reacting," said Winston, saying the same thing he said to calm himself down while studying that upright toilet seat.

"Mr. Chandler, if someone is competent enough to, what's the word in English?" Ohi said, "to orchestrate a conspiracy of this scale, don't you think they would have us bribed, blackmailed, kidnapped, brainwashed or assassinated already? They should at least have the courtesy of hanging us upside down above a pit of hounds, with electrodes attached to our testicles and centipedes crawling into our ears, until we swear to never reveal their secret."

"Stop giving *Them* ideas!"

"But you just said no one was overhearing..."

"Ugh, I don't need this," Chandler said in distress. He walked to the cockpit to grab his suitcase and was going to leave the plane. "I can't be part of this anymore. I need to get off the grid." Before stepping out, he spun and pleaded, "Wins, promise me you won't show anyone those videos."

Chandler was referring to the video records that would prove Eratosthenes was just a myth. When the trio were in custody, the airport police informed them that a group of Siberians just initiated a class action to restrain Kane Shotto Studio from releasing any footage filmed on their lands. Apparently, the locals were backed by some American legal financing companies. Although Winston's laptop was confiscated by the police and probably would never be returned to him before the lawyers could suck them dry, Chandler knew that he must have got a backup somewhere else.

Winston thought for a while before opening his mouth. "I swear I won't show those videos to anyone," which was another line he said to himself on that fatal morning in Bangkok.

Upon hearing those words, Chandler walked down the airstairs.

With the pilot out of earshot, Winston added, "until I have enough ammo to take *Them* down."

After bidding farewell to his panicked friend, not a single second had Winston wasted in the past three weeks.

Under the pretext of documentary making, he interviewed people who purportedly designed bridges, built railroads, programed GPS devices, drew maps, taught geology, or had travelled to Antarctica. All of them gave extensive accounts of how their professions, products and experience were compatible with the spherical Earth model. Nonetheless, Winston felt that their stories were too good to be true.

Those phonies were just trying to blow me off with big words like curvature, planetary movement and science.

He then turned to reading books about flat Earth, which he found very empowering as they gave him a sense of secret knowledge and confirmed all the beliefs he wanted to believe. He was only slightly disappointed that the books posed the same questions he already asked his earlier interviewees. To a teeny, tiny degree, he was also surprised that none of the books featured a picture of the Earth's edge, anecdote of Antarctica trips, or a non-spherical model that could explain sunset, seasons and eclipse all at the same time.

Notwithstanding the minor setback, he was undeterred and continued with his research. After going through a few more hoops and rabbit holes on YouTube, he finally identified a disgruntled NASA employee that was willing to talk. Initially the meeting seemed quite promising, as this cat lady could prove that she had really worked at the Public Communication Department (or Pub Comm) of NASA. She went on and on about how she always felt left out in NASA, was banned from the staff lounge, couldn't get employee discount for cat food, didn't get invited to annual dinners, and got seconded to JAXA when she petitioned to end the segregation. After listening for hours to her early life, which she heavy-handedly compared to Rosa Parks, Winston finally asked if she knew any dirt about NASA, and she said, "Yes, I will say anything you want me to say at the right price. What's it you want? Alien on Mars or Moon landing hoax?"

Winston would not have been disappointed if he had known that Pub Comm was the only department in NASA whose staff were not required – or allowed – to attend the P-clearance Induction & Mentoring Program. It was partly because the Pub Comm staff were industry elites who could just make things up as they went without knowing anything about the organization they spoke for. But mostly it was because NASA had made a CSR commitment to mitigate the agency-wide occupation hazard of secret keeping, which studies had shown could induce insomnia, digestive problems, chest pain, impotence and baldness in the case of women.

Dispirited, Winston decided to look for some cheerful videos on the ride back to his studio, and fatefully stumbled upon an ad about the True Earth Summit. Thirty years later when biographers looked back at this very moment, they called it the moment that reshaped the world as we knew it.

* * *

"So... Sensei, about this event," Ohi asked and kept his head faced to the backseat, "should I clear your schedule for next week and book two tickets to Toronto?"

"Make it three," answered Winston, "but not before you help me crochet a message to that chicken in hiding."

Chapter 17

It would be a mistake to think of the True Earth Summit as an event exclusive for flat Earth believers, as it was in fact open to the skeptics of globe hypothesis from all schools of thoughts, who collectively referred to themselves as True Earth Seekers, or Seekers in short.

It is an even bigger mistake to think of the Seekers as simply people practicing another form of religion. A comedian once made such a comparison in public and soon found himself at the bottom of the Thames, because a passer-by found the connation offensively negative. The police never pieced together whether the passer-by was a Seeker or a theist.

"I still have a hard time believing Gina is a flatee," Smith said while pacing around the meeting room, "or a Seeker, or whatever you call it. Even though she never attended the orientation, her peers, the education curriculum, and all the space movies we uncreditedly co-produced should be enough to keep her in the line."

Britta ignored his moaning the way people ignore the complaint about insulin price from a dying diabetes patient who always vote for Republicans. She couldn't take her eyes off the files Smith just received from Dr. Stinson.

"I mean, the fact that a movie like *Truman Show* is produced in the first place," Smith continued his monologue, apparently forgetting that it was a status meeting for the R.D.G.A.R. operation, "should be enough evidence that the entertainment industry is *not* part of the conspiracy. Before I joined, I used to think, 'If *They* exist, why would *They* allow such a movie to be made when it warns people that everything they believe in could be a meticulously calculated lie?' Do people think it is a reverse psychology trick?"

The Round Ops representative, Charles Peralta, thought the question was directed at him and stopped texting with his phone.

"I wasn't here yet when that movie was made," he said with a shrug, "but I heard we green-lighted it because some lobbyists made a good case of how much profit would be brought to the psychiatry industry by exacerbating what we now call the Truman Show delusion."

"Thank you for jumping in, Charles," Smith said without any hint of sarcasm, "but I was just asking a rhetorical question like all those conspiracy theorists do," he then continued with his oration, "the very people who should have known better, picked up the clue and left Hollywood out of the equation."

"For any academics who didn't go through the induction program," said Britta and closed her laptop, "their lives would be spent on doing research and writing papers on false premises like 'gravity is real' and 'the Earth spins around the Sun.' They will always be chasing the non-existent graviton or busy at counting how many dimensions there are. Normally no one gets to do any *real* science until they get P level clearance. And even then, they can only do it discretely and need to keep publishing papers to promote false science."

"And to attend prize ceremonies that award them for their fake discoveries," Charles jumped in again, "but you would be pleased to know that nowadays they can delegate the publication duties to the AI we developed. No one can tell any difference."

"*Normally* that's the case," Britta said, "but Stinson is not normal. She ignores and then rediscovers all the science since Aristotle, adding new ideas along the way. She is basically Albert Einstein with a vagina *and* a stylist."

"Language!" said Mosby from the Human Resources department. No one in the room knew why he was in the meeting, or the last meeting, or the meeting before that, but assumed other attendees knew why.

"Seriously, did you just *language* me for saying out loud a body party that I have?" Britta retorted.

"I would do the same if Robin or Peralta brings up their reproductive organ unwarrantedly," said Mosby unflinchingly. "It's a two-way street."

Britta turned to Smith and asked him quietly, "Why the flat did you invite HR to our meetups?"

"I..." Smith whispered and seemed uncomfortable with the question, "didn't. Every time I walked into the meeting room, he was already here. He didn't seem to mind staying or being kept in the loop of minutes, so I thought some of you must have invited him..."

Honest mistakes – like arriving to the wrong meetings, sending emails to unexpected recipients, leaving classified files on the subway, or taking selfies with the Earth replica in staff library – happened every day in NASA. That was why part of NSD's job was to surveil NASA employees, and some NSD analysts specialized in monitoring NSD staff, which were in turn spied by another group of NSD staff, and so on and so forth.

Unbeknown to Britta, Mosby was *not* one of those surveillants; he simply walked into the wrong room and didn't mind coming back.

Fighting off her anxiety of being watched, Britta returned to face the room and said, "Anyway, enough on who Dr. Stinson is; let's focus on what she will reveal to the Seekers."

After waiting a full minute for the screen behind her to drop down and spending another ten minutes with IT to fix the display issues, she managed to put on screen the presentation materials that Dr. Stinson was going to use in the summit.

"Since she didn't share her full speech with Robin," Britta said, still insisting on last-name basis, "we can only speculate what she will say based on the presentation slides we got."

Britta then rapidly clicked through several slides showing pictures of plain, river, sunset, eclipse, and constellations.

"Apparently, Dr. Stinson is going to begin with why one can only see the horizon up to three miles away," Britta said, "which, according to our storytellers from Sci-Edu, is because the Earth has a curvature."

Everyone in the room chuckled, except Mosby, who was counting how long it was before lunch.

"This is not funny. The flaters had made up this eight-inches-per-mile-squared rule of thumb to counter us," said Britta, referring to the increasing number of memes where the drop height of distant objects deviated from expectation.

"About that," said Charles, "my team is developing an App for people to calculate how much a distant object is obstructed by curvature. We will claim that our results are more accurate because it accounts for the observer's height and atmospheric refraction."

Saying the word "refraction" cracked Charles up again.

"Speaking of refraction," said Britta, "I assume Stinson is also going to explain the concept of re-refraction and how it distorts the sightline. Then, presumably she will talk about the Bedford Level experiment. As I am sure all of you can recall from our orientation, the Bedford Level experiment conducted by Samuel Rowbotham and Lady Elizabeth Blount successfully showed that the Earth is flat. But the findings were discredited by our English counterpart, contesting that the experiments failed to account for refraction."

The room burst into laughter again.

"O my, I remember that story," said Charles with tears in his eyes.

"Poor Rowbotham and Blount, they completely fell for the refraction BS. It's a shame that they never heard of the *real* science of re-refraction," Smith said and laughed hysterically.

Mosby still kept a straight face, trying to recall the menu of cafeteria.

"Guys, this is serious," Britta said with a straight face, "if my guess is correct, it will be the first time for the public to learn of re-refraction."

The whole room instantly fell into silence, because they – besides Mosby, who was deciding on the drinks – understood the implication, even though they had no idea how re-refraction actually worked.

It is no exaggeration to say that refraction and its sister re-refraction (short for real refraction) were at the very center of scientific disputes over the shape of our planet. Refraction as a scientific concept was first made up and used by the supporters of round Earth fallacy (i.e., present-day globeheads or globetards) in the 19th century, who desperately wanted to win a wager against the supporter of Rowbotham. In order to discredit the Bedford Level experiment, the globeheads claimed that light travelled slower in air and the varying air density in atmosphere bended the path of light, which of course was nonsense.

About a century later, this made-up word was appropriated by Seekers who were confronted by natural phenomena they could not explain with their own models of Earth, such as sunset, eclipse, and shift of constellations. Since refraction was a make-up concept to begin with, globeheads and Seekers could never agree on what it meant and neither of them ever succeeded in convincing another that the Earth was or was not a globe.

While globetards and Seekers were busy mocking each other's scientific illiteracy, the *real* scientists (i.e., scientists that had gone through the baptism of PIMP and hence were allowed to do research for *real* science) discovered re-refraction in the late 20th century. This powerful concept could explain the aforementioned phenomena without the crutch of round Earth model, and had been the most safely guarded secret in the *real* scientific community. Even in the orientation materials of PIMP, re-refraction was only briefly mentioned as "a natural phenomenon by which light works in a mysterious way."

"It may not be as bad as it sounds," Smith spoke after a long silence. "Re-refraction is like $E = mc^2$; anyone can print it on their T-shirt, but few truly understand what it means."

"Agree," Charles concurred. "If that's all Dr. Stinson has to say, then I don't see any need for Round Ops to get involved."

"Boys, I only showed the first six pages of her slides," Britta said, eyerolling at the room's naïve optimism. From her vantage point, only Mosby appreciated the gravity of the issue at hand. She resumed clicking through the slides rapidly, all of which were full of mathematics formulas.

"At the risk of stating the obvious," Britta added, "we are busted."

"I see," said Smith as if he did. "Just for the benefit for Charles over there, do you mind elaborating a bit more?"

"Stinson found holes in all the pillars of modern physics," Britta answered while flipping through the slides. "Here, she shows that gravity can never fit into the Standard Model. There, she catches us using a sleight of hand to prove the string theory. You know, the only way we could prove the theory is by saying the sum of all natural numbers is equal to negative one over twelve."

"What, she actually read the proof?" Charles said in surprise. "No one ever read the proofs. People just take scientific theories as given and incorporate them into pop culture."

"And that's not even the worst part," Britta continued. "We can maneuver around those loopholes by smearing her reputation or having some Nobel laureates publicly rebuke her, but apparently she got something even more damning."

Britta jumped to the last slide of the presentation, which only had one line of text highlighted in yellow:

<Placeholder for "The Proof" video >

Chapter 18

Agent B was visibly annoyed that Britta Geller didn't read out loud what was so damning in Dr. Stinson's slides. She didn't know what to write on the report.

Watching agent B scratch her head, agent F found her quite cute. She was always his favorite, because she kept everything neat and tidy, easy to read even with his moderately powerful binoculars.

Chapter 19

Mosby Dent was the office equivalent of a cameraman in animal documentaries, that is to say he strictly followed the cardinal rule of not letting his presence interfere with the outcome of decision making.

The outsourcing of head hunting, automation of benefit calculation, and use of consultants for training, survey, resources planning, etc. essentially meant that Mosby had no place to break the rule even if he dreamed to. That was why he was so used to making absolutely no contribution to any meeting he attended. Conscious of the risk of brain death due to prolonged inactivity, Mosby's mind was actively philosophizing whenever he was not expected to speak, which was basically all the time.

How much time left before lunch?

When will they be done with the PowerPoint?

Why do they get all worked up by this PowerPoint?
Is there any point?
What is the point of power?
Where does the power reside?
Do They *have power?*
Who are They?

"Who are *They?*" is indeed the most intriguing question in philosophy. The question pre-supposes *They* are real and not just some metaphysical construct developed for argument's sake, that is, *They* exist as much as Tooth Fairies don't. And since this question is often asked out of context, its underlying assumption is that both the questioner and would-be respondent know exactly who or what the word "*They*" refer to. This bold assumption unfailingly leads one to believe that the question itself is rhetorical, when most of the time it isn't. As soon as the would-be respondent realizes the question's non-rhetorical nature and its ambiguous use of pronoun, they will always seek clarification by asking, "Who are *They?*" A loop of question and counter question will then ensue.

Mosby steered clear of that loop by pre-defining *Them* as those who were ultimately behind the Global Lie. "Ultimately" was the operative word. Surely, he was aware that the scientific community, construction industry, airline companies, SpaceX travelers, movie producers, GPS manufacturers, cartography associations, etc. were all in bed with NASA and its equivalents in allied as well as hostile nations to tell the Big Lie. But he still couldn't figure out who was behind all that. For a moment, he thought NASA was the ultimate beneficiary, stealing from its annual budget that accounted for as much as 4% of the federal budget in mid 1960s. But its declining funding since 1970s and the extent of collaboration required from private sectors convinced him that NASA couldn't be making enough to pay the kickback.

Mosby then suspected that Uncle Sam was scheming with the ultra-rich to control the people, but had a hard time figuring out why China and Russia would play ball with the U.S.

It's not like our eastern friends need any excuse to misappropriate taxpayers' money.

Eventually he deduced, boldly but logically, that all the

geopolitical conflicts were just a front.

Cold War was an act, NATO is a foil, sanctions is a prop and trade war is plot device.

He couldn't quite put his finger on what was behind that front, so he continued to call it *Them* for now but he could already see the answer clearly in his mind. His brilliant mind concluded that he had solved the most elusive question since "How are you doing?"

They are the most powerful and discrete beings on earth, capable of controlling the G12 to do their biddings while staying completely out of sight.

Mosby was quite pleased with his reasoning, feeling like he just discovered between the Earth and Mars an orbiting china teapot hitherto undetected. With so much accomplished before lunch, he decided to stop spacing out and rejoin his colleagues. He noticed the NSD Analyst had come to the last slide of her presentation, with nothing but a placeholder for video.

Well, it would be great if someone makes a video to explain why They want to lie about the Earth's shape.

Britta had gone through a few possible candidates of what she guessed would be the contents of Dr. Stinson's video, but soon realized it was futile.

I need more data, she thought.

Meanwhile, Smith just got off the phone with Dr. Stinson.

"You were right. She said she had evidence that can destroy the globe once and for all."

"And she told you what it is?"

"No, she just said she wanted to keep it a secret but would think about giving me a teaser if I buy her a drink," said Smith, without concealing the pride in his charm, "so I guess agent Robin will need to be on the field again."

"We are way past discovery now," Britta said. "Just knowing what she found is not enough; we need to stop it from being shown to the flaters."

"Did you mean I should..." Smith asked while having his index finger cross his throat.

"No, taking her out now would give too much credit to the flaters.

Take it from me, nothing makes conspiracy theorists happier than seeing one of their own mysteriously die." Britta's eyes dashed to Charles and continued, "What I meant is Round Ops should step in and sabotage her presentation."

"What?" the Round Ops agent said in incredulity and stood up. "No way, next week is Columbus Day. Do you have any ideas how many STEM projects across the country my team will need to round off? Not to mention our BAU task of making ships progressively disappear over the horizon. I don't have extra hands to help with you little sabotage."

"But doesn't Round Ops always attend flatees' events on standby, in case an intervention is needed?" asked Smith.

"Yeah, but the problem is..." said Charles reluctantly, "the boys and I have a rather specific role to play in the summit. I am not sure if we can help."

Before Britta could redefine the problem, Smith gave her a wink to signal that he could handle it with the problem-solving skills he had picked from his previous employer.

He cleared his throat to command Charles' attention and said, "I am afraid you, and you alone, have the problem. As your colleague and project manager, I am more than happy to discuss any of your problem and recommend you a few books on problem solving. But, I have to say, at no point of our discussion shall your problem become my problem, because once your problem becomes my problem, I will have two problems. First, I will have your original problem. Second, since you no longer have your problem, I am left to wonder why we were discussing your problem. You see, this can become quite a problem."

Charles found himself involuntarily nodding along, while Britta wondered if Smith just redefined the concept of problem solving.

"So I guess the best way forward is," Smith added, "you and I go together to Toronto, while we discuss the little problem of yours on our flight. You will leave the conversation with the problem still being exclusively your problem, while I will go to meet Gina, find out where the video and its backups are, and give you the signal when the time is right."

"The signal to do what?" Charles asked, having already forgot what the problem was.

"Did you not get a copy of my A3 laminated R.D.G.A.R. chart?" howled Smith, taking the question personally. "Attack. We will attack."

Chapter 20

The official website of the United Ways, an international organization whose purpose was to maintain friendly relationships among Seekers and provided advice on tax avoidance, had the following description of the summit:

The True Earth Summit to the Seekers is what the Parliament of the World's Religions is to the faithful. Both of them pave the path for people who literally see the worlds differently to meet in the middle. The Summit was created to bring the world's enlightened communities closer, encourage productive exchanges of ideas, and promote tolerance among geocentric creeds.

Nothing could be further away from the truth.

The True Earth Summit (formerly known as the Council of Four and the Congress of Seekers) was created by and originally exclusive to the *Big Four*, namely All-Ways, Treeism, TYDF and Zetetic Society (the spiritual ancestor of present-day Disk Earth Society). The Big Four convened the first Council of Four in 1893 with the intention to settle their intellectual differences once and for all. They informally described their objective as "to debate the hell out of each other and have the victor lead the rest of us in waging the war on globalists." Because of the cultural differences in interpreting the coordinates of meeting venue, the first Council meeting was adjourned due to insufficient quorum. They tried to meet again in 1903, but Zetetic Society's insistence on using a sidereal day calendar – according to which one day was equal to the time it took a distant star, rather than the Sun, to return to its position – thwarted that attempt. They finally managed to meet in 1913, with a minor wording change in their meeting objective: To avoid being mistaken as a protectionism movement, the word "globalists" was replaced with the less controversial and more politically neutral term "globetards."

As fate would have it, the Big Four's meeting/debate was prematurely ended due to an incident in the All-Ways camp. Its representative, Kunal Kutner, was supposed to cite empirical evidence in support of his people's belief that the Earth rested on the back of the Cosmic Turtle, but he went off the book when describing the turtle's favorite sport. He claimed that the world-bearing turtle swam breaststroke on an infinite ocean, which directly contradicted the canons of All-Ways. The teachings of orthodox All-Ways unambiguously stated that the world extended all the way down, that is, the turtle stood on top of another turtle, which stood on another turtle, which in turn was another turtle on an infinite tower of turtles. Upon hearing the heresy, Kunal's father, which was also the leader of All-Ways at that time, jumped onto the stage and gave his son what we nowadays call a Batman's slap. The incident not only brought the council's meeting to an abrupt end, but also resulted in the First Schism of modern geocentrism. Kunal and his followers left All-Ways and triggered the so-called Ratlonallst Movement (not to be confused with rationalist, which spells with *i*'s and embraces the epistemological view of rationalism) by founding numerous branches of All-Ways, each adhering to a rational number of turtles in their doctrines. They rejected the dogma of infinite turtles and criticized imaginary numbers for blasphemy. The favorite sport of ratlonallsts was to offer wager that their chosen number of turtles couldn't be proven wrong. No one had won such wagers, ever.

Due to the Ratlonallst Movement, All-Ways had been largely weakened and was only the third largest belief system among the Big Four.

"Has Dr. Stinson arrived yet?" Pandit Abed Kutner asked as he got off from the backseat of a SUV. On the back of the SUV was a bumper sticker that read "Always All-Ways."

"I am afraid not, your Excellency," said Seth Nadir, the right-hand man of Kutner. He, Kutner and the dozens of men behind them were all dressed in black Sherwani and wore the same armband printed with a tower of turtles. Below that was the slogan "WE GO ALL THE WAY DOWN." The only difference between their armbands was that Kutner's was in golden yellow while the rest in blue.

The pandit did not speak another word as he walked through the main entrance of Greendale Convention Centre. A sign next to it said, "Attendees of True Earth Summit, welcome to Greendale, your one-stop shop for conference, vacation, dinning, sports, and affairs. As a pioneer in hospitality market, we provide 100% guarantee that our facilities are not haunted." Below the statement was a QR code that would direct the customers to submit refund claims along with ghost sighting evidence.

Nadir took the pandit's silence as a sign that he was in a fit of pique, or constipation. He rather erred on the side of caution and humbly said, "I was told that Dr. Stinson will attend the banquet tonight. If it makes sense, maybe I arrange her to sit at—"

Nadir stopped speaking as Kutner waved his hand. He stared at the pandit's slender fingers in dread.

So it was constipation after all?!

"Seth," Kutner said and stopped in tracks, "I don't want her under the wrong impression that it is a social gathering. I expect the doctor to walk me through what she will present this Thursday. As her sponsor, don't you think it is the least I am owed?"

"Certainly, I will arrange it immediately." While Nadir pulled out his phone, the pandit resumed walking to the exhibition floor. Pandit Kutner was usually in a much better mood when not having digestive problem, but the summit rendered him tense.

I will lead All-Ways to reclaim its long-lost glory, thought the pandit. *The keynote speech. The debate. The election. Everything must be perfect.*

Although there was still some time before the summit's opening event, a number of merchandise booths had already been set up at the exhibition space outside of the ballroom. A small number of attendees had also finished checking in to the hotel upstairs and were wandering between the exhibits. The pandit was too proud to get a good look at them, but at a glance he saw that most of the booths bore the logo of a transparent, umbrella-shaped tree.

Despicable profiteers. Once I am elected, the only goods you get to sell will be the replica of Cosmic Turtle and merchandises featuring President Abed Kutner's face.

Just before entering the ballroom, the pandit walked past three men intensely staring at a carrot-shaped object. Two of them, in Hawaiian shirts, appeared to be Southeast Asians but could speak fluent English, while the other one with light skin, in a jacket with elbow patches, was holding a carrot in silence. Kutner did a double take at them, trying to figure out what this unlikely trio were up to.

They don't seem to be from any of the Big Four. That means they are swing votes. I should go shake some hands, give some bows, or kiss some cheeks, depending on their cultural disposition.

The pandit had barely taken a step when someone from one of those booths greeted the trio and dragged them over. Disheartened, the pandit spun and entered the ballroom.

Your loss.

Chapter 21

"Dudes," Chandler said as he took off his sunglasses, "I am beginning to think this is not the Canada Aviation Tradeshow."

"What," said Winston with an awkward smile, "what gives you this silly and factually unsound idea?"

"You know what is the most common merch in an aviation tradeshow?"

"Moveable action figures of flight attendants with changeable cloths and body parts?"

"No, they never take up my ideas," Chandler said bitterly. "It's plane models, sometimes bundled with a disproportionate globe underneath. But the people around here are selling disks, trees and cubes printed with a map. And the two forty-plus-year-old dudes in a brawl over there almost killed each other when arguing how many angels can stand on one corner of the Earth. Please tell me you didn't bring me to the Church of Satan for human sacrifice."

"Nonsense," Winston said dismissively. "This is how the Canadians do aviation tradeshow. They are just more innovative and passionate about their trade. Remember I told you they would have a stewardess pageant?"

"Sensei," Ohi interjected, "now that Mr. Chandler is with us, maybe we can tell him the truth?”

Winston closed his eyes for a moment and turned to his slightly unhinged friend, who had been hiding from imaginary assassins for almost a month and started naming the carrots in his plant house.

“OK, I made Ohi lie to you about the whole tradeshow thing, but I couldn’t think of other ways to bring you up here. And I did this only because I wanted to help you.”

“O my...,” Chandler said in shock and disgust. “*You wanted to help?* This is exactly what a Satanist would say before cutting the sacrifice open on an altar. I would be so pissed at you if the pageant does not have a swimsuit competition.”

“Dude, knock it off already,” Winston snapped, “we stopped doing human sacrifice years ago, and there will be no flight attendant pageant, with or without swimsuit competition.”

“I am sorry for lying to you, Mr. Chandler,” Ohi pleaded on his boss’ behalf, “but Sensei did this only because he wanted to show that you are not in any real danger just because you know a thing or two about flat Earth. Look around you,” Ohi drew Chandler’s attention to the signs and booths around them, “you can see disk Earthers, cube Earthers, tree Earthers, prism Earthers, triangular pyramid Earthers, square pyramid Earthers, hexagonal pyramid Earthers, and, oh my, phallic Earthers.”

“No, I think they just believe the Earth is a circular conic frustum, with the Sun and Moon orbiting it,” Winston corrected him.

“True, that would make more sense,” Ohi said and wonder why he hadn’t seen that. “My point is, if someone is willing to kill for covering up the big lie, none of these people would still be alive and kicking, except for the two dudes over there. They definitely stopped kicking.”

“So you brought me to a freakshow to show that I don’t have a reason to freak out?”

“Yes.”

“And neither of you are going to cut me for blood ritual?”

“Absolutely not. At least not today.”

“And you are sure the theatre down there is not going to host any beauty contest?”

“Yes. Seriously, why are you still asking?”

Chandler took in the information and reflected on his behaviors in the past four weeks. He breathed a sigh of both relief and disappointment, and took out the carrot in his jacket.

Wilson, it is time for me to move on. So long. And sorry for what I did to Barbara.

Before Chandler could kiss his orange friend good bye, a woman with similar skin pigment as Wilson came to greet the trio.

"Morning early birds," said the cheerful lady in a blue long sleeve shirt, the front of which read "THE JEWS LIE!" To pre-emptively address the most likely follow-up question, the back of her shirt clarified "I AM NOT ANTI-SEMITIC."

"I am BigLoveMaeve2E731 or you can just call me Maeve. Before you ask, I am not biologically related to Trump; I just got a really bad artificial tanner."

For a moment, the trio thought they were going to hear a Mormon sermon or a pitch about their cars' extended warranty, but remembered they were in the venue of True Earth Summit, which was something on a totally different level.

"Um... Maeve, thank you for the offer of whatever you are going to offer," said Winston, "but on our way here, we already subscribed to three newsletters, signed up for a dating service, funded a Kickstarter game, and our bags are now full of obviously overpriced T-shirts, posters and bumper stickers, some of which even you would find offensive."

"No, no, no, no, that's not what it's about," Maeve clarified and dragged them to her booth. "I am not here for sales. With that said, if you are interested, you may still visit booths E616-E632 down the vendor hall that will be open between ten and six. We don't do toys. We sell mattresses, dining tables, digital scales and frozen pizza, all in the shape of Earth."

Maeve knew exactly how confusing this sales pitch would be in a forum promoting diverse ideas of the Earth's shape. She was not really into making some sales commission, although it wouldn't hurt, considering her husband just left her for being "a flatard." She was trying to gauge the trio's geological orientation.

"That sounds... interesting," Winston said and really meant it, "although I don't have a round bed frame for your mattress."

Praise the Earth, thought Maeve.

"That's fine. As I said, I am not trying to sell you anything," Maeve pulled a document from her booth and leaned in to the trio. "I was just wondering if you have any thoughts on the election."

As the only one from the group who had read through the 128-page brochure, Ohi knew Maeve was referring to the main event on day four: Election of the president of the United Ways (POTUWS). The brochure explained that the word "way" took its meaning from Taoism, by which *the way* (or *Tao*) could refer to a path, tradition or doctrine. It also stated the POTUWS would have the power to control the doctrine of all registered members of geocentric creeds.

"Wait a second," Chandler cried out, "so there *is* a vote for pageant?"

"No, Mr. Chandler," Ohi interrupted before the retired pilot could further embarrass himself, "and Ms. Maeve, we didn't plan to vote. We are here for exploration."

"O honey, I didn't mean to ask if you will vote for the POTUWS," Maeve said with a grin. "I just wanted to know if any of you are interested in *running* for the POTUWS."

Chapter 22

The Disk Earth Society (DES), whose ancestor was the second largest geocentric creed for the better part of the 20th century, had no one but itself to blame for its fall from grace.

As YouTube became the chief source of knowledge in 2000s, the School of Flat Earth (an intermediary between the Zetetic Society and DES) saw an unprecedented number of recruits. It was on its way to overtake the Indo-European Treeism and make America proud again, but inexplicably it started shooting its own feet. Like really hard. With an intent to kill. As if its feet murdered its significant other and then drew their signature happy feet in blood to taunt it.

What happened was that a number of vocal, well-intentioned flat Earthers publicly – that is, on YouTube channels with up to hundreds of subscribers – accused each other of being ingenuine believers. Before long, flat Earthers turned their attention from productive research to name calling, as if they were debating how to eradicate poverty, provide accessible medicine or fund public schools. They called each other controlled opposition, movie studio's plant, CIA agent, and false prophet. As a matter of fact, it was this toxic dispute that gave Smith Robin the idea to penetrate into the flat Earthers' circle.

The mutual sabotage was one of the triggers to the Second Schism, dissolving the School of Flat Earth into multiple small creeds, the biggest of which was the modern-day Disk Earth Society. This reorganization not only made DES the smallest among the Big Four, but also put it in a very embarrassing position in the True Earth Summit: No one was willing to run as a DES presidential candidate.

"Maeve, I don't know what to tell you," Winston said meekly. "Call me traditional, but I am not used to being asked by a woman I just meet to run for election."

"But... will you stay in Toronto in the coming four days?" asked Maeve.

"Er... we will."

"Do you plan to go anywhere besides the summit's events?"

"Well, we haven't had time to figure that out yet. You know, it is Canada."

"Were you previously indicted or convicted in any countries?"

"Umm... yes, but it was a misunderstanding. I drank a lot of water that day..."

"It doesn't matter; it won't affect your candidacy. And in case it is what you were worried about, there is no application fee. No service charge. You will even get a free lapel pin like the one I have here."

"Cute, it looks like a humanoid magnifying glass with arms, legs and..." Winston looked more closely to the cartoon Seeker, "whatever body part it is, being held by a hand to observe the Earth."

"See, there is absolutely no downside and unbounded upside for running."

Winston did not find any weakness in Maeve's arguments.

"Now, what do you say? Sign here and complete a short form,

then you will be our POTUWS candidate," Maeve said and handed a pen and a pile of forms to Winston.

"I will do it," Chandler interrupted and attempted to grab the papers from Maeve.

"Sorry, honey," Maeve said unapologetically and withdrew the papers. "You are too white for that. If we want to appeal to the far left, we need to be more woke."

"Is it why *you* didn't run for the office?" asked Chandler. "By it, I didn't mean how much you sound like my racist grandma."

"No worry, I get that a lot," Maeve said with a genuine smile. "I know how much I sound like a person of refined wisdom. But that's not the reason why I, the vice-chairwoman of Disk Earth Society, cannot put my name in the ticket. My name *is* the reason why it cannot be on the ticket."

"What's wrong with your name?" asked Ohi when Maeve began to write her last name on the back of POTUWS application form.

Walsh

All three men looked attentively at the letters, racing to find an anagram that might suggest she was the Antichrist or reincarnation of Hitler.

"This is my last name, and if you put the *l* in front of the capital *W*, then it looks like this," Maeve said as she kept writing.

lWash

English is so confusing; the lower-case of L looks like an upper-case i, Ohi thought.

It looks like the name of an Apple product, Chandler thought.

What do I wash? Winston wondered.

"Now, if you look closely, you will notice that the *l* and *W*, when written closely together, look like two *N*'s written in one stroke. Something like this."

NNash

Ohi wondered why anyone would write *l* and *W* like that, Chandler found his head spinning, and Winston's brain just completely shut down.

"Then, if you re-arrange the letters this way… you get this. Now you see where the problem is?"

Nsa Nh

All three men were wondering if they were incredibly stupid or the word "problem" had a definition they were never made aware of. Ohi happily concluded it must be the latter since English was not his mother tongue.

"Oh, sorry, I forgot to give you some context," Maeve added. "I am from New Hampshire."

Winston was still in denial but Chandler was beginning to accept his stupidity.

"National Security Agency, New Hampshire," Maeve revealed the answer. "I have spent years trying to explain to my fellow flat Earthers it is just a coincidence that my family name can spell the acronym of my home state *and* the most secret intelligence agency…" Maeve felt like crying as she spoke, "but people still don't believe me."

"This is…" said Ohi, "very hard to explain away." He had tried to think of something nice to console her, but he also found the coincidence uncanny. "For what it's worth, I would have volunteered to run if my employment contract didn't prohibit employment, partnership, joint venture, directorship, or equivalents in any organizations not affiliated with Kane Shotto Studio."

Maeve began weeping like she was the only person in the family photo not being tagged.

"So…," said Winston, "will you transfer my personal data to any third party without my consent if I sign this form?"

"No, we would never do that," Maeve sprang to life instantly and resumed her pitching. "If you tick this box, your data will be exclusively shared with the sponsors of True Earth Summit, their parent companies, subsidiaries, affiliates, venture partners, licensees, and the designated organizations on this website that is updated from time to time. All of these organizations have comprehensive privacy policies written by excellent lawyers."

"Sensei, are you sure about that?" Ohi whispered uneasily. "We don't know what impact it will have on your income tax residency status."

"Listen up, both of you," Winston quietly said as he put on the lapel pin from Maeve, "besides helping Chandler with his paranoia problem, we are here to validate what we discovered a month ago. What's a better way than telling the constituents what we know and let them do the homework for us? I am sure they will exercise the wisdom of crowds and fact check everything I say like a sensible voter."

Both Chandler and Ohi took a moment to take in Winston's optimism. They respectively thought of Brexit and the frequent change of prime minister in Japan. They could never get the hang of those dramas, but the dramas were what millions of eligible adults had voted for. Those voters must have collectively thought it through and validated all available options before casting the votes. Following this line of thought, both men came to the same conclusion: A bunch of average persons could see things they alone couldn't.

They both nodded to Winston.

With his best friends' approval, Winston picked up Maeve's pen and started filling out the form."

"You only need to fill in this page and I will do the rest for you," Maeve explained and guided Winston through the single-spaced text wall in 8pt font. "Finally, sign here. You can download and read the terms of conditions later. While I help you fill out the rest of the form and plagiarize a two-thousand-word platform, you may start preparing your speech."

"Well, fair point," said Winston. "I am sure I can come up with something after absorbing all the information this summit will throw at me."

"Sensei," Ohi beat Maeve to it, "you may not have that luxury of research. According to the brochure, all POTUWS candidates will deliver the keynote speech, slash, election speech at 9 a.m., which is like, now."

Chapter 23

"... and that's how the model of Cosmic Turtle can explain days and nights, seasons, tides, eclipses and climate change. Combine it with the watchmaker argument I put forward earlier, I suppose I have convinced you that the world as we know it rests on an infinite number of turtles and turtle warming is real," said Pandit Kutner. "Thank you all. Praise the Earth."

Damn it, I missed the opening, Smith groaned as he entered Sapphire Dome, the main ballroom of Greendale Convention Centre.

Closing the doors behind, he could barely see the podium at the far end of the dome. The pandit of All-Ways had just delivered his keynote address to the six hundred participants. Seeing the ballroom was almost at its full capacity, Smith began to worry that he could only sit at some gym rat in moist discolored shirt with unsubtle armpit stains.

He was not supposed to be at the Greendale Convention Centre until his meeting with Dr. Stinson tonight, but he decided to come in the morning anyway. He could not resist the curiosity to find out what kind of self-respecting adults would take four days off from work to join an event about geocentrism.

I thought flatees would be too unemployed to pay five hundred and ninety-nine Canadian dollars before tax for a four-day pass.

It didn't take long for him to realize how unjustified and stereotypical his presumption was, because at the registration counter he bumped into his former colleagues from MacCheddar & Co. One of them explained that they came for the annual corporate retreat and the theme this year was "Bleeding Open Mind and Impossible Sales Pitch." They were all excited to expand their horizon and pick up some speaking skills from the summit. Because of the chit-chat, Smith had missed out on the most scientific argument for world-bearing turtle. Luckily, he could still find an empty seat near the stage and his neighbors actually smelt pretty nice.

By the time he put on the translation headset, the chairman of

TYDF, Ben Song, who Smith estimated was between sixty and four hundred years old, had already slogged his way to the podium and begun his emotionless speech.

TYDF was arguably the most ancient creed among the Big Four. The chronicle of its rise and fall was comparable to Shakespearean tragedy, and much more interesting than its current chairman's speech.

The root of TYDF could be traced all the way back to the 220s BC. Its doctrine originated from the literal interpretation of the ancient concept *Tian Yuan Di Fang*, meaning round sky and square earth. It was the most popular, the least contested, and the only geographical thought in East Asia at that time. Hundreds of books were written about it, but all of them were destroyed along with their authors when an emperor ordered the burning of books and burial of scholars between 213 and 212 BC. After that incident, eastern scholars dared not conduct any more geological research, and *Tian Yuan Di Fang* was repurposed as a philosophical idea related to *Yin* and *Yang*.

The suppression on TYDF movement sustained for almost two thousand years. When the last imperial dynasty was overthrown in 1912, the TYDF adherents in hiding thought they could finally be left alone to do their research. They studied, published, lectured and were on their way to reclaim the glorious days that TYDF had lost to book barbecue. Unfortunately, most of those scholars were wiped out because of a great famine that kill tens of millions during 1959-1961. The lucky ones who survived on cannibalism dedicated themselves to estimate the death toll of the famine. Before they could agree on a number that would not sound too bad, almost all of them were cruelly killed or driven to insanity in a sociopolitical movement during 1966-1976.

Despite all the hardship, the remaining adherents of TYDF never abandoned their research. In the 21st century, their perseverance was finally answered by the miracle called Second Schism, which revived the dying creed of TYDF and made it the second most influential geocentric creed.

* * *

Smith was awakened by a thundering ovation and startled to learn that it was already 10:32am.

Shoot, I slept for almost an hour.

Before he could ask his neighbor what he had missed, he noticed the chairman of TYDF was just leaving the stage.

As it turned out, the speech – or more accurately, the reading of scripts – by Chairman Song lasted seventy bloody minutes. The audience mistakenly thought the translation headset malfunctioned because the interpreter fell asleep five minutes after Song began. Curiously, the standing ovation did not come from the TYDF fellows; it came from the bottom of the hearts of those who were grateful for the end of a virtual (or verbal) lobotomy.

After the host jokingly reminded audience not to mock TYDF adherents' belief because they had a pinky heart of glass, he made another joke about the taboo of mentioning their fragile egos, and was escorted away from the stage by security guards, for his own safety.

Without the host's introduction, a man in Hawaiian shirt stepped onto the stage and picked up the microphone. Some audience expected he was the DES chairman who purportedly had been hiding from the Illuminati for over a decade.

Isn't their chairman still in a coma caused by type 2 diabetes? Smith wondered.

The man on stage had a care-free demeanor, striking the audience as a confident leader. He unconsciously adjusted the lapel pin on his left chest pocket, which some interpreted as a heartfelt salute to the United Ways. Before he spoke, he took a few rapid, involuntary breathes and did a two-hundred-decibel sneeze, confirming his importance in the room and seizing everyone's attention.

"Morning my fellow Seekers, my name is Winston Kanshū."

Chapter 24

There are many things Winston didn't know, almost as many as the things he didn't know that he didn't know. For instance, the story behind the lapel pin on his chest.

Ever since the first Council of Four meeting, adherents of geocentrism had been lovingly referring to themselves as *Geochapes*. Two things led to the name change in the late 20th century. First, in 1970s the fans of Arsenal Football Club started embracing *Gooners* as their nickname, which was intended by rival teams as an insult on the Arsenal fans who called themselves *Gunners*. The Geochapes then thought, *Hey, we are obviously very open-minded people, and if those Gooners can take an insult and turn it into a prideful identity, so can we. Well, we have been called suckers for the majority of our adult lives, so why don't we start calling ourselves Sucker… Supper… Sister… Seeker. Yes, Seekers!*

The second reason for the nickname change is that some outsiders began to confuse the Geochape with the name of a certain rock Pokémon. Since the video game franchise was at that time construed as a devious scheme to promote Satanism and, much more importantly, one of the franchise owners had a team of famously aggressive copyright lawyers, the nickname Geochape was largely abandoned in late 1990s.

No, it never occurred to the Geochapes that some of their fellow believers did not have Y chromosome, so the name change had nothing to do with the use of gender-neutral language.

Even though Winston was not yet indoctrinated with all the rich culture and fascinating history of the United Ways and geocentrism, he had watched enough Fox News to know what to say in a formal speech.

"I am very, very happy to be here today. This is a great place. A wonderful conference center, even though it's in Canada."

Some audience giggled.

"It gives me tremendous pleasure to talk to you folks about the many great things I have in my head, which is very bright. Many people say it is the brightest thing they ever saw, and those people are very intelligent people. They all like me, and I like them. I respect them, like a lot.

"Before I tell you my great ideas, I would like to say a few words on behalf of my vice-chairwoman, Maeve. Look over there, she is a wonderful person. Very wonderful."

For a few seconds, Maeve appeared on the wall screen behind Winston, minding her business of nose mining.

"She wanted me to say that we miss our fellow flat Earthers from North Korea. Despite the different opinions we have on whether Kim Il-sung is the Sun, we and the North Koreans see eyes to eyes on a lot of things. A lot. They actually have people who were going to join us, you know. They got the travel permission for attending scientific conference and flew all the way to Canada. But... um... for some reasons they disappeared after getting off the plane. Maybe they got lost. I am sure they will show up any minute. It could happen. It could happen even to the brightest among us. I remember something similar happened when I stayed in France last year. A French producer wanted to meet me on the first floor of an office building. *Le premier étage*, that's how they call it. I went to the first floor and waited and waited and waited, and he never showed up. I made sure I was on the first floor of that building – it was actually a pretty small building, unlike the beautiful skyscrapers we have in Manhattan; you know what Freud said how we symbolize power using big, high building, don't you – so I was damn sure I was on the right floor. But damn, that frog went to the second floor. He got lost, at the building he chose to meet me. Believe me, I am not trying to make fun of him or the French people in general. I love him, despite his being retarded and too stubborn to admit his mistakes. I am just telling you: Anyone may get lost once in a while. That's all."

In the span of a few minutes, Winston talked about the North Koreans' geocentric model, narrated a short episode of Winston@Paris, compared the commercial buildings in Paris and Manhattan, mused on their symbolic significance, expressed his complex feeling of a French colleague, before reverting to the message from Maeve: *North Korean flater Earthers can't join us today and I don't know why.* While it almost made the interpreter and transcriber commit double suicide, the conversational speech style completely captivated the audience. To some of them, it was the first conversation they had with a human being in the last decade.

"OK, OK, enough of the foreplay," Winston continued with his speech. "This is not about the North Koreans. This is not about Maeve, or the microchip some of you allege is in planted in her NSA nose. No. It is about *me*. Me! Some of you may recognize me as a movie director and wonder why I never came out as a flat Earther before. You may question if I belong to here. But actually, you and I are not that different. I have been called many names in my life. Mostly animal names. And I am sure most of you do. You over there. Yes, you. Tell me, have you been called any names before?"

"They call me idiot," a man in the front row shouted.

"Very good, anyone else?" Winston opened his arms to invite the audience.

"Flatard," Maeve yelled from the crowd.

"Good."

"Turdiot," another man with a blue armband said.

"Great."

"Pervert," a man sitting near the entrance said, with a hand in his pants.

"Dude, you deserve that. And stop doing it."

The floor was hysterical and kept shouting out names, as if they were brainstorming how to call their newborn baby. They felt like they finally found the company who would understand them.

"Awesome, awesome," Winston spoke again and gestured the crowd to calm down. "You all have met some very creative people. Especially the German ones. Wow, they really know how to pack all reproductive organs into one word.

"But, you know, are those people right in calling us those names? Of course not. Except for that guy at the back. Jeez, stop doing it and don't put him on the screen behind me.

"Phew, they are wrong. You are all very intelligent people. Very, very smart. Believe me. I know, because I talked to some of you before I came up. I know some of you are physicians."

Someone from the crowd whistled aloud in response.

"Yeah, thanks for the hot tip of ivermectin," Winston acknowledged the whistle and said, "Some of you are teachers."

Another group of people cheered from the crowd.

"Missing you guys already," Winston said and pointed to the

source of cheering. "No one ever explained to me as well as you could why the fossils are fake.

"And a lot of you are creators, writing books, making podcasts, uploading videos. You guys are amazing. You are the best. The best. *They* don't see that. *They* are blind to what you are. *They* are liars. *They* tell this big fat lie about the Earth being a spinning ball so that they can sell more balls. *They* know people love buying balls. Footballs, basketballs, softballs, volleyballs, handballs, disco balls, you name it. You know, ball making and selling is an industry that makes hundreds of billions. *They* are afraid people would stop buying balls and only buy frisbees. That's why *They* lie."

The crowd cheered again.

"Grab *Their* balls," someone from the crowd shouted. Seconds later, everyone in the room was rhythmically chanting the same three words.

The enthusiasm in Sapphire Dome reached a surreal level not seen since lynching was made a federal crime.

Amid the chanting, someone shouted, "What are we gonna do about it?"

"Good question. Excellent question," Winston pointed at the source of that question. "We need to stop fighting among ourselves. We need to unite our voices. Our influence. Our will power. We should stand together to purge the world of the spherical Earth nonsense. Those who say the Earth is round, we will send them to the round hole that sees no sunlight."

One after another, the audience rose to their feet in excitement. Some of them even had a minor orgasm.

Even Winston found himself got carried away. He didn't care much about the presidency before getting onto the stage, but now he wanted to win. He felt like the possessed girl from *The Exorcist*, speaking in a commanding voice and projectile vomiting words.

"If I get elected, I won't touch a word of your doctrines, because they are all beautiful. Very beautiful. I won't change a thing. You know what needs to be changed? Everything outside of this room.

"I am gonna lead you to lobby for a change in our education system. Flat Earth, turtle Earth, phallic Earth will all get equal time in science classrooms. They will be taught along with intelligent design by God or by that big turtle this gentleman in Sherwani mentioned.

"And then, we will purge our language. Whenever you hear someone uses the expression 'around the globe,' call them out as being insensitive. Whenever a corporation describes itself as a global conglomerate, boycott its product. Whenever someone asks you to think globally, ask them to think again and gain a little more perspective. Whenever someone describes the world as a global village, make sure they know how offended you are and cancel them. We will deny global warming to our death, because there is no such thing as *global* warming."

Another standing ovation.

A 380-pound man from the back even took off his clothing and started streaking across the Sapphire Dome, unironically chanting the three-word phrase of today.

While waiting for the applause to die down, Winston calmed down a bit and organized his thoughts on the closing.

"I have a dream," Winston said in a deeper voice and more gentle tone, "that one day globes will be artifacts only seen in the museum and fetish porn.

"I have a dream that one day the sons of globetards and the sons of flatards can sit together at the fine dining tables we sell at booths E616-E632.

"I have a dream that one day the round Earth map will have the same social status as the swastika symbol and Confederate flag outside of Southern United States.

"I have a dream today, and I invite you to make the dream come true!

"Praise the Earth!!!"

With that said, Winston dropped the microphone and walked down from the stage amid thunderous applause. Carefully avoiding the streaking man who wanted a hug, he returned to the row reserved for the keynote speech speakers.

The POTUWS candidates from All-Ways and TYDF both eyed him in awe. Without citing a single fact in support of the Earth's flatness, that outsider managed to flip even some of the firmest adherents of All-Ways and TYDF into his groupies. His words were responsible for the endorphins skyrocketing through the audience's skulls, inducing the mental state known as natural high.

Between the two of them, however, one man remained untroubled. Noticing it was his turn to make the keynote speech, this man wrapped up the call with his broker and steadily walked onto the stage.

When he picked up the microphone from where Winston left it, a screeching echo pierced from the speakers around the ballroom. The frenzy stirred up by Winston died down instantly and everyone's attention turned to the six-foot-four man on stage. His name was Gabriel Odinson, the First of His Name, Protector of the World Tree, Beacon of Grass Sea, the Last Prophet, Odinson the Wise, the Enlightened, Prince of Truth. Sometimes, just sometimes, people called him White Jesus.

Chapter 25

Literally rooted in the Norse mythology, Treeism had always been the most influential school of thoughts in geocentrism, but Odinson still managed to bring it to the next level of greatness in the 21st century.

He ran the Church of Treeism like a typical successful American corporation, i.e., ruthlessly maximizing the bottom line through predatory and legally questionable business practices. He incited hundreds of undergraduates majoring in Environmental Science to harness Corporate America until tree planting became part of their balanced scorecards. He used bots to thumb up / subscribe to / upvote / like pop culture featuring Norse mythology, including but definitely not limited to *God of War, American Gods, Record of Ragnarök, Vikings,* and *Yu-Gi-Oh! Trading Card Game.* He even personally persuaded Marvel Studio to pay Vin Diesel an awful lot of money to voice an animated tree whose vocabulary consists of exactly three words. Odinson primed everyone to associate trees with good, softening them up for the teachings of Treeism and making it a brand almost as profitable as Goop.

In the early 21st century, the Church of Treeism not only had the highest number of believers among the Big Four, but also had pension scheme and medical benefits for its senior priests. It was once voted as the third best choice for theology graduates to jump start their careers, right after screenwriter and sign designer.

Although Treeism mostly operated outside of NASA's jurisdiction, even Smith was familiar with the name of Gabriel Odinson, the First of His Name, Protector of the World Tree, Beacon of Grass Sea, the Last Prophet, Odinson the Wise, the Enlightened, Prince of Truth, because his counterparts at European Space Agency couldn't shut up about him:

"I wish the ESA policy does not forbid staff from attending his sermon."

"Why can't I use White Jesus as my wall paper?"

"Odinson denial is the new Holocaust denial!"

That was why *gambling-grandma55699.com.uk* quoted 1.25 odds for Odinson winning the POTUWS race. But having seen the wild rally of Disk Earth Society, Smith began to doubt that even Odinson's surreal charisma and raw sexual magnetism could not salvage the election.

You better start walking on water again *if you want to win,* Smith thought.

Odinson's demeanor was the exact opposite of Winston's. When introducing himself, which was quite unnecessary given his fame in the geocentric circle, he spoke in a solemn yet soft tone. In his signature black turtleneck, he struck the audience as someone who cared less about formality than substance. The way he carried himself made one feel welcome to his community of Treeple, i.e., the followers of Treeism. After making a joke about his increasingly long title, he began his preaching.

"*They* want you to believe you are a product of randomness. *They* want you to feel like a survival machine that happens to be born on a spinning rock in an infinite, purposeless universe. *They* want you to accept that life, your life, is meaningless.

"*They* are lying.

"No, you are not an accident. You are much more than that. In fact, you are literally at the center of the universe, a universe that was built for *you*. Fossils were laid underground to provide fuel for modern vehicles, so don't let *Them* get to you with the climate change nonsense. Animals were created for your consumption, so don't hold back on enslaving and torturing animals in ways you see fit."

People from the TYDF camp vigorously nodded to that remark.

"Some people – some of them are sitting among you today – asked me, 'How do you know the world is a big-ass tree, instead of a pancake?' Well, I simply asked them to look around themselves.

"When you walk on a street, any street, what is the most commonly seen living thing besides humans? Trees. Isn't it a clue?

"Even with all the industrialization and urbanization in the last two centuries, forests still account for almost one third of the Earth's landmass. Isn't it a clue?

"Look at the logo of World Health Organization, with a serpent coiling on a trunk erected on a map. Doesn't that trunk look like the world tree described in the *Prose Edda*? Isn't the WHO logo itself a metaphor that the world is a tree? Isn't it a clue?

"The Greek philosopher Pythagoras called three the perfect number. And you know what rhymes with three? Tree! Isn't it a clue?"

Hell no, Smith thought in protest, *the Earth is flat, you sexy piece of smooth-talking smartass.*

"There are clues all around you. You just need to look. When you look closely, you will see."

White Jesus stopped talking and simply let his words sink in.

Almost a minute of silence ensued, forcing the summit participants to do what World Health Organization knew was the heathiest thing to do but never told people about: thinking.

A lot of the participants began to see the clues in their minds and started connecting the dots. Some of them pictured green notes in their pockets and associated them with trees. Some thought of how much they loved things that were free and then they thought of trees. The possibilities were endless. The more they thought about it, the more World Tree clues they saw.

Suddenly, a bang on the doors awakened everyone from their spiritual pursuit. Their attention was stolen away from the pope of Treeism to the main entrance opposite to the podium. The double doors there just blasted open.

Now what, another streaker or hand in the pants? Smith thought, and realized it was probably the weirdest sentence he ever formulated in his head.

Tracing to the objects that burst through the door, Smith saw a familiar face.

What am I looking at?

There were seven to eight transparent spheres *walking* into Sapphire Dome. Each of them was six feet long in diameter, with a person inside. The persons inside those inflatable balls were all in blue hazmat suits, pushing the giant orbs from within in an awkward position to keep them moving. Watching from their left flank, it looked like a very bad reenactment of the 007's gun barrel sequence. In front of those rolling spheres sat a man on electronic wheelchair. Unlike his companions, this man didn't wear a hazmat helmet. A banner reading "Zorbists Roll!" was flying in the back of the wheelchair, while its occupant was doing an impression of Stephen Hawking. Despite the distance, Smith could recognize that man was Charles Peralta from Round Ops.

This is inappropriate on so many levels, Smith thought.

He had been told that Charles and his team would play as "controlled opposition" in the summit, but was not privy to the details of their operations. His look of surprise invited unsolicited explanation from a woman on his left, who wore glasses typically worn by psychiatrists in TV shows.

"They are Zorbists, you know what a Zorbist is?" said the woman with a British accent that was deemed stereotypically sexy by Americans in '90s sitcoms.

Smith mildly shook his head. He had never been involved in projects that were not related to flat Earthers.

"Zorbists are like Solipsists, but more *down to earth*, if you know what I mean," said the woman in a tone typical of psychotherapists portrayed in movies. "They assert there is no objective shape of the Earth. They neither accept nor deny the spherical Earth model. The foundation of their belief is that everyone just lives in their own reality bubbles, hence those orbs.

"Zorbists argue that natural phenomena like sunrise and sunset are subjective experiences, which people happen to share in a similar but not strictly the same manner. You see what they are doing? They are trying to reconcile all the geocentric schools of thoughts."

All I see is a bunch of adults playing indoor water balls, thought Smith.

"Underlying Zorbism is the most powerful theoretical model that can explain the physical world without resorting to a spherical Earth. It is rumored that the Zorbists have started using their model to make falsifiable predictions and will publish them early next year. Sounds pretty exciting, doesn't it?"

"It certainly does," Smith replied half-heartedly, thinking it was the most deliberate troll ever pulled off by Round Ops.

When Smith returned his attention to the rolling balls, Charles was already less than a foot away from the stage and Odinson had got down from it.

"We urge," the Round Ops agent spoke in a robotic voice through the speech generating device on his wheelchair, "the United Ways to re-consider our membership and accept my nomination for POTUWS."

"Zorbism is not a registered member of the United Ways, because it refuses to condemn the globe," said the archetype of psychologist, unprompted. Smith began to suspect she was hitting on him.

"Brother," Odinson said and kneeled down, without regard to whether the white Americans in presence would be offended by the posture, "I am afraid you are speaking to the wrong person. I cannot speak on behalf of the United Ways."

"So I came all the way to here, for nothing?" said the robotic voice.

Charles tried to squeeze out a tear, but in vain. Smith was like the famous statue *Caïn venant de tuer son frère Abel*, in facepalm.

"I hope I can make this worth your while," Odinson said and laid his right hand on the wheelchair user's forehead. He closed his eyes and his lips began rapidly moving. Not a single word he murmured was audible, but some well-read onlookers figured he was casting the healing spells from *Harry Potter*. Before long, the man in wheelchair also closed his eyes with his head tilted backward. He started speaking in tongues and his chest gradually heaved as if an invisible bully was grabbing his collar for lunch money. As his speaking in tongues got increasingly louder, his body began to leave the wheelchair.

Some onlookers fell down on their knees in disbelief. Some of them ecstatically rushed to Odinson but were stopped cold by the Treeple. Smith was doing a double facepalm.

The man who was quadriplegic a minute ago was now standing on his own feet. Odinson took a deep breath and re-opened his eyes.

"In the name of Yggdrasil, I command – you walk again," he howled.

The man under his palm awakened from stupor and looked around himself in bewilderment. Speechless, he stared at the floor in hesitation. A mix of hope and determination replaced the incredulity on his face. He upper body slowly leaned backward before swinging itself forward. His body was at a tilt of around forty-five degrees and dropping fast, but his legs remained unhelpfully still. Everyone around him almost screamed in anticipation of a man-shaped hole on the ground, except Odinson, who just stood in front of the falling man and did not reach out to catch him. Just a moment before the man hit the floor, his freefall abruptly stopped as his right foot took a quick step forward.

He had walked.

The whole room exploded into frenzy.

Chapter 26

The participants of True Earth Summit had barely recovered from the hysteria following White Jesus' miracle, but the host already returned to the podium. He thanked the Zorbists for peacefully leaving the venue, repeated that the United Ways reserved its rights to press charges, and presented the updated rundown of day one without so much as implying a hint of how it could possibly have anything to do with TYDF chairman's prolonged speech.

Original time	Revised time	Event
9:00 – 10:15	9:00 – **11:10**	1. Opening ceremony 2. Keynote speeches by distinguished guests
10:15 – 10:30	-	Break **(cancelled)**
10:30 – 12:00	**11:10 – 12:30**	Parallel Sessions (sponsored by Church of Treeism): - Mindshift: Blockchain in Treeism - Robotics on World Tree – A Business Case - Age of Hyper-automation in One, Two, Tree - Bring Big Data to Yggdrasil - Building an AI Playbook for Treeple - NFTs Incoming, Guard Your Greenfield - Take a VR Deep Dive into Our Root - A Leafy Guide for Navigating Extended Reality - Strategies to Protect Your Tree Research on Distributed Cloud
12:00 – 14:00	**12:30** – 14:00	1. Lunch 2. Ceremony for Content Creator Awards 3. Presentation: 2,000 years A Warrior – 3 ups & 3 downs of TYDF **(regrettably cancelled)**
14:00 – 15:30	14:00 – 15:30	Parallel Sessions (cont.')
15:30 – 15:45	15:30 – 15:45	Break
15:45 – 17:00	15:45 – 17:00	True Earth Research Workshop – Fake or Deep Fake
17:00 – 18:00	17:00 – 18:00	Panel Discussion: The Future of Geopolitics and Antarctic Treaty in 20 Years
18:00 – 19:00	18:00 – 19:00	Evening Reception Remarks: BYOB **Complimentary drinks sponsored by Church of Treeism**
19:00 – 21:00	19:00 – 21:00	True Earth Banquet

The audience was visibly devastated by the cancellation of a break and shortening of lunch time.

Coming to realize he was in deep water again, the host swiftly urged the participants to leave Sapphire Dome and go to the breakout rooms for the parallel sessions of their choices.

As everyone was swarming to leave the ballroom, Smith stood up from his seat and took a glance at the front row for no particular reason. The pandit of All-Ways and pope of Treeism had already left, while the chairman of TYDF appeared to be whispering in the ears of the speaker from Disk Earth Society. The chairman then left a card on his chair and took off.

Smith tried to make sense of what he had seen, but got interrupted by his neighbor who might or might not practice psychology.

"Hey, neighbor," said the woman with glasses, "which session do you fancy to join first?"

"Um... I haven't given much thought about it yet," said Smith and looked at the screen on stage. When he took another peek at the front row, it was already empty.

"The VR session seems fun but I don't want to put on a headset that just sat on an oily sweaty baldy scalp, which is surprisingly common around here. Maybe I will check out the NFT one first." Smith thought NFT meant national football team.

"Cool, you mind if we buddy up?" asked the bespectacled woman, who thought NFT stood for non-fungible token.

Of course they were both wrong.

"God bless you, God bless you so much," Maeve yelled across the corridor. She just spotted Ohi from the flock leaving the ballroom, and rushed to give him a hug.

"O ma'am, I am not too sure about that," said Ohi in panic, seeing his whole life in flashback 0.1 second before being tackled by a 220-pound woman.

"Why is he getting all the candies? He didn't do a thing," Chandler protested over the two bodies that just crash-landed on the ground.

"O... you are also here," Maeve said as she supported herself to stand up, "the carrot-talking weirdo who can't shut up about the demeaning contest that objectifies women and serves the male gazes under the pretense of celebrating beauty."

Coming from a profession overwhelmingly dominated by men, Chandler didn't understand a single word she said.

"And how dare you say he did nothing," Maeve added. "*He* gave a hell of a speech back there."

"Ma'am," Ohi sluggishly got up and spoke, pressing his own chest to check for broken rips, "I am afraid you have mistaken me for Sensei."

After several minutes of heated discussion, Maeve eventually acknowledged that Ohi and Chandler were probably not pulling a prank on her.

"I am sorry, Ohi," Maeve said. "It was the aloha shirt. I swear I can totally distinguish you and Winston based on your facial features alone."

"It's OK, don't worry about it," said Ohi, putting a Band-Aid on his bruised knee.

"By the way, where is your Sensei? I wanted to thank him for standing up for the Disk Earth."

"He texted us," said Chandler while checking Ohi's another arm for dislocation, "saying he needed to meet Song from TYDF first. We are still waiting for him to join us."

"What," Maeve said in awe, "our guy is alone with that Song?!"

Twelve floors above the summit's venue, Winston was standing outside of room 1221, holding the keycard from Song.

As an experienced movie director, he was keenly aware that it might be one of those #MeToo situations, so he had brought a letter opener from his own room.

If he dared to lock me up in the bathroom, I am going to Wick him up.

Holding the paper knife in reverse grip, Winston used it to rapidly stab the face of his imaginary opponent in air, like he was John Wick with a pencil. A hotel room cleaner walking by thought he was a male escort rehearsing his routine.

Feeling ready, Winston put the knife in his back pocket, and swiped the keycard.

Here goes nothing.

As he slowly opened the door, a figure in Mao suit came into view.

It was Song standing in front of the floor-to-ceiling windows, overlooking the view of Lake Ontario. He undoubtedly heard Winston's entry, but still kept his back to the door for dramatic effect.

Okay, he still got his pants on, Winston thought and breathed a sigh of relief.

He was not surprised that Song came alone without an interpreter, as he always assumed everyone on earth could speak English. He gently closed the door behind himself and walked in Song's direction, while scanning the room for any sign of ambush. As he carefully paced through the narrow corridor connecting the foyer and the bedroom, he found a video camera on tripod quietly standing next to the king size bed.

You sick, dirty bastard!

Chapter 27

Inside the Fairmont Theatre, also known as "NFTs Incoming, Guard Your Greenfield" breakout room, Smith felt like he was one of those self-claimed flat Earthers from North Korea, who ran like hell from the airport to the nearest immigration office for asylum, only to discover that he had come to the embassy of China.

"Thank you everyone for coming in. Please take a seat," said the facilitator, whose track jacket bore the emblem of Treeism. She and two other helpers in the same outfit ushered the participants to find a seat in the small theatre. "In the next thirty minutes, I am going to talk to you about how to handle Internet trolls that say 'No Freaking Trees' in your face."

Crap, I should have known better. The Treeple are just spraying buzzwords to make their lame presentations look cool. Smith blamed himself and took a seat in the midsection, figuring that if he had sat at the back, he would only be called out and then put at the front row.

"Why the long face?" asked the "buddy" of Smith. "It isn't what you expected?"

"What? You *knew* this session was about how to make memes and retaliate trolling?!"

"No," the woman replied with a giggle, "but I keep an open mind to new experience. Seeing you were late for the opening and didn't buy any of the merch, I thought you would be a non-believer, slash, explorer."

"Well... you weren't wrong. A friend of mine gave me a free pass for this... thing, so I just came to see what the fuss is all about."

"O... me too," said the woman with glee, "I mean, I am also a non-believer. I came here for business." She extended her left hand. "Frey, Jean Frey, but I hate being called Frey."

She is definitely trying to tell me she is single and wants to take my surname, Smith thought while studying her ring finger.

"Johansson, Smith Johansson," Smith shook Jean's hand and began to worry that he might get into a love triangle relationship with Gian and Jean, compromising the R.D.G.A.R. operation. "Nice to meet you, Frey-Jean-Frey-But-I-Hate-Being-Called-Frey. That was not mouthful at all. What exactly do you do for a living?"

"You could never guess it," said Jean without acknowledging Smith's attempt to be cute. "I am a psychiatrist. And you, let me guess, are some sort of consultant? Judging from your frequent hand gestures and dream-talking about timesheet."

"I did that in the ballroom?" said Smith, still a bit upset that he had forgot his timesheets again in the nightmare. "You were pretty close; I am a public speaking guru. Just came to see if there are any business opportunities and look for ideas for my next book." Smith had created a list of book titles for his undercover identity, but suddenly had trouble to recall their publication order. He panicked and his hand gestures got even weirder.

"No way, I am also here scouting for potential clients," said Jean. "This summit to a psychotherapist is like Russia to a HIV specialist."

"You mean the people here are... mental?" Smith wanted to find a more politically correct adjective but his mind was too occupied to reconstruct the backstory of his alter ago. *Is Smith Johansson a con man who exploits the emotionally vulnerable clients or simply delusional about his professional qualifications, which don't exist?*

"No, not at all, and it is not cool to use the M word," whispered Jean in a hurry. "Are you trying to get us both killed?"

Smith understood the question was intended as a joke, because the summit participants must all be numb to that word.

"Joking aside," Jean added, "just because someone has a different idea of the Earth's shape, it doesn't necessarily mean they have mental illnesses. For one thing, I myself have a very different idea of psychic model from Freud and my colleagues."

"How so?"

"I think there are more in us than just Id, ego and super-ego. Like, a super-duper-ego that asks the other three to shut up and do stuff."

"Well... I guess we will never know if it exists or not... unlike the shape of Earth..."

"My point is," said Jean with zero interest in defending her thesis, "you can just as easily find people who believe Columbus was friendly to Indigenous Americans, North Korea has a nuclear program for peaceful purpose, or *A Song of Ice and Fire* will ever be finished.

"I am not here looking for people with mental disorder; I am trying to find people with trust issue, and help them rebuild that trust."

Smith began to find this conversation more interesting than the ongoing presentation about "Civilized ways to counter name calling by offering unsolicited suicide advice."

"Flat Earthers, tree Earthers and whatnot," the psychiatrist continued, "are fundamentally the same: They distrust established institutions.

"Some people think the conspiracy theorists have problems with authority figures or have inferiority complex. Well, I can't say they got it 100% right. On the one hand, you have conspiracy theorists who don't take vaccination advices from professionals who have spent at least seven years in medical school and residency, but merrily chow down horse dewormer simply because a senator – still an authority figure, who just happened not to have a medical degree – called it the miracle drug. On the other hand, you have one of the best, if not *the* best, chess players of all time openly endorse the new chronology, effectively saying that all mainstream archaeological dating methods are wrong and that Jesus Christ was born in Crimea in 1152 AD and crucified at modern-day Istanbul in 1185 AD. I would be hard pressed to say he has an inferiority complex."

"So it is all about trust, huh?" Smith felt like he was back to those marriage therapy sessions with his second strike, and regretted not paying more attention instead to the presentation slide headlined "All hope is not lost: how to implicate internet bullies in your suicide notes." He saw a lot of practical values in that.

"Yeah. And if they are willing to receive my help, I will help them identify which experiences they had with established institutions led them to where they are."

"Interesting value proposition. I just don't understand why you can't simply walk up to any random participant and give them your name card. As far as I am concerned, they are all conspiracy theorists with what you call trust issues."

"It's not that simple. For one, almost half of the people in this room don't have any sort of geocentric belief."

What? Besides Round Ops, there are other controlled oppositions?! Wait, does it mean our covers are blown? Smith panicked again. He was still trying to decide on Smith Johansson's opinion on abortion. He had grave trouble in reconciling the makeup persona's pro-life stance and his apathy for lives outside of wombs.

"Take that lad as an example," Jean pointed to a young man in the front row, who was industrially taking notes. "I recognize him from a wedding officiated in the Church of Treeism. He never had a doubt if the Earth is round. In fact, like most sane adults with lives to deal with, he never gave much thought about the shape of Earth. He goes to all these geocentric gatherings for writing his papers."

"On... astronomy?"

"No, on social science. He figures flat Earthers and the like are either radiantly bright underachievers or irredeemable waste of skin. If the former, then he wants to understand why brilliant minds like those – capable of seeing through the big lie that conned billions of people – devote their valuable time to make YouTube videos rather than cure cancer. He conjectures that the apparently inefficient allocation of talent is a clever ploy to avoid over-saturation of human resources in non-tradable sectors."

"That sounds research-worthy, but what if they are already flying as high as their talents can take them?"

"I asked him the exact same thing. He said at least he would get a laugh and could always repurpose his paper to explore why natural selection fails to weed out stupidity from our gene pool."

"OK, OK, is there any other non-believer you spotted in the room?"

"That blonde two rows behind us," Jean whispered without turning her head, "she has been filming the whole thing and didn't mind you used the M word. I bet she is a journalist or vlogger, milking the United Ways for contents."

Smith was going to turn his head around but was stopped by Jean. She guided his gaze to a row in front of them.

"That nerdy guy on the right is a psychologist and the rest on the row are his subjects."

"As in he rules and collects taxes from them?"

"That may be his next step, but now they are just his experiment subjects. You can see from his notepad that he is doing an intelligence test on those participants to see how long it takes for conspiracy theories to melt their brains."

"Cool, anyone else, Sherlock?

"And those two who just barged in the door are explorers like you, apparently looking for someone."

Smith followed Jean's finger and looked to his right. Five feet away stood two men who just came into the theater, both scanning the room up and down. One of them was dressed in the same aloha shirt as the DES presidential candidate and another dressed like a professor. Behind them was a woman panting to catch up, whom Smith recognized as the vice-chairwoman of DES.

"Winston is not here either," Chandler said and turned to Maeve, who could barely feel her feet.

"I am alright, thanks for asking," Maeve said and breathed in with an asthma inhaler.

"Ma'am, you're sure we didn't miss any room reserved for the summit?"

"Hell no, we got them all." Maeve collapsed on an aisle seat. Barely anyone in the theater noticed the three of them, as the presentation had come to its climax, "How far is too far: Lawyer up before Swatting.”

“Damn, he may be meeting Song outside of this building,” Chandler said exhaustedly. “There is no way we can find him in time.”

“Hey both, maybe we are overreacting,” said Ohi. “I am sure Sensei will be okay. It is not like he never met a godfather or kingpin. He probably got himself armed before meeting this TYDF guy.”

“Dear, you have no idea,” Maeve said weakly. “Gangsters make you watch when they cut off your balls, but Song is a snake. If Winston is not careful, he may end up in a ten-year diabetic coma.”

Chapter 28

“Mr. Kanshū, welcome,” the TYDF chairman turned around to greet Winston. “Please, make yourself at home.”

How does he know about my bedroom's camera setup? Winston recoiled in shock.

A small metal object dropped from Winston's back pocket onto the carpeted floor. It appeared to be a letter opener, because it was.

Both Winston and Song stared at the sharp blade for a while with no words.

“Ur...” Winston broke the awkward silence, “I mean...” he already regretted speaking first, “what I was trying to say was...” he decided to stop his brain from thinking and let his mouth do the talking, “as a movie director, I often receive lots of fan letters, handwritten and sealed in envelops, so it is very natural for me to carry around a paper knife.”

He then casually picked up the knife, very casually put it in his chest pocket, and even more casually checked Song's face for any trace of suspicion.

“I am also a great admirer of your movies,” Song said with no inflection whatsoever and took a seat at the lounge chair against windows, apparently having accepted Winston's explanation, “although sometimes they hurt the feelings of my people.

What? Did I use the wrong pronouns or film someone kneeling during the national anthem? It can neither be the F nor the N word, because they never got anyone into trouble. Oh, it could be the F word followed by an a. Wait, if this guy is from Russia, which I can't tell because no one ever mentioned his nationality or ethnicity, then I would have crossed the red line simply by featuring a black person in my movie's poster.

As he narrowed down what could have offended his interlocutor, Winston settled himself into the armchair opposite to Song. He was startled when Song's hand reached into his chest pocket.

Should I start stabbing him now? Winston wondered.

A moment later, Song took out a folded A4 paper, unfolded it, and continued speaking tonelessly.

"I appreciate that you are a busy man, so I will just cut to the chase. I would like to form a partnership with you."

Winston kept a poker face and awaited Song's elaboration on the word "partnership," conscious that he might have misinterpreted it.

"I am sure you are aware that your Disk Earth Society and my TYDF share a lot of similarities," Song spoke as he used his peripheral vision to read from the paper. "Both of us believe in a spherical heaven, although you call it firmament and I call it egg. Neither of us believe the Earth's surface is curved, although you think it is round as a disk and I think it is a perfect square."

Winston felt like he knew where it was going, but didn't want to take any chance, so he kept nodding to everything Song said.

"Isn't it silly that we let our differences in terminology or the number of Earth's sides divide ourselves? We should reject the cold war mentality. You and I are not enemies. If anything, I consider ourselves cousins."

Winston felt confused again because he knew people treated their cousins very differently, depending on whether they were from Alabama or not.

"The Tur and the Treeple, they are the enemies. They are, what people of your culture call, witches. In the good old days, they would be burnt at stake, alive."

Winston guessed "Tur" was a slang for the All-Ways followers, and was impressed by Song's candidness in using witch hunt to justify elimination of competition. Believing Song was a stand-up guy, he finally opened up.

"So... what exactly do you expect me to do?"

"I have a suggestion," Song said after taking another peek at his notes. "We jointly appeal to our constituents to pool their votes to one single candidate. With our bases combined, we will out-vote Odinson for sure."

"And that candidate would be…"

"Of course it would be you, Mr. Kanshū," Song said with a forced smile and patted Winston's lap in a very nonsexual way.

"I am happy to be the vice president on your ticket. Look." He directed Winston's gaze to the video camera on tripod. "If this arrangement sounds good to you, we must not waste another second. While we speak, Odinson and his minions are brainwashing the summit attendees with their heresy. We have to release a video as soon as possible to announce our partnership."

Ooooooo, it never occurred to me the camera is for this purpose, Winston thought.

He took a moment to consider Song's offer. Since he was more a visual thinker, he first pictured in his mind a balance whose weighing platforms read "pros" and "cons," held by a scantily clad lady justice. Finding it distracting, he removed the balance altogether and started chatting with his attractive mental projection, who didn't complain about the unnecessarily revealing clothing at all. After a few drinks and what must feel like three minutes from Song's perspective, Winston concluded there was no downside to working with Song.

"Mr. Chairman, thank you for the offer," Winston extended his right hand. "I will be happ—"

Before they could shake hands to it, a bang came from the door behind Winston. Panicked, Winston instinctively looked for his pants, but realized he was not in an affair. He then recognized a muffled but familiar voice from behind the door.

"Sensei, are you OK?"

Song was unpleased and going to say something, but Winston already rose from the chair and went to open the door.

"Thank god," said Chandler, "or Satan or however you call it, you are not being force-fed refined carbohydrate."

"How did you guys find me?" Winston asked, almost obligatorily.

"We were looking for you all over the exhibition floor, and then an American told us he saw Song give you a card back in the ballroom. We figure he is meeting you in his room, so we asked the concierge for the room number." Ohi explained like he was giving an obligatorily deliberate explanation for the unsurprising plot development in a soap opera.

"Mr. Kanshū, I thought we were going to speak in private," Song said in a slightly less emotionless tone, as he approached the foyer.

Maeve ignored Song's protest and got between him and Winston. "What did he want from you?"

"All of you chill out," Winston said breezily like a man whose adultery is just discovered and the only way out is to casually suggest a ménage à trois, "Chairman Song was offering to help with the election. We are going to pool our votes together, and he is willing to be my VP on the ticket."

"And when you win the election, he will incapacitate you, like what he did to Robert."

"Nonsense, I don't even know the English word 'incapacitate,'" Song objected with an almost imperceptible hint of anger. "Ms. Walsh, your words have deeply hurt the feelings of me and my people."

"As if you have feelings in the first place," Maeve rebutted without missing a bit. "Ten years ago, you said the same thing to our chairman, offering to merge TYDF into the School of Flat Earth. You then started attending our gatherings, smoking our weeds, and preaching to our friends. You quoted the Bible and then accused our disk Earth model of contradicting the Book of Revelation."

"Miss, I didn't make it up," Song interrupted and all the hints of emotion had disappeared again from his face. "The Bible clearly states that four angels stand at the Earth's four corners. Your disk is a heresy."

Maeve was getting furious, while the three men behind her were enjoying the nerd fights, especially Ohi. He was still inclined to think that the shape of Earth was of as little consequence as who was the fastest superhero in comics books or whether George Lucas's interview remarks were part of *Star Wars* canon.

"You didn't talk to my brothers and sisters because you wanted to have 'an intellectual discussion'; you did that to convert them into

TYDF. *You* caused the Second Schism. And when Robert confronted you about this, the next thing I know is he was lying unconsciously in his mom's basement surrounded by energy drinks."

"Is there a chance he got himself a blood sugar overdose?" Chandler asked, purely to fuel her fume.

"No, Robert never drank anything with soya flavor, so I knew it must be this snake."

Hot damn, Winston gasped, *Song is guilty as charged.*

"I will not entertain such baseless accusation," Song took out another cheat card and spoke. "Mr. Kanshū, the words of your colleagues are very hurtful. I have nothing more to say to you. See you in the debate tomorrow."

With that said, Song closed the door in Maeve's face.

None of the three men spoke, as Maeve was obviously still in rage. They did what bored people did; they found something to read. Ohi took out the summit brochure for revision; Chandler read the non-antisemitic message on Maeve's back and admired its font design; Winston noticed a *manji* tattoo on the back of her neck and reflected on its rich meaning in Buddhism. Eventually they ran out of things to read, so Winston broke the silence.

"Did he say there would be a debate tomorrow?"

"O honey, don't you worry about it now," Maeve spun around and said, apparently having regained her composure. "Let's worry about the panel discussion first."

Inside room 1221, Song had returned to the floor-to-ceiling windows to make a hands-behind-the-back pose. Breathing a quiet sigh, he took out a business card from his chest pocket and made a phone call.

"I have re-considered your offer. Let's talk money."

Chapter 29

Balancing the risk of stating the obvious and providing a truthful account, here is a short version of the chronicle of Second Schism, extracted from a Wikipedia article dated ten years from present day:

On September 11 1999, Robert "Whale" Milburn was elected the sixth chairperson of the School of Flat Earth. Some historians boldly speculated the election was as rigged as the stock market, based on nothing but flimsy circumstantial evidence. They cited that the only polling place was in the middle of a fifty-thousand-square-foot fenced property at Glasgow, Montana in the name of a Phoebe Jennings Milburn, who happened to be the biological mother of Robert Milburn. Historians with opposing view pointed out that voters who had difficulty in accessing the physical polling place were more than welcome to cast their ballot through e-voting via the Internet, which was made available on September 9 1999. They further argued it was purely a coincidence that the e-voting system's database program voided all the e-votes, whose vote-in dates 9/9/99 were misinterpreted as the 9999 value commonly used in the 20th century to represent unspecified date. Both camps continued to have a fierce debate over the election's legitimacy until they had enough arguments to meet the minimum word count requirement of The American Historical Review, *which sadly rejected their co-authored submission.*

Despite the aforementioned controversy, Milburn had no trouble in governing the School of Flat Earth. Not that there was much to govern in the first place. To fulfil his election promise, he dedicated all his energy to canonicalizing flat Earth thoughts and theories into a unified tenet, whenever he got off from Wendy's. All went well until YouTube replaced broadcast television as the dominant source of knowledge. The new ecosystem transformed the flat Earth circle from a peaceful community that fostered harmony and love among socioeconomic underdogs who shared a unique insight into how the world functioned, to a bloody gladiator arena that bred malice and hatred among socioeconomic underdogs who believed no one but themselves had such secret knowledge. Besides mutually accusing each other of being controlled opposition, the community was deeply divided on whether the flat Earth was a disk, a square or an infinite horizontal plane.

Looking for ways to calm the quarrel, Milburn first consulted his vice-chairwoman. However, her blaming the Jewish and Obama for the feuding did not seem too useful, so Milburn reached out to most united creed of geocentrism, TYDF, for advice.

Chairman Song suggested a democratic approach: merging TYDF with the School of Flat Earth so that the squared Earthers could outnumber and suppress the voices of the minority with dissenting views. Milburn saw the appeal in it and got on board.

As part of the merger, Milburn started doing roadshows with Song around the States, unwittingly providing a platform for Song to preach his squared Earth teachings. Belonging to the minority who actually read through the Bible from front to back, Song impressed the roadshow participants with his impeccable literacy in scriptures. By the end of the roadshows, more than half of flat Earthers had abandoned the School of Flat Earth and converted to TYDF.

Devastated as he was by the mass apostasy, Milburn still believed the merger would proceed as planned and had faith that his work-in-progress Gospel of Flat Earth would unify TYDF and the School of Flat Earth. He quitted his job as the French fries heating specialist, and worked on the book night and day. To make sure he could finish it before the merger referendum, he slept only eight hours a day and drank nothing but energy drinks for two weeks in row. The blood sugar level finally caught up to him when he was about to finish the last paragraph in chapter one.

On the day of referendum, Song came to Milburn's place to call off the merger, but was startled to find the man lying among stacks of beverage cans filled with suspiciously yellow liquid. Fearing implication in a foul play, Song ran away in panic and left behind a pack of soya milk, which Maeve Walsh correctly deduced was from the TYDF chairman.

After the merger was called off, Walsh rebranded the School of Flat Earth into the Disk Earth Society on behalf of Milburn, who ostensibly had gone into hiding from the Illuminati's assassins.

Years later, the manuscript of Gospel of Flat Earth was discovered by an aspiring historian that was researching for his submission to The American Historical Review. *He shared it with his university colleagues and spent days studying its prose. Despite its incompleteness, they unanimously remarked that it was without a doubt the greatest attack on the English language.*

They proceeded to burn the manuscript into ashes.

Here is an even shorter version of the chronicle of Second Schism, extracted from the glossary of the True Earth Summit brochure:

An ill-advised merger that led to the corporate restructuring of the School of Flat Earth.

In the absence of time travel, the shorter version was all Maeve could make use of to explain the entire conflict between DES and TYDF during an elevator ride.

"What did I just read?" asked Winston, holding Ohi's copy of the brochure. "It seems like the CEO's statement from an insolvent company's annual report."

"It is the gist of what I was trying to tell you," said Maeve. "Because of the Second Schism, there are now several flat Earth denominations out there. They were neither converted to TYDF or absorbed by DES, and all of them will attend the panel discussion this afternoon."

"I am supposed to get all this information from that one-liner?!"

"Why not? It is as clear as high quality crystal meth," Maeve turned to Ohi and Chandler for agreement; both vigorously nodded.

"What I am trying to say is, if *you* can ace the panel discussion this afternoon, then those pagans may vote for you this Friday.

"Me again? Jeez, I thought *you* are the vice-chairwoman of DES?"

"I can't be seen publicly with you, remember? The whole flat Earth community still thinks I work for the New Hemisphere office of NSA. I don't want to taint your name, so you have to do everything on your own."

"Ma'am, I think I can help you with that," Ohi said and handed his phone to Maeve. "I just checked the NSA's website. Look, none of their office locations are in New Hemisphere. It can clear your name."

"It won't work," Maeve said without looking at the "Why Work At NSA?" webpage. "They will say 'Absence of evidence is not evidence of absence' or 'Why would the NSA website honestly tell you where their people work at?' and then call you idiots or something."

"Seriously?" Chandler asked in surprise, apparently having

trouble to understand the mentality of flat Earthers. "Just for argument's sake, what evidence would be considered sufficient to persuade people that you are *not* an undercover agent working in an NSA office that *no records* show it ever exists? Your 401K statements? Location data of your cell phone? GPS records of your car? CCTV records that could reconstruct your day-to-day life? Statements from your colleagues that you never skipped work to do NSA's bidding?"

"Um... that's an interesting question... it never occurred to me I can think of it this way." Maeve mumbled and did a hand on chin pose to indicate she was giving serious thoughts about it.

She simulated in her head what an average flat Earther would say when presented each piece of the evidence suggested by Chandler. She shook her head and then considered the scenarios where different combinations of corroborating evidences were used to clear her name. Once she went through all thirty-two possible permutations twice, she let her imagination go wide and considered other possibilities. That led her to a revelatory conclusion.

"No, nothing can change their mind. All of the records could be fabricated, and any evidence that proves their authenticity can also be fake."

"So... I guess we have established that Sensei will have to do that seminar *alone*," Ohi said and then turned to Winston.

"Sensei, have your ever heard of the Antarctic Treaty System?"

"No idea what you are talking about," Winston said with no hesitation whatsoever.

"And do you have any thoughts on how the geopolitical environment may impact the system in the next two decades?"

"I understand every word you said, but not the question you were asking."

"Ma'am, I think we *may* have a problem," Ohi said to Maeve.

"I got this all figured out." Maeve took the brochure from Winston's hands and said to him, "All you need to do is to browse Wikipedia to cram before the seminar, use the talking points I have prepared to deflect all difficult questions, and—"

"Swing it the way I did this morning," Winston said smugly.

"Hey guys, I don't want to sound cynical here," Chandler

interrupted before anyone can ascertain whether Winston correctly finished Maeve's sentence, "but do any of you feel like something is off?"

The rest of the group exchanged a look and shook their heads.

"We have been doing an awful lot of talking and thinking and talking in this lift, but the lift door still hasn't opened."

"O did I forget to press the floor button again?" Maeve hastily asked with a hint of guilt. "Every time I pressed the call button for help, they told me the elevator didn't move because no floor was selected. So I know exactly what to do. Stay calm, check the button panel and don't bang your head against the door until you are absolutely sure the elevator is stuck."

Maeve approached the button panel, swiped her hotel keycard, pressed a few buttons, swiped her card again, pressed more buttons and turned around to face the men.

"Hey guys, I am beginning to think that we are stuck. Care to join me in headbanging the door?"

Chapter 30

Back in his days at MacCheddar & Co., Smith used to think there were only two reasons for going to an industry forum: easy credits for his PMP qualification and legitimate reasons to swipe the corporate card.

He would assiduously exchange name cards with anyone he met; buy wine, dinners, lap dance, concert tickets, amusement park packages, ammo at gun range, or anything else that occurred to him as a good idea at the time; and submit reimbursement claims for client entertainment, enclosed with the said name cards as supporting evidence. He wasn't proud of it, but this lifestyle enabled him to pay two ex-wives alimony and father a child.

While the True Earth Summit offered no pretext for such shenanigans, it did give Smith a new perspective on the epistemic values of forum going.

From "Building an AI Playbook for Treeple" he acquired a few awe-inspiring catch-phrases to use in future presentation. From "Mindshift: Blockchain in Treeism" he picked up the most efficient way to chain block people with opposing geophysical, political, metaphysical or grammatical views. From "Age of Hyper-automation in One, Two, Tree" he learnt a few passive income schemes that he had no reasons to suspect were scam.

He always knew flat Earthers, or Seekers in general, were menaces to the Global Lie, but never realized how systematic they were in organizing and educating themselves. He now had no doubt that if Dr. Gina Stinson's discovery was announced in the summit, the Seekers would be able to weaponize it and cause irreversible damage to NASA, effectively rendering himself unemployed and in default on spousal support.

And yet, here I am, still without a solid plan to sabotage Gina's presentation, Smith moaned as he wandered on the exhibition floor, which was crowded with Seekers enjoying their break.

Smith was like an unsuccessful satire writer who thought the plot would come together as he went along, so he only had very vague idea what he should do or say when meeting Dr. Stinson in the evening. To tackle this problem head-on, he did what an unsuccessful satire writer would do to resolve a writer's block: put the problem aside and open himself to new experience in hope of getting an epiphany.

From one of the book stands, he picked up a few books with adhesive labels or taglines whose sole purpose was to scare the faint-hearted shitless, such as "You have been warned – get ready to be smacked flat," "I will be shot dead if *They* know I am telling you this," "Proceed after getting your affairs in order," and "Disclaimer: globe and coffin not included." Despite their unfriendly advertising, Smith found them real page turners. Their above-average font size, generous use of spacing and abundance of illustrations made them very appealing as bathroom reading materials. The books' heavy use of quote mining, reciting words from George Orwell to Adolf Hitler, even made him feel smarter. His only complaint was that the books sometimes detoured too much to talk about the authors' favorite movies or criticize certain Christian churches' tolerance for heliocentrism.

Holy cow, they have figured out that gravity is not real and their geocentric models are almost exactly the same as the one displayed in staff library. These flatees know their science.

Leaving the non-fiction book area, Smith walked into the intangible goods section. The first stand greeting him was a dating service agency specializing in clients who were, in its own words, too flat to find true love. Heeding the advice from his divorce lawyer, Smith steered clear of it and went to another side of the floor.

Before he knew it, he was standing next to a booth that promoted itself as "The One and Only Reformed Astrology Consultant." It was hosted by a young lady with dreadlock braids, who was either in a trance or stoned on weed, or both. He was about to walk past it when the fortune teller snapped out from trance and/or highness and asked him for a few minutes.

"Monsieur, may I interest you in some non-fraudulent measurable predictions?" said the astrologer with a Canadian French accent. "If you find my prediction ambiguous, not expressed in probability, or without a time frame, you don't have to pay."

"No need to tell me more," said Smith with his right hand raised to head level. "You made the sale when you said non-fraudulent."

Smith eagerly walked to the booth and seated himself opposite to the self-proclaimed consultant. He noticed a name card on her desk bearing what could only be her YouTube user name, True3Oracle5U.

True Tree Oracle Find You, what an enigmatic name, Smith thought with admiration.

As an experienced consultant, Smith always had great respect for astrologers, *feng shui sifu*, Tarot guru and the like who make a living by talking a great game. He also sympathized with their predicament of being mistaken as charlatans, because he always considered their work nature identical to his own.

"Before I begin," said True3Oracle5U, "you must know that my methodology is based on the constellation of Treeism[5], so it is not directly comparable to the predictions made by orthodox fortune telling, tarot card playing, spirit talking, crystal-gazing, rooster observing, tea leave reading or any other divination methods that rhymed with 'thing.'"

"That's terribly specific," Smith gasped in awe and had no follow-up question at all, because he already learnt from the summit brochure what Treeism[5] was and how to properly pronounce it and its derivatives.

In a nutshell, Treeism[5] was the Mayan branch of Treeism. Treeism bore the same ideological relationship to Treeism[5] as socialism to socialism with Chinese characteristics. They were the same, but different in the sense that Treeism[5] adherents believed the world consisted of five world trees rather than one. Since the difference between them could be rounded down to zero, universally they were considered the same geocentric creed.

"Now, please write down your birth place, date and time on this piece of paper," True3Oracle5U said as she passed a pen to Smith. "Be as precise as possible. If you are unsure of the exact time you got popped out, then at least try to write down AM or PM."

Smith paused for a moment to consider whether he should provide his personal particulars or those he made up for Smith Johansson. He carefully weighted the consequences in his mind while True3Oracle5U intensely stared at him. To minimize the risk exposure of R.D.G.A.R., at last he decided to use his real personal information to get the most accurate prediction.

When Smith was done, the astrologer took a quick glance at the paper and burnt it with a lighter she pulled out from nowhere. The burning paper was waved around in the air for a few seconds, before being thrown into a glass of water on the desk. While Smith watched the glass with the same enthusiasm as one would watch a man jump from the Empire State Building, True3Oracle5U closed her eyes, formed a triangle with her palms and started talking in tongues.

After approximately 8.81 seconds, which was theoretically the time it would take to freefall to the ground from the top of Empire State Building (ignoring air resistance), True3Oracle5U stopped mumbling and reopened her eyes.

"Monsieur, the Trees[5] told me you are dealing with a matter of life and death. You are anxious, because you have looked everywhere and still couldn't find the answer you need. Am I correct?"

"Yes, figuratively speaking," Smith spoke in a low voice.

"Look no further, Monsieur," said True3Oracle5U and pointed at Smith's forehead. "You have already found what you seek. You just don't know yet. There is a 99% probability that your problem will go away in one to 18 months."

Ooh la la, probability based, unambiguous and with a specified timeframe. It is a measurable predication. A prediction that no one in her trade would dare to make because it would hold them accountable. But she just did it with impunity.

While Smith was impressed by the fortune telling, he saw a familiar figure reflected on the astrologer's crystal nail. He squinted to take a better look and recognized it as a person he was looking for.

He hastily put down a fifty, took a name card from the desk, and got up to chase that person wearing a baseball cap, which would have been the perfect disguise in American superhero movies.

The afternoon break was just over and hundreds of people were flocking to the main ballroom for the "True Earth Research Workshop – Fake or Deep Fake." Smith and that person were the only two walking in the opposite direction.

Weaving through the swarm of Seekers who referred to each other as their YouTube user names, Smith finally caught up to that person.

"Hey, where have you been?" Smith asked. "You phony Zorbist plant."

Chapter 31

Elevator N4 had been stuck between the seventh and eighth floors for more than four hours. And yet, it and its occupants were completely free of stress or any negative emotions normally connoted with an elevator in its position. Instead, it was literally choked with joy, imagination and marijuana smoke.

"Chandler, did you get any signal?" asked a slothful voice in the smog.

"Ugh... nope, just like what I told you twenty minutes ago," slurred another voice.

"You're sure it has been only twenty minutes? I feel like starving," said the first voice.

"Sensei, I heard smoking joints would stimulate the production of hunger hormone, so it is normal to feel hungry," said politely a stoned voice.

"Great to know that, although it doesn't make me any less famished."

"Wins, when we are trapped here, maybe the world out there has already been overrun by zombies like one of your deer movies. Maybe we should have *that talk.*"

"Oooooooh *that talk,*" said the slothful voice, whose inflection made it hard to judge if its owner truly knew what it was talking about.

"Sensei, Mr. Chandler, you really want to have *that talk* now? She is right there."

"What?" cried a female voice, which sounded deceptively attractive in the thick smog. "I am not going to let you use my body to re-populate the planet."

The three male voices' owners exchanged a look the way three noncorporeal beings would.

"Ms. Maeve, I think I can swear on behalf of the three of us. What you were thinking has never, ever, had the chance..."

"... of even coming close, in any meaningful way, to materialize itself..."

"... even in the most remote and underdeveloped corner of our consciousnesses," categorically said the slurring voice.

"I feel reassured," said the female voice, "as much as I am flattered."

"Just so we are clear," the slurring voice said again, "*that talk* is merely about who should do the first stabbing if we are going to have a successful survival cannibalism."

Seven and half floors below elevator N4, Smith Robin and Charles Peralta were in a pose commonly referred to as *kabedon* in Japanese romance manga (or *bìdōng* in Chinese TV dramas), which literally means wall bang. That is, Smith forced Charles against the wall with one hand, making a banging sound, while leaning into Charles' face. Despite its misleadingly sexual translation in English, it is indeed a platonic gesture often made in the course of love confession, which was more or less what Smith was trying to do.

"Hooray, no time no see bro," Charles talked like a ventriloquist without his dummy. "I am fine, thanks for asking. I was just going to take a leak. And how about you, having fun with the hottie you met in the ballroom? I love your shirt by the way. Mine? Please, I bought it from a thrift shop."

"Give me a break. I have no idea what you are talking about," Smith hollered and almost shared a kiss with Charles. "You said you would be too busy 'playing controlled opposition' to support *my* operations. But you and your team were just helping Odinson play Jesus."

"*That* is controlled opposition," said Charles and discreetly looked around to make sure no one was in earshot. The two of them were now standing in front of the washroom entrance, around thirty feet away from the nearest sales booth. Besides them and a few entrepreneurial booth hosts, the whole exhibition floor looked empty.

"The infighting of flatees gave me the idea of fighting weirdos with weirdos," said Charles, while looking for ways to get past Smith into the bathroom, "so years ago Round Ops decided to found its own geocentric creed. We held focus group to brainstorm ideas, hired consultants to teach us design thinking, and then we had this wonderful idea from Jenkins—"

"Jenkins from Accounting, who looks like the white version of Homer Simpson?"

"No, Jenkins from Finance, who looks like Peter Griffin without the chin balls."

"I think we are talking about the same woman."

"Anyway," said Charles, whose legs began to twitch involuntarily, "she came up with this idea of denying all other geocentric creeds as products of subjective experiences. And that's how I became a Zorbist chaplain."

"I kind of figured that out already. I once saw those inflatable balls in pantry and needled them. Then Mosby gave me a warning letter for obstructing Round Ops operations."

"*You* were the Orb Rapist?"

"I prefer to go by Smith the Poker. Anyway, why would you be working for the Treeple? Are you a double agent? Oh my god, I shouldn't have asked that. You are going to gun me down after I say something extremely dumb, aren't you?"

"As much as I would love to indulge myself in that scenario right away," Charles said in a trembling voice, with both hands on his waist, "I did not double-cross NASA. You know, my team didn't have the budget to get Zorbism off the ground, so the operation was not exactly a success, for which I partially blamed the over sophisticated doctrine and partially you for vandalizing our props."

Smith recalled he had recently cut the budget for a Round Ops' spending item called "Projects brought forward," but decided not to overtax Charles with this information.

"For several fiscal years, the whole Zorbism project was on life support," Charles spoke like he was holding a lot of emotion in himself, "until Odinson reached out and said we could help each other out. I would help him with his healing stunt, and he would help put Zorbism on the map."

"That's it? For publicity? Then how are you different from those jerks who took their vaccination booster and then made memes to mock the vaxxed as sheep?"

"The difference is," said Charles with veins popping on his face, "I don't have my supporters' blood on my hands *and* now we have a leverage on the Treeple. Think about it, if Odinson wins the election and I come forward to expose his lie, then the whole United Ways would take a big hit."

Smith did think about it.

Undermine the flatees' leader and destroy them from within... how come it sounds so familiar?

"Alright, I can't say what you did is wrong because it is basically R.D.G.A.R." was what Charles expected to hear.

"Who cares if we can undermine the United Ways or even bring down the Church of Treeism?" was what he actually heard.

"Excuse me?"

"Odinson and his folks operate exclusively outside of the American soil and the United Way is a tax evasion shell registered in Cayman Islands. Neither of them is within our jurisdiction," Smith presented his case with the air of a criminal defense lawyer who is about to get his client's charge dismissed because the prosecutor's key witness statement has a glaring split infinitive.

"Now, tell me what you plan to write on *your* performance appraisal when your little Zorbist project leads to Odinson's impeachment?"

As a Round Ops agent who swore to protect America's No.1 national security interest, namely the Global Lie, Charles had never thought about himself.

"If anything," Smith continued as he saw no comeback from his dumbfounded colleague, who appeared to be literally bending to his argument, "we should let the Disk Earth Society or its sister denominations win the election before we undermine them."

Smith felt his case was strong enough and rested it. Meanwhile, several emotions rapidly swapped place on Charles' face.

"You mean," Charles said, "it would be a bad idea to help Odinson's campaign..."

"Correct."

"... by preventing DES from re-uniting with its flat Earth cousins."

"Yup, you got it."

"By corollary, if we foresee the DES presidential candidate may use the panel discussion to swing the flatees outside of DES to vote for him..."

"Then we should wish him luck."

"And make sure we don't stand in the way..."

"Hell yeah, you don't wanna do that."

"Specifically, we should never trap him and his aides in an elevator, disable the emergency phone, and jam mobile signal in the shaft?"

"Oh boy, it would be a very silly thing to do."

"Great," Charles said and looked at his watch in an unusually conspicuous manner, "then I am glad that no one ever did it. You know what, why don't we re-group after you meet with Dr. Stinson tonight? I really need to hit the bathroom now and need to make a few phone calls that had nothing to do with what we just discussed."

Seven and half floors above the exhibition floor, Maeve, Chandler and Ohi were in a position that professional wrestlers would refer to as a double cross-face. As occupied as she was, Maeve was also having a Mexican standoff with Winston at the other corner of the elevator.

"Don't you dare to take another step," bellowed Maeve with a joint on her lips. In a bridge position applying pressure on both Chandler and Ohi's backs, she had wrapped her hands around each of their necks and pulled them backward, performing the signature move "Bank Statement" of wrestler Sasha Banks.

"Chill out, chill out, I won't," said Winston, with his back on the wall and both hands raised in the air, one of which was still holding a weed joint. "I promise, we won't eat you, regardless of whether the world out there is in a nuclear war or alien invasion."

"We can even let you take a bite at Mr. Chandler," moaned Ohi, with his stomach and right arm nailed to the floor, "if it pleases you, of course."

"Screw you Ohi," yapped Chandler, who was in a similar prone position on Ohi's right and no longer slurring.

Despite the chaotic situation, Winston was unnaturally calm. Partly because he was as stoned as a diamond, and partly because he always knew a day like this would happen.

It is happening now, thought Winston, *the day I have to choose which of my best friends to feed to a slavering jaw for the greater good.*

A lesser man would have fainted in dread and a noble one would have scarified himself, but Winston Kanshū was neither of them. He was giving dead serious thought about which of his friends should be fed to the vice-chairwoman of Disk Earth Society.

Since this wasn't the first time Winston meditated on this unsavory yet thrilling prospect, he had already devised a neo-utilitarian approach to facilitate his decision making, namely weighting the financial consequences of each option.

He quickly calculated the amount of unpaid salary and unvested employee benefits to Ohi, minus the cost of replacement hiring and work injury compensation. He then did a quick netting between the debts owed to and by Chandler, neglecting interests. The last time he did so much math was when his fund manager told him that his investment had seen an unprecedented growth of -99%.

"Ohi, Chandler, no biggie," said Winston, unconsciously impersonating his fund manager's voice. "You are in good hands."

Both Ohi and Chandler expected Winston would trade himself as a hostage, while Maeve had no idea what to expect.

"Maeve, I got an offer for you. I will give you my—"

Before Winston could finish his sentence the elevator re-animated, which was what Maeve thought had happened.

But what actually happened was, Winston flicked the joint over Maeve's head and crouched down as if a portal just opened up on the floor and sucked him in. Before Maeve could react to the sudden movements, Winston had exploded from the squatting position and launched himself toward Maeve's 220-pound body, wrapping her neck with both arms. The moment Maeve lost her balance, Ohi and Chandler raised themselves and joined Winston in pinning down Maeve. They were all too stoned to perform any wrestling hold, so they were basically just sitting on her arms.

"Oh my god, you are going to eat me," cried Maeve, whose cigarette was still miraculously on her lips. She tried to kick Ohi and Chandler with her free legs but in vain. She couldn't tell whether it was because the two men were out of kick range, or because her legs just gave up moving.

"No one is eating anyone here," Winston hollered. "We are not having *that talk* anymore. And damn the entertainment industry for turning us into animals who can't get enough of apocalyptic genre."

"Sensei, thanks for saving us. I thought my soul was getting squeezed out from the mouth."

"Phew, I thought you were going to feed Ohi boy to this cow."

"I would never do anything like that to you two," said Winston, whose mind was still boggled by the mind-boggling amount of work injury compensation and the otherwise irrecoverable loans made to Chandler."

Suddenly the elevator re-animated, which was what Maeve hoped to happen. Coincidentally, it was also what indeed happened.

As the elevator resumed moving downward, four smartphones simultaneously vibrated, which was enough to bring the quartet back to their civilized selves. The three men released Maeve and started checking their phones.

"Oh my god, we have been stuck for almost five hours," said Chandler.

"And only five new likes on the story I posted this morning?!" exclaimed Winston.

"So I was wrong about the hunger hormone," grunted Ohi.

"We don't have time to discuss your deprived ego and stomachs," Maeve said as she struggled to get back up on her feet. "The panel discussion will start in forty minutes."

The elevator door finally reopened, bringing them back to the virtually empty exhibition hall.

"No problem, I remember everything you downloaded to me when we were trapped," Winston said as he staggered through the door.

"What, I didn't give you any prep," Maeve said in surprise. "We started rolling joints as soon as we stopped headbanging the door. You don't remember?"

"Oh..." Winston said as his eyes ballistically dashed around, like a pinball bouncing among several closely situated bumpers, "it makes sense now... I also find it strange that you would teach me *kung fu*, implant a chip into my neck and then take off your face mask to reveal you are a goldfish. I think none of that is real."

"You *think*?" Maeve asked.

"Chill, you said we still have forty—"

Before he could finish, Winston's face had landed onto the carpeted floor.

Both Ohi and Chandler wanted to help him, but both were too scared to step on the carpet.

"Is it just me or they have replaced the floor with a trampoline? It is floating up and down wildly," said Chandler.

"It must be you, Mr. Chandler," said Ohi, "because I don't see any floor. How come we are on a sky walk?"

"Don't press the close button, we still need to get off," Maeve yelled at Ohi. "Just follow my lead and *crawl*." Maeve saw a concave floor, but denied the curvature like an average flat Earther would.

"Yes, you crawl," said relaxedly Winston, whose face was still on the floor. "I will go grab a late lunch and join you guys in the ballroom."

Winston's upper body heaved and lunged forward, but dropped to the floor around half a second later. After catching a breath, it projected itself forward again for another inch. As far as he was concerned, he was walking with his chin at full speed.

Chapter 32

"Look at this and tell me what it is," hollered the facilitator, pointing at a picture of the Earth allegedly taken on a hot-air balloon.

"*Fake!!!*" bawled the participants, who just did a hands-on exercise to reproduce the curvature using cameras with fisheye lens.

"And this?" the facilitator clicked on his laser pointer and the wall screen behind him refreshed. It now displayed a picture of Buzz Aldrin standing next to the American flag, both on what appeared to be the Moon's surface.

"*Fake!!!*" the audience shouted louder, all holding a leaflet that summarized the one hundred clues for fake Moon landing.

"How about this?" another click on the laser pointer and a live stream from the International Space Station was played.

"*Fake, fake, fake!!!*" chanted the attendees, most of which had previously watched it on YouTube and received free mental health advice from the chat room.

Seated at the very back of Sapphire Dome, Smith Robin was getting a bit uncomfortable. Next to him was, he thought, a gym rat in moist discolored shirt with unsubtle armpit stains. Actually, that dude just got a bit too excited to be in the "True Earth Research Workshop – Fake or Deep Fake." And actually, that sweaty man had little to do with the lack of comfort Smith was feeling.

Oh my god, Smith recoiled in horror, *they saw through all of those.*

Smith's fear and concern were not unwarranted, as NASA had spent an awful lot of money to produce those realistic pictures and footages, especially the ISS live stream. A lot of creative efforts went into the camera work and selection of background music, keeping the supposedly silent stream less uninteresting. To NASA's dismay, the stream's live view count usually hovered in the low three digits, shadowed by dances of scantily clad teenagers, video game playthrough, and scantily clad teenagers doing video game playthrough.

The initial shock notwithstanding, Smith's fear receded as he continued to watch the facilitator's debunking and listen to the one-syllable chanting.

"*Fake!!!*" shouted at a picture of SpaceX launch.

"*Fake!!!*" shouted at a picture of solar eclipse.

"*Fake!!!*" shouted at a picture of lunar eclipse.

As everything was dismissed as fake, Smith started to doubt the meaning of fake.

Many linguists, and many more chronicle swearers, had long been aware of the bizarre phenomenon that if a word was repeated successively it would begin to seemingly lose its meaning. A number of psychologists had come up with different names to describe the same phenomenon and published papers to discuss its root causes, such as loss of short-term memory, brain's fatigue in associating words with meaning, and economic use of cognitive resources. To their disappointments, none of the names they coined really sticked and they continued to have a miserable time during high school reunions. Some economists had taken it upon themselves to further study that bizarre phenomenon and conjectured it was a result of adaptive evolution, "designed" to increase the survivability of psychologists by boosting their publishing rates. A small number of anthropologists had published peer review of the aforementioned researches, commented on their methodologies, concluded they all had their merits, and recommended further research into this interesting area with a bit more focus on practical application.

While academics from various disciplines continued to mine publishing values from that bizarre phenomenon, the Project Management Director of NASA just came up with an airtight theory that could comprehensively explain its root cause. Luckily for those scholars, Smith didn't bother to write down his theory and immediately forgot about it, because he just saw a saving opportunity for NASA.

The eclipses are not fake, thought Smith, *although all the other things are. These flatees have no idea how much our real scientists wish to find out how eclipses actually happen.*

Seeing that the flatees would simply dismiss all inconvenient evidences as fake regardless of how carefully NASA fabricated them, Smith felt confident in his decision of keeping the Arts Department's budget flat. He suppressed a devious grin and joined the others in applauding at the end of the workshop.

Moments later, the host returned to the stage. While he cracked a joke about two globetards walking into a bar, two helpers swiftly came to the ballroom's stage. They moved the podium to a side and put in the middle four chairs with writing tables, each bearing a plastic name plate. They were gone before the host could finish telling his joke that was offensive to Mexicans, Democrats, autistic people, gay rights activists, vegans, and Siberian tigers, in that order.

"... all jokes aside," said the host, pulling a clue card from his golden metallic leather jacket, "it is time for the final event of today – Panel Discussion of the Future of Geopolitics and Antarctic Treaty in Twenty Years, also known as the four flat Earthers who get between you and the banquet."

Adherents of All-Ways and Treeism laughed unnaturally loud at the host's bad joke, while it flew completely over the heads of TYDF followers.

"Without further ado, I present to you our distinguished speakers. First, Karenna Plain—" the host paused as Plain mouthed some words to him from her seat. "Sorry, I mean, Dr. Karenna Plain from Plane Rite. Besides her veterinary practice, Dr. Plain dedicates her life to advocate the infiniteness of our flat planet. Some of you may have read her recent op-ed, arguing that Syrian refugees should be relocated to the other side of Antarctic ice wall."

Plain walked onto the stage and waved to acknowledge the applause, mostly attributed to her creative solution for refugee crises. Despite her congenial smile and gentle gesture, her blue pant suit and reading glasses unhelpfully reminded those undereducated attendees that she was a professional living on a higher plane.

"Following Dr. Plain, we have Leonard Roundy from Wraparound's Witness, also known as the worst critic of Dr. Plain. Personally, I am a big fan of his mind-warping, or I should say, dimension-wrapping theory that the Antarctic ice wall is like the screen of *Asteroids*. If one goes over the edge of, say, the East side of the ice wall, they will immediately find themselves within the

West side. Very interesting theory!"

Roundy made quite an entrance by directly leaping onto the stage from his front row seat. He barely acknowledged the applause before seating himself next to Plain, whose suit sharply contrasted his superhero T-shirt and jean shorts.

"Coming next, we have Pierce Gerry from Neo Gerrymandered Temple, or NGT," said the host and flipped his clue card to the next page. For some reason, he didn't seem to believe what he saw and switched to another card, then another. Running out of notes, he started patting his jacket. Before he resumed his introduction, Gerry had waddled past him.

"You know what," said the host carefreely, "we all know about NGT, right? Who doesn't? You don't need me to tell you what Gerry and his pack are up to." The host scanned around the floor for an approving nod, but failed to spot any. "Well, but just in case some of our attendees are new to this community, maybe I will pass the mic to Gerry for a few quick words about his temple."

Being unexpectedly handed the microphone did not surprise or annoy Gerry. Instead, he seemed to enjoy the attention drawn to himself. His silver head, wrinkled smile, expensive-looking black suit and silk pocket square suggested he just came from his granddaughter's wedding or his ex-wife's funeral, or both.

"I am, hello, I am an old friend of Robert, Robert Milburn. You know, the on-the-run chairman of Disk Earth Society. He and I, we see eye to eye on a lot of things. Things like, the Earth is flat, the atheists try to hide it, and women should just stay at home. But, erm... we had this little fallout many years ago. He was trying to – what was it again? – canonize – boy, that was a four-dollar word – he was trying to canonize how the Earth's perimeter is like. You know, like a circle, oval, square, or whatnot. I couldn't agree with what he was doing. It felt wrong, it just did. Because do you know who drew the perimeter of the Earth? Huh? It was God. And God, he works in a mysterious way. It is silly of us to try to discern how God created this world. If, and it is not even a big if, if he wanted it to be in the shape of a, say, salamander or a pair of earmuffs, he can just, snap, and make it. See? Who says the Earth is always in the same two-dimensional shape?"

"So basically you think God gerrymanders the Earth like an electoral district," bluntly said Roundy from behind Gerry.

"It is not what I think, kiddo" corrected Gerry without turning to face the zoomer, "it is what I know."

Although he still wasn't sure what to make of NGT, the host believed the audience had been exposed long enough to the boomer's thoughts and retrieved the microphone from him. He guided Gerry to his designated seat in a way that didn't make the old man feel senile and dependent, before returning to the podium.

"Last but certainly not the least," said the host with unabated enthusiasm, "we will have Winston Kanshū, the presidential candidate from Disk Earth Society."

Perfectly synchronizing with the host's introduction and the thundering applause, the main entrance of Sapphire Dome burst opened. Everyone turned around and expected to see a dramatic entrance like the Zorbists this morning, but were surprised to see no one at the door.

Actually, some of those at the aisle seats did see someone come in. Looking down, they could see a human centipede in aloha shirt slowly wiggle on the carpet. Of course it was the DES presidential candidate, Winston Kanshū.

Chapter 33

Among the three famous slogans from *Nineteen Eighty-Four*, "Ignorance is strength" is the most underappreciated piece of wisdom. Most literature analysts believe it simply serves to highlight the contradictory nature of totalitarian indoctrination and to warn of how an authoritarian government can cement its power by keeping people ignorant. They overlook the most obvious: It is a literal and factual statement with unbounded possibilities of practical applications.

For instance, investment bankers pocketing the biggest bonus checks would never ask their quantitative engineers what models and dog shit are used to cook up their synthetic products, because such knowledge is not only irrelevant but indeed detrimental for a convincing, clear-conscience sales pitch. Defense attorneys who hate disciplinary hearing often also hate being told by a client to plead not guilty *and* how much the client enjoyed stabbing his wife. Partners of audit firms, if they are shrewd, will go to great length to prevent themselves from having access to the audit work papers (e.g., restricting read-access to shared folders in the name of least-privilege principle or deploying an audit software that takes a minute to load one attachment) so that their lawyers would have an easier time to defend against a professional negligence case.

With the right amount of ignorance (also known as the epistemic Goldilocks zone), a person can attain confidence, deniability, conscience, or even the most important job in the world. Since Winston Kanshū was too busy smoking weed and crawling his way to Sapphire Dome, he only got three talking points from Maeve Walsh before his head could bang open the ballroom's doors. The limited intel and mild concussion were, however, exactly what he needed to arrive at the Goldilocks zone.

"You're sure you still want to do this?" asked the host.

"I am OK," Winston spoke into the microphone on his writing desk. "*They* wanted to silence me because I know too much, but I won't let *Them* have *Their* way."

The audience audibly gasped when they put together that the DES presidential candidate just survived an assassination attempt by *Them*. They automatically assumed that Winston Kanshū was in the possession of vitally important information. They further granted him the license to dodge any fact-finding questions that might come his way, with the presumption that such evasion was for the sake of the questioners. Moreover, their dot-connecting engines had been dialed up a few notches to connect whatever he said or didn't say with whatever they believed he would say.

"In that case," said the host and returned to the podium, "let's begin our panel discussion."

With a flick on the laser pointer, the host put on the screen wall a logo of the Secretariat of the Antarctic Treaty, which allegedly was established in 2003 to support the treaty's implementation.

"For decades," the host said, "the Antarctic Treaty had been in our way to the truth. To enlightenment. To the edge of our world."

Plain raised her hand in protest against the host's choice of words, but he pretended not to see her and continued. "Since its inception in 1959, more than fifty countries have entered into the multilateral agreement, with the pretense of protecting the freedom of scientific investigation, which we all know is horseshit."

The audience cheered. Nothing touched people's hearts as much as a word of profanity. The host savored the wowing, clapping and whistling for a moment, before he continued.

"The treaty seems to be expanding its sphere of influence and it looks increasingly hopeless for us to get definite proof that the Earth is not a ball. But the tides have been changing in our favor recently. With the trade war between China and the States, Russia's invasion into Ukraine, and the rising number of sanctions imposed by both Eastern and Western countries on each other, the tension among the treaty signatories is escalating by the minute. That brings us to the topic of discussion today: What will happen to the treaty because of the geopolitical dynamics? And what are the opportunities for us, the Seekers?"

Having finished his introduction, the host finally stopped ignoring Plain and said, "Dr. Plain, what is your thought?"

"Before I begin," said Plain and pushed up her glasses, "I would like to clarify that the ice wall at Antarctica is *not* the edge of Earth. It is just the barrier between our world and the infinite horizon beyond the wall."

The host pretended he did not hear Plain's complaint. As a Delist – that is, the follower of The Second Coming of Delta Del – the host never doubted that the Earth was an inverted pyramid and that our civilization thrived on its base, fenced by the ice wall in Antarctica. Similar to his ancestors who supposedly built polyhedrons to honor Delta Del four thousand and five hundred years ago, he firmly believed the Earth was an unfinished octahedron and someday the creator would return to make the world *whole*. According to their Book of Octahedron, one day Delta Del would create another Earth, flip it upside down, and bang it onto the face of our Earth, effectively wiping out all globeheads and Israelis. Only the Delists would survive the bang and be rewarded with ninety-nine virgins of their preferred gender and age.

Getting no response from the Delist host, Plain was visibly annoyed and a heartbeat away from asking for the manager, but managed to contain her irritation and returned to the discussion.

"Back to your question, I don't think the geopolitics will have much impact on the treaty system. Think about it. Why would *They* go to such trouble to hide from us the world beyond the ice wall? Because *They* feel threatened by whatever is out there."

"Can you be more specific about threats you mentioned?" asked the host without a hint of aggression. He trusted the God would crush this spectacled pagan with the full weight of another Earth and therefore saw no need of hostility. *Delta Del doesn't need me to speak for Himself,* he thought. He asked Plain the question only to facilitate the discussion.

"It could be anything," answered Plain, "maybe it is an oil field or a diamond mine, which *They* would like to hide from us in order not to shock the oil price or bankrupt the jewelry industry. Or aliens. Or zombies."

"Or a bunch of cashiers who got fired because a Karen spoke to their managers," interjected Roundy.

"Whatever threats they are," Plain continued after giving Roundy a mean look, "the stakes are simply too high for the status quo to change."

"Interesting insight," the hosted jumped in to diffuse the tension between Roundy and Plain. "How about you, Gerry? Any prediction on the treaty?"

Everyone in Sapphire Dome unwillingly turned their gazes to the unsightly boomer sitting silently between Winston and Roundy. His eyes were open but didn't blink for almost half a minute. People began to wonder if he was dead, but it turned out he was just taking his time to process the question.

"My prediction," Gerry blinked and spoke, "is war. The Communist Bloc will be the first to exit the treaty and start building military bases at Antarctica. Then NATO will be like 'Screw it, I am gonna put some missiles there as well.'"

"Interesting," the host repeated his favorite non-word, "so you actually believe the Antarctic Treaty is an arms control agreement. A by-product of the Cold War. You don't think it was established to prevent people from exposing the Global Lie?"

Gerry froze again. He was so still that the host thought there was a connection problem, only to remember he wasn't in a video conference.

Not just Gerry, all of his fellow NGT members below the stage froze. All five of them.

"While we wait for Gerry to come back," the host changed the subject again, "from wherever he is right now, why don't we hear from Roundy what he thinks of the treaty's future?"

"I have to disagree with Dr. Plain," said Roundy. "I don't believe the treaty will continue to be observed when its most powerful signatories turned against each other."

"So you also expect a war, like Gerry?" asked the host.

"No, that's extreme," the young man said. "Just something in between, you know. Like, the States may let some billionaires break the treaty and go over the wall like visiting an amusement park. You see, the ice wall is basically a Ferris wheel. Instead of taking you up and down, it wraps you from east to west or from north to south instantly."

"That's a very curious prospect, I must say," the host enthused. "If I understand it correctly, you are saying the ice wall will be like the private spaceflight. Only the filthy rich can afford and be let into the know about the Global Lie."

"Exactly like private spaceflights," said the zoomer affirmatively, "except that no one will publicly advertise it, because people outside of this room think travelling to Antarctica has always been a thing."

"So you are saying the 1% would spend a fortune and then not brag about it?" Plain asked with disdain. "That doesn't sound characteristic of them. Why did they get that rich in the first place?"

"Interesting, very interesting," the host stepped in again. "We have covered a few unique angles. Kanshū, how about you? Any thoughts?"

The attention of everyone in the ballroom, except the six NGT fellows in suspended animation, gravitated towards Winston, who had regained approximately 30% of his motor functions. Flat Earthers were curious what insight he could possibly bring to the table, given that the representatives from Plane Rite, NGT and

Wraparound's Witness had covered virtually all possible scenarios of the treaty system's future. Seekers outside of the flat Earth community, on the other hand, wondered if the DES presidential candidate would utter the same nonsense as his fellow flat Earthers.

"What's going to happen to the treaty system?" asked Winston rhetorically. "That's a silly question. I can't believe you all fell for *Their* trick."

The host didn't know what to make of this comment. Plain felt insulted and wanted to speak to the manager. Gerry came back to live and wondered who pissed in his pants. Roundy just sat back and watched the show.

Meanwhile, Winston recalled the first talking point Maeve had downloaded to him. *Support the argument by citing a lack of evidence. If there is indeed some unfavorable evidence, assert it doesn't exist anyway.*

"I am sorry if I was being rude," apologized Winston unapologetically, "but I just found it amusing that you three went back and forth on what would or would not happen to the Antarctic Treaty, without stopping to consider the possibility that the treaty is itself a lie. A conspiracy within a conspiracy."

Generally, a highhanded remark like that would have made the Seekers lose their minds, because they used to be the ones pointing out accepted truth was a lie. However, the assassination-survivor halo around Winston made his argument more compelling than repelling.

"Excuse me," said Plain, whose voice was two pitch higher than usual. "Are you seriously telling me the Antarctic Treaty never existed?"

"Dr. Plain, have you ever seen the treaty?" asked Winston.

"Personally, I haven't—"

"How about the rest of you?" asked Winston and turned to the other panelists. "Do any of you have evidence that the supposed signatories actually signed on the treaty?"

Both the panelists and audience grew restless. They felt like there was something wrong with the question but could not put their fingers on it. Granted, they were no strangers to questions with similar syntactic structure, but often they were the ones who did the asking.

"There is a bloody website run by the Secretariat of the Antarctic Treaty," bellowed Plain and showed the screen of her phone to Winston across the stage.

"Doctor," said Winston calmly, "there is no evidence that the Antarctic Treaty Secretariat is appointed by the so-called treaty parties. I am sure you can find a website with its history, missions and meeting documents archive. But I can just as easily google for you the website of the Church of the Flying Spaghetti Monster, which provides propaganda materials and witness stories. A website doesn't make the subject matter any realer."

"There are people out there enforcing the treaty," Gerry joined Plain in protest.

Winston was getting a bit bored of the where-is-the-evidence trick, so he turned to the second talking point from Maeve. *Question the doubter's qualifications, but don't shy away from conceding that you are not an expert, preemptively striking down similar challenges.*

"Really, are you some kind of military inspector from the United Nations?" asked Winston like a vax denier who just did his medical research on the loo and argued with immunologists on Facebook. "And before you tell me someone told you what they saw or what they knew, what are their qualifications?"

"Erm... if I might," the host gently said, "why would anyone make up the Antarctic Treaty?"

"Why wouldn't *They*?" Winston countered. "Certainly I am not an expert of international affairs, but you said it yourself: The treaty was first opened for signing during the Cold War, a period of high geopolitical tension. *They* obviously needed to keep the Global Lie a secret, but the First and Second World nations couldn't agree on anything. So what could *They* do?"

Winston paused for a moment to make sure he was playing it right.

He knew he was.

"The easiest way to do it," Winston continued, "is to tell the world that a treaty has been signed to prevent Antarctica exploration. And when the age of Internet comes, hire an intern to make a website for the treaty system. Problem solved."

"That's a nice theory," said Plain reluctantly, "but what proof do you have to support your theory?"

Viola, time to wrap it up with the final trick, Winston thought. *Poke a hole, or anything that looks like a hole, in the reality and take it as evidence for your case.*

"Give me a minute," Winston said and shifted his weight to face the host. "Lenny, can I call you Lenny?"

"Eh... but my name is Yusuf Adel," said the host in bewilderment. "How did you jump from it to Lenny?"

"O, Yusuf," Winston established the first-name basis without explaining. "Can you put onto the screen the list of countries that supposedly have signed the treaty?"

Yusuf "Lenny" Adel complied. Less than a minute later, the list of Antarctic Treaty signatories was displayed on the screen wall behind the panelists.

"Cool, now can you further google the list of countries that reportedly have launched satellites into the space? Please display both lists on the screen."

Plain wondered what tricks he was playing. Gerry was impressed that text appeared on the wall. Roundy continued to look amused.

"Now, Dr. Plain," Winston addressed the Plane Rite speaker when the setup was completed, "do you notice anything from the lists?"

"Eh...," Plain was caught off guard and struggled to make sense of the lists of country names. There were fifty-four names on the treaty list and thirteen on the satellite list, the latter of which included North Korea even though all its launches were sabotaged.

"The treaty list has two Korea's."

"They refer to South Korea and North Korea, which are both on the satellite list."

"The spelling of Ukraine is wrong on both lists."

"No, they aren't."

"There is a fictional country on both lists: Japan. It and the Pearl Harbor attack were made up to justify the States' entry into the World War II."

"Jeez, my father was born there. What's your problem?"

"Then it must be Kazakhstan. It was from the Borat movies."

"Thank you for your participation, doc," Winston felt she had embarrassed herself enough and moved on. "If you compare the two lists carefully, you will notice two countries that are supposed to be on the treaty list are missing. If you need one more hint, they both start with an *i*."

"*Iran and Israel!!!*" Roundy blurted out. "Both of them have placed satellites on orbit and should be in the know about the Global Lie, but neither of them is on the treaty list."

"Bingo," Winston said. He felt his strength had come back and stood up in front of the screen wall.

"All these years, you guys have been saying the treaty is enforced by the countries behind the Global Lie. Well, shouldn't Iran and Israel be part of them? If they are, which I believe they are, then why didn't they sign the treaty?"

Winston paused again for the question to sink in. He knew the audience would connect the dots on their own and take ownership of the idea he just fed them. And they all did. Hook, line and sinker. Except, of course, Smith Robin, who knew the two G12 members did not sign the treaty because they had other issues to work out on their own, such as whose signatures should go in first.

"I believe," resumed Winston and paced around the stage like he was doing a product announcement, "enough has been said about the treaty conspiracy, and I will leave it to you to draw your own conclusion. I just want to say one more thing."

The catchphrase from Steve Jobs, trademarked by a Swiss watch maker but first popularized by the TV show *Columbo*, pricked up the audience's ears. This wasn't a talking point from Maeve; it was another ad lib from Winston Kanshū.

"Regardless of whether *They* are guarding the ice wall with a bluff, or an army, or a nuke submarine, I give you my words," announced Winston and every cell in his body. Actually, less than 1% of his cells did the talking, while the rest of them contracted, expanded, multiplied, dissolved, rolled, died, or did whatever cells usually did when their host got very excited in making a point. The details didn't really matter; the effect was that they all added weight to his closing remarks.

"If I am elected the president of the United Ways, I will lead you to the ice wall.

"I will show you the edge of our world.

"I will spare no expenses, even if it means bankrupting the United Ways shell corporation!"

Winston's words hit a button in the audience's brains with the full force of every tax dollar that the United Ways had saved by registering in Cayman Islands. Once again, their brains exploded with endorphins, their ideological conflicts gave way to common goals, and Sapphire Dome erupted into deafening applause.

Spoiler: Three days later, Winston Kanshū received all the votes from Plane Rite, Wraparound's Witness and Neo Gerrymandered Temple.

Chapter 34

It is interesting that many words related to psychology can refer to the same thing. For instance, a psychologist may be referred to as a behavioral economist and receive the Nobel Memorial Prize in Economics Science.

It is also interesting that familiarity can override rationality and make people believe, or prefer to believe, a statement simply because they are repeatedly exposed to it.

Less interestingly, this phenomenon is called mere-exposure effect, familiarity principle or illusory truth effect, depending on which psychologist you ask, what time of the day you ask them, and how well their favorable football team did last weekend.

Slightly less uninterestingly, the said phenomenon can also affect whoever makes up the statement. For instance, after making hyperbolically exquisite election promises on two occasions, Winston Kanshū began to lose track of why he was running for the POTUWS office in the first place.

Did it have something to do with my discovery in Russia?

Or was it because of Maeve's fake tears?

Well, I did get a kick out of doing these speeches. Perhaps I did it for the fun.

O, maybe it was because I wanted to lead these people, to expose the Global Lie!

It is why I am doing what I am doing, right? Right...?!

Before he could come to a closure, a mildly disturbing sensation brought Winston back from his trance. That sensation came from his hands. It reminded him of the time a slavering deer in Nara Park swallowed his whole hand when he was feeding it crackers. The moisture. The warmth. The germs.

Winston fought off the residual THC in his nerve cells and regained control over his dilated pupils. His gaze stumbled to locate the hands and finally found them after some confusion with the ears and mishap with the armpits. To his delight, they (the hands) were simply being held in the sweaty palms of Leonard Roundy.

"Congratulations on destroying Plain," said the theorist of Wraparound's Witness. "Big fan of your movies, by the way. Can I get you something to drink before the banquet?"

While the two flat Earthers were holding hands on the stage, Smith Robin quietly slipped out of the ballroom. Not because his makeup persona was a homophobic (Gerry from NGT was, by the way, and asked the host to break them off), but because he had a date to catch.

He quickly ran to the washroom to check for anything stuck in the teeth, plucked some nasal hair with quarters, did a few push-ups under the illusion that they would give him bulging biceps, and washed the armpits with soap and water.

"I am Smith Muriel Johansson Jr.," whispered Smith to the mirror, "born in New Jersey, raised in a fundamental creationist family.

"I believe all lives are sacred, including and especially fetus, and condemn to hell anyone who is engaged in homosexual relations, supports abortion, worships pagan gods, or writes jokes about religious people. My faith entitles me to my physical health and economic prosperity, while the poor and the sick are being either tested for their faith or punished for what they deserve.

"I believe in free market, antagonize international trade, stigmatize those receiving social benefits, and vote for whoever advocates government subsidies and pledges to create jobs in my industry.

"I know my rights. I say whatever I want to say, and my opinion is worth as much as anyone's facts. I respect the freedom of expression, both mine and others', as long as they don't offend me.

"I think global warming is a hoax, feminism discriminates against men, and racial disparity is exaggerated. I'm not racist, but—"

Smith's rehearsal was cut short as the alarm on his phone went on. He quickly dried his underarm and put on his shirt. A shirt that was too light and comfortable to be business casual but too dark and formal for smart casual. A shirt that used to drive the HR of MacCheddar & Co. nuts in enforcing the workplace dress code.

It's time for the love machine.

Two minutes later, Smith found himself sitting in the reception lobby of Greendale Convention Centre. He sat in such a way that whoever came in from the main entrance would be at a 45-degree angle to him. A life coach like Smith Johansson would say that the 45-degree angle was exactly what one needed to look approachable. Smith Robin, on the other hand, would say that it was the perfect angle for observing the entrance while the glare from sunset would not impact his gameplay of *KrazyCoral*, a coral simulation game that was universally deemed too violent for active brain cells.

Attending to both the lobby entrance and the eventful adventure in Great Barrier Reef was no easy task, which was probably the reason why Gina could sneak upon him.

"The video game that redefines the concept of gameplay and cutscenes?" Gina giggled from behind Smith. "Why didn't you tell me you also play it?"

Startled, Smith turned around and found a lithe and genial face just inches from his shoulder. Her hazel eyes were staring at his screen, beaming with glee and mischief like a child who just found her parent's credit card.

Before Smith could regain control of his jaw muscles, Gina had gracefully walked around his sofa and sat across him, leaving behind a faint scent of jasmine.

"Nice shirt, by the way."

"Oh, thanks," Smith recollected himself, "and I love your new hair and rose vale long overcoat."

It was not inexplicable that Smith could accurately tell the color of Gina's attire, whose chromaticity in standard RGB was 171, 78, 82.

It was also unremarkable that Smith noticed Gina's curly hair was trimmed by 0.5 inch and otherwise looked exactly the same as last week.

And it was certainly not surprising that Smith had an incredibly large range when it came to casual conversation. He was basically Viola Davis in small talks. He could traverse from the Neo-Cubism paintings in the lobby; to the connection between the foyer's fake plants and bee extinction; to the psychological effect of having an over-sized, glamorous reception lobby that might appear as a waste of rent; to a remark that the hotel's Wi-Fi password was the longest palindrome in English, first coined by James Joyce in *Ulysses*.

What was indeed remarkably surprising in an inexplicable way was that a man who was capable of detecting inconsequential nuances in appearances and thrived on having trivial conversations still managed to have three failed marriages.

Thirty years later, in his bestselling memoir *I Am Telling You All*, Smith would theorize that his repeated marriage failures *might* have something to do with the prenup he insisted on signing. In his follow-up memoir *I Didn't Tell You All*, however, he would revise his stance on that matter. On the book's back cover, he triumphantly stated that his latest marriage had proven beyond reasonable doubt that he "only needed some time to find the soulmate." Curiously, that paragraph was removed in the second edition.

While Smith was telling a joke about Canadians that only American white girls on the Internet would find offensive, he found himself sneaked upon again. He knew it was a man because that person's cologne had made a pungently musky statement to announce his entry.

"Dr. Stinson," that man spoke without acknowledging Smith's presence, "this is Seth Nadir from All-Ways. Glad to finally meet you in person. I was expecting you at the coffee shop upstairs, thirty minutes ago."

"That's fascinating," said Gina, unfascinated, "because I already texted you that I couldn't make it."

Gina's bluntness surprised not only Nadir but also Smith, who had never seen this side of hers. He found her even more attractive now.

"As I told you earlier today," said Nadir, "it is imperative that you and I have a pre-meeting before your first mock interview with his Excellency's deputy. We need to make sure you digest all the lessons learnt and pass the second mock interview, before you can meet with his Excellency. Please tell me you have finished your pre-course work."

Holly molly, Smith thought, *has All-Ways hired MacCheddar & Co. to streamline its executive workflow?*

"Sorry, I didn't realize there was coursework in the four-hundred-page manual," said Gina. "I must have missed it when I deleted that file. Look, if your Excellency—"

"Not mine," Nadir hastily corrected. "His. His Excellency."

"If," Gina blew a raspberry and continued, "your Excellency wanted to talk, I'm more than happy to. I'd also like to thank him for his hospitability, but I am not doing any of your bureaucratic BS. You know what, I actually want to meet him now."

Before Nadir could find the correct response from the *Playbook for Upward Management: 99 Lessons from Eunuchs* published by MacCheddar Press, Gina and Smith had disappeared from the corridor that led to the exhibition floor.

Chapter 35

"Sensei, I am beginning to worry about your heart," said Ohi, watching Winston devour the nuts on their bar table.

"Really?" grunted Winston. "I was obviously trapped by someone in a bloody elevator, smoked my lung out for four hours straight, wrestled with a 220-pound woman, ground my face across the germ-infested floor, and now you worry about how much calorie I am taking in?"

"Don't let him upset you," said Maeve, putting a handful of limp chips in her mouth. "I also get grumpy when I am hungry."

"Yeah, we have seen how it goes," said Chandler grimly and

turned to Winston. "What did that kid say to you? Another I-will-do-anything-for-a-role or remember-me-from-Bangkok?"

"No, fortunately," said Winston and took a sap of his root beer. The mug was printed with the trademarked logo of Treeism and a line that read, "Even when you drink to forget, don't forget to pay your tithe."

After looking over both his shoulders, Winston whispered, "He just told me he is a troll."

"What?" Ohi almost screamed. "I thought the last of them died in the Battle of the Bastards."

"You were thinking of giant," said Winston, "I meant troll, which is kind of a giant, but Roundy is neither of those. You see what I am saying?"

Chandler stared blankly at Winston for a moment. "Do you?"

He went on to empty his mug, which had a different customed text, "Looking for guaranteed return? Tithe NOW."

"He is an Internet troll," hissed Winston. "He told me he started trolling flat Earthers around six years ago. At first he was being sarcastic, saying things like, 'No wonder I can jump and land on the same spot,' but soon got frustrated when his sarcasm went undetected. He then started writing a satirical novel to make fun of, sorry Maeve, the flatards, but he could never finish it."

"Why not?" asked Ohi, holding a mug that read, "You may lose your job. You may lose your saving. But never lose the habit of tithing."

"Well, he was worried that if he debuted with a book about flat Earth, he would never be taken seriously. Anyway, he then decided to turn a few notches up his trolling game. He made up this theory that the Earth is like the wrap screen of classic platformers, produced several YouTube videos about it, and used bots to take the view count off the ground. Before he knew it, he was signing autographs for fans and fighting a holy war against the Plane Rite."

"And he told *you* all about that?!" asked Chandler.

Winston shrugged.

"He said I would need the votes from 'his bros' to win, so he could freely brag about his trolling in my face with no repercussion. That's some high-quality trolling if you think about it. By the way..."

Winston looked at Maeve, whose mug shouted, "DON'T YOU DARE STOP TITHING." He struggled a bit but felt she deserved to know the truth.

"Um…," Winston fumbled with the right words, "Roundy wanted me to tell you he is the one who spread the rumor that you are an undercover agent from NSA. He also asked me to give him a detailed description of how you would react to it, you know, for his satisfaction."

While Maeve Walsh composed the longest curse sentence in English history, Winston saw an attractive woman out of the corner of his eye, which would have been nothing to write home about, should he not be in the venue of True Earth Summit.

She was in her late twenties, wearing a red long overcoat, tight jeans, ivory flats, and a white blouse. Next to her was a man in a nice shirt, which probably was her date. The two of them were making a bee line to Pandit Abed Kutner in the middle of the exhibition floor, followed by a panting All-Ways follower.

"Mr. Kutner?" said Gina.

Kutner looked more annoyed than surprised to see his guest's unannounced arrival. An impromptu meeting like this, according to the Human Capital Optimization model of MacCheddar & Co., was not the best use of his time. He peeped at Nadir over her shoulder and grudgingly excused himself from his company.

"Dr. Stinson, I didn't expect to see you here," said Kutner, while counting how many more voters he could have met if Nadir had done his job right. To save time, he kind of skipped the handshake and greeting, had no choice but to keep the small talk to the minimum, and politely used the most polished words possible to ask the one thing he wanted from Gina.

"Tell me about your discovery, now."

Smith's pupils dilated.

It won't work, he thought, *Britta's intel shows that Gina's psychological reactance is on par with vaccination deniers. You need reverse psychology to steer her into your way.*

"It will be shared with you and the world in two days," calmly said Gina, while the amygdala in her brain was violently strangulating the prefrontal cortex. The waiter passing by offered her a glass of champagne but she opted for a juice on account of her stomach ulcer.

"You may not be aware of this," said Kutner, in a way he thought was not blunt, "but I have an election to run here, and I need to make sure your presentation will not contradict the messages of my platform."

From Smith's position, he could not see Gina's expression, but he imagined it would be a combination of bared teeth, flaring nostrils, contorted face, lasering eyes, burning cheeks, or the like commonly described in novels but rarely seen in real life. The only thing he was certain of was that Kutner's attempt to censor Gina's scientific discovery would not be welcome.

"I see," said Gina. "Sure, I am happy to show it to you after the banquet."

Chapter 36

Winston awoke with a start. His watch said it was just past one, which didn't feel right. He would never go to bed that early. But then he saw the sunlight creeping below the curtain.

That makes more sense.

He just had a nightmare in which Chris Rock announced his exposé of the Global Lie had earned him an Oscar for Best Documentary Feature. He was hugged by Scarlett Johansson, received the award from Michael Moore, said a clever joke that cracked Dave Chappelle up, and gave a tear-jerking speech. Before leaving the stage, he kissed the golden man statue and discovered it was wrapped with yeast.

Awakened, Winston found himself holding the foot of Chandler. He got up and looked around the room. Everything looked as ordinary as a hotel room could be after a party night. The dripping bottles. The emptied minibar. The juvenile drawings on Chandler's face. Ohi dry humping a pillow on the floor. A rock python leaving through the ventilation duct.

Winston tried to retrace his steps leading to the fungus on Chandler's feet.

I joined the boys for drinks after the banquet, he thought, *wait, they were also at the banquet. Why didn't we come back together?*

He groped for his phone and found a small card on the nightstand. It was a wholesome message that encouraged Seekers to respect each other's way of explaining away gravity and included several examples: "Universal upward acceleration: the whole Earth accelerates upward at 9.8 m/s^2," "Dielectric acceleration: differences in electrical charges cause objects to fall," "Density: differences in density cause objects to fall," and "Aristotle's natural teleology: everything has a natural purpose and most them just want to fall."

Weird. Why would I keep a card like this?

Confused, Winston flipped the card over and saw a message less wholesome, "If convenient, come alone to the Fairmont Theatre at nine. It's OK if that's inconvenient; you can still come."

This brought back some of his memory. He got this card last night when he returned to his seat at the banquet. He initially thought it was from Roundy and prepared to ignore it, but the jasmine scent lingering on the card got him intrigued.

So he went to the theatre with no regard for convenience.

When he arrived, he was pleased to see the woman in red coat on the stage, but disappointed to find Odinson, Kutner, Song and the nice-shirt guy in the front row. He correctly deduced that the odds of him getting laid were astronomical.

There was some argument between Kutner and the lady who called herself doctor something. For simplicity, he decided to call her Hot Girl. Kutner didn't want Hot Girl to do something in certain way but she insisted on doing it in hers. Winston guessed Kutner was either her dad or a micromanaging boss who cared about obedience more than outcome.

Everything else that happened in the theatre was quite foggy now, but Winston could clearly remember one thing.

Hot Girl had positive evidence to debunk the Global Lie.

There was no ambiguity, no margin of error, no room for spinning, and no space for reinterpretation.

Her proof packed as hefty a punch as Superman, had as much weight as he could lift, and was as tight as his speedo.

It was so simple that it made Song smile.

It was so beautiful that it made Odinson cry.

It was so revolutionary that it made Kutner scream.

Winston closed his eyes and recalled the exact moment he was enlightened. He tried to feel the goosebumps again. He wanted to re-experience the joy of knowledge.

After a few deep breaths, he slowly reopened his eyes and peered into the black television screen across the room. He fixed his reflection with a dignified look.

"What the freak did she show me again?"

Chapter 37

Three blocks away from the Greendale Convention Centre, in a three-star hotel room whose daily rate was the maximum claimable amount for NASA personnel at salary grade D, Smith Robin and Charles Peralta were in a touch-base call with the NASA Director.

"Gents," said Miranda over the phone, "I have thought over what Smith reported to me last night. The objective of R.D.G.A.R. needs to be updated."

Charles' gaze puzzledly darted back and forth between Smith and his laptop. Neither of them would tell him what Dr. Stinson had discovered. He never felt so much like one of those Pub Comm losers before.

"Simply undermining the flatees is not enough," she added. "You need to make sure Dr. Stinson's findings never get revealed to the world."

"But," said Smith, "I thought we don't do assassination anymore? At least not with our budget."

"It won't be necessary. Stinson already told you where she kept her data backup, right? I will take care of the one on cloud, while you two will dispose of those on her laptop and backup drive before her announcement. No one will need to get hurt."

"But how about Gina and those guys from Big Four?"

"Don't you worry about your girlfriend now. When she has nothing to show for tomorrow, no one will ever take her seriously again. We can then approach her to see if she wants to do some *real* science for us. As for the four flatees…"

"No one outside of their echo chamber will believe them," supplemented Charles.

"Precisely," said Miranda. "Gentlemen, you have less than twenty-five hours to complete your mission."

Chapter 38

Agent A found his heart pounding as hard as it did the first time he stole his dad's *Playboy*. He hadn't told anyone about Robin's debrief to Miranda, not even to agent B. Rationally, he knew there was no reason to hide anything from her, but he loved the feeling of possessing secret knowledge. He thought he would keep it as his little secret until the next weekly team meeting.

Chapter 39

Maeve Walsh not only believed the Earth was a flat disk; she was also a believer in fate.

When her son was twelve and started searching for the meaning of life, he asked her why she gave birth to him. She thought it was a strange question. *Like I need a reason to bring a life to this world.* She said something along the line of "because I always wanted to be a mom," "because it is selfish not to raise a child," and "because I love you and want to show you this beautiful world." Her son was upset by the answer and never spoke to her again.

Since her husband wasn't much of a talker either, she took up the job as cab driver just to have someone to chat with. On the first day on her job, she picked up a middle-aged man who said he was catching a flight back to Montana. As they chatted on the way to the airport, she learnt that this man was recently elected as the chairperson of School of Flat Earth, whose mission was to "expose the Jews' scheme in controlling our minds." She was instantly hooked. In less than thirty minutes, she was converted into a flat Earther. She called it fate.

Years after that fateful encounter, she was made the vice-chairwoman of School of Flat Earth. In her acceptance speech for that honor, which had a view count of exactly 420 thanks to Leonard Roundy and his bots, she explained that Robert Milburn had changed her life by telling her there was no transatlantic flight in the Southern Hemisphere. Her belief in fate remained unshaken even though someone subsequently pointed out to her there *were* regular flights across the Southern Hemisphere.

She never regretted losing her husband for her flat Earth belief.

She never lost faith when all her friends on social media cut her off.

She never feared when other flat Earthers threated to "cut her NSA throat."

She believed everything she went through since the day her son stopped talking to her was part of a grand scheme. To fulfil her destiny as a king maker. To put Winston Kanshū on the throne of POTUWS.

If there was a new testament of the *Gospel of Flat Earth*, she would be the holy mother, adopting the prophesied Japanese American, raising him and his two brothers with all-you-can-eat buffet of Canadian comfort foods. Tourtière, ginger beef, butter tart, poutine, pierogi, Nanaimo bar and so on, all dipped/dressed/glazed/served/soaked/whipped with maple syrup. At least, that was what she thought she was doing.

"Alright, now I am physically ready," said contentedly Winston, wiping the syrup from his aloha shirt. "Prep me up."

"First thing first, optics," said Maeve and handed a bag to Winston. "These should fit you."

Winston took a peek at its contents and felt insulted.

Was it how those girls felt when I handed them a bag of lingerie before audition? wondered Winston.

"I am not putting them on," Winston protested. "What am I, Chandler the boring pilot? I did fine yesterday without pants and blazer, and I will just do the same today."

Chandler didn't seem to mind the comment and forked another hash brown from Ohi's syrup-saturated dish. The diners sitting behind them were warily browsing their phones for news of anyone who just escaped from a nearby institution.

"Yesterday you were letting the Seekers know you as a person," said Maeve maternally, "so it was okay to dress down. But today you are going to the war. You need all the help you can get."

Winston had already learnt from Ohi that the debate among Big Four was the most important tradition of True Earth Summit. However, he was not aware of the real nature of debates.

Like an average idiot, he thought debates were about truth. He thought it was a civilized, structured way to compare the arguments for and against a thesis so that humanity as a whole could get one step closer to enlightenment.

As a cab driver, Maeve of course had it all figured out and knew debates were never about truth, let alone *the* truth. She thought that if debates were sentient organisms, they would give as much damn to objective truth as politicians gave to ideological principles, which was none.

"Listen," said Maeve and fixed Winston with a stern look, "if you think you know what you will be up against, then you are dead wrong."

"Boring Song, uptight Kutner and—" said Winston and counted with his hand, "holy Odinson. Hot damn, he made that ball guy walk again." He paused and thought for a moment if that miracle was legit. "Do you think if I buy him a lunch, he will cure my hemorrhoid?"

"Winston, we talked about this," said Maeve and swallowed a Figgy Duff. "Stop bringing up your anal inflammation when I am eating." She gulped down another Figgy to help the first one move along. It was an anatomical mystery that she could keep talking.

"And you were wrong about your opponents. Big Four can send anyone to represent themselves in the debate. It doesn't have to be a POTUWS candidate. It doesn't even have to be a Seeker for crying out loud," Maeve washed the pudding down with a jar of syrup. "I am not sure about All-Ways and TYDF, but the rumor is Odinson has hired Ross Maximoff to represent Treeism."

Both Chandler and Ohi looked up from their plates and did a three-way look exchange with Winston. They were so skilled in doing it that no side would suffer from any exchange loss due to volatility in the market.

"*The* Ross Maximoff?"

Chapter 40

In the middle of the east royal suite of Greendale Convention Centre, Abed Kutner seamlessly transitioned from *tittibhasana*, the firefly pose, to *taraksvasana*, the handstand scorpion pose. He carefully controlled his breath and moved his legs backward, upward and forward. They stopped when the toes gently rested on his head. His body was as still as the crystal chandeliers overhead/feet. To maintain balance in this naturally untenable position, Kutner had to completely clear his mind, which was a task he could *normally* perform with no effort whatsoever.

It was a mistake to invite her to the summit, Kutner mused involuntarily.

Before he knew it, the thought already disrupted his breathing. Sensing he was about to lose his balance, Kutner unfolded his body and gracefully landed on the mat. He rolled over and stared blankly into the suspended lamp.

He wished he could fall asleep right away, but couldn't. Not only because the great debate was about to start, but because of the troubling presentation from Dr. Stinson.

The world is NOT on the back of a turtle, or for that matter an infinite tower of turtles?! I never thought it was possible.

Having seen Stinson's shocking discovery, Kutner could barely sleep last night and didn't attend any of the events in the morning. He could no longer ask with a clear conscience for donation to stop turtle warming. He found it ridiculous to reveal the 1:6500000 actionable figure of Cosmic Turtle, even though it was predicted to be a bestseller in the EMEA market. He didn't even want to defend All-Ways teachings in the great debate.

While he was sulking, the phone next to his yoga mat rang.

"Your Excellency," Seth Nadir's voice sounded in Kutner's Bluetooth earpiece, "sorry to disturb you before the debate, but you must see this."

Before the pandit could respond, a notification prompted up on his phone. He unlocked the screen and saw a GIF file capturing the screens of several world-renowned astrophysicists' Twitter accounts, all with the hashtag #globe2go.

"That hashtag," Nadir added, "appeared to originate from Dr. Stinson's account."

Kutner could already guess what his right-hand man was about to say. His breathing was getting out of control again.

Didn't I ask her to keep it low profile last night?

"Since last evening," Nadir continued, "Dr. Stinson has been, for lack of a better word, harassing these scientists and their followers. She taunted them for their unrigorous proofs and dogma of inductive reasoning. One thing led to another, she announced she would live-stream her debunking the round Earth fallacy at 2 p.m. Eastern Day Time tomorrow, with that globe-to-go hashtag."

Kutner lay on his back again and wished the chandelier would just come down and crush his skull. To minimize the chance of leaking Dr. Stinson's discovery, he had assigned Nadir to a stakeout outside of her room, but now realized he underestimated this woman again.

Seeing the chandelier had no intention to depart from the ceiling, he finally spoke to Nadir on the phone.

"I don't have time for her right now. Just keep a close eye on her. I will deal with her stunt after the debate."

"Sure, your Excellency," said Nadir. "Before you go, there is one more thing I think you should know."

Kutner's hand froze before it could press on the Bluetooth device.

"I may not be the only one surveilling Dr. Stinson. I feel like someone is watching me from one of those door peepholes."

Chapter 41

Smith Robin found himself in Sapphire Dome again simply because he had nothing better to do. According to Round Ops' intel, Gina hadn't left the room since last night, apparently busy in cyber-bulling.

Checking his phone again for any messages from her, Smith seated himself in the mid-section of the ballroom, without noticing who were in the row.

"Hi, flat Earther?" asked the bespectacled young man next to Smith. His peers on the left, who looked old enough to buy guns but definitely couldn't buy booze, also curiously gazed at Smith.

If the same question was asked outside of the True Earth Summit, it would be considered a witty insult, but Smith understood it was just a friendly greeting.

"Not exactly," said hesitatingly Smith, conscious that he might offend those youngsters and get beat to death like those TYDF scholars in 1970s. "Just learning, with an open mind."

"So are we," the teen enthused. "I am Pete, by the way. These are Jon and Nydia. We are from Klynveld Early College High School."

For a moment Smith thought modern education had failed to brain wash the young minds because Sci-Edu was under-funded, but was relieved upon learning that they only feigned as flatees because they wanted to blend in.

Pete explained that they were from a high school debate team and professed to believe in flat Earth only as an intellectual exercise.

"The idea is," said Nydia pridefully, "If we can argue the Earth is flat, then we can win on any position."

It suddenly dawned on Smith that he might be talking to a future senator, elite lobbyist, advertising tycoon, law firm partner, political pundit, or at worst a theologian. The practical applications of sophistry were limitless.

"Don't listen to her," interjected Jon. "She only came to get a selfie with Ross Maximoff."

It did not surprise Smith at all. Maximoff was a household name even to debate noobs like himself.

Less than a year after obtaining his doctoral degree in philosophy, Maximoff made the national news (U.S. national news, for the minority who do not live in the greatest country on Earth) with his twenty-match winning streak of "Does God exist?" debates. He destroyed the oppositions by a landslide, be them biologists, astrophysicists, philosophy professors, communist propagandists, or atheist comedians. Most of them were atheist comedians, by the way.

For the sake of variety, he slightly modified his proposition in his following debates as "Does God exist and tolerate evil?", "Does God exist and have a butthole?", "Does God exist and ride on an invisible pink unicorn?", etc., and went on to win every single one of them. His undefeated records were taken by some apologists as a revelation from God and a controversy around the God's hole-ness ensued.

After his fame came the fortune. He was hired by multiple religious groups to debate on their behalf, taking the proposition side for "Does the Christian God exist?", "Does the Islamic God exist?", "Does Zeus exist?", "Does Odin exist?", and so on. Soon he went international and had to hire an agent to handle the pipeline.

Curiously, a year ago his pipeline went completely dry. No more requests were received by his agent and Maximoff had to foreclose most of his properties. While the exact reason remained unknown, some bitter millionaire comedians speculated that it might be because Maximoff had taken their offer to debate on "Does Tooth Fairy exist?", and won.

Despite his deteriorating financial status, Maximoff's name remained untainted. He was still considered the sharpest tongue alive, and *gambling-grandma55699.com.uk* quoted 1.1 odds for him winning the debate of Big Four.

Smith learnt of the odds from Jon, who further explained that the odds were quoted without knowing whether Maximoff got to make the opening statement first.

"What's the big deal about going first or not?" asked Smith.

"Look," said Jon, "although this debate is not exactly a traditional LD, whoever goes first still gets to do what one usually does in an AC."

With a thoughtful expression, Smith nodded along without betraying his ignorance of the terminology. It was one of the survival skills he had picked up from MacCheddar & Co. and got him through countless otherwise embarrassing or career-ending situations. What did he do when a client said their PWM got a LOPR problem due to the bespoke swaption in omnibus? He just nodded along, agreed it was a common problem among whoever had similar problems, and said he would come back with a price proposal. What did he do when another client complained their virtualization backbone was brought down by a SYN-ACK flood because his fellow consultant recalibrated their HIPS settings before a production DR? He just nodded along, remarked on how devastating the incident was, and cross-sold an incident response training to them.

While nodding along, Smith also waited for Pete or Nydia to jump in and expand the abbreviations. To encourage them, he slowed down his nodding, increased the frequency of blinking, and slightly tilted his head. He didn't fail to convince the three high-schoolers that he was following the conversation.

"So if Maximoff goes first," Jon continued, "he can do his routine."

"Which is?" asked Smith, boldly assuming it was not a stupid question.

"First, pepper his opponents with so many arguments that they cannot logistically address in their speaking time. Second, frame the winning criteria by saying that his opponents only win if they can refute all his arguments *and* present arguments that positively support their positions. Third, after all opponents finish their prepared speeches but before they can do rebuttal, call drops. Fourth, profit. That's his flow."

Smith sensed that maybe he still looked too comfortable for the teens to realize he only understood half of what was said, so he asked what he thought was a stupid question.

"What do you mean by calling drops?"

"As in using the chance to extend the arguments."

"Alright."

No, it wasn't alright, and Smith still had no idea what was going on.

Relieved that the conversation was finally over, he looked around the ballroom and noticed it was already fully seated, with the Delist host walking onto the stage. Today he was in a metallic leather jacket that was more yellow than golden, but no less distracting than yesterday.

To Smith's surprise, Adel did not make any racist joke and went straight to introduce the three impartial judges who were invited from an isolated Amazonian tribe. Seated in the front row, they were all wearing translation headsets and N95 face masks.

According to a journalist covering the summit, none of the judges contracted any modern diseases or consumerism and were safely sent back to their habitat after the debate. The journalist would also report that the three previously uncontacted people had agreed to leave the jungle because they had been promised twenty pounds of salt, which they successfully obtained and consumed within a week. They all died mysteriously after a violent seizure and were posthumously sainted by the locals as the Three Wise Men of Prosperity. After their death, an indigenist belief system called North Cult arose, where the tribe would face the direction where the Three Wise Men returned from, dance like they had a seizure, and pray three times a day. Their tribe also became the first civilization to develop a word for "acute salt poisoning," which literally meant "ascension" in local dialect, before it had a word for "sea."

"The objective of the debate," Adel said, "was to convince our judges here that the Earth is either a cube, a tree, a flat disk, or a tower of turtles. For those of you who are old enough to have attended the previous debates in the last century, you may recall that the question 'What is the true shape of our world?' remains unsettled because we made the mistake of inviting biased globeheads to be the judges. And I am both proud and humble to announce that we have ingeniously resolved this problem thanks to our sponsor Macrosalt International Pte Ltd."

Big hands followed.

"The format of the debate," the host continued, "will be the same as usual, which means it will be divided into three rounds. In the first round, each Big Four representative will present the arguments in favor of their own schools of thoughts. Their speaking order will be determined by a draw. Afterwards, there will be a cross-examination where the debaters can freely question, answer, and preferably insult each other."

Another round of applause ensued. Seekers were quite honest about their expectations, compared to F1 fans who watched the race for crashes, stand-up fans who bought tickets expecting the comedian to get attacked, or generally anyone who bothered to watch an election debate.

"Finally," added Adel, "each participant will present their closing statements and our judges will decide on which side, or I should say, which shape of the world they stand. Without further ado, our judges will draw from the box in front of them the first debater to speak."

The air inside Sapphire Dome froze instantly. Not because they wanted to beat the bookies at *gambling-grandma55699.com.uk* for the best odds. Not because they understood the technical advantage Maximoff would gain from going first. It was because they never saw anyone as amused of a 12" x 10" x 4" box as the Amazon people. They were uncontrollably chuckling, which in their culture was the expression of the worst fear.

Having explained to the indigenous people that the box was not a Gilbert's Naval[1], and failed, the host drew a card from the box and showed it to the audience who could not possibly see it from the distance.

"The first debater will be," announced Adel from the top of his lung, "the representative of Treeism. The magician of words. The warlock of logic. The rapist of minds. *Ross Maximoff!!!*"

Chapter 42

Ross Maximoff was a stand-up guy, which was the first impression he unfailingly gave. His perfectly symmetrical face, high cheek bone, prominent chin, blue eyes and undying smile all contributed towards blurring the line between attractiveness and goodness.

Despite his reputation as a tongue for hire, his tall stature and neat cool-youth-pastor attire were more than enough to convince the audience that he came to inquire into the true shape of Earth in good faith.

Besides the three teenagers next to Smith, the ballroom was not short of Maximoff's fans. Their clapping, screaming, wowing, raving and whistling took a good minute to die down before Maximoff could begin his five-minute speech.

"Thank you everyone, I am very excited to be here," said

---

[1] Depending on which tribesman you ask, Gilbert's Naval can mean either the gate to hell, or the womb of a man-sized scorpion that kills, eats and mates with anyone who approaches it, exclusively in that order. Etymologists are still killing themselves to understand why it is called Gilbert's Naval.

Maximoff and laid his notes over the lectern, "to address the ultimate question, 'What is the true shape of Earth?'"

Ben Song on the second row wondered why Americans always mentioned how excited they were when beginning a speech, announcing a new product, or telling to-be-fired employees that their companies would be more focused on core values.

"This question," Maximoff continued, "is philosophically important, for reasons that are too obvious to be repeated here."

Everyone in Sapphire Dome nodded along.

"I am convinced there are better arguments for Treeism than for the competing schools of thoughts, including but certainly not limited to, heliocentrism. There are two reasons for my convictions. First, there are good arguments that Treeism is true. Second, there are no good arguments that other competing ideas are true."

How about the "The Earth is flat," duh, thought Winston in the second row. Heeding Maeve's advice to take notes, he had asked Ohi behind him to summarize Maximoff's arguments.

"I will elaborate on my second point," added Maximoff, "during the cross-examination, but let me briefly say this: There is no conclusive evidence that our world is *not* a tree. Millions upon millions of people have tried to prove it, but failed."

Of course, thought Odinson, *until Gina Stinson.*

Compared to Pandit Kutner and Chairman Song, Pope Odinson was the least troubled by Dr. Stinson's discovery. He never really cared much about the shape of Earth to begin with.

"For now," Maximoff said, "I will focus on arguing why Treeism is true. My first argument is the fractal argument. The term 'fractal' was coined by the mathematician Benoit Mandelbrot, describing self-similarity in nature."

Bloody hell, he didn't make this up, thought Chandler, assigned by Winston to do fact-check. Having googled Benoit Mandelbrot, he shook his head to Ohi next to him.

"The science historian," said Maximoff, picking up speed, "James Gleick said in his *Nature's Chaos* that a river's basic shape is not a line, but a tree. I couldn't agree more."

"You see what he is doing?" whispered Pete smugly to Smith. "This is Maximoff's signature name-drop special. I calculated that

99% of his quotes are genuine."

"Only 99%?" hissed Smith.

"That's his genius," admired the fan boy. "The 1% is his get-out-of-jail-free card for making a point when he absolutely has no point to make. Plus, since 99% of the time his quotes are genuinely research-based, more often than not his opponents will just waste valuable time on fact-checking rather than on preparing arguments."

"Let's imagine," the magician of words continued his opening arguments at a deceptively high speed, "you are a caterpillar crawling from one leaf to another for food. The leaves will be your whole world, but they are just extension of one branch. If you are a snail that lives on tree branches, your world is made up of branches, which are nothing more than an extension of the trunk. And if you are a koala bear always clinging to the trunk, you may never realize how big the tree is."

Smith instinctively nodded along, even though he didn't know whether he with still with Maximoff.

"As for us, humans," said Maximoff without losing a beat, "whose ancestors lived among the trees, we may think the world is just a plate planted with trees. But when you think about the self-similar pattern in the nature, isn't it obvious that we are simply living in a bigger organism? The World Tree?"

A million questions galloped over Winston's mind. He found Maximoff's argument so stupid that he didn't even bother to come up with a counter-argument.

What Winston didn't realize was that stupidity of an argument was never a weakness in an argument. Since Maximoff came fully scripted and prepared, it took him only forty seconds to make his first point. As stupid as that argument was, it would take an unprepared debater easily more than a minute to address it. The opposition might quip on how bad Maximoff's analogy was, detour to address his misunderstanding of fractal geometry, point out the lack of logical necessity for our planet to be a fractal, *but* still fail to convince the judges that his argument was invalid.

That was why Maximoff was nicknamed "Hyperinflation" by his contemporaries. He destroyed the word economy of his adversary.

"My second argument for Treeism," said Ross "Hyperinflation"

Maximoff, "is the moral argument. The philosopher Michael Ruse has argued that morality is an illusion put in place by genes to make humans social cooperators. And many scientists have agreed with that position. They basically are saying that morality is subjective. However, their explanation for morality cannot explain why we, human beings, feel that elderly abuse is wrong, even though it is evolutionarily advantageous to dispose of homo-specifics who consume resources but no longer reproduce. In other words, there must be an objective source of moral values. Some of you call it God, I call it World Tree."

"Genius, it is genius," whispered Pete. "He re-purposed the moral argument he used to prove the existence of Odin, Yahweh and Zeus."

"And it only took him nineteen seconds," Jon extolled. "It's a new record."

Smith looked at the fan boys and wondered why debates were not as popular as reality shows and zombie dramas.

"My third argument," said Maximoff, flipping his notes to another page, "is the ontological argument."

"Here it comes," said Pete to Smith with a disturbing grin. "This is gonna mess your mind up sooooo bad."

Smith was disturbed.

"World Tree," said Maximoff, "is defined as the tree than which no greater tree can be conceived. It is perfect in every possible way. Such a perfect tree can and does exist in your mind, no matter how little sunlight shines on it. Now, if the greatest possible tree finds its root in your mind, it must also be rooted in reality. Why? If it *only* exists in your mind, then a greater tree must be possible, that is, one that exists both in the mind and reality. Therefore, the greatest possible tree must exist in reality."

Smith's disturbed mind was blown, but at least he thought it was over.

For some unknown reasons, number three always has a special place in human psychology. The rule of thirds in photography. The rule of three in writing. The rule of whatever has the number three in it that can make this paragraph punchier.

Thinking of number three, Smith took a glance at the three judges at front row. The distance and their masks made it impossible to make out their reactions. It certainly didn't help that they were neither nodding nor shaking their heads. They all vertically rotated their heads clockwise as if they were drawing an invisible circle with their chins.

"Argument number four," Maximoff spoke in defiance of the rule of three, "the historical consent on World Tree's existence. Unlike Ahura Mazda in the *Avesta*, Yahweh in the *Bible*, or *Kotoamatsukami* in the *Kojiki*, World Tree is featured across multiple cultures."

Ohi and Chandler looked at each other for help to spell "Ahura."

"Also Known as Yggdrasil in the old Norse textbook *Prose Edda*, World Tree is prominently featured in Lithuanian folk painting, described in the Russian verse *Dove Book*, sung in the Estonian runic songs, recorded in the Gnostic text *On the Origin of the World*, depicted in the pre-Columbian culture of America. Just to name a few. Don't even get me started on the folklores in Africa and North Asia, tree symbols in Mongolic and Indian religions, or the sacred trees in Roman and Greek mythologies."

Ohi and Chandler decided to respect the rule of three and ignored argument number four altogether.

"Is it a coincidence that so many cultures, both geographically and temporally separated, all share a narrative of World Tree? No one in their right mind would think so. There is only one plausible explanation for the prominence of World Tree across cultures and history – World Tree is real."

"Was it a double tap?" asked Nydia reverently.

"No, it was a triple," praised Jon.

Smith simply gave up on understanding their fanspeak and wished they would not elaborate.

"What Jon was saying is," Pete elaborated, "Maximoff has packed three punches in one argument. The core of his argument is that the prominence of World Tree seems too good to be a coincidence, so it *isn't* a coincidence. He then added an ad hominem attack, calling anyone who disagrees not in their right mind. Finally, he took a leap to the conclusion that there is only one plausible explanation, effectively asking those without a better explanation to shut up and stop questioning him."

That was considered ad hominem? Smith moaned.

Smith's failure to detect *argumentum ad hominem*, or argument to the person, was not surprising, as it was too commonplace in the 21st century. Across the political spectrum, people who disagreed with each other on gun control, abortion, gender pronoun, etc. labelled each other gun nuts and gun bigots, evangelical bigots and baby murders, unsensitive bigots and entitled millennials, etc. On the bright side, it reduced the pressure on Twitter to raise its word limit. On a much brighter side, it stigmatized the most outspoken comedians and created opportunities for the unfunny ones. On a much, much brighter side, it saved people the trouble of having time-consuming, thoughtful discussion of issues that they truly cared about.

"Finally," said Maximoff, finally, "number five, the immediate experience of World Tree. I must say, this is not a rational proof for the existence of World Tree, but a way for us to find it simply through personal experience."

"This is so beautiful," Pete said with tear in his eyes. "You see what he did there?"

Raping my mind? Smith frowned.

"A moment ago," sobbed Pete fannishly, "he was spewing technical terms, mined quotes and cherry-picked facts that no layman can properly assess. Now, he shows his humility by conceding one of his arguments is not based on reason," Pete shut his eyes so hard that Smith thought he had an orgasm. "Who would think a humble man like him is intellectually dishonest?"

I see, the bulb in Smith's head lighted up, *so he switches position when assaulting my mind, probably for variety's sake, incidentally convincing me he is a good lover.*

"Many philosophers, including Aristotle, David Hume, John Locke, and Bertrand Russel, accepted what is generally called foundationalism."

I thought David Hume and John Locke are TV characters, thought Winston.

"This philosophical theory argues there are two types of beliefs. Type one, beliefs derived from justified beliefs, which in turn require justifications by other beliefs, and so on and so forth. Type two, *properly basic beliefs* that do not require justification by other beliefs. For instance, anthropologists believe the past exists even though they cannot prove that the universe was *not* created a minute ago along with all the ruins, artifacts and witnesses' memories. Psychologist believe people have conscious experience, even though there is no way to tell if a person on fire is screaming in pain or just an unfeeling zombie acting like it scored a goal. Most scientists believe induction is a valid process of reasoning, even though the only reason to believe it will work is that it has worked. And you believe the chairs supporting your weight will continue to do so, even though you cannot prove the laws of physics are permanent."

What are you trying to say? groaned Winston. *You lost me at "anthropologists."*

"What I am trying to say is," said Maximoff, "while there are beliefs that cannot be scientifically proved, they are not groundless. They are *rooted* on personal experience."

"Oh, puns," Ohi laughed. "What, I love puns."

Winston had turned to fix him with a murderous look.

Seriously?

Seriously, in a debate setting people love puns, punch lines and retweet-able zingers more than substance. They also love to disrupt the proceedings with cheers and sneers, and get their emotions played by those on stage. Fortunately, since the Seekers were much more civilized than the average goers of presidential primary debate, no such disruption happened.

"If you know World Tree," continued Maximoff on stage, "your belief in it is a properly basic belief. If you are willing to open your mind, you will hear the inner voice of World Tree. If you free yourself from the external arguments and let World Tree enter your soul, World Tree will become a self-evident being to you."

The magician of words stole a peek at his wrist and calculated he still had twenty seconds to frame the winning criteria.

"To sum up, there are five good arguments in support of Treeism. If other debaters think otherwise, they must first refute those five arguments *and* present arguments for their own geophysical ideas. Otherwise, the only logical conclusion we can arrive at is that the

Earth is a tree. Thank you."

Amidst a storm of applause, Maximoff returned the stage to Adel, who noticed the judges had stopped rotating their heads. Without burdening them with the fear of Gilbert's Naval, the host volunteered to draw another name from the box.

For reasons even Winston could not fully grasp, he expected "Winston Kanshū (DES)" would be drawn. Subconsciously he thought it would make for a better narrative of the Big Four debate.

And of course, he was wrong.

The card on Adel's hand read "Kanshū Winston (DES)," respecting the Japanese government's decree to write surname first.

Chapter 43

Winston had got to the lectern without bringing a piece of paper, but he wasn't unprepared. To begin with, he no longer looked like a tourist to Hawaii; today he looked like a tourist to Hawaii who has to put on a dark blue blazer because his mom has told him to. Besides, he had prepared the most powerful tool to make his points. A PowerPoint presentation. Due to an oversight of the United Ways, visual aids were not disallowed in the Big Four debate.

To support his assertion that the Earth was flat, Winston began by showing side by side the shadows of statues he captured a month ago in Russia. In case his explanation for the shadows' implications was not compelling enough, he then showed a portrait of Eratosthenes on the wall screen. After a click on his laser pointer, a cartoon machine gun pinwheeled into the screen and graphically blew up the Greek polymath's head.

Waiting for the ten-second animation to end, Winston peeked at the Amazonian judges and found them vertically spinning their heads again, but counterclockwise.

Maybe they think I am..., Winston squinted, *special?*

He then went on to demonstrate the incorrect scale of round Earth map by showing a small table of numbers. More precisely, it was an underexposed picture of a napkin scribbled with boxes of numbers. The low production value would have made a self-respecting director blush, but Winston believed it helped him come across as raw and authentic. He wasn't entirely wrong.

He explained that the numbers on the left boxes referred to the theoretical flight times for flying between Singapore and Japan at 470 mph, while those on the right were the actual times he personally recorded using a correctly calibrated airspeed indicator.

The judges' head spinning accelerated and Winston could almost feel the cool air coming from their direction.

Seeing that he still had almost a minute to spare, Winston thought it wouldn't hurt to show the final slide that Maeve had prepared for him. It was the official emblem of the United Nations.

"My third argument for the Earth being a flat disk," said Winston, unconsciously imitating Maximoff, "is the UN logo. Look at the world map in this picture. At its center is not Brazil, or Kenya, or any country supposedly on the equator. It is the Arctic. Bizarre, right? Not only that, if you look more closely, you will see that this logo is missing a significant landmass."

Winston took a pause to build the suspense.

He also noticed the judges had started spinning their heads clockwise again.

Damn you Maeve, Winston thought to himself, *I told you this argument is too strong for the mortal.*

"The logo," Winston overcame his anxiety and continued, "does not have Antarctica. You may ask, 'Where is it?'" Winston did an impression of confused Travolta.

Luckily for him, the reference to *Pulp Fiction* didn't seem to bother the judges, who never saw any '90s movies, or hardly any movies at all. They had their first taste of cinematography only a few hours ago during their flight, and were still convinced that the pale men cruelly imprisoned dwarfs in little boxes for entertainment.

Actually, most of those sitting in Sapphire Dome should feel lucky that the only movies available on that flight were *The Purge* series, warming the judges up to the idea that pale people were extremely violent. If not for this mildly incorrect stereotype, the three glorious fighters from eastern Amazon rainforest would have indulged in their xenophobia and joyfully wiped out half of the Seeker population.

"Well," said Winston, oblivious to how lucky he was, "*They* didn't put Antarctica in the logo because they don't want you to know it's actually an ice wall surrounding the disk Earth. If you add the ice wall back to this picture, the UN logo will be a perfect replica of the disk Earth model. Do you think it's just a coincidence? If not – and you are right in thinking it isn't – then the only logical explanation is that the Earth is a flat disk."

Winston was going to sum up his arguments but his microphone had already been disabled because his time was up.

Whatever, Winston thought, *it was a great show.*

"It was a complete disaster," said Pete.

"Really?" said Smith. "Except for the UN part, I thought it was pretty well researched and the visuals' quality is on par with the videos normally consumed by flat Earthers."

"Oooh, mister," Jon said in a tone very inviting to an uppercut, "debate is not about numbers. It is not even about facts. It is all about rhetoric."

"And he shouldn't have sticked with his prepared presentation," said Nydia, "although I am not sure how prepared he was."

"What she meant is," added Pete, "Kanshū Winston should have modified his flow to quote Maximoff out of context; twist, strawman and hyperbolize his arguments; and plant some tangentially related criticism that would either undermine Maximoff's character or take him valuable time to respond."

Smith frowned so hard that Pete thought his forehead was going to collapse into a black hole.

"Basically," Pete added, "talk like a commentator on night-time talk show."

While Smith was lectured by the high schoolers, Adel had already drawn the name of the third debater. Smith's mind drifted back to his skull just in time to catch the name, but swung itself out a moment later out of confusion.

What the flat? Smith thought. *This is the representative of All-Ways?!*

Chapter 44

Before he became the henchman of Pandit Kutner, Seth Nadir was a financial engineer at Dalal Street.

His transformation journey, from a high paid quantitative analyst who brought creative solutions to problems that didn't need to be solved, to an All-Ways volunteer that couldn't look away from the spiritual deficiencies in mankind, was tear jerking to say the least. In a nutshell, it involved the collapse of Enron, an incorrect proof of Fermat's Last Theorem, a can of expired peanut butter, and an expensive lawsuit to trademark *lusty gallant*, a light reddish-pink color similar to orange in hue.

"Why is it important?" one might ask.

The backstory of Seth Nadir would be indispensable for understanding Abed Kutner's rationale to select Nadir as the All-Ways representative in Big Four debate. No less importantly, it would help humor researchers understand tons of inside jokes among All-Ways adherents, and bring some perspective to mathematicians who tried to apply imaginary numbers in financial reporting.

However, since Seth Nadir was never selected to represent All-Ways and both humor researchers and mathematicians had better things to do, no one ever formally documented the early years of Seth Nadir.

The only mention of Nadir in the official chronicle of Seekers, which would be published in the same month as Smith Robin's third memoir, *Oops, I Forgot to Tell You These*, would be that he had "brokered a freakishly good deal for All-Ways in hiring its representative in the Big Four debate."

Watching the All-Ways representative climb up the stairs to the stage, Winston could not believe his eyes. He turned to ask Maeve to give him a slap, but realized there was no way for her to be around. His brethren, his mentor and his friend was not on his side.

Not at the moment.

She was on her shift at booth E616 doing a fire-sale of disk Earth themed furniture.

So he did the next best thing that came to his mind. He fiercely bit his lips and immediately regretted it.

If I am not dreaming, Winston concluded, *then he must be and I am now in his dream.*

The "he" that Winston referred to wasn't dreaming, though. He couldn't afford to. He knew it would take everything he got to dance with a formidable opponent like Ross Maximoff.

Indeed, if anyone could stand a chance against Ross Maximoff, it must be him, now standing behind the lectern and adjusting his name tag.

It read, "Ross Maximoff (All-Ways)."

Sensing the confusion of the audience, Adel got in front of the lectern and pulled out the Big Four debate rulebook. He claimed it was the original copy and carbon dating subsequently showed he was truthful, even though no Seekers ever believed in carbon dating.

Partly for formality and mostly for vanity, the rulebook was written in French, double-sided, on a wrinkled brown napkin that was once swan white. It was, the host explained, primarily written to stipulate the dress code, language guide, branding color, theme music and length of coffee breaks, and therefore didn't elaborate on the eligibility of Big Four debaters. He did, however, mention that the rulebook could be amended or expanded anytime without prior notification by the designated board members of the United Ways. He further pointed out that the list of authorized board members was written on the napkin margin. All the names were still very, very legible and their bearers very, very dead.

After the host's patient explanation and a coffee break of permissible length, the audience had come to terms with the rules, or the absence thereof, and Maximoff could begin his opening arguments for All-Ways, which were no less convincing than those for Treeism.

Maximoff began with the historical consent of Cosmic Turtle, citing Hindu literature, Chinese mythology and folklore in North America. He then strengthened his position using the immediate experience of world-bearing turtle.

When the audience began to doubt if Maximoff was simply recycling his talking points, he subtly showed that any similarities between his arguments were coincidental and no actual turtles were harmed in the production of his speech.

For the first time in the debate, he used a modified version of the cosmological argument, asserting that a wonderfully complex universe must be created by an even more wonderfully complex designer. Maximoff had slightly tweaked this classical argument and contended that our wonderfully complex planet must be supported by a wonderfully complex turtle. He even took it one step further and argued that such a god-like world-bearing turtle must be supported by another god-like turtle. Following this logic, he successfully demonstrated that the tower of turtles must be infinite. It not only destroyed the Ratlonallst Movement once and for all, but also made scholars of the Kalm cosmological arguments reevaluate their position on whether the universe was caused by an uncaused creator. Fortunately, after a pack of cigarettes, those scholars were relaxed to report that their postulated creator didn't need to be created by another creator, for good reasons. The most promising one was that the uncaused creator could travel back in time to create itself.

Once Maximoff established the existence of Turtle Tower, he used the ontological and objective morality arguments to show that each of the Cosmic Turtle must be perfect, exist in both mind and reality, and provide the source of moral values.

Taking in all those mind-blowing arguments was intellectually taxing; doing so while spinning the heads clockwise even more so. Just when the three Amazonians thought it was over, Maximoff had already changed his name tag and begun to make his case for TYDF.

As usual, Maximoff's arguments were research-based, carefully structured, packed with quotes, supported by authority, and eloquently delivered, especially the one he put forth to replace the fractal and cosmological arguments.

Without a doubt, it was the greatest debate of all time. It would forever be remembered as Ross Maximoff v. Kanshū Winston v. Ross Maximoff v. Ross Maximoff.

Chapter 45

"You didn't find anything?" hissed Winston to Chandler sitting behind him.

"Eh..." Chandler thought for a moment if it was worth mentioning the challenge he had in spelling those foreign names. Personally, he hated people who boasted of their hardship to play martyr. Since he liked to think of himself as someone with coherent values, he decided to keep his problems to himself.

"No, no alternative fact could be found in his speeches."

Before the debate, Winston thought it would clear his doubt about the shape of Earth, or at least jog his memory of what Hot Girl had told him. Holding the transcript scribbled by Ohi, however, he began to think perhaps he wasn't open-minded enough. After all, nothing would stop a disk Earth from being compatible with Treeism or All-Ways teachings. The only thing that bugged him was how to reconcile disk Earth with the TYDF doctrine.

"Mr. Kanshū, or Mr. Winston," said gently the host, who appeared to be sniffing Winston's aftershave. It was less weird than it sounded, because he didn't use any.

"Oh, Lenny," said Winston, gathering himself from thoughts. He would swear he had a clear vision of a squared disk in his mind, but lost it forever because of Lenny.

"Just Winston is OK."

"Likewise," said Yusuf Adel, "just Yusuf is fine."

"What now, Just-Yusuf?"

"May you go up to the stage and join Maximoff for the cross-examination?"

Winston dropped his head and took another look at the yellow papers with Ohi's scribbling. Calling them writings would be more appropriate if, and only if, those papers survived an extinction level event that happened to wipe out all civilizations, and then were discovered by an extraterrestrial being.

"Do you insist?" asked Winston, hoping Just-Yusuf wouldn't.

"I am afraid I do," said Adel, wondering if it was a tactic to buy time.

"What if I insist harder?"

"Then I must either insist harder or declare DES forfeits."

"OK, if you insist."

In the interest of time, another lectern had been put onto the stage. It was identical to the one in front of Maximoff, except that it had two less name plates.

"During the cross-examination," spoke the host to his microphone, "each debater will have two minutes to ask as many questions as possible. In Maximoff's case, it would be eight."

"What?" Winston suspected if he just asked a stupid question.

"Oh sorry," said Adel with a blush, "I should have elaborated. It's two to the power of three."

"... huh?"

"Two times two times two," Adel said matter-of-factly.

"Ooo, I see." Winston was convinced now he had asked a stupid question.

"Without further ado," said Adel with no ado at all, "you maaaaaay, start now."

"Mr. Kanshū," said Maximoff, slightly pushing his Treeism name plate forward, "I didn't hear any arguments from you against Treeism. Am I correct in thinking you have none?"

"I already made my case for disk Earth, which is the best evidence why the Earth is not a tree."

"I see, so Mr. Kanshū is saying he doesn't have positive evidence that the Earth is not a tree," Maximoff rapidly drew his Treeism plate backward and pushed the All-Ways one, before Winston got to fire back. "Regarding your first argument for a flat disk Earth, where did you get those pictures?"

"I took them, actually my cameraman took them when I was shooting a commercial in Russia."

"The cameraman worked for *you*, a representative from DES?"

"Yes, he worked for me, but I wasn't—"

"Thank you, you already answered my question." Maximoff pushed the TYDF plate forward and continued, "and for your second argument, what is the evidence for your flight times, besides the napkin with Greendale Convention Centre's logo?"

"I told you already, the airport police took away the black box and must have twitched my plane's speedometer when I was in custody."

"I take it as a no."

"I do, my friends over there saw the whole thing."

The three judges turned their heads and saw two pale men in the direction pointed by Winston. They returned to face the stage with the air of an Amazonian who just saw two cane toads copulate, unsightly and inedible.

"So your only witnesses are your friends?" Maximoff kept pressing.

"Wrong, the airport police and whoever touched my plane—"

"Both conveniently not in presence."

Winston thought it was indeed quite convenient, as he had a thing with the police.

"And for your third argument," said Maximoff on Treeism's behalf, "why would the United Nations put a disk Earth on its flag when its biggest benefactors are backing the Global Lie?"

"Because they are stupid."

"Then why didn't they include the ice wall on the flag?"

"Because they are stupid."

"And why didn't *They* make the UN replace the emblem after your peers call it out as disk Earth evidence?"

"Because *They* are stupid!"

Maximoff didn't seem to mind the curt responses, while a lot of emotions ran over Winston's face, most of them starting with the letter *R*.

Resolution. Remorse. Self-reproach. Relish. Ridicule. Rage.

This was because Winston decided it was time to fight back like Rocky, but remembered he lost in the first movie and regretted the cultural reference. He felt like he was jinxing himself, before coming to realize he was just thinking to himself, which he found quite funny. A moment later, though, he got angry at himself for wasting all the mental energy on introspection.

"Mr. Maximoff," said Winston, no longer mindfully, "do you find it weird that you are arguing for three competing ideas for the shape of Earth?"

"Facts don't respect feelings," said Maximoff righteously, "so my feelings are irrelevant."

"If the Earth is a tree, then why can't I see its trunk?"

"Just because you can't see it doesn't mean it is not there. Absence of evidence is not evidence of absence."

Maximoff's reply recalled the bitter memory of quite a few Seekers. They all had asked globeheads why they couldn't see gravity if gravity were real, and got a similar reply preceded by pseudo-science and alternative facts. However, Seekers were all open-minded people so they didn't let their disaffection prevent them from accepting Maximoff's explanation.

Meanwhile, Winston wished his aloha shirt would come to life and squeezed some intelligent questions out of his lung. He had, of course, prepared more than two questions, but they all kind of required Maximoff to provide positive evidence that the Earth had roots, a shell, or corners.

As his brain raced to find the next question, his jaw stayed relaxed and his vocal cord hummed a single syllable sound that kept the transcriber wondering if it was an "eh" or "uh." It is amazing how the dumbness of one's face is inversely proportional to the amount of thinking going between the ears, thought Winston's Id. The ego stumbled to find spare memory to jog down this insight and got a ballpark budget for making a movie about it, while the super-ego, in the shape of Maeve Walsh, asked how any of these were helping. Thankfully, the super-duper-ego shoved them all back to the asylum of unfalsifiable constructs and came to Winston's rescue.

"Besides your fancy arguments and personal experience," said Winston, "do you have any direct proof that the Earth is a tree, a turtle or a cube?"

Maximoff didn't immediately fire back. He didn't touch any of his name plates either. He reached for his glass of water and took a sip.

I have him by the balls, Winston thought to himself.

"I believe," said Maximoff, "I already provided some very good arguments in support of Treeism, All-Ways and TYDF doctrines."

"But they don't prove the shape of Earth one way or the other," said Winston, clenching his fists.

"By 'proof,' you mean like a mathematical proof?"

"Yup."

"Like, no positive integers x, y and z can make x to the power of n plus y to the power of n equal to z to the power of n for any integer value of n greater than two? That kind of proof?”

"Precisely what I meant. I couldn't have put it better myself."

"Mr. Kanshū," said Maximoff with the politeness of a car salesman explaining the no refund policy to a customer who has bought his car seven years and one hundred thousand miles ago, "it is not possible."

I have him, Winston repeated to himself. He felt like something just exploded in his palms.

"Not possible," added Maximoff, "because a proof as rigorous as a mathematical proof is only feasible in mathematics." He then took out the brochure of True Earth Summit and flipped to page forty-six. "In fact, it is not even necessary for me to produce proof, because paragraph d of subsection three of section twenty-one of the by-laws of the United Ways clearly states that registered members of the United Ways and their affiliates disclaim the responsibility to bear the burden of proof."

Nope, I don't have him, Winston thought.

"But can you—"

"Winston," said Adel, "your two minutes is up. No more question is allowed."

"What—"

"Please stop."

"How—"

"I said stop."

The influence of stress hormone on dorsolateral prefrontal right cortex and the disturbance of space-time continuum due to a recent solar flare had absolutely nothing to do with Winston's misperception of time. He had simply spent too much time on meaninglessly saying "eh."

With no more question time left and Maximoff's carefully framing all his questions as binary traps, Winston had no more way to fight back or dodge. In the remaining time of cross-examination, he felt like the Irish potato from *Sausage Party*, Unit-02 from *The End of Evangelion*, and Superman's adopted father from *Man of Steel*. Since all those references flew over the super-duper-ego's figurative head, the hyper-super-duper-ego came in, tucked it up in the bed, and explained that all those side characters went on to live happily on a farm upstate.

Chapter 46

It is a perplexing fact that the majority of children aspire to become police officers, doctors, lawyers, inventors, writers, directors, actors, singers, dancers, and, increasingly, opinion influencers. So few ever dream of becoming an insurance adjuster, pesticide trader, internal auditor, concrete surveyor, or toad researcher. Even rarer are those who resolve to become an interpreter. Maria Santiago was one of those.

Specifically, she dreamed of becoming an interpreter working at the United Nations back when she was four, an age at which she was not even supposed to know what the United Nations was. That particular career choice had nothing to do with hunger for social contact, fascination with languages, or ambition to subtly influence international relations.

She wanted to do it simply because she wanted to do it, although she made up several reasons as she grew up.

After getting her bachelor degree in translation, Maria started working her way up as a legal interpreter. Court of first instance. Juvenile court. Criminal court. Things were going quite well and by her own estimation her dream would come true in fifteen to twenty years. However, it all went south when one day a court clerk asked if she was interested in an opening of interpreter at supreme court.

She gave a lousy interview to a lousier interviewer and got the job in two weeks, only to be fired a week later when it was revealed that she only spoke three and a half of the eight languages she put on the resume, one of which was sign language. For a long time, she firmly believed she would have nailed that plea of guilty if the deaf defendant's hysterical sobbing did not inconveniently betray the inaccuracy of her interpretation.

That incident meant that she would never get a call back from UN recruitment without some serious shenanigans, so she did the next best thing she could do. She worked for the United Ways.

Putting aside the awkwardness at family gatherings and class reunion, Maria really loved the perks from working at the United Ways. Valuable exposure to international tax knowledge. Free lectures on buoyance and density. Access to White Jesus for selfies. Today she added one more to her list of reasons to work at UW – a free ticket to watch Ross Maximoff take apart Winston Kanshū piece by piece.

Despite not being a big fan of debating, she still enjoyed watching the sharpest tongue alive cut through the realist director's arguments piece by piece. When she translated Maximoff's closing speech for Treeism, she didn't detect the selective quoting, buried insults and definition twisting, but she heard loud and clear how his opponent had failed to address his arguments.

She wasn't quite sure how she felt about the Earth being a tree before, but now she was inclined to think it was.

Sitting in the sound-proof booth of Sapphire Dome, Maria wondered if the three judges listening to her translation had come to the same conclusion.

They all spin their heads counterclockwise as soon as Kanshū starts speaking, Maria thought. *It can't be a good sign for him.*

"I only want to say two things before I return the stage to Mr. Maximoff for his closing speeches," said Winston. On a second thought, he thought he should have said three things, because people liked three things rather than two things, but it was too late to walk back on it.

"First, in response to Mr. Maximoff's attempt to undermine the evidence I presented, I just want to say they are all real. The photos are authentic. The flight times are accurate. And the UN logo is really the UN logo.

"If you have ever watched my movies, you would know I always keep it real. The telepaths in my movies are real psychics. The tornado is real tornado. The dead bodies are real dead bodies."

It was really tricky to translate "tornado" for the Amazonians living outside of Tornado Alley, so Maria took the liberty to call it "the divine act that sends everything up for ungeared skydiving."

The judges showed no sign of confusion at all.

"The second thing I want to say is," Winston thought for a moment and continued, "I have no arguments against the Earth

*

being a cube, a tree or the back of a turtle."

He forfeited, Maria thought as she carefully structured the sentence to keep the cube, tree and turtle gender-neutral.

"Mr. Maximoff surely knows his ways around words, and I have no wish to challenge his rhetoric. But don't get me wrong, it doesn't give me a shred of doubt about the flatness of our world. I still believe disk Earth is as valid as All-Ways, Treeism and TYDF.

"As I said yesterday during the keynote speech, all your beliefs are beautiful. As far as I am concerned, they are all facts. I have no intention to contest any of them, and I humbly ask you to do the same. Let's put down our doctrinal differences and work together to expose the Global Lie.

"I am Winston Kanshū, and I approve your diverse geocentric views."

Except for the challenge in translating "facts," which was getting increasingly difficult nowadays, Maria effortlessly interpreted the DES debater's tactical concession. While doing so, she couldn't help but think it was the cheesiest way to salvage an unwinnable debate.

Chapter 47

Winston Kanshū might have – actually, must have – failed to meet the winning criteria set by Ross Maximoff, but he still had good reasons to think he would win the debate.

As a starter, he never operated with the assumption that he might lose or be wrong. For the better part of his adolescence, he believed he was a white pyromancer who could remember his past life as a wet nurse in medieval France. He protested against affirmative actions, accused his teachers of being historically inaccurate, and printed flyers to promote the use of pie/pim/pir/pis/pieself pronouns to respect people whose gender identities differed from those of their (or pir) past lives. The delusion persisted until the cardboard sign guy in his neighborhood was arrested for serial arson, thereby failing to sustain Winston's faith in his own pyrokinesis and coincidentally shattering his whole belief system. Since then, he identified himself as an agnostic of reincarnation.

Another reason for his surreal self-confidence had everything to do with the countless clutch wins engraved in his sweet memory. His Hail Mary passes always found their ways to a receiver. His video game playthroughs were always saved by clipping glitches, sequence break or memory leak that caused the AI to malfunction. Most importantly, he had a poor memory of all the things that didn't work out for him.

With the profound confidence substantiated by selected facts, Winston remained undisturbed when Maximoff punched down on him in his closing speeches. From an omniscient observer's point of view, he was as optimistic about his chance of winning as the nice-shirt guy he met last night about re-re-remarriage.

"Everyone," said the host with the cheerfulness of a cold call marketer, "standing with me is Maria, who has been speaking in the judges' ears this afternoon. She is going to announce the results on behalf of our open-minded judges. Maria, please, has Maximoff convinced them that the Earth is a tree?"

Maria repeated the loaded question in Tapu Guajá, a dying Tupi–Guarani language spoken by less than four hundred indigenous people, interpreters who desperately sought a market niche, and language preservationists who recorded endangered languages in case there would be a revolution in the society's pedagogical needs.

Her reaction to the Tapu Guajá reply suggested that she was just informed of an unexpected pregnancy or an unheard-of household debt, which infrequently amounted to the same thing.

She re-repeated the loaded question and the judges re-repeated their answer. Since experimental studies suggest that nouns are easier to learn than verbs, a hyperpolyglot listening to this exchange should have by now learnt the Tapu Guajá words for "son of toad," "earth" and "tree."

"Eh... they said," Maria paused to double-check in her mind whether she misheard a silent *s* or mistook a homonym. After all, the word for "son of a toad" in Tapu Guajá can mean many things in English. To give a few examples, it can mean (1) another cane toad once sat on it, (2) since when cannibalism is out of the equation, (3) I would rather be fed to Gilbert's Naval than fed on this, (4) geez, you think I am a pale man, and twenty other expressions that playfully indicate something is inedible. However, none of them seemed semantically consistent with the rest of the message.

"They said," repeated Maria, in case someone would take it as a personal attack from her, "'Son of a toad, the Earth is no tree.'"

With so much suspense built beforehand, one would expect the audience to have expected a similar answer, give or take the "son of a toad." However, they still let out an audible gasp as if they were doing it for effect. Even Odinson puzzledly turned to Maximoff, who obviously avoided eye contact with him.

Nothing pleased the host more than the expectedly unexpected twist. He seized the opportunity to play with the audience's emotion and sensationally asked if the judges believed the Earth was a tower of turtles. The answer didn't disappoint him.

"'Son a of toad, the Earth is no turtle' was the answer," reported Maria.

Maximoff's eyes insisted on not meeting anyone's.

"They also said, 'geez, you think I am a pale man? The Earth is no cube,'" said Maria, who just realized there was more than one way to interpret the judges' answer without compromising its expression of annoyance.

"Finally," asked Adel, "are the judges convinced that the Earth is a flat disk?"

The ensuing exchange between Maria and the three Amazonians was notably longer and richer in vocabulary, giving those in earshot a chance to appreciate the beauty of their endangered language. According to a post-event survey conducted by Klynveld College, only 32% of the attendees of True Earth Summit were "mildly bothered" or "extremely distressed" by hearing foreign languages, compared to 98% of the heliocentric respondents who identified themselves with far-right ideologies. The study went on to conclude that 2% of the respondents were liars.

"Eh... I will try to interpret it as faithfully as possible," said Maria and scanned the crowd to look for Kanshū. She found him smugly smiling at Maximoff while weirdly squeezing his fists. "The judges said, 'We have seen good evidence that the Earth is a flat disk.'"

Winston jumped from his seat and turned around to hug Chandler and Ohi, in exactly the way they had rehearsed for an Oscar win.

"'... but none was presented today. Balancing all the arguments we have heard, we conclude that the Earth is a cube lodged on a giant tree erected on the back of a tower of turtles. Now, pay us the salt.' That's it."

Chapter 48

Gina had been staring at the ceiling for exactly nine minutes and thirty-two seconds, in a sitting position not unlike a gangster who has shot herself in the mouth. The ceiling itself was not that interesting, and Gina herself was not that dead. She was simply listening to a harp rendition of the Toccata and Fugue in D minor, BWV 565.

It fits, she mused.

She straightened her back and returned her gaze to the laptop. At the top right corner of its desktop was a file called "The Proof." As she added that piece of Bach to the video, she kept whining why she didn't think of adding a background music earlier. Her mildly obsessive-compulsive disorder compelled her to apply the same change to all the backups, but she knew it was too late to do so.

Replacing the cloud backup was a no brainer, but over-writing the backup drive was technically impossible. Encrypted in a WORM (write once read many) hard disk drive, the raw data of her research and a copy of "The Proof" were immutable and could only be deleted by physically destroying the disk itself. If she wanted to save a copy of the edited video on a portable drive, she would need to do some shopping.

But if I leave the room, I will lose.

For reasons she could no longer remember or care, she had resolved not to leave her room until Seth Nadir was bored to nap or his bladder gave way to the call of nature. So far, he was winning.

She took another look through the peephole and found her worthy opponent standing still. By her calculation, his phone battery would go dry in four hours of Instagram. In her own words, the real battle had not even begun.

She decided to re-schedule her dinner with Smith as a breakfast and stay on stakeout at her own room. The attrition nature of this warfare didn't escape her notice, so she had planned to put her time to good use with some serious *KrazyCoral* farming.

Meanwhile, the edited version of "The Proof" was played on her laptop. Against the backdrop of BMV 565's signature toccata, the video showed a geocentric model that was compatible with earthshine, diurnal motion, stellar parallax, annual motion of stars, relative position of the Sun, constant size of Moon and Sun throughout the day, change in Orion constellation's angle according to observer's latitude, mid-night sun at poles during summer, same face of Moon being observed everywhere on Earth, and shadow of mountain casted on cloud before sunrise or after sunset. As the fugal section of BWV 565 began, the true shape of Earth was revealed on the screen.

Chapter 49

Watching Maximoff quietly disappear from the back entrance of Sapphire Dome, Ben Song received an automatically generated email from Supermax Defense LLC, which was solely founded, owned and staffed by Ross Maximoff to provide ideology defense services. The email contained a net-30 invoice, several discount coupons, a pre-filled application form for Supermax Premium Deluxe Loyalty Club, and a service evaluation form. The email also mentioned that customers returning a completed evaluation form would receive five service credits, whatever that meant.

The survey questionnaire put Song in an uncomfortable position. Partly because it asked him to rate whether the service was satisfactorily completed, and partly because it was only in English.

What an egocentric imperialist, Song thought.

Ben Song was hard to upset, or please, or have any emotion. The last time he felt anything was during his stay in Australia forty years ago.

Back then he was an undergraduate in civil engineering, studying abroad in Melbourne. Naïve and heliocentric, he used to believe gravity was real, his motherland was always right, and everything in Australia was upside down, but the two years he spent in Australia completely changed his world view.

At the beginning of his stay, he convinced himself that the lack of upside-downness was a side effect of jet lag, but he grew uneasy with the spherical Earth model as his courses progressed. On the one hand, the Earth's curvature was completely ignored when discussing the design of small bridges. On the other hand, students were asking all sorts of challenging questions that fundamentally shook his understanding in physics, which never happened in his homeland. Neither the questions nor the questioning.

Some questioned why limousines were not in an arch shape to account for the curvature. Some queried why shoe soles were not convex if the Earth was round. Some even went so far to ask why a computer mouse, which was a bleeding edge technology at that time, could work if the Earth was not flat. Granted, the professor deflected all those questions by dismissing them as trolling, but the seed of doubt had gently landed on Song's heart.

He became increasingly disillusioned with the jet lag explanation and started taking seriously the possibility that Australia wasn't on the lower halve of a globe. But he got a problem. The same problem that always stood in the way of dreamers who dared to fly.

Gravity.

If gravity were real, then the Earth must be round, because the gravitational force would pull materials toward its center in all directions, smoothing its surface into a ball. Even if the Earth was stubborn enough to maintain its flatness (perhaps as a cosmic affirmative action for Australia), gravity would make people feel like climbing up an increasingly steep hill as they moved away from the Earth's center to, say, Melbourne.

But Song didn't struggle long with that problem before coming across the theory of ether, which was postulated by Isaac Newton in his *Opticks* and further developed by James Clerk Maxwell. Rather than the Earth greedily pulling matters to itself, Song found it more believable that the Earth was passively propelled by ether wind to accelerate upward at 9.8 m/s^2.

As someone with tertiary training in physics, of course he didn't stop at theorizing. He conducted multiple experiments, involving a wide variety of objects released mid-air. He measured, re-measured, and measured the measure used in measuring the speed of freefall objects, one of which was a measure. After months of research and noise complaints, he still couldn't disapprove the ether propelling hypothesis.

He was furious.

He had always known his home country suppressed academic freedom, but he thought it was the problem of humanities and social sciences. He never thought it would be *his* problem.

The anger and disgust transformed him overnight. Should Song have a slightly different upbringing, he would have gone on to commit mass shooting, blow himself up publicly or at least ram a car into pedestrians. But his contempt for imperialists and their puppet states held him back from those extracurricular activities. Instead, he swore to reinvent physics and disseminate the truth.

Not long after his return to home, he re-invented the equation for buoyancy force such that it no longer contained the constant of gravitational acceleration, and exclusively used the Earth's upward acceleration, buoyancy and density to explain phenomena that would otherwise entail gravity.

One thing led to many others, he found that his BUD Theory (less elegantly known as the Unified Theory of Buoyancy, Upward Acceleration and Density) was compatible with, and only with, a cubic Earth where all known civilizations lived on one side only. As if by destiny or for narration convenience, he learnt of the existence of TYDF two months after this discovery. So he dedicated the most productive years of his life to expand the influence of TYDF while continuing to refine his BUD model.

Over the next forty years, he encountered one challenge after another to the BUD Theory, but he stayed true to his science.

Did he flinch when the Eötvös effect implied the Earth was spinning and gravity was real? No, he wrote pages of assumptions to preemptively explain away why the upward acceleration of Earth (previously known as gravitational acceleration) would change as the observer moved eastward or westward.

Did he yield to meteorological phenomena that normally were explained by the Coriolis force of a spinning Earth? Nope, he added a dozen parameters to re-write the law of inertia.

Did he give up when the model's prediction of Mercury's orbit was off by ninety degrees? Not a chance, he wrote a book to argue that the orbital shift of celestial bodies was a stochastic process and therefore not deterministically predictable.

After elegantly overcoming one hundred of the one thousand challenges to his model, he recently felt that the BUD Theory was ready to be shared with the world. He just needed a platform. A prestigious platform for him to announce the intellectual triumph. And he had chosen the throne of POTUWS.

At least we didn't lose the debate, Song thought to himself as he clicked four stars on the service evaluation form. *Now the problem is Dr. Stinson. If she talks, then everyone will know I am a fool who spent forty years for nothing.*

Before he left the ballroom to attend the "Through the Convex Glass: Earth and Abstract Expressionism" exhibition, he received another email. It wasn't the confirmation of service credits from Supermax Defense LCC, but pleased him just as much (or little). The message was so simple that it had half as many letters as the mathematical expression of BUD Theory.

Dear Comrade, they will be ready by the morning. – Chu

Should Song be easier to please, he would have laughed like a Batman villain while the invisible camera slowly zoomed into his nostril.

Chapter 50

Finding themselves once again in the restaurant of Greendale Convention Centre, Chandler and Ohi felt like they were two strangers in the middle of a threesome. They had a common interest, didn't know the right moves, and were in tacit agreement not to look at each other.

The erotic parallel, sadly, could not be drawn further, as they were both fully dressed and sitting across a sulking Winston. Neither of them mentioned anything about the debate, as they understood there was a chance that his selective memory was already working in their favor. They figured it wouldn't hurt if they just quietly waited for the restaurant to start serving afternoon tea, but the silence and non-sexual tension were taking a toll on them.

"Did you notice there was a snake in our room?" Chandler gave in first. He thought this topic would keep themselves entertained till the waiter replaced all the menus.

"Is it another English expression that involves animals in an enclosed space?" wondered Ohi. "Like 'ants in the pants?'"

Chandler wasn't crazy about where the conversation was going but still wanted to give it a go.

"We do metaphorically confine a lot of animals, like 'elephant in the room.'"

"I got another one," Ohi raised his hand. He was the only one genuinely enjoying this chat. "Something about 'cat out of the bag.'"

"Guys, how did the debate go?" asked Maeve, waddling past their backs.

"And 'snakes on a plane,'" said Chandler, hoping it was not too late to change the subject.

Maeve looked at Chandler the way one would look at a "Turn Left" sign in the shape of a right-pointing arrow. She decided against engaging him any further, as she had no tea time to waste. She ordered everything under "Wednesday's Specials" and steered the conversation back to where it just came from, much to its confusion.

"Hey, big guy, did you ask White Jesus to help with your hemorrhoid?"

Chandler thought maybe a discussion about the swollen veins in Winston's anal canal was not too bad an idea during tea time. *I have some experience in that arena*, he thought, which might or might not refer to the medical condition.

He was going to weigh in on that matter, but Winston beat him to it.

"I lost. Specifically, I was the only loser in the four-way debate."

"Oh," uttered Maeve while drinking her water with Zen like tranquility.

"I can understand it if you are upset, but in my defense—"

"I am not."

"You are not?"

"Nope. It was kind of expected."

Winston squinted at her as if she just bragged that there were millions of flat Earthers around the globe.

"But you were so nervous about it during lunch."

"It was probably the low blood sugar," said Maeve and thanked the waiter for the three-tier tray of finger foods, "and good sportsmanship, of course."

"It doesn't bother you that the judges would rather believe in a cubic Earth on turtle tree rather than a disk Earth?"

"Come on," said Maeve with a mouthful of scones, "how often do you think we win an argument with strangers on the Internet? And do we lose sleep or modify our belief system every time we lose? Hell no. Only the weaklings do that. We know we are right. We know." Maeve seemed a bit tired from all the talking, so she took a short break and fed herself with several finger sandwiches.

"Plus, you said it was a three-way tie, so it didn't hurt your chance of winning POTUWS that much."

"About that," said Winston softly, "I am not sure if I still want to run for it. You know, I only put my name in because I wanted to share my flat Earth evidence and get some feedback. Now that it is done and makes virtually zero impact, I guess I have no business around here anymore."

"No," said Maeve, "no, no, no, no," she might be tired again, so she put some desserts in her mouth and continued, "no, no, no, no, no, no, no, no."

Seeing she had made her point perfectly clear, she supped up the herbal tea that just arrived on the table.

"Just because you didn't win the debate doesn't mean it has no impact. And if you really want to make an impact, stay and film a documentary about flat Earth."

"I *am* making that documentary, but you guys look too normal to be in it. When people watch a documentary about flat Earthers, they expect to see a bunch of socially ostracized losers who had no remarkable talents or meaningful accomplishments but yearned for attentions, hence desperately setting themselves apart by clinging to bizarre beliefs. That's what people pay to watch, but you guys are not any of those things."

"But can't you just stay for two more days till the election? I swear you won't have to do another speech or shake another hand. Just stick around. You won't even have to try to win."

"But in the unlikely event that he wins and doesn't want to do the job anymore?" asked Chandler.

"Then just delegate all duties to me," said Maeve. "You won't even have to answer a call. If you don't believe it, you can ask Robert, or the psychic I hire for talking to him."

"Why do you care so much if Sensei stays in the race?" asked Ohi.

"Because running in an election is a fun experience and I want you all to have fun. You know me, I am all about fun."

The three men – who, by the way, had been collectively referred to as COW boys by fun Maeve – squinted at her.

"Because I believe a voice representing Disk Earth Society should be in the presidential race, regardless of the chance of winning."

The COW boys squinted harder, doing exactly what a real cowboy would do to make his opposing duelist realize the foolishness of risking one's life for a public display of courage

"Because I have fallen in love with Winston and want to spend as much time with him as possible."

Chandler's eye lids were trembling, Ohi's optic nerve dying, and Winston's posterior chamber internally bleeding.

"Because, eh... you know... there is this reason for, um..."

The men's eyes had become a line so thin that only a subatomic particle could past through them.

"OK, OK, stop peering into my soul," cried Maeve. "If you quit then I will have to return the campaign donations, which I already spent on settling a taxi accident claim."

"Wha... what?" said Ohi. "How bad was the accident?"

"That's your first question?" said Chandler. "Who cares if she killed someone? She is stealing money from us, I mean, from the campaign."

"But since when do we have a campaign?" asked Ohi.

"Technically," said Maeve, "we do have a campaign. It just isn't very active. So technically, I didn't break any of the GoFundMe rules because keeping your campaign manager, aka me, out of an expensive lawsuit is essential expenditure for the POTUWS election."

"Wait a minute, did you just use me as an excuse for funding?" said Winston. "Oh my god, I feel so used. I feel dirty."

"No, I do care about who will become POTUWS as much as I cared who would be my cellmate. And I truly believe you can win. Look at this."

Maeve showed Winston her phone, which was playing an ad about online chat with lonely housewives.

"I don't think distracting me with pornography is the solution here."

"Oops, stupid ads," Maeve closed it without waiting for the skip ads button and scrolled the page down. "Look at this, the comment. I post the same message to all the most viewed videos."

Below the message praising the camera work and above the one analyzing the plot, there was a message by BigLoveMaeve2E731. It was concise enough to capitalize on the readers' short-lived post nuts clarity.

You think you have balls?	o_O
He has the balls for change.	(▇Ĺ▇つ
He has the balls for truth.	(▇Ĺ▇つ
He has the balls to take on The Ball.	(▇Ĺ▇つ
Vote for Winston Kanshū.	└(^o^)X(^o^)┘

"Well, it is... adorable," said Winston, "and graphical, which is saying a lot in this context."

"Isn't it?" said Maeve with the pride of a mother who just walked into her son exploring his body. "If I didn't truly support you, would I have soiled my eyes with all these sinful, degenerate, step-brother-and-sister grotesque? Seriously, this is like the only genre out there."

"True, I can't imagine why anyone else would have done that," said Winston with a straight face, "and I promise you I won't drop out."

"Good, that's good enough. As long as you stay, then there is still a chance to win and for Disk Earth Society to unite the Seekers."

"But seriously," asked Chandler, "you still think Wins has a chance? You just promised he won't even need to try anymore."

"Of course," Maeve's eyes glittered as another dessert arrived.

"Who knows what stupid things the other candidates will do tomorrow?"

Chapter 51

Duh, Thursday again.

Smith Robin got up and put on another nice shirt of his. He just had a lousy Wednesday and hoped Thursday would go gentle on him.

The lousiness of Wednesday had nothing to do with the fact that he made absolutely no progress on R.D.G.A.R. He knew how to swing a thirty-minute status catchup with nothing to show for, and he did. Some chit-chat on the weather. A recap of the action log. Going through the threat rating on risk register. Patting himself on the back when reviewing the milestones. Some remarks about the updated definitions of green, amber and red status. Some much shorter remarks about why everything on the project timeline got shifted to its right. Before anyone knew it, he was already wrapping up the call with a summary of the next steps.

The lousiness also had nothing to do with the paper work he had to do last night. It was not exactly pleasant, but he was no stranger to doing tasks whose sole purpose was to cover one's behind, regardless of whether that rectum in question belonged to him or not.

His Wednesday was lousy because the only time he got to spend with Gina was via *KrazyCoral* co-op. As fun as it was to protect coastline from waves, he was hoping something less virtually nautical.

He knew he shouldn't feel that way. He really did. He already had a girlfriend. And, incidentally, the whole NASA relied on him to cover up the Global Lie. If he didn't act in the next six hours, Gina would destroy everything NASA had worked decades to build, or pretend to build.

Fifteen minutes later, he arrived at the floor of Gina's room. As expected, a man wearing an All-Ways armband was stationed outside of her room.

"What do you mean I can't knock on the door," said Smith.

"Because you don't have an appointment with His Excellency," said Nadir.

Smith took another look at his phone and the door number behind the All-Ways apostle. For good measure, he also tried to remember how he got here. It wasn't conclusive but he found it unlikely that he was still in a dream.

"Isn't it the room of Gina Stinson?"

"Yes, it is."

"Then what is your egg salad C doing in my date's room?" hollered Smith.

Before Nadir could enforce the punishment for blasphemy, which could be either a pinch on the elbow or a slap on the wrist, the door behind him swung open.

"Let's go, Seth," said Abed Kutner as he emerged from the room. Behind him was Gina with eye bags that could carry two sodas worth of changes.

To preempt any misunderstanding that he was about to make a wish for success, the pandit slowly turned his head around and fixed the young physicist with a menacingly cold look.

"Good luck with your presentation, doctor."

Inside the west royal suite of Greendale Convention Centre, Gabriel Odinson, the First of His Name, Protector of the World Tree, Beacon of Grass Sea, the Last Prophet, Odinson the Wise, the Enlightened, Prince of Truth put down his tablet and poured himself a cup of cappuccino.

He just reviewed the daily summary for yesterday and it had nothing for him to worry. The merchandises were selling themselves, the traffic on his podcast and YouTube channels was steadily rising, and one of his crowdfunding campaigns just hit the target. Starting from next week, the senior priests of Treeism would be preaching across Norway in a limo.

So far everything was going as he planned. Maximoff's triple dealing wasn't in his script, but it didn't hurt the outcome. The only hiccup was the physicist invited by Kutner.

I was right about him, Odinson thought as he tasted the coffee.

He is an idiot.

Around a month ago, Odinson caught wind of the latest project of All-Ways – a partnership with Red Hot Toys to produce collectible figures of Cosmic Turtle. The data from qualitative interviews, focus groups, social media analytics, and double-blind trials all suggested that the authentic figurine would be a disaster, if disaster meant monopolization of the doll market.

That news came as a revelation to Odinson.

He used to think World Tree was the most marketable geocentric idea. "Who doesn't like trees?" he always said. He could put a tree figure inside a snowball and sell it in Christmas, or put some candle holders on its top for sale during Hanukkah. He could print it on a gun and sell it to the right, or carve it into a reusable coffee mug and market it to the left. He even had this inscription painted across the wooden beams of his office as if he was Michel de Montaigne: "If it rhymes with tree, then it isn't free," and trademarked the phrase in eighteen European countries.

But he overlooked the toy market. Besides life-size silicone dolls, the most profitable toys in the adult segment were collectible figurines, masculinely referred to as action figures, or traditionally known as dolls. The inconveniently inanimate nature of trees and lack of doctrinal support for World Tree to have swivel joints meant that Odinson stood no chance to capture the market share that would soon be in Abed Kutner's pocket.

So he did what a reasonable businessman would do, after exhausting all other means such as suing All-Ways for copyright infringement, lobbying to restrict the sale of chelonian toys in EU countries, spreading rumor that Red Hot Toys used child labor, and smearing Kutner with accusations of animal cruelty. He offered to help market All-Ways' turtle collection figures across western Europe.

Hands were shaken, champagnes were opened and a contract drafted, but White Jesus had to walk out of the deal at godspeed in the last minute, upon learning that Kutner would donate all the proceeds to combat turtle warming.

Abed Kutner's fundamentalism, Odinson thought, was the recipe for self-destruction, so he was not too surprised when Dr. Gina

Stinson revealed her discovery that would render All-Ways irrelevant, with Treeism as collateral damage.

What surprised him was the constraint Kutner showed in the past thirty-five hours.

Kutner boy, if you ain't doing nothing, thought Odinson rather grammatically incorrectly as his shaving blade slid on his sexy cheekbone, *then someone else will have to step up.*

Smith grew wary of Gina's grumpiness.

She didn't laugh at his jokes, refused to take her ulcer meds, and requested to speak to the manager of the customer service manager who refused to refund the bacteria she had purchased to feed her coral avatar. Apparently there was some login problem with her *KrazyCoral* account.

Once he learnt that Gina was sleep deprived after a night of, in her own words, war of attrition, his palms started sweating.

If she goes back to her room for sleep now, Smith thought, *then there is no way in.*

He wasn't euphemistically thinking of his chance to have sex. He was professionally assessing the practical challenge against penetrating – again, nothing sexual – into Gina's room to erase her research and discovery.

In an ideal world free of fart, shit (both physical and metaphorical) and consequently rectum, Charles and his team could have pulled a break and enter while Smith and Gina were dining two blocks away from Greendale.

In a less than ideal world where people do have an ass to cover, however, it was not possible. Not until the Administration Department of NASA (less formally known as Admin, or more passionately known as freaking Admin) accepted the P-46K form he re-submitted last evening.

Without a duly processed P-46K, the Legal Department of NASA would not provide free in-house legal services to staff facing prosecution for burglary and/or trespassing in North America. As a result, no Round Ops staff could perform a break and enter in Canada, according to their departmental policy.

Smith was of course aware of the delicacy of Round Ops' policies and the reputation of Admin. He submitted the form more than two weeks ago and had taken reasonable steps to ensure the correct form[2] was used, the form was duly received and acknowledged in writing, and no inquiries from Admin were unattended. As a matter of fact, he hadn't heard from them until yesterday afternoon, fifteen minutes before the end of working hours, or five minutes after the de facto close of business.

He was regrettably informed by a salutation-less email that his "P-46K and its enclosure were not completed without material omissions or errors."

With no recourse to clarify the "material omissions or errors" – which, to be fair, had little to do with the email's untimeliness, but more with the permanently silent mode of Admin's phones – Smith spent the whole evening to triple-check everything. At last, he located a mistake he made in answering "Did you previously apply for similar services?" He still wasn't entirely sure why that question was relevant, but was certain that the "material omissions or errors" referred to the dangling preposition in his answer.

"Do you have any plan after breakfast?" asked Smith, having checked his phone for any news from Admin. "Maybe we can gang up to bully a Canadian or something."

Gina was visibly shocked by the suggestion. She gracefully stared at Smith.

"But won't you have a workshop about hyperbole and legally false advertising this morning?"

Smith's palms almost froze the dripping sweat.

"Yeah, I almost forgot," said Smith Johansson while doing a professionally fake laugh. "Thanks for reminding me. I'm going to give a talk about how obviously exaggerated statements can absolve corporate executives from liability."

"It is sweet of you to ditch work for me, but I am okay. I have somewhere I want to go. See you in the crowd during my presentation."

---

[2] Many Round Ops rookies made the mistake of submitting the less frequently used P-47K form, which was for trespassing *to* North America. Most of them were bankrupted by civil lawsuit or ended up getting raped in federal prisons. Some NASA employees speculated that the P-47K form itself was a conspiracy engineered by the freaking Admin.

Chapter 52

Robin Smith wished he was giving a seminar about responsible use of innocent exaggeration in business context. It would bring back a lot of fond memories he had at MacCheddar & Co. He used to tell the new joiners that they could say whatever they wanted as long as it couldn't be proved false. And if it could be falsified, then they might just as well go over the top so that they could defend it as a rhetorical expression.

He missed those good days. No Global Lie to cover up. No theoretical physicist to seduce. And certainly no burglary to seek approval for. Granted, at MacCheddar & Co he also had his fair share of lies to tell, red tape to cut and fresh graduate chicks who wanted a grown-up man to date. But he wouldn't be held accountable for the collapse of a six-decade-old deception. More importantly, if he was still an Ops Transformation SME, he wouldn't be watching woke comedy with Charles Peralta in Sapphire Dome.

"Did the approval come through yet?" whispered Charles, with his gaze fixed on Yusuf Adel performing on stage.

"It is as approved as it was five minutes ago," hissed Smith, also looking straight ahead.

"Geez, only five minutes? I like him better when he didn't have to follow the stupid woke rules for stand-up. Some of his jokes really cracked me up yesterday."

"That is soooo insensitive. He shouldn't be punching down on those people."

"What? What's wrong with making fun of pedophiles and people who claim to have past-live memories?"

"It is just offensive. You know, pedophilia is a psychiatric disorder that compels an otherwise healthy adult to be sexually attracted to children. It is just wrong to make fun of people with mental illness. And, and past-live memory? It is a core part of a person's identity. We should accept that. By the way, reincarnation-phobia may increase the suicide rate of reincarnation believers."

Charles turned his head to Smith and then rapidly turned it the other way around, pretending he was looking for his car keys. Logically speaking, in order for that pretense to work, people around him must be open to the idea that lost car keys could remain airborne while waiting to be recovered. Fortunately, Charles was in an environment where disbelief was not only suspended, but hanged by the neck and dried to the bones for good measure.

"I saw you laughed at those jokes yesterday."

"No, I didn't. And don't you dare to say I am virtual-signaling. I'm—"

"You know that sorority chick is no longer sitting behind us, right?"

"She isn't?" asked Smith and did the same car-keys-search routine, thereby successfully signaling that he and Charles were not undercover agents from NASA.

"Phew, of course I loved those jokes. Damn those moral Taliban and their terrorism on comedy."

It was only 9:12 a.m., but Britta Geller already met the Fitbit step goal for 9 a.m. – 10 a.m. It was nothing short of bragworthy, as she rarely hit the target within NASA office, or anywhere at all. The only time she did was when she was at home, walking her dog. For the avoidance of doubt, the step goal was met when she remained absolutely still on couch, while her dog enthusiastically chased its Fitbit-wearing tail.

Despite her chronic lack of exercise, Britta did not have an inch of excessive body fat on her waist. When she arrived at the stuffy windowless Admin office, populated by grimy office-chair potatoes who collectively had zero career ambition and seventeen unpublished erotic fan fictions, Britta felt like she was Miss America visiting McAllen, Texas. That was the magic of Admin office. It could make visitors feel either extremely good about their life decisions or so depressed that they wanted to kill themselves.

But Britta did not come down for slum tourism. Not only for that.

Smith Robin had escalated the P-46K situation to the Head of Administration Department, who naturally ignored it, so he re-escalated it to Miranda. The NASA Director didn't want to upset her fellow members of NASA writing club, so she decided to de-escalate it to the next person who would walk into her office, who turned out to be janitor Alex. Not too eager to overstep above his pay grade,

Alex horizontally escalated the issue to his smoking buddy. That chronic smoker, who happened to be the deputy head of NSD, already had a lot of problems on his hands and in his lungs, so he turned Alex's problem into Britta's problem.

All of the above happened within the span of twelve minutes, categorically debunking the myth of government inefficiency.

"What is the status of P46K000ED20-Z?" Britta asked the first person she saw in Admin office. "I need it approved this morning."

For a moment, Britta thought her Admin colleague didn't hear her or pretended he didn't hear her. That misunderstanding was resolved a few moments later when the Admin officer, whose name plate implied he was Clark Earl Jr. Jr., reacted to the question.

Since Clark Jr. Jr. was completely bald, when he slowly raised his head to face Britta, she thought she was watching the Earth's rotation from space. That was certainly an absurd feeling, because the Earth never spun, which had been empirically confirmed by the nine thousand satellites that had been launched solely or jointly by more than forty countries around the world.

In the past six decades, millions of hours of satellite images had been received, analyzed, censored, edited, re-mastered, and re-distributed by the designated ground stations maintained or tampered by G12 agencies. The raw images had informed the *real* scientists in developing a much simpler version of BUD Theory. Similar to Ben Song's BUD Theory, the NASA version (called DUB Theory) had some limitations in explaining certain astronomical and meteorological phenomena, but it was not exclusively compatible with a cubic Earth. In itself, the theory's promiscuous compatibility didn't bother the involuntarily chaste *real* astrophysicists, but it presented a huge mathematical challenge to solving a few non-linear partial differential Diophantine equations. It would be tremendously helpful to the research if one of those satellites could climb to a higher orbit or travel to a sharper angle against the ground and confirm what was beyond the Antarctic ice wall. But somehow all the attempts had failed. It was as if a fifth dimensional wall, or the transparent hand of a supreme being, or the face of a certain invisible goal keeper named Scott Sterling was hell-bent on halting scientific progress.

It takes as much time for an average person to read through the previous paragraph twice as it took Clark Jr. Jr.'s gaze to rise to meet Britta's. His eyes were so hollow that Britta was not sure if she was talking to a philosophical zombie. She thought she should find another Admin officer to help, but Clark Jr. Jr. immediately showed her it was a silly idea. He turned to the cubical behind him and said to the lady named Amy that she should be addressing Britta's query.

Amy politely complied and requested Britta to repeat the form number.

"P forty-six K zero zero zero—"

"Sorry, honey, you lost me at *B*."

"There was no *B*. It was *P* for papa!"

"No need to yell, honey. I am not deaf. So it was P twenty-six—"

"No, Papa forty-six kilo. You know what, maybe I just write it down for you."

"Sure, if you want to borrow any stationery for writing, please fill in the SW4Gamma form here."

Britta looked at the pink form in Amy's hand and then at her bespectacled face, just to make sure she could fully appreciate Amy's sense of humor. She failed, because there was none.

"But I don't have any pen on me to fill in the form."

"You can borrow one if you submit this form."

"But if I have a pen, why would I need to fill in the form to borrow a pen?"

"Hey, young lady," Amy seemed offended, "don't turn your problem into my problem."

"Alright, let's do it verbally again. Papa forty-six Kilo zero zero zero Echo—"

"Was it three zeros or four zeros?"

"Three. Triple zero."

"Why didn't you just say triple zero? And did you say *E* for echo?"

"Yes. Is there a problem?"

"No," Amy smiled, "not my problem anymore. Any P-46K with an *E* in its eighth digit is handled by Earl over there. Have a nice one."

Smith thought Adel would run out of permissible jokes before his P-

46K got approved, but he had moderately overestimated Admin's work morale on a Thursday morning and vastly underestimated the number of ways to poke fun at heliocentric believers. Apparently, flatees had invented more than seven hundred words to describe the believers and perpetuators of Global Lie so that they could keep their podcast colorful for almost two years without repeating the vocabulary from previous episodes.

Aflatiests. Ageocentrist. Anal sheep. Anti-planes. Arch asses. Arch backs. Archdiots. Arch feet. Archliars. Ballasses. Ball clowns. Balldiots. Ballface. Ballgoblin. Ballgots. Ballheads. Ballists. Ballmen/Ballmaids. Ball monkeys. Basic globeface. Basic globeheads. Basic globetards. Basic sheep. Borks. Just to name a few in alphabetical order, having excluded the slurs that are too susceptible to be misinterpretation (e.g., ball breathers and ball suckers).

To distract himself from the offensive jokes directed at aflatiests, Smith kept spamming Admin's general mailbox with capitalized subject lines to expedite his application process.

Adel finished his gig and Ben Song returned from what must have been a very long bathroom break. No news from Admin.

A reputable theologian gave a seminar about biblical text proving the age and flatness of Earth. No news from Admin.

Several celebrities shared the hardship they went through to prove the absence of curvature, through first-hand observations made on ball courts, cruise ships, penthouses, private choppers, and Red Mountain, Aspen. Still no news from Admin.

The accountants of the United Ways made a donation pitch for the non-profit organization's GoFundMe campaigns, raising funds for a twelve-day Antarctica tour package, development of a genuinely working compass, a second-hand private jet for serving the God/Tree/Turtle, building a telescope powerful enough to see the (absence of) U.S. flag on the Moon, two economy-class SpaceX tickets. Not a blip from Admin.

The main course of networking lunch was served and Charles had asked for the third refill of spritzer. Not even one photon had been transmitted from the Admin office to Smith's mailbox.

"Man," said Smith to the half-drunk Charles, "I am beginning to worry."

"You are?" slurred Charles half-soberly.

"What do you say if we change the plan? You kidnap Gina before she steps onto the stage, and we will take care of her data after we get the greenlight from Admin."

"That sounds brilliant," mumbled Charles. He debated with himself if he was in no condition to carry out his Round Ops duties. He won. He just couldn't tell which side did, which kind of proved the point one side was making. To get out of his half-drunkenness and settle the internal debate, he emptied another glass of spritzer. It worked exactly as intended.

"But – hic – there is a tiny, teeny, little – hic – technical problem with your new plan."

As he always considered himself a generalist, Smith hated it when people got technical. Triply so when they were drunken.

"You – hic – need to have a properly processed P-99K before Round Ops can perform any abduction or hijacking in North America."

"Would it be simpler if the target is outside of the continent?"

"Absolutely. But why?"

"Nope, just asking for a friend."

Smith opened an album on his phone. It was full of pictures of his younger son, taken with his stepfather in Argentina.

Seeing two Smiths reminiscently look at their phones, it finally hit Charles that Gina Stinson would soon put his whole department out of work. He might lose the first job he got since graduation. Over his ten-year career, the only skills he had acquired were bomb making, blackmailing, lock picking, kidnapping, hot-wiring, breaking and entering, pickpocketing, high-speed chasing, reverse-driving, and flatee impersonating. As employable as they were, he would still be hard pressed to explain the ten-year experience gap after Harvard BBA.

It finally dawned on Charles that maybe he shouldn't be waiting for the fourth refill. Perhaps he should stop worrying about those stupid policies. Possibly it was a good idea for him to do something now. Probably he should start working on his resume.

Let me put a positive spin on the two years I spent on messing with Foucault pendulums.

With a newfound resolve, Charles supported himself to get out of the chair, but was pressed down immediately by three Smiths, all coherently yelling something at him. He couldn't hear what they said until their palms, at least one of them, made direct impact with his cheek in a very unpleasant manner.

"Get the flat up," said the re-unified Smith, incidentally proving trinity was not logically impossible. "We got the greenlight. Now move your P-46K covered ass and round off the Earth."

Chapter 53

Chairman Song's blinking frequency had reduced by roughly 20% since his return to Sapphire Dome this morning. Everyone on the Central Committee of TYDF noticed it and understood its implication. Whatever was on their leader's mind, they supposed, must be related to his brief disappearance after the banquet on Tuesday.

Those sharing the same table with Song barely touched their dishes. They all wanted to find out what had happened to their beloved chairman, but none wanted to be the nail that stuck out. That was also the reason why none of them had said anything about the black thing in Song's teeth. They just kept refiling the chairman's cup with tea.

A likely candidate for the chairman's notably worse mood, they speculated, was that he finally realized his BUD Theory failed to explain why other planets were spheres, something the Central Committee noticed around a decade ago.

They could not be more wrong, though. Song had already got around that ostensible challenge by adding the axiom "We are special."

Only Song's secretary had the right idea and the courage to check with the chairman.

"Chairman," said the secretary, "did they do what you wanted them to do?"

Song didn't say a word but imperceptibly squinted at his tea. He drank it and said he didn't know what his secretary was talking about.

The secretary didn't press for more, as he believed he had got the answer he asked for. He was quite confident he got it right. The Central Committee members also thought he got it right. Even Song thought everyone on the table got whatever they were thinking right.

They continued to dine in silence.

The black thing remained in Song's teeth.

Chapter 54

Somewhere between the small table formerly occupied by Charles Peralta and the square table surrounded by TYDF officials was a round table seated by Winston Kanshū, his dormant POTUWS campaign team, and three DES members who had introduced themselves as Winston's biggest fans. Winston didn't quite catch their names, because he made no attempt to, so he had named them Nazi Forehead, Four-eyes Maeve and Racial Token.

Over the course of lunch, Winston discovered the three fans shared two things cinematic in common: They had repeatedly watched *The Truman Show* and never seen any of his movies. Hence he had stopped making further attempts to discuss cinema and let it slide into a how-many-conspiracies-do-you-believe quiz.

"For the record, I would call them conspiracy facts rather than theories," said Maeve. "Chemtrails."

"Great Replacement," said Nazi Forehead.

"Deep state," said Four-eyes Maeve.

"Pizzagate," said Racial Token.

"Eh... flat Earth?" said Chandler.

"Moon landing," said Ohi.

"Area 51," said Winston.

"Everything related to Freemasonry," said Maeve.

"Sandy Hook," said Nazi Forehead.

"Wait a second," said Four-eyes Maeve. "What do you mean by Sandy Hook?"

"I meant," said the man who supported the Nazi symbol with his brows, "it never happened, like Holocaust. It's pretty obvious."

"*Hell no!*"

"Hell yeah, no way six million Jews were killed when there were only seventeen million of them. Duh."

"No," cried the bespectacled woman, "of course Holocaust is a hoax. I meant the Sandy Hook shooting. My child was murdered there!"

The temperature of that table dropped to absolute zero.

Chandler was a bit skeptical if she was just playing victim to get sympathy, but kept his mouth shut out of respect. Winston and Ohi also didn't say a thing, in case Four-eyes Maeve's child was the shooter. Maeve wanted to comfort her sobbing doppelgänger, but her fellow Jew hater was in her way. So she did the next best thing she could do.

"I am sure he didn't mean that. I think, I think what he was trying to say is the shooting was staged by the left so that they can take away our guns. The shooting happened. It did happen, right?"

Both Nazi Forehead and Racial Token nodded, after Maeve winked at them.

"Let's talk about something else," Maeve said with a forced smile. "Let's move on to the next conspiracy fact."

It was enough to light up Four-eyes Maeve. Having blown her nose like Scottish Highland bagpipes, she resumed the game.

"Er... this one may not count," said the grieving woman, "because it's as plain as the day. Obama is the anti-Christ and not an American."

"Woo, woo, woo," said Racial Token, "it's a bit racist, don't you think? And how could you believe in both deep state and birtherism but not San—"

The woman blew another tone.

"Anyway, the next one," said Racial Token, feeling rather hurt. "This one is about 9/11. I know it's a bit out there, but I have checked the footage frame by frame with my own eyes, so it is a fact." He took a moment to look around the table and build the suspense. "There were no planes involved. The towers were hit by missiles surrounded by state-of-the-art hologram."

"BS, no freaking way," exploded Nazi Forehead. "It was the Jews. They did it!"

Before the friendly nerd flight escalated into a deadly fist fight, Maeve and the COW boys had returned to Sapphire Dome, expecting the "Missing Link Between Modern Physics and Figure of Earth" presentation to begin in five minutes.

Chandler noticed Winston was unusually enthusiastic about this seminar. "Unusual" because he must have had a rough morning. From what Chandler had heard, the events in the morning were the conference equivalents of a married man's life. All he got was chattering, more chattering, bitching and some money asking.

Ohi had the same observation, but he figured it was because his Sensei really looked forward to this seminar. Winston had mentioned how eye-opening Dr. Stinson's discovery was, how much goosebumps it gave him, and how regretful that he couldn't recall a single thing she said. Ohi had recommended him to receive a Scientology auditing, but Winston rejected on the ground that he had "a thing with Cruise," which had banned him for life from the Church of Scientology.

Winston was not alone in anticipating Dr. Stinson's announcement. There were more journalists and cameras in Sapphire Dome than before. Even more than day one.

Originally, most of the journalists who had come to cover the True Earth Summit had left after the first day. Most of them left disappointedly because the attendees were not freakish enough. Some of them quitted their jobs and flew to Norway to serve the World Tree. A few of them ran away in panic and rented the bunkers next to Chandler's. A couple of them had to go because they had left the stoves on. One of them took leave to cover the breaking news that two suspicious women armed with vacuum cleaners, toilet brushes, mops and buckets full of hideous sponges had entered an unlocked house in Nova Scotia, cleaned it and left without taking anything, which was the second time in five years.

Except for the one who was still investigating the mysterious serial cleaning, all the journalists had returned to cover what would be either the most cringe inducing fail in science community or the biggest paradigm shift in natural science since Copernican heliocentrism.

Finally, it was two o'clock Eastern Day Time.

Close to a million of netizens had tuned in for the outcome of another Twitter argument and some schadenfreude. The prepared ones had got themselves some snacks. The few exceptional ones had pulled their pants down.

Through the Internet, they watched Dr. Gina Stinson step into the screen and began explaining the illusion of curvature. It was due to refraction here and refraction there. Sometimes the refraction here went into the refraction there and caused more refraction somewhere. For obvious reasons, refraction could not be everywhere, but for more subtle reasons it must not be nowhere at all. Following that train of thoughts, the livestream viewers were made to understand how a non-spherical Earth could cast a round shadow on the Moon during a lunar eclipse.

After the warm-up, the presenter got a bit more technical and stated that the spherical Earth model bore an inalienable relationship with gravity. If gravity was real, then a flat Earth would either collapse into a sphere under its own gravity, or be a plate where trees grew diagonally while too much air and water were drawn to the Earth's center, eliminating life. However, with some mathematical gymnastics that the audience was warned not to try at home, it was shown that gravity could be replaced with density and buoyancy.

Having established the possibility to do without gravity, the young scientist attacked why a planet with no core could still have geomagnetic field holding the atmosphere in place. That one was a biggie, but with some eye-catching animations and soul-stirring classical music, the audience learnt that the diamagnetic force of Earth displaced black body radiation to drag the anti-neutron toward itself, creating a ferromagnetic field that centripetally held the atmosphere together.

"Wow... that's," whispered Ohi to Winston, "that's really deep. No wonder Sensei you need a second viewing."

Winston didn't say anything. He appeared to be troubled by those big words, but he wasn't. By the time "refraction" was mentioned for the fifteenth time, Winston had done what 99.98% of the livestream viewers did. He simply gave up on understanding the words and enjoyed the visuals. But he was still genuinely troubled.

"Wins, Dr. Gina is nothing like what you told us. Don't get me wrong. I'm not saying she is not attractive, but I didn't know she is," said Chandler hesitatingly, "I didn't know she is a man."

"Hey, you insensitive privileged elitist," interjected Ohi. *"Zie is a man!"*

Chapter 55

Smith Robin was as confused as the DES presidential candidate sitting five rows behind him. Somehow he was even more confused than those watching the presentation online with their pants down. He had expected some flatee would say the presentation was cancelled or re-scheduled due to a technical error. He never thought All-Ways would substitute Gina with someone else, let alone someone he personally knew.

The chubby neat young man who just delivered an astrophysical mumbo jumbo was William "Bill" Parker, who used to be a junior consultant at MacCheddar & Co. Smith could still recall interviewing him four years ago at the New York office. Bill had worked in three boutique companies over two years, didn't have a single typo in his resume, gave a firm and moist-free handshake, came across as a standup guy, carried himself like a bold risk taker, maintained the right amount of eye contact and fake smile, said nothing too stupid to the behavioral interview questions, sent a beautifully handwritten thank-you note afterwards, and was fired four weeks after he got on board.

According to the 360-degree feedbacks, Bill had all the right traits as an effective associate director, but was completely useless at his pay grade. Hiring him was one of the biggest mistakes made by Smith at MacCheddar & Co. That and the three times he gratuitously hit reply all.

Smith had heard that Bill went on to explore other career options, relocated from New York, embarked on a spiritual journey, shed all material possessions, reconnected with his ancestral lineage, took over his family business, and devoted himself to serve the emotional needs of niche market sector.

What Smith didn't hear was that Bill had several equally successful careers at consulting, got evicted from his apartment, joined a cult, lost all his savings, moved back to his parents' basement, became a third-generation gunsmith, and specialized in modifying semiautomatic weapons into fully automatic firearms, ideal for American citizens with enormous psychological problems or racial hatred to take their problems out during an un-scheduled school visit.

The less than perfect life trajectory not only incurred ridicule from the neighboring farmers who survived on government subsidies, but also made Bill question the meaning of life. He had made multiple creative attempts to end his miserable existence, such as decorating his shop as an abortion clinic or walking in the street while wearing black make-up. Unexpectedly, the worst he got was a few broken ribs.

Thus, he took his unsuccessful suicide attempts as a sign. A sign that his life was not an accident. A sign that his life mattered to someone. A sign that his life had an objective meaning, rather than a purpose that individuals could arbitrarily assign to themselves. A sign that he was at the center of the universe, which must mean that the Earth was not a spinning ball revolving around a star orbiting around a supermassive black hole being dragged around by gravitational field in an ever-expanding cosmos borne out of a singularity event.

Emboldened by his newfound meaning, Bill embarked on another spiritual journey and found his way to All-Ways. Having taken out multiple loans for his previous cult, Bill was initially skeptical of its *All The Way Down* doctrine. However, the moment he met Abed Kutner, he saw another sign indicating Kutner's legitimacy.

Two men walking by Bill high-fived each other.

Bill's favorite number was five.

Kutner's first name contained the first five letters in the alphabet except the letter *c*.

C for *conman.*

Therefore, Abed Kutner must not be a conman. Q.E.D.

As fate would have it, the pandit really didn't con a single cent out of Bill, and confirmed all his prior beliefs about life, the universe and everything. Among others, Bill learnt that the world-bearing turtle did care about him, so he proudly put on the blue All-Ways armband and accepted his role in the grand design of Cosmic Turtle. He didn't worry too much about the technical details of why the planning of a supernatural being would give more meaning to his life than a blacksmith to a nail.

In the past three years, Bill didn't pass a day without thinking what the Cosmic Turtle had in store for him. Imposing All-Ways beliefs onto everyone in the name of salvation? Brainwashing children with All-Ways doctrine before they developed critical thinking? Collecting donation to build a temple glorifying the Turtle? Establishing a theocratic state of All-Ways to enforce anti-blasphemy law? Waging war on aflatiests, geocentric pagans and people who never heard of All-Ways?

Bill didn't have the answer, but he knew for sure that the Cosmic Turtle didn't just want him to do medical research, promote literacy, reduce poverty, advocate for human rights or combat terrorism. These causes sounded too mundane and aflatiest-ish.

So he kept waiting.

He awaited the next sign.

He didn't take any of his meds so that he wouldn't miss any subtle sign.

He didn't move from his parents' place in case the sign sent him a mail.

He came to the True Earth Summit, reasoning that maybe the sign had some trouble with border control.

Thirty minutes ago, the sign finally paid him a visit, in the form of a mass email from Seth Nadir. Apparently, Dr. Gina Stinson had gone missing and a volunteer was needed to take over her stage and wing it.

Bill didn't know any better what had happened to Dr. Stinson and couldn't care less. He had found his calling and was using his talents to fulfil it. To be fair, he did quite a job. The MacCheddar & Co. staff who came to the summit for corporate retreat thought perhaps they should give Bill another shot. A week later they re-hired him as the Crypto Insight Lead, focused on sales.

The livestream viewers didn't know what to make of the word salad and dropped off one by one. They would, however, spend the next few weeks debating among themselves if it was the most groundbreaking presentation or the worst troll ever.

Meanwhile, Smith Robin could not hear a word coming from his ex-colleague. All he could think of was what terrible things could possibly have happened to an attractive sleep-deprived woman in expensive clothing, wandering alone in a foreign country.

His mind was saturated with plots of slasher movies and horrible news headlines, which in all fairness had nothing to do with the lives of 99.9999% of their readers.

He began to scare himself and had to close his eyes to block the ideas out.

Trembling, he reminded himself he was in Canada, and reran the simulations in his head with this information.

After a while, he had come up with another worst-case scenario.

It was still pretty gloomy, but he could not shake it out of his head.

It kept coming back to him, in the form of a question.

Did she oversleep on a bus or something?

Chapter 56

Even before joining NASA, Smith Robin had always believed some conspiracy theories were true. What truly distinguished his conspiratorial beliefs from, say, the Global Lie was that in his theories the perpetuator always had some obvious, tangible benefits to gain.

For instance, he believed that daytime television was financed by foreign governments to curb the U.S. productivity, child beauty pageant was organized by the FBI to catch pedophiles, body shaming was promoted by beauty product companies, anti-body shaming was initiated by fast food producers, and voicemail was invented by psychiatrists to drive people crazy.

As the usage of voicemail became increasingly polarized, Smith got extremely confident in his voicemail theory. He observed that people either expected a 100% retrieval rate of voice messages or aggressively ignored the existence of that technology. He belonged to the pro-voicemail camp and suspected that Gina came from its archnemesis.

To confirm his suspicion, Smith had returned to the floor of Gina's room. Besides the manifest absence of Seth Nadir, the floor felt different from the morning. Smith could no longer sense someone watching him as he passed through the corridor. He figured it was because Round Ops had withdrawn.

Stopping at Gina's door, he thought he would give it a knock and then find her crying about the lost laptop, but something told him to forget about it.

The exposed wires of the electronic lock suggested that someone had tried to hack the door open.

The scratch on the key hole indicated that hacker also attempted to pick the door lock.

The removed peephole implied that the intruder then used a tool to turn the door handle from within.

The knob on the floor subtly hinted that whoever tried to break in eventually got frustrated and just hacked the bloody lock off.

Half expecting a trashed hotel room, Smith pushed the door open, and found a trashed hotel room with the body of Charles Peralta.

More precisely, it was the butt-naked body of Charles Peralta, sitting on the bed, watching daytime soap opera and blowing dry his hair.

"What the—"

"Close the door," hissed Charles. "I haven't got dressed."

Smith had never felt so confused about priorities before.

"Why are you still here? Ain't you supposed to grab the data and run?"

"I was," said Charles and pointed to the laptop next to his butt, "but I also needed to confirm I got the right disk drive, so I ran a decryption on it while I went to take a shower. Breaking down that damn door made me all sweaty."

"Can't you just do this later? What if Gina walks in now?"

"Why would she walk in? Isn't she supposed to be doing a presentation now?"

Smith was utterly speechless.

He looked at the laptop, which was running a program to decrypt the backup without using password. He looked closer and noticed its screen reflected the darkest side of Charles that he wished he could unsee. He was sure at least one person in this room was mad, but wasn't sure who. He decided to figure it out later.

"No time to do this. You have told Miranda to delete the cloud backup, right?" said Smith and packed the disk drive and laptop into a nearby carryall. The bag already contained another laptop, with a battered sticker that read "Property of Gina Stinson."

Looking quite dejected, Charles reached for his pants, but Smith suddenly did a finger-on-lip gesture that could either call for silence or invoke a *shinobi-jutsu*. Applying the game theory training he had received from Harvard BBA, Charles determined staying quiet was the dominant strategy regardless of what Smith intended to do.

"Someone is coming," whispered Smith, clearing any doubt that he was trying to perform a ninja technique.

"They can't see me like this," panicked Charles.

"I don't think anyone is supposed to."

Smith estimated, correctly, that he had time to brainstorm exactly three solutions with Charles before the footstep came to the half-closed door.

"I got an idea," said Charles. "When someone walks in, we kiss. I heard public display of affection can make people very uncomfortable. When they look away, we—"

"It does make me uncomfortable. Any other idea?"

"OK, OK. How about this. You pin me down, or I pin you down. You scream for help while I rip your pants off, and then when someone walks in—"

"How come all your ideas are sexual?"

"I got another one. It is nothing sexual and can explain my pantlessness. You pretend to be possessed by a demon, and I use my pants to hit you, as a kind of exorcism."

"Putting aside its exorcistic effectiveness, who would use their pants to hit someone?"

"My dad did, repeatedly," said Charles as matter-of-factly as an obituary, "except that he did it when he was still wearing it."

"So you two have seen the hot— I mean, Dr. Stinson this morning?"

asked Winston as he led Chandler and Ohi down the corridor like Dr. House doing a differential diagnosis with his team, but without his cane and an unrealistically attractive physician.

"We did," said Chandler, "but we just referred to her as the hottie from the banquet."

Winston felt offended on behalf of Dr. Stinson. He found it inappropriate to sexually objectify another human being. If anything, he felt Stinson should be intellectually objectified, because she was the key to overthrow the Global Lie.

Before he could protest against Chandler's male chauvinist remarks, Winston had stepped on a broken knob lying rather innocently outside of Dr. Stinson's room.

"Sensei, are you thinking what I am thinking?" said Ohi, staring intently at the lifeless knob.

"I think I am. And you, Chandler?"

"Me too. You were wondering why someone would install a knob on the carpet. I guess there is a trap door on the floor."

"No, man," said Winston with intellectual contempt. "I was thinking Dr. Stinson is freakishly strong, so don't shake her hand."

"Sensei, Mr. Chandler, am I the only one who thinks a crime has happened?"

Before Ohi could hear the "No," the half-opened door became completely opened, from which a naked man carrying a pile of clothing and a bag emerged. He looked familiar but was too naked for anyone to unblushingly study his face.

"What am I doing? Where am I?" asked the naked man unconvincingly.

"Mister, just go. No more nakedly wandering business," said another voice within the trashed room. "Or I will call the cops."

The naked man then pushed aside Winston, ran down the corridor and disappeared from a corner. None of the COW boys had said anything or tried to stop him.

"Geez, can you believe it?" said the other man who came out from the room. "That man just barged in, took off his clothes and watched TV at a stranger's room. Can you believe it is what just happened?"

Winston looked around himself to see if anyone would volunteer an answer.

"No… it sounds uncanny," said Ohi.

"Exactly!" said the man in a nice shirt. "It's so unbelievable."

The trio took another look at the knob under Winston's shoe, the damaged door, and that nice-shirt man. They were expecting more elaboration from him but that man seemed content with how things stood.

They all agreed that it was very unlikely for a man to wander into a stranger's room and take off his clothing for some TV entertainment. But they also surmised that if anything nefarious was going on, then an explanation better than this would have been offered. Therefore, they all logically accepted the said explanation and moved on from it.

"I think we have met before. You were with Dr. Stinson, weren't you?" said Winston. "Can I speak to her? I'm—"

"I know who you are. My name is Smith Johansson, by the way," said Smith Robin. "I was also looking for Gina, but she didn't pick up my calls. The door and everything else were already like this when I came in. Well, before that man unbelievably walked in and unbelievably gave a free strip show."

Smith wondered if he had pressed his luck with the too-fake-to-be-fake (or more academically known as TFTBF) line. It was the first time he applied this consulting technique, although he had read it countless times in business journals. Case studies had shown that TFTBF had a wide range of applications, from turning pet psychics into a respectable profession, to selling egg-shaped minerals for vaginal weightlifting purpose, to promoting urine drinking / ear candling / colon cleansing / crystal touching / prayer healing as alternative cancer treatments, to convincing customers that corporate America had their best interests in heart. As long as one kept a straight face, 40% of the time this technique worked every time.

"Have you called the police?" asked Ohi.

"I am about to," said Smith and walked past the three men, "and I am going to search for her. I suspect her disappearance had something to do with her presentation."

"Wait a minute," said Winston.

Smith stopped cold on his track. The hair on his back shot up and he could almost hear his own heartbeat. He slowly spun around to face the three men as he re-examined what went wrong with his TFTBF execution. He then realized the lessons learned exercise could wait and he must say something clever.

"..." was the best line he came up with.

"Let me come with you," said Winston. "I want to speak with her before the election tomorrow, and my friends have told me where they saw her this morning."

"..." repeated Smith, seeing it worked like a charm.

"Chandler, you call the cops and stay here until they come. Tell them to check the alibi of all summit attendees and call me if Dr. Stinson is found. Ohi, you go back to the summit and keep an eye on Kutner, Odinson and Song. I think one of them did it."

"Wins."

"Sensei."

"I know. I know. I know how cool I am right now."

"No, that's not what I am trying to say. Not at all," said Chandler. "You are doing this because you don't want the cops to find the weeds on you, right?" He took out a small plastic bag from his pants and tuck it in Winston's. "Take mine as well. And don't smoke it all in one go, son."

Chapter 57

Agent B felt confused by a call she just eavesdropped between Charles Peralta and Miranda Lin. It involved the retrieval of certain packages, taking care of something on the cloud, a lengthy discussion about Peralta's nudity, and what to do about it. She deduced they were having an affair. To help whoever would read her report make sense of it, agent B put in this conjecture as her closing remarks.

That conjecture successfully confused agent F, who was reading her screen from a distance.

Chapter 58

"... oh, so that's why you became a filmmaker in the first place?" said Smith while doing his witch-like hand gestures. "In a way, it is like why I became a life coach and a father. You know, to mess with people's minds."

"In my line of trade," said Winston with a grin, "it's called subverting expectation."

Ever since they left Gina's room, Smith had been steering the conversation like he was driving on the wrong side of a freeway. The technique he used was not entirely different from those employed by conversational narcissists. What he thought of the broken door knob? He had exactly the same model installed in his vacation house at Paris, the one he inherited from his great-grandmother, who was a nurse during World War I and allegedly had slept with Charlie Chaplin's second cousin. What about the trashed hotel room? He saw the exact same thing after the after-after-party of Kanye West' 40th birthday party, to which he was invited because he (not Kanye West) had won an award for third-party risk management.

So far, so good.

The unbelievability of his TFTBF line remained unscathed.

In fact, Winston was extremely glad that his new acquaintance always drew the conversation back to himself, as he was tired of explaining how he captured the horror in his movie characters or what it felt like to be a director famous for fending off lawsuits. The only thing that bugged him was Smith never asked if he really believed the Earth was flat. Should he have asked, Winston would be able to tell him how much this question bugged him. Since this question never came up, Winston had been looking for a chance to bring it up and his endeavor had been going nowhere.

"Tell me. Do you believe...," said Smith and paused, who had all Winston's attention in a split second, "this is the coffee shop your friends mentioned?"

It was a small café in the middle of nowhere, at least five blocks away from the nearest commercial building. The ideal location for aspiring writers to stare at a blank page for ten hours straight with two federally mandated coffee breaks.

When the duo walked in, there was only one aspiring writer sitting, and staring, at the corner. Winston ordered two coffees and asked the barista if she had seen a woman in red.

"Sorry, didn't see no woman like that."

"How about a woman in rose vale long overcoat?" asked Smith. "Rose vale as in moderate red in ISCC-NBS System of Color Designation."

"Oh, sorry, I did," said the barista and went to the back of the house. A moment later, she returned with a purse.

"When I yelled at her about the purse, she was already through the door and didn't look back. I must be not loud enough. I'm terribly sorry about that."

"Did she come alone?"

"Eh...," the barista thought hard about it, "sorry, can't remember. See, I have too many customers around."

Smith looked around the coffee shop and realized that "many" was a very subjective concept.

After listening to a bit more apology, Smith opened the purse with Winston at a nearby table. Inside it were a smaller purse, some cosmetics, a pill bottle, some papers and her phone.

"I don't know what to make of this," said both of them, each holding an item from the bigger purse. "Let me see yours."

They exchanged what they were looking at and said, "This shouldn't be here. What? Yours too? Why are you copying what I say? Stop."

Before they could say another word, Winston's phone rang.

"It was my assistant," said Winston a minute later. "He got an update about the summit attendees' alibi. Between 10:30 a.m., which was the last time my friends saw Dr. Stinson around here, and 2 p.m., everyone's alibi checked out."

"That's weird," said Smith as he unlocked Gina's cellphone using the hack he had read from a Dan Brown novel. "There is this unread message asking Gina to meet at 2 p.m. I thought whoever sent this must have kidnapped her, but—"

Buzz, buzz.

This time it was Smith's phone.

"It was a government friend of mine," said Smith like he was humbly bragging. "Gina has been found. She's in the holding cell of a Toronto police station."

"Wait, isn't it like the first place we looked at?" said Winston. "We did the whole routine of *The Hangover* before we got here. We checked the precinct, the zoo, hospitals, tattoo shops, strip clubs, pawn shops and all the buddha temples in Toronto."

"The thing is," added Smith, who was still unsure why they couldn't just come straight to this coffee house, "it is in Toronto, Jefferson, Ohio, United States."

Chapter 59

The Sapphire Dome ballroom of Greendale Convention Centre had gone through a lot of ups and downs. In its less glorious days, it was the venue of dictionary trade fair and annual director conferences of MacCheddar & Co. In its better days, it hosted the first International Forum for Handrail Sanitizers, the 40th – 46th Design Awards for Shoe Sole Patterns, the KrazyCoral National Championship 2020, and the first, the last and the most successful Economist Beauty Pageant. Depending on who was asked, the election day of the president of the United Ways was either the peak of its history or a page intentionally left blank in its biography.

Waiting outside were hundreds of impatient voters. Fifteen minutes had passed since the supposed opening hour of Sapphire Dome but they still couldn't get in to cast the votes that, statistically speaking, had a lot more impact than all the other votes they had ever casted in life, combined. They were getting anxious, however, not so much because they deeply cared about the democracy of geocentric organizations, but more because they needed the receipt for attending the movie premiere of *Them (Part I)*. We will come back to this movie next chapter, which is a lot more interesting than this one.

Minute by minute, the friendly chatter outside of the ballroom was drowned out by moaning and grumble. Fortunately, not all Seekers were fond of venting their frustration through verbal violence. The more civilized ones understood that no amount of swearing or jeering would magically open the door, so they wrote some threatening notes to be slipped under the door.

As any educated adults would reasonably expect, this brainy approach worked like a charm.

As soon as the papers were slipped in, the door swung open. Adel ushered the voters to the ballroom / polling station, collected their cell phones, and invited them to wait behind the stanchions. On the other side of the stanchions stood the four POTUWS presidential candidates.

"Sorry for the waiting," said Adel. "I was having a discussion with the election committee about an impromptu request from Mr. Kanshū, who wishes to speak to you before the voting. Initially we were worried if it would be a violation to the election silence rule, but then we confirmed we don't really have that rule in place. So we're good."

Adel took a glance at the Big Four representatives on his left and wondered whether they were too lazy or too stupid to raise any objection. He understood there was only a very fine line between those qualities.

"Therefore, before the voting begins, I am going to pass the mic to Mr. Kanshū. Please keep it short."

Under the gazes of more than six hundred people, Winston came to the front. He had thought of a less dramatic way to do this, but Smith had convinced him that the Seekers deserved to know the truth of their future leader.

"What I am going to tell you is about Dr. Gina Stinson. Not the stand-in we saw yesterday. I mean the real one who has diamond-solid evidence to debunk the Global Lie.

"Three days ago, she gave all presidential candidates, including myself, a preview of the materials she was going to present yesterday. Apparently, her discovery had upset someone among us. And that *someone* has tried to keep it as a secret from you. From all of you."

The Seekers looked to each other to make sense of what they just heard. A few dramatic ones even let out an audible gasp.

With that, Winston knew he had hit all the right buttons.

Inside knowledge.

Secrecy.

Cover-up.

He scanned around the crowd of Seekers, and gave a nod to the man approaching from his right.

"The man here is Smith Johansson, a close friend of Dr. Stinson. He has evidence to support my claim."

Without saying a word, Smith took the microphone from Winston and pressed it against a dark red object on his palm."

"Dr. Stinson," said the synthetic voice coming from his palm, "if you want your level eighty *KrazyCoral* account back, come to the address I just texted you at 2 p.m. sharp."

"This message," said Winston, "was sent to Dr. Stinson's cellphone yesterday morning. And we are going to find out together who sent it."

"Oh, oh, oh," said Adel in excitement. "Are you going to reverse the voice masking and analyze the acoustic frequency spectrum?"

"No."

"You have traced the anonymous message back to the burner phone that sent it and then you cross-checked the CCTV footage of the shop that sold the phone?"

"Nope."

"You used the message's timestamp and file size to find the cell towers that handled the message, triangulated its originating location, compared it to the GPS history of—"

"No, seriously, stop it. Let me show you."

Winston and Smith exchanged a look.

The silent tension among them quickly spread across the room.

The only sound lingering within Sapphire Dome was the humming of its air-conditioners.

For a few seconds, everyone held their breath in anticipation of the evidence.

Smith raised Gina's phone and pressed a button on its screen.

"... *leaves, trunk, whateeeever you are... I believe that the heartwood is strooong... once more, you kneeeel down to Thor...*"

The tone of "My Heartwood Goes On," whose copyright status was still in dispute, drew everyone's attention back to the box of cell phones collected by Adel.

"Wait a minute," said Adel and turned to one of the men behind the stanchions. "This is yours, Mr. Odinson. You blackmailed Dr. Stinson?! What did you do to her?"

Another audible gasp from the crowd.

"No, I didn't do anything," said Odinson, "other than sending that message. For the Tree's sake, she didn't even read it. It wasn't blue tick yesterday."

"Actually," said Winston while slowly walking around the other candidates, "White Jesus was telling the truth. He certainly has blackmailed Dr. Stinson, but he didn't do anything to her. He didn't even meet her at all. Someone else got to her before she could see the message." He stopped and fixed a look at one of them. "YOU."

Adel followed Winston's line of sight and found himself staring at a broccoli. He zoomed out and noted it was stuck in Chairman Song's teeth.

"I don't knew what you is talking about," Song disagreed so strongly that his verbs did not agree with the subjects.

"So Chairman Song also blackmailed Dr. Stinson?!"

"No, I would never do things like that," said Song. "Yes, we met, but I didn't blackmail her. I only—"

"You only offered a bag of gold bricks in exchange for her silence, didn't you?" said Winston, holding the papers he found in Gina's purse. "Seriously, why would you leave your cue cards to her? Those words are not even that hard to pronounce."

"She complained I was reading too slow. You have any idea how heavy one million dollars' worth of gold bars are? They almost killed me."

Adel was overwhelmingly underwhelmed by how quickly Song confessed. Having observed numerous flat Earth experiments that got covertly rounded off by NASA, he had seen his fair share of anticlimactic events. He just didn't think he would see two in the short span of five minutes.

"Okay, I got it now," he tried to summarize. "Ben paid Dr. Stinson off before she could be extorted by Odinson. Half of the POTUWS candidates are bad at covering their tracks. Got it. End of story. Now, let's get the polling started. We have a movie to—"

"No, it is not yet over"

Adel's eyes rolled so far back that he could see his own cranium.

"Dr. Stinson didn't take the bribe," said Winston. "In fact, she left the coffeehouse without any of her belongings, stole a firetruck, kidnapped a beaver, crossed the border without paper, robbed a gangster, hijacked a school bus and ended up in an Ohio precinct for DUI."

"And for those who care," said Smith, "the firetruck, the kidnapped beaver and Gina are all on their way back to here as we speak."

"O. M. G," spelled one of the voters, after a sigh of relief. "Chairman Song roofied her?"

"I have no idea what you mean," said Song and used his phone to translate the word "roofied." "Okay, now I know what you meant, but I didn't drug her."

"He is telling the truth," said Smith. "I have checked the pills in Gina's purse. Someone has replaced her ulcer meds with Rohypnol. And there is only one person who knows about her condition *and* had a chance to replace her meds."

Adel looked at his watch very deliberately as if he wanted to impress people with his expensive watch, but that wasn't his purpose. He simply wished the excessively explanatory dialogue would come to an end.

"Mr. Kutner," added Smith, "I remember you went to Gina's room yesterday morning."

Hundreds of gazes turned to the pandit.

Adel didn't bother to ask how the drug switch was forensically confirmed, but wished Kutner would make a clever comeback. Otherwise, he didn't see the point of continuing with the election.

"What," said Kutner, "I was... I mean, I didn't...eh... you know. You see what I am saying?"

Chapter 60

It is finally time to talk about the fictional documentary *Them (Part I)*. We will come to why it is important to talk about it in a bit.

Originally known as *Lie, Kill & Rule: Step into the Darkness – A Complete Chronicle,* it was meant to be a self-contained direct-to-streaming movie that would declare the United Ways' canonical view of *Their* identities and motives. From casting to hairstyling to score composing to shooting to editing to dubbing to sound mixing to color grading to re-shooting and everything between editing and color grading again, that crowd-funded movie was in development limbo.

However, the previous statement didn't do justice to how relatively smooth the movie's production was. If, for whatever reasons – for instance, to meet the word count of a film analysis assignment or to achieve some romantic effect when writing a movie review – one draws an analogy between the production of *Them (Part I)* and a journey through Dante's nine circles of hell, it was the scripting that went through the second to nineth circles of inferno.

For a long time, the screenplay co-writers could only agree on one thing: The scripts would be written in Courier font. They couldn't even get past the font size and spacing, let alone where the page number should be put. Their irreconcilable differences, however, helped them agree on one more thing: They couldn't work together.

After working independently for a few months, the four screenwriters re-grouped and were pleased to discover that their creative differences didn't get worse. The investors were also happy to learn that they now had four equally filmable scripts for the price of one. A party was thrown, champagnes were popped, toasts were raised, people got drunk, and luckily no one got pregnant.

All things went well, until the first day of table read.

According to the script developed by Disk Earth Society, the movie should go all the way back to a lunch more than two thousand years ago, where a bunch of Jews who had too much wine after breakfast played with the idea of nailing another Jew. Several meals later, that Jew was nailed, his fans were upset and many other Jews got hated for that. In the absence of social media, the hatred didn't get the Jews' careers cancelled and their descendants did pretty well at whatever they did, be it business or science. Naturally, they got more hated than before. Very, very, very, very naturally, they thought that if their haters knew the Earth was a flat disk, then they would be even more hated, so they did what anyone with the same influence and power as they did would naturally do in their position. They lied. *They* lied the Earth was a ball. Scene.

As appealing as DES's historical epic was, the actors found it didn't sit too well with the light-hearted comedy written by TYDF. In the latter, the movie would begin with a montage of the USSR's launch of *Sputnik 1* in 1957 and *Vostok 1* in 1961, followed by the Moon landing in 1969, and ended with the announcement of Shuttle-*Mir* program in 1993. After that, the movie would follow the NASA and Roscosmos representatives from a meeting room to a washroom, to a taxi, to a restaurant, to a riverside, to a balcony, to another restaurant, and to a train station, in a style not dissimilar with *Before Sunrise*, not too different from *Before Sunset* and almost identical with *Before Midnight*. The two heterosexual males would talk about the futility of space race, budget cut of NASA, non-existence of the Russian space station *Mir*, fabrication of Moon landing, and failed attempts to launch satellites. In the movie's climax, the NASA guy would be surprised that nothing was ever sent to the space by Russians, while the Roscosmos guy would realize nothing was sent to the space, ever. Before parting their ways at the train station, the duo would share a passionate handshake and agree to keep the Earth spherical.

With a stroke of genius, the director found a way to seamlessly combine the two stories, by treating the DES version as flashback of the NASA guy. However, he then found the main characters' biological makeup didn't match the plot of All-Ways version, where *They* were shapeshifting reptilian aliens whose ruling over humanity mysteriously depended on the unquestioning belief in a spherical Earth.

Making a self-consistent movie that could please all three geocentric creeds became a tad challenging, but the producer proved it wasn't impossible. With a bit of retconning, the arrival and evolution of kitten-eating reptilians were perfectly integrated with the rise of Hebrew civilization. It not only justified the five-thousand-dollar budget for visual effects, but also had the unforeseen benefit of explaining the lack of archaeological evidence for the biblical Exodus.

But then a supporting cast member noticed that the backstory of extraterrestrial reptilian-turned-Jewish elites flatly contradicted the script approved by White Jesus. In that version, *They* had dual membership in Freemasonry and Illuminati, sent their children to the same schools as the Rothschild family, engineered the New World Order during the day, and worshiped the Satan at night. So far so good. The problem was: Rather than being aliens, *They* discovered aliens. The movie would start with *Their* first contact at Antarctica in the 1820s, and ended with *Their* establishment of Area 51 in the 1950s. Morgan Freeman, or someone who could do a good Morgan Freeman impression, would supposedly lend his voice to explain that all the probes, satellites, rockets and shuttles sent to space were just props to distract the public from the underground experiments on alien technology.

That contradiction almost ruined the best geocentric movie ever made. But it didn't, because the movie editor had a brilliant idea that saved the day.

At her suggestion, all four scripts were filmed without changing a single word. No flashback. No retcon. No time travel shenanigans. *Lie, Kill & Rule: Step into the Darkness – A Complete Chronicle* was retooled as, to use the words of its synopsis, "the first-of-its-kind trilogy that faithfully depicts the rise of Global Lie perpetuators in four equally real parallel universes."

Now we come to the part of why it is important to talk about the movie *Them (Part I)*.

After the little whodunit drama in last chapter, there was no doubt that the DES presidential candidate would win the POTUWS race. In the absence of any cliffhanger, Day 4 of the True Earth Summit would have been incredibly uneventful, had the United Ways not scheduled the world premiere of *Them (Part I)* in between the polling of POTUWS and the election announcement.

No, none of the four scripts got *Their* identities right. We will come back to that bit later.

Chapter 61

As repeatedly mentioned and implied, there was no suspense

whatsoever regarding who would become the first president of the United Ways. One may therefore reasonably assume that when the votes were counted, Pandit Kutner, Chairman Song and Pope Odinson would be smoking, drinking, praying, sobbing, self-harming, high-speed driving, suicide contemplating, or doing whatever rituals they needed to go through the stressful moment.

That is where a reasonable assumption could go horribly wrong.

To begin with, Kutner had boarded the first flight that would go anywhere but the countries with extradition treaties with Canada. According to his lawyer, the pandit had gone on a self-imposed exile to obtain the sacred text *Sutra of Cosmic Turtle*, but promised to return before the Great Turbulation.

On the other hand, Song was occupied by an extraordinary general meeting called by the TYDF Central Committee, who demanded to know why the gold bars were written off as "loss on asset disposal." Song insisted the accounting treatment had been audited, the auditor insisted the audit working papers existed, and the auditor's lawyer insisted the audit working papers must not be disclosed on grounds of national security and state secrets.

As for Odinson, he didn't go anywhere. He just quietly watched his phone with a half-suppressed smile, while the election results were announced.

"Abed Kutner, thirty-seven votes.

"Ben Song, sixty-four votes.

"Gabriel Odinson, one hundred and eighty-two votes.

"And finally, Winston Kanshū, three hundred and seventeen votes!"

For the penultimate time in the summit, Winston was showered with applause as he walked up to the stage for a speech. He was almost as excited as Odinson, who had taken a loan to bet on Winston when *gambling-grandma55699.com.uk* was still quoting 51 odds for the DES presidential candidate.

"Thank you. Thank you for putting me here," said Winston, finishing the whole victory speech he had prepared.

He was about to leave the stage when Maeve handed him a card from the crowd and pointed him back to the microphone.

"I would," read Winston reluctantly, "also like to thank my

campaign manager, Maeve Walsh, who is standing over there and not an NSA agent. I repeat, she is not an NSA agent.

"And er... I would like to thank Maeve's parents, her friends, her high school teacher Mr. Henderson, and everyone who donated to 'Make America Flat Again.' Maeve and I could not have done this without these wonderful people.

"Now, say something about your election promises."

It took a moment before Winston could hear what he just said.

He took another moment to process it and see if it made sense.

It didn't.

He thought he might have missed a line or misremembered the context, so he took another look at the script, which read exactly the way he had said it.

A few more moments later, he finally noticed the last sentence was underlined.

"I mean," continued Winston, "I will talk to you about *my* election promises, which I certainly remember. Don't you, ever, ever, ever doubt if I have forgotten about them. I don't need anyone to remind me of what I said," he felt his words might be too harsh and therefore added, "although I respect your rights to do that."

"*Antarctica!*" someone shouted from the crowd.

"Of course," said Winston, letting out a sigh from his nostrils, "of course I remember that. I promised you a trip to the edge of the world and I am going to deliver."

Sapphire Dome burst into wild applause again. Until this very moment, it never occurred to the Seekers that they might see the seven-hundred-foot ice wall at Antarctica with their very own eyes.

"When?" asked another, who cared deeply about the shape of Earth.

"Er... I heard the best weather there is in December, so I would suggest—"

"Some of us have holiday plans already," shouted the same person.

"Then let's do it one month from now. I will work out the details with my vice-chairwoman."

Winston looked up and saw Maeve gesture him to flip the script around.

"Until next time, don't forget to like, comment, share and subscribe to Maeve's channel BigLoveMaeve2E731."

* * *

Smith didn't hear the benefits of BigLoveMaeve2E731 channel membership. He had left the ballroom to take a phone call.

"Gina? Where are you now?

"Sure, I will help you find a lawyer and meet you there.

"Your computer? Er… I am not sure about it. You know, apparently someone broke into your room yesterday. The police said whoever did it also cleared your minibar and watched a dirty movie.

"Yes, this is the worst crime I have ever seen.

"Hello? I didn't catch you.

"What do you mean the beaver is gone?

"Hello? Hello?

"Er… I want to hear the good news first.

"Good that you found it. What about the bad news?

"It sounds pretty bad. I hope the driver is not allergic to pet or biting in general. Let me guess, the good news is your car is waiting for red light, right?

"No? O, I forgot, you already told me the good one.

"What was that sound?

"Hello? Hello? Is everything OK?"

Chapter 62

"Breaking news.

"A police car was caught on tape losing control on Highway 401. The policeman behind the wheel said he was attacked by a beaver, which was kidnapped earlier by an American tourist. Fortunately, neither the policeman nor the beaver sustained any injury.

"The police are still investigating if the incident was a terrorist attack and if it has any connection to the thief of firetruck from yesterday. So far, Bleach White Movement, KKK 2.0, Proud Racists and True Canadians have claimed responsibilities for the attack.

"The mayor of Toronto also addressed the incident during a fundraiser this afternoon. He condemned the American kidnapper and urged for building a wall along the Canada-America border. He repeatedly emphasized he was not xenophobic and the wall was only meant to keep away people with lots of problems, like, quote, those poor bastards who covet our affordable insulin, would-be criminals who fancy our low incarceration rate, and cowards who run away from their mass shooting lunatics, end quote."

"Thank you, Jim. Another news. The two women who committed mysterious serial cleaning are still at large. The RCMP cautions citizens to remain diligent but do not panic..."

Chapter 63

Why the flat is he here again? Britta thought as she took a seat across Mosby from HR, who had no business in the status meetings of R.D.G.A.R.

Normally she would have asked Smith the same question, but he still looked rather bummed out by the accident of Gina Stinson, who had been in a coma for two weeks. Not that she cared about her colleague's emotional state. No. She simply didn't want to hear another human being's whining.

She had heard enough from herself.

To be fair, it hadn't been her day. This morning Britta was assigned to run a background check on everyone who made a donation to "Show BOB the Curve," because her boss found it probable that the donors were "onto something big." This task was much more daunting than she initially thought. Although the campaign only raised a few thousand dollars for the purchase of a satellite, falling a bit short of its aspirational goal of one million dollars, the sheer number of five-dollar donors meant that it would be weeks before she had a chance to take on another interesting assignment, should it exist.

To provide more context, it hadn't been her week either. Britta had spent forty hours listening to the locker room talks of Draymond Green, Kyrie Irving, and several other NBA stars who were not entirely sure if the Earth was round. Topics related to balls came up a lot, but she couldn't be sure if they were discussing the shape of Earth, the games, or certain body parts. To get more context, she had made a formal request to her boss for remotely activating the targets' cell phone cameras, but the reply was, "Nice try. We are not helping you make porn again."

To make the case even stronger, although one might argue it was unnecessary, it hadn't been her month either. Last month she was assigned to investigate the increasing number of athletes who allegedly subscribed to flat Earth belief. It was quite an undertaking. For weeks, Britta struggled to find any connection among former professional boxer Carl Froch, football wide receiver Stefon Diggs, wrestler AJ Styles, and football quarterback Geno Smith. She checked their text messages, phone records, Internet browsing histories (that was a biggie), psychological profiles, travel histories, bank statements, play statistics, Netflix watch lists, and library checkout records. Nothing turned up, and "nothing" didn't just refer to library checkout records. In her final report, she reluctantly concluded that the only thing the alleged flaters had in common were that the sports they played had a high chance of causing traumatic brain injury.

To round things up, it hadn't been her year either, but that had absolutely nothing to do with her job as a NSD senior analyst, so let's just leave it there.

What *did* have something to do with her job was the video she played to her R.D.G.A.R. working group colleagues.

It was the first video on BigLoveMaeve2E731 channel that had more than one thousand likes. A woman who must have either eaten too many carrots or had a really bad artificial tanner appeared on the screen and introduced herself as the vice-chairwoman of Disk Earth Society, slash, the vice-president of the United Ways. Having reminded the viewers to like and subscribe, she began mumbling about the lunch she just had.

Conscious that the three-hour-long video might be too much for the uninitiated, Britta fast-forwarded to twenty minutes later, when the video became a split screen. A man in aloha shirt appeared on the right panel and introduced himself as the newly elected POTUWS, which sounded exactly the same as POTUS, except that the speaker must be having a seizure when it came to the TU sound.

The video was sped up again to skip past the next thirty minutes, where the two hosts discussed the latest season of *Stranger Things*. Charles, who had been sitting at the corner, asked what if some cryptic messages were buried in the chit chat. Smith agreed and created an action item for thoroughly analyzing the full video. It was assigned to Britta.

When the video resumed playing at normal speed, the two hosts mentioned they had some exciting news to share. The teasing of how exciting the news was went on for about five minutes, before it was interrupted by an unskippable YouTube ad. It was followed by another skippable ad and five more minutes of teasing. When the excitement in meeting room 5C of Mary W. Jackson NASA Headquarters building reached the historical peak, the POTUWS broke the bloody news.

"The United Ways and its registered members would be restructured as one global – correction – one international organization known as the Big Flat Earth Federation, or BFEF in short. As we speak, our lawyers and consultants are doing their best to obtain tax exempt status in the seventy countries we operate.

"To ensure a smooth transition and avoid unnecessary confusion, my title will continue to be POTUWS, and our branding adviser will work out its full name within twenty billable hours. We appreciate your patience and support during the transition period."

Britta put the video on pause to give her colleagues some time to process the information.

A lifetime of silence ensued.

The R.D.G.A.R. working group tried to imagine the impact coming from the consolidation of all geocentric creeds. They tried to make sense of what it would mean to them and to the world at large.

They couldn't.

Because it was too huge.

"Is BFEF going to be in our jurisdiction?" Charles burst out nervously. "Will we be using U.S. taxpayers' money to round off those flatees' activities in Russia? Will we need to play balls with JAXA and CNSA? You know how much I hate people speaking foreign languages. And, and does our union know about this? Can we get the same benefits as ESA? Wait, you don't think our pay will be cut to match those losers in ISRO, do you? O god, will *They* dissolve NASA or merge it with the other seventy-six government space agencies? Most of them still think the Earth is spherical for crying out loud!"

"Don't panic," shouted Britta in a friendly manner. "Procurement is drafting a tender to hire consultants to provide advice on this. All the short-listed candidates must have worked on Brexit, so we will be in good hands."

Smith knew they were not.

Smith's skepticism was not unfound. In fact, whenever a consulting firm says in a proposal that they have "rich experience" in certain challenges, or sectors, or technologies, or regulations, or solutions, or projects, what they often mean is that their network of international affiliates, as a whole, have those experiences.

One shouldn't get too excited about those credentials either, because the chance is that the staff with hands-on experience have already left the network firms.

If those experienced staff happen to remain employed, there is still a good chance that they have been promoted to a very senior level. So senior that you will only see their faces in the proposal's "Our SME" section and, if the project is lucrative enough, several status meetings.

In the event that those experienced staff are not yet made partners, more often than not they work in an overseas office and will never fly in or contribute in any meaningful way to the project due to a wide variety of reasons, such as other work commitments, dispute over revenue sharing, risk management policies, long-outstanding inter-office bills, or simply poor leadership.

If those experienced staff are indeed at the working level *and* employed in the local office, there is still a very high chance that they have worked on similar challenges, sectors, technologies, regulations, solutions or projects once and only once. One is infinitely better than zero, but usually not the number people intuitively gather from "rich experience."

Smith didn't share his concerns with his colleagues, partly because it would be against *The Code*, and partly because Britta didn't play the video to discuss the corporate restructuring of the United Ways. She said there was another troubling news, exactly ninety minutes after the BFEF announcement.

"Before we go," said the POTUWS, "I want to give you an update of the 'Edge of the World' trip.

"Some of you have sent me some very passionate DM in graphic language, saying such a trip is impossible because of the Antarctic Treaty. You know what, Maeve has got it figured out.

"If you come from a country that isn't a treaty party, like Iran or Israel, then you don't need anyone's permission to get there. And for the rest of us, the operators of Antarctica cruise tours will get the permit for you. Do your own research, please.

"By the way, I want to give a shoutout to MFwithaPHD69, who claims that those trips are impossible because they always start at Australia, New Zealand or South American, none of which truly exist. Well, I don't know about your research methodology, but I have personally been Australia. And I can confirm it is not upside down."

Two seconds later, Maeve on the left panel laughed at her boss's remark.

"Okay, back to the trip itself. Now, you know it is *possible* to happen. Hear this out.

"It is. Going. To happen.

"Using the proceeds from *Them (Part I)*, which by the way has become the Netflix Top Ten in comedy, BFEF will fully sponsor five lucky Seekers to take a cruise trip from Hobart, Australia to Eastern Antarctica. Application for the trip is completely free for BFEE members."

"That's it?" asked Charles with a healthy amount of conceit, while the video described the fee structure for BFEE three-tier membership plans. "Come on, we have dealt with this before. Those cruise ships will follow our designated route and no one will see the ice wall covered by dynamic hologram."

Britta didn't say a word and let the video continue.

"Now, some of you may think, 'Hey, how do I know if the Antarctica we are seeing is not a hologram or a huge dome like the one in *Truman Show*?' That's a good question. A very good question. I have got it—"

A skippable-after-five-seconds ad popped up.

Britta clicked skip.

It was followed by another fifteen-second unskippable ad, which successfully convinced Britta to never buy the advertised product.

"… figured out." The video continued, "Four days after the cruise ship leaves Hobart, another group of lottery winners will depart from Ushuaia, Argentina. Their destination will be… (drum roll)"

The screen cut to a conventional map of Antarctica. At its bottom right quadrant was a red cross, marking the destination of the crew from Hobart. A moment later, another blue cross appeared at its top left quadrant, marking the destination of the crew from Ushuaia.

"Antarctica Peninsula.

"If the global map is correct, the red team from Hobart and the blue team from Ushuaia will arrive at the east and west coasts on the same day. In five or six days, they would meet each other on Ross Sea."

The screen refreshed to show a red arrow travelling leftward from the red cross, and a blue arrow— Okay, you got the idea. At the end, they met at the bottom left quadrant of the map.

"However, if the global map is wrong, which you and I believe is the case, then red and blue teams will literally be a world apart from each other."

The screen then cut to the flat Earth map that was audaciously incorporated into the United Nations logo. The red cross was located at the top right quadrant while the blue one— You know what, you probably don't need the visuals.

"It will take weeks, if not months, for the two ships to cross path. In other words, if the two teams do not run into each other within a week, we can conclude the Earth is not spherical even without seeing the edge."

Another ad popped up.

Chapter 64

"Whoa, whoa, whoa. Don't click skip. I have some very important message to share with you.

"This is Tina Phalange, who just earned one hundred and thirty thousand dollars last month in passive income, because she listened to me and started selling BleedCoins on the Internet.

"This is Joey Adam, who just paid off his student loan, bought a Porsche, crashed it, bought two more, one for himself and another for the kid whose mother he crashed, and never has to spend a day working.

"How did they do that?

"It doesn't require any prior experience, training, talents, skills, education, intelligence, or anything valued by our society. With minimal amount of initial investment, you can just sit there, with pants at your ankles, watching old movies from your mom's basement, while generating six-figure income per month. For those of you who are less math-savvy, six-figure income means at least a hundred thousand dollars. Are you still with me?

"All you need to do is to spend less than thirty minutes a week to manage your BleedCoin business. And when you get good at it, you only need fifteen minutes per week.

"And if you don't know what BleedCoins are, it is totally okay. I don't expect you to.

"It's something totally new, invented in Germany, refined by the Japanese, and getting momentum in China. It's not MLM. It's not e-Commerce. It's not drop shipping. It's not penis enlargement surgery or anything like that.

"Since we are in an ad with only ninety seconds, it is not possible to fully explain it to you right now. But if you check out the link here, you can register for free to my online course about BleedCoins. You will also get a discount for my advanced courses on how to use the YTB method to sell BleedCoins.

"Hundreds of thousands of people have taken my courses and have their lives forever changed for the better.

"It is very easy, I guarantee. And if you don't find the paid courses helpful, you can always ask for a refund. Under my forty-day refund policy, all it takes is one click of a button for you to get your money back.

"Click the link now. I really want you to be as successful as I am.

Because. Why wouldn't I?"

Chapter 65

If one lacked the incentive to commit suicide during office hours, one might try working as an analyst at NASA's National Surveillance Department, also known as No Such Department. If the incentive was still not strong enough, one might further volunteer to run background check on the donors of "Show BOB the curve."

This task might sound simple, but was extremely soul-crushing.

Besides diligently checking the donors for any affiliation with geocentric organizations, the background check involved a thirty-minute phone interview, which per se was quasi-impossible in the 21st century. Under the pretense of academic research or, much more often, phone sex, the interviewer would gauge, among others, whether the interviewee believed in the existence of Wyoming. If the reply was affirmative, the interviewer would further ask "Have you been to Wyoming?", "Do you know anyone from Wyoming?", and "Do you know anybody who has been to Wyoming?" If all the replies were "No" and the respondent still insisted the state of Wyoming existed, then they were considered by NSD a red flag. The idea was that anyone stubborn enough to have unshakable faith in Wyoming's existence must have the psychological make-up required for debunking the Global Lie.

If the respondent happened to be a Wyoming resident or answered "Yes" to any of the three questions, then the interviewer would repeat the same process, replacing Wyoming with the state of Idaho or the whole country of Finland. So on and so forth.

As mentioned above, it was a criminally mind-numbing task. Anyone doing this for more than eight hours a day would develop unconditional disgust of phone screen, dial pad, speaker, microphone and basically anything related to telecommunication technology.

That was why Britta got uncharacteristically worked up when her R.D.G.A.R. work phone rang.

"What's this?"

"This is beta. I have visual on Pizzaman. Over."

"This is Britta. Who the flat is beta and what the flat is Pizzaman? Over."

"This is beta again, I am Charles. Didn't we agree that my code name is beta and the POTUWS is Pizzaman? You know, because of the Pizza Earth map. Over."

"No, we never agreed on that. And where do you see the POTUWS again?"

"He just got off from a taxi at the port of Ushuaia," whispered Charles. "He is now approaching *Rey Azul*, which will leave the port of Ushuaia in about an hour. He is greeted by five flatees, who, judging from their behaviors, I can only assume have never seen the sea. Over."

"This is alpha."

"And who the flat is alpha!"

"My bad, this is Smith. Charles, did you say you saw Winston Kanshū at the port? But his Instagram shows he is taking a dump at the airport."

"It must be him," said Charles. "Hold on a second, I will send you guys his picture."

Despite being on the line, Mosby remained completely silent. He was still trying to figure out why he was assigned to surveil the BFEF red team that departed from the Port of Hobart four days ago.

Actually, saying Mosby was on surveillance duty was as much an overstatement as saying all men in a van distributing free candies must be pedophiles. Among the fifty passengers aboard *Bloody Helm*, he was only one of the forty-four plants placed by NASA, Roscosmos, ISA, ISA again[3], and six other space agencies whose acronyms were uninspiringly a combination of the founding countries' initials and the letters *A*, *I*, and/or *S*. None of them will be spelt out because none of them is important for understanding Mosby's duties.

But to understand Mosby's assignment, one must first understand what the other forty-three plants were doing on *Bloody Helm*.

What they did was not entirely differently from what an ordinary

---

[3] The rumor goes that Iranian Space Agency deliberatively chose its English name to take a piss out of Israeli Space Agency.

date rapist did on an average night. They spiked the flatees' drinks, waited till they passed out, and gently carried them away. What distinguished their behaviors from those acquaintance raping citizens was that they took the unconscious flatees to a seaplane and then flew to an identical ship a thousand miles away, before platonically tucking them in.

Mosby was tasked to observe if any of the plants were indeed date rapists. For humanity, rights, morality, principles, equality, and similar reasons.

After repeating the same maneuver four nights in a row, he began to dream of sleeping when he slept in the morning. That was why when the picture from Charles came through, he genuinely thought the man in aloha shirt was the president of Big Flat Earth Federation.

"You face-blind racist," said Britta politically correctly, "it is not Winston Kanshū. That's his personal assistant!"

"What?" said Charles. "Isn't he supposed to lead the blue team?"

Before Charles could finish his sentence, Britta had pulled up the movie maker's Instagram and confirmed that he just took a selfie in the washroom of Ministro Pistarini International Airport, more than one thousand eight hundred miles away from the port of Ushuaia.

She found it very confusing.

And by "it" she didn't mean the brown, floating object she saw in the picture.

"Robin," said Britta, "call Kanshū. Call him now!"

Chapter 66

Buzz. Buzz.

"Hey, amigo. Didn't expect a call from you. It has been a month. How is everything?

"Cool. And... how is Dr. Stinson?

"O... I am sorry to hear that.

"I am telling you, the NASA bastards who did this to her will pay for it.

"Of course it was NASA. That beaver is just a scape-beaver.

"Anyway, I will prove it to you after proving the Earth is flat.

"Yeah, you saw that too?

"Yes, I am in Argentina now. It's pretty nice.

"You know what, I am not supposed to tell you, but I am not exactly in Ushuaia. I just arrived at Buenos Aires.

"I can't tell you. I really can't, but I will be able to show the world real soon."

"Well, yes, I can, but then you have to be here.

"No way, you are coming to Argentina for a vacation?

"And you are on your way to the airport now?!

"And you haven't planned where to go?!!

"That is unbelievable!!!

"OK, I am staying anyway until tomorrow morning. You can try this number again when you get here."

Chapter 67

Agent A had lost count of how many times the Global Lie was almost blown. Off the top of his head were the *#miss_you#blue_balls* fiasco, the *12 Years Hanged in Balance* scandal, and, most recently, "The Proof" near-miss.

Comparing the "Edge of the World" trip to those close calls, he thought Kanshū's little science project would be rounded off before it could even take off, but the agitation in Britta Geller's voice made him re-evaluate the situation.

He went off the daily surveillance reports in the last two months. Until now, he didn't realize the name *Winston Kanshū* had been all over the place. The experiment in Russia, terrorist attack in Singapore, POTUWS election in Canada, orgy in South Korea.

Agent A feared his operation might soon be made redundant.

With a mixed feeling, he consulted agent B if they should fly down to Argentina. Notwithstanding the budget constraint, he said, it would be nice to do some fieldwork.

Agent B stopped doing whatever she was doing on the computer, resumed briefly, stopped again, and then turned to agent A.

She tenderly shook her head and said she got a different idea.

Chapter 68

The United Ways' apparently smooth restructuring might give one the idea that corporate reorganization was an easy business, like gaining weight or losing money. The prominent absence of any war or terrorist attack against BFEF might give one hope that ideological differences among human beings might be settled in a non-violent way. The audacious lack of mentions of All-Ways, Treeism and TYDF might even give one the impression that they were nothing more than a bunch of spineless apologists who just rolled over and accepted the POTUWS' decree. Most importantly, the abruptly rapid development of the "Edge of the World" trip might lead one to believe that the chronicler had forgotten to wrap up the arcs of the Big Three creeds.

Since at least 75% of the above ideas are falsehood, it is important to set the records straight here.

Not long after the POTUWS election, the United Ways was at the edge of two very promising wars. Promising in the sense that they had an awful lot of potential to do what wars are good at doing, which is to hack the heads off from whoever show up in the wrong uniforms. Fortunately, both of them were motivated by glorious reasons, so the head hacking part didn't bother too much the initiating parties. In case anyone does take an interest in those glorious reasons – which may seem unlikely now, but one should never underestimate what whimsical academic interest may spark up tomorrow – they are not too terribly unorthodox. They revolve around the themes of "liberating so-and-so from so-and-so undesirable conditions," "defending so-and-so interests from so-and-so evil," and "restoring peace among so-and-so people."

The first party that waged a war on the United Ways was All-Ways. Claiming their divine rights to liberate/defend/restore so and-so, it declared a special military operation against the POTUWS and the Disk Earth Society he belonged. The exact scale or combat mode of the operation was never made clear, as their acting leader Seth Nadir was invited to a summit meeting in South Korea not long after the declaration was made. In defiance of all expectations, the meeting was overwhelmingly unsuccessful. No items on the agenda were discussed, no ideas were exchanged and no feelings were acknowledged. It was hard to know exactly what went wrong in the meeting, partly because the POTUWS didn't bring any notes to the one-on-one meeting, on account of his "greatest memory of all time." Another reason was that the POTUWS didn't bring himself to the meeting either and it got cancelled altogether. He and the newly appointed pandit of All-Ways got pretty drunk at the cocktail reception, which was insanely successful.

During the insanely successful cocktail party, Nadir acknowledged that All-Ways waged the war because they had a few problems. Not knowing what to do with their problems, they thought the best way was to distract everyone from the problems. Besides the exile of its leader and the universal problem of not being sufficiently rich, the biggest problem facing All-Ways was the Ratlonallst Movement, which was literally getting irrational. Nadir predicted that a civil war would soon erupt among the believers of Cosmic Turtle because more and more people believed the Earth rested on an irrational number of world-bearing turtles.

Thanks to the open dialogue, Winston and Nadir came to a mutual understanding and entered into the first geocentric trade agreement in history. According to the napkin-based treaty, Disk Earth Society would share its know-how in developing flat Earth products with All-Ways, who would use all the proceeds to educate pre-school children on All-Ways doctrine. They reasoned, drunkenly but correctly, that indoctrinating children before they developed the faculty of independent thinking was the most effective way to eradicate heresy.

Almost concurrent with that peace-making cocktail party, TYDF also declared its intention to go to war with the United Ways. The details were a bit foggy to those who went to the party, but the gist was that TYDF demanded its One-TYDF principle to be respected by the reorganization and warned, "Whoever plays with fire will perish by it." After getting no responses in three days, TYDF declared victory and agreed to be part of the Big Flat Earth Federation. To this day, historians still argue among themselves what the heck happened.

However, neither of the two wars posed as much challenge to the formation of BFEF as the lawsuit between the Church of Treeism and the United Ways.

As soon as Odinson cashed out his winning at *gambling-grandma55699.com.uk*, he filed an injunction order against rebranding the United Ways, citing its impact on the sales of Treeism merchandises. That move shocked the church's pastors to the core, as they never thought of the Church as a litigious, profit-seeking vehicle engaged in predatory business practices. They naively thought it was a profit-seeking vehicle engaged in predatory business practices, period.

What happened next was, according to the lawyers who refused to elaborate unless they could start the clock for billable hours, a bit technical. The United Ways countersued the Church, which had used the WHO logo as evidence for the World Tree, for infringing Disk Earth Society's UN-logo-is-flat-Earth-map idea. The Church counter-countersued the United Ways for three counts of defamation, each claiming fifty bazillion dollars in damages. It was immediately followed by a counter-claim filed by the United Ways that claimed damages of a hundred bazillion dollars.

The crossfire court case soon caught the attention of Seekers, who expected it would be the next trail by TikTok. Hashtags were drafted, meme templates were prepared, and reaction videos were choreographed in anticipation of the virtual sport.

Then, the trial was cancelled abruptly.

In the statements issued jointly by the involved lawyers, the decision to settle out of court was attributed to mutual understanding and technicalities. Specifically, the Church of Treeism and the United Ways had come to understand that bazillion dollars technically did not exist and fifty Brazilian reais were technically around ten dollars.

As part of the settlement, Odinson got the golden parachute he bargained for an early retirement, while the United Ways was awarded with a Bombardier Global 8000. It was the second plane crowdfunded by Treeple who believed their priests should not travel in a long tube filled with demons. The first one could still fly but got decommissioned, as it couldn't fly everywhere at one stop.

How this settlement arrangement came about was quite

technical and could only be explained over several hundred billable hours. The key takeaway was that now Winston had at his disposal a three-suite business jet that could carry up to nineteen passengers, with a range of nine thousand miles.

Chapter 69

When the Treeple said commercial airlines were full of demons, they were entirely onto something.

Smith almost missed his flight to Buenos Aires because the family in his check-in line punched the service assistant who had the audacity to say that they were late for their flight by an hour. Fortunately, his flight's departure was delayed by a vlogger who licked the plane's toilet and got food poisoning. He got aboard just in time to see another two passengers get escorted away, one for bringing parrots as service animals and another for refusing to sit next to a BLM-shirt man. The flight itself was less eventful, with only one brawl among drunken passengers and one couple who demanded to be dropped off at Santa Fe.

Despite all the arrests and delays, Smith managed to reach Winston before he left the airport.

"I hope you didn't bring anything besides that carryall," said Winston as he power walked down the private jet terminal, "because we don't have time for you to wait for the baggage. We are taking off in fifteen minutes."

"Great," said Smith, with the laid-backness of a man who doesn't have fifty pounds of luggage checked in.

The two of them got on the Global 8000 just in time to hear Chandler's voice over the PA system, reminding the passengers to please consume or otherwise get rid of all the cocaine on them before their destination. They were greeted by Leonard Roundy from Wraparound's Witness.

"Now, ask me again the question you asked me minutes ago," said Winston as he threw a bag out of the cabin, "and ignore Leo's camera. He is helping us record the whole thing."

"Eh… where exactly are we going?"

"Figuratively speaking," said Winston figuratively, "the edge of the world." He winked at Roundy behind the hand-held camera and continued, "now act like you are surprised at my reply and ask me, 'What do you mean?'"

"What do you mean?" Smith complied, minus the part about pretending.

"Geographically speaking," said Winston geographically, "we are heading to Perth, Australia."

The camera completely ignored Smith and followed Winston as he walked through two of the jet's suites. He passed by Karenna Plain from Plane Rite, Pierce Gerry from Neo Gerrymandered Temple, Yusuf Adel from The Second Coming of Del, Seth Nadir from All-Ways, and several flat Earthers he colloquially referred to as Nazi Forehead, Four-eyes Maeve and Racial Token.

"At Big Flat Earth Federation," said Winston as he turned to the camera again, "we are tired of debating with globetards whether nonstop flights between Melbourne and Santiago or between Auckland and Buenos Aires exist.

"Even if they *do* exist with non-delusional passengers – about which a lot of us are still skeptical – it doesn't mean Antarctica is not an ice wall, because such flights do not fly over Antarctica.

"To end this debate once and all, today we are going to do something no one has even done before. We are going to fly across the South Pole."

From a nearby table, Winston picked up a globe and spun to its lower halve.

"Here is the plan, assuming the Earth is a ball. We will take off from Buenos Aires, go all the way to the south, fly over the South Pole, and then find ourselves flying due north toward Perth."

While Winston put down the globe, Adel walked by and acted like he just discovered the camera. He looked directly at it and asked what if the Earth was not a ball.

"If it isn't, then depending on how high the ice wall is," said Winston to the camera, "we will either fly straight to it in a few hours or, as Dr. Plain has predicted, have a very rough mandatory landing after nine thousand miles."

Chapter 70

"Are you sure?"

"Positive, their thirsty gazes are ravenously staring at her, worshiping her elegant body like it belongs to a goddess, a goddess of moaning and flapping," whispered Charles. "I can practically see their loins on blaze and hear their rhythmical breath, heavy but not without pleasure."

"We have talked about this, Charles," said Britta. "No graphical narration! Just tell me. Are the flatees doing anything besides bird watching?"

"No, that's all they do in the morning. To be fair, we don't have much to do anyway."

Britta put down her headset before Charles could elaborate on the flapping.

She wasn't too bothered by the workplace sexual harassment; she was just puzzled by how uneventful the journeys on *Rey Azul* and *Bloody Helm* had been. She had expected the flaters would conduct some sort of experiments on the ships, like searching for inconsistency in the constellations at nights. Such efforts would, of course, be futile because the 24/7/365 drone light shows paid by G12 ensured that the same set of stars would be seen everywhere in the Southern Hemisphere.

"Hello, is anyone still on the line?" spoke Charles loudly.

"What is it now? More erotic description of pecking and stroking?"

"No, but we will get to that part later. I think there is something wrong with the phone."

"Huh?"

"Can't you hear that? The tapping. Is someone watching one of those ASMR videos at work?"

Instead of asking what kind of life Charles had been leading, Britta pricked up her ears.

Besides the roar of waves, Mosby's snore and Charles' inexplicably heavy breathing, there was indeed some oddly satisfying sound in the background.

"Di-dah-dah-dit, dit, di-dah-dit, dah, di-di-di-dit."

Its gentle mannerism and random pattern stimulated a tingling sensation in the listeners. To someone as imaginative as Charles, it sounded like someone trying to compose music on a primitive organ. To someone as banal as Britta, it felt like someone tapping the word "Perth" in morse code.

Chapter 71

"Flat ladies and gentlemen, this is your captain speaking. In about two minutes, we will descend to six thousand feet at full speed, breaking a bunch of aviation regulations. Please return to your seats, fasten your seatbelts and finish your drinks."

Smith quickly finished his coffee and submitted his application for electronic visa. Compared to his fellow passengers, he had slightly more faith that this flight would arrive at Perth in one piece.

Looking around himself, Smith found that he was the only one not doing or filming some sort of flat Earth experiments.

Pierce Gerry had been lying on the floor with his bubble level for four hours straight. Once in a while Roundy would walk by and asked if he was dead yet, and he would go off on a tangent, either remarking that the plane didn't dip its nose or proclaiming that his faith in flat Earth was never misplaced.

Not far away from where Gerry horizontally lay was where Karenna Plain vertically jumped. Before she boarded the plane, she had posted a TikTok video of herself jumping and landing on the same spot, brilliantly disproving that the Earth rotated at a thousand miles per hour. To her surprise, she got the same result when she repeated the feat inside a moving plane. After some careful consideration, she declared that globetards were wrong in comparing a rotating Earth to a moving plane, because people were on, not inside, the Earth. In order not to confuse the twenty followers of hers, she decided not to upload the sequel video.

Newton might be wrong about gravity but at least he got inertia right, thought Smith as he turned his gaze to the kitchen scale across his desk. Yusuf Adel had brought it onboard to prove that weight had nothing to do with gravity and everything to do with density. He expected the lower air pressure would make his phone weight *more* now than it was before the takeoff. And he still expected that after fifty disappointing re-experiments. As an ordinary Seeker, he began to suspect a serious leak in his phone battery, serious enough to over-compensate for the weight gained from higher altitude; he didn't think there was anything wrong with the scale. He never imagined that all the manufacturers of scales would conspire with *Them*. He didn't even begin to fathom the possibility that all the kitchen scales on the market were secretly installed with a barometer that would trigger the scale to misrepresent the weight as air pressure changed.

Poor man, Smith thought rather sympathetically.

"You may want to lift the window shade," said Winston as he emerged from the adjacent suite. He buckled up next to Smith and added, "Or you will miss the show."

"You mean the curvature?"

"Not exactly. I used to think the Earth was round because I could see the curvature from a plane, but Maeve has talked some sense into me. You see, the horizon seems a little bit curved only because of the circular windows. They distort the view."

Smith nodded along as if he had never heard of it from the brown bag lunch sharing hosted by Round Ops.

"My friend Chandler said the windows are designed this way to withstand air pressure, but it doesn't make sense."

"How so?" asked Smith as sweat trickled down his back.

"If round windows are so much more durable than flat windows, why are they not installed in every school? You know, to protect the kids from getting shot. I am telling you, the mass shooting problem in America has nothing to do with windows."

The plane took a dip, pushing everything inside Smith's stomach up.

"It has everything to do with the doors," added Winston, "we need less doors for the intruders. Don't let the leftists fool you into thinking it is about the guns. It never is."

Seeing no fault in Winston's logic and, more importantly, having his lungs pressed to his back, Smith didn't say another word. After what felt like a lifetime of dropping, his internal organs slowly rolled back to where they should be.

"Flat ladies and gentlemen, this is your captain again. If your geography is right, you will see the ice wall at any minute now."

Chapter 72

The myth that the lands and waters we know as Earth are surrounded by a seven-hundred-foot wall at Antarctica is, of course, false.

The Antarctic ice wall is thirty thousand feet tall, just enough to give a finger to Mount Everest.

Mythologists trace the root of that myth back to a heliocentric, undocumented immigrant who had a slightly inaccurate idea of the Great Wall of China. That idea got increasingly inaccurate by the time it was, allegedly, passed on by word of mouth to the creator of *Attack on Titan*, in which the xenophobic humans built walls to keep the otherwise harmless Titans from eating them alive. Some researchers believed this Japanese manga series indirectly, but not too remotely, gave birth to the idea of Trump Wall, which would keep away the compatriots of the very immigrant who started the whole Wall thing. That curious chain of events is, of course, ignored by the mythologists, who are too busy arguing among themselves at which point of those events a flat Earther culturally appropriated the Wall idea.

Equally controversial is when the ice wall was discovered. Among those in the know, some Americans believed it was discovered in 1821, when American Captain John Davis became the first human to set foot on Antarctica. Some Russians argued it was first sighted along with the Fimbul Ice Shelf in 1820, by the Russian expedition led by Fabian Gottlieb von Bellingshausen and Mikhail Lazarev. Some Britons even claimed that since the ice wall was "so bloody huge," the British explorer James Cook must have seen it during his second voyage.

Similar to Captain Cook's sixty-thousand-mile voyage, which had been retconned by *Them* from an Antarctica circumnavigation to a search for the hypothetical continent *Terra Australis*, the exact date of the ice wall's discovery had been muddled beyond oblivion. More generally speaking, everything generally known about Antarctica had been fabricated, retold, modernized, refined, corrected, over-corrected and completely rewritten so many times that hardly anyone alive knew if they knew what they knew was true.

Quite a number of people claimed they had crossed Antarctica or explored the South Pole. They weren't all liars. Of course not. Except for those who lied for a book deal, the majority of them honestly thought they had been there, although in fact they only visited the Truman Domes. Named after their designer Gill Truman, the Truman Domes were the two biggest studios / refrigerators / swimming pools ever built. Located in the middle of South Atlantic Ocean and Indian Ocean respectively, the two studios were equipped with movable platforms, electromagnets, snow machines, and 9.1 surround sound systems to re-create the homicidal nature of Antarctica. They were also incidentally the inspiration for *The Truman Show*.

Those who knew about the ice wall generally agreed, or assumed they agreed, that no one had ever seen the other side of the wall. They were curious, for sure, but never climbed over it, because they were told not to. The people who gave the order explained that they had been told it was a bad idea, who heard it from those who had better things to do, who in turn were grounded by those who swore to have a good reason not to go over the wall but had it temporarily escaped from their minds.

In a nutshell, no one went over the ice wall for the same reason why so many people believed in the ice wall myth.

"Am I dreaming?"

"I would say 'No' but you first have to believe I am not a projection of your subconsciousness."

Winston turned his gaze to Smith and thought about it for a moment. As he tried to dial down his skepticism, he recalled the story about Lisa Simson.

That lady came up to shake his hands after he finished the victory speech. She was kind, sweet and, like all DES members, didn't look stupid, mental or socially rejected at all. She said she recently became a flat Earther after watching his *400 Proofs Earth is Not a Spinning Pear*. Thinking it would be rude to correct her, Winston didn't mention he never heard of that movie. He nodded to her remarks on proof #21, thanked her for appreciating #101, and laughed with her at a pun in #289. He still remembered how much she loved #45-46, #118-130 and #301-314. She said those proofs, which were basically identical and pointed to the unperceived motion of Earth, gave her renewed confidence in human senses. They led her to become a vocal activist against the big pharma and medical institutions, educating the public that germ theory was just a theory. Unfortunately, one week after their meeting, Lisa died from a complicated case of cholera and hepatitis, with a new breed of microorganism discovered on her hands.

Having relegated his skepticism to a healthy degree, Winston approached the window again. This time he accepted what he saw.

Through the oval-shaped window, he confirmed with his very own eyes the ice wall's majestically striking and imposing absence.

Smith was no less surprised than the flatees running up and down the cabin. When subsequently told what had happened, he would call this rounding operation (code named Two Birds One Sewn; ad hoc project ID: 2B1S) the craziest shoot he had ever funky heard. Except he didn't say "shoot" or "funky."

He didn't expect Round Ops would remotely hijack the plane minutes after its takeoff. He never would have guessed that two stealth fighters had sneaked upon the Global 8000, locked wings with it, and deployed 4K displays on its windows when it ascended through clouds. And it was completely outside of his imagination that dozens of fighter jets would take turns to propel the plane in order to cut the thirty-hour trip in half.

To anyone who thought the global conspiracy was just an ad hoc hypothesis dreamed up by flat Earthers, 2B1S must seem highly improbable.

To anyone unfamiliar with *Their* determination to maintain the Global Lie, 2B1S must trigger millions of questions about the logistics.

To anyone who never gave more than two seconds of thought about the shape of Earth, 2B1S must be too far stretched to be true.

But to the Project Management Director of NASA, 2B1S was just another example of poor spending control.

Geez, I thought Britta would just call ground control to redirect the flight or something.

Chapter 73

Mistakes – not flat Earthers, although their parents and spouses use the two terms rather interchangeably – are always the biggest threats to NASA. In that sense, NASA's Arts Department (Arts for short, or ArtsHole for fun) is the motherland of NASA's arch enemies.

The most famous mistakes of ArtsHole were made in late 1960s, captured forever in the Moon landing photos: the absence of stars in the lunar sky, waving of the American flag in space, unparallel shadows on the moon surface, visibility of objects within shadow, and invisibility of Armstrong's camera.

Those mistakes are not only famous, but also costly. It took years of propaganda to convince the public that the camera's exposure was too short to capture the stars, the flag had a horizontal rod, the shadows were distorted by perspective, the moon surface reflected sunlight, and Armstrong's camera was mounted on his suit. NASA was also obliged to spend millions of dollars on root cause analysis. Consultants would come in, do a gap analysis, produce a hundred recommendations, conduct a follow-up study six months later, provide another list of best practices, come in again in six months, run a diagnostic, and so on and so forth.

Even after decades of improvement, reengineering, overhaul, upgrade, revamp, strategic turnaround and technical refreshment, mistakes still popped up now and then. Sometimes they were intentional, like that time when a disgruntled employee wrote "SEX" on the atmosphere. Sometimes they were flat out you-had-one-job memes, like uploading the behind-the-scene footage to YouTube, which showed that space mission was filmed in a swimming pool.

Round Ops was, of course, aware of the ArtsHole's reputation. That was why they didn't involve their Arts colleagues in producing the wall-free aerial view of Antarctica. Instead, they outsourced the task to the in-house studio of China National Space Administration. In their delivery note, the CNSA studio promised that no one could prove the video was made by CGI.

"It must be CGI," yelled Seth Nadir at the cabin window on his right. "If you look very closely, you can see the pixels. Here, look at here. Does it look blur to you?"

Roundy put down his camera and pressed his face at where Nadir was pointing. He briefly touched that spot to confirm his suspicion.

"Dude, it was your booger," said Roundy in disgust as his camera was aimed at Nadir again. "Besides your knee-jerk reaction, is there anything else that makes you think the view we're seeing is fake?"

"Look at the shadow. Look at the sunlight. And look at the shape of clouds! You don't see anything unusual?"

Nadir paused, expecting Roundy to say something stupid. Roundy didn't say anything, lest he should say something stupid. The camera kept rolling, wishing someone else would say something stupid.

"They don't look right."

"How so?"

"I don't have all the answers. You should do your own research," said Nadir as he stormed off.

Feeling unwelcomed, Roundy moved to the front suite to find someone who would share their insight into the absence of ice wall. He was met by a group of flat Earthers enlightening each other on what was going on.

"It is the heaven energy," said Plain. "It bounces off the ice wall and affects our vision. That's why we can't see it."

"What is this heaven energy?" asked Adel. "You said the same thing when your gyroscope showed the Earth was spinning."

"What? You never heard of it?"

"No."

"What do you want me to do? Give you a definition of heaven energy?"

"Yeah."

"OK, I will give you one."

"Great."

"Heaven energy is," said Plain as Roundy zoomed in on her face, "the energy of heaven. It comes from the heaven and bounces off gyroscope and ice wall."

"It doesn't sound..." said Adel, "as good as my explanation. You know, people are going to think you just make things up. I prefer to explain it with more established ideas."

Roundy saw it coming light years away, but he maintained his professionalism and only said those words in his mind.

"Refraction and perspective," said Adel outwardly and Roundy inwardly.

"Huh?"

"You know, the atmosphere and moisture play tricks with the light. And then there is the law of perspective, making things far away disappear."

At Adel's request, Roundy pressed the camera against the cabin window and zoomed in.

Still, no wall was seen.

"It doesn't change anything. I am sure we would have seen the wall under the right weather, with the right equipment."

"You are all full of BS," shouted Gerry. "Who cares about the explanation? I don't need to know all his tricks to know that a magician only performs illusions. We all know the ice wall is there and *They* have covered it up. The question we should ask is: Why do *They* do it? No one outside of this plane is supposed to know about our flight."

"You are saying we have a mole?" asked Plain, "and we should tie him up, strip him naked, show him our tools, give a menacing speech, and pull out his nails one by one until he talks?"

"I didn't think of the part beyond tying them up..."

"But we are all hardcore, vetted Seekers," said Adel.

"Yes, we are," said Gerry as he spun to face the president, "except for him."

"How dare you," said Winston and jumped up from his seat. "I opened every single hidden folder on my computer in front of you already. I have told you many times. I don't know how those pictures and videos got in there. And I swear, I am not—"

"I didn't mean you. I mean the guy your brought."

"O... er... Leo, you would cut out that part, right?"

"That's your concern?" said Smith as the three other Seekers closed in on him. Instinctively, his tongue searched for the fake tooth containing cyanide while his hand reached for the Walther PPK in his back pocket. Rather unfortunately, neither of them existed.

At Plain's signal, Roundy stopped the camera, Gerry took off his belt and Adel swung himself upon Smith.

Nothing sexual or too violent ensued. It was simply some good ol' American guy-on-guy action that resulted in Smith being tied up with a premium recliner seat, which promised to make its user at home.

"Winston, let me go," said Smith, who didn't feel quite at home.

"All of you chill out," said Winston. "I believe Smith is not a mole."

"Phew, thanks."

"But I also respect the rest of you who have legitimate concern that plan C may be jeopardized, so let's keep things as they are until the press conference is over."

Chapter 74

"I want you to imagine this. In the dimly lit, barely decorated room, there was no one other than me and nothing other than – well, there is no subtle way to put this – the stick of joy. I called her Joyce. Not just for euphemism. I really felt that was a she.

"For a very long time, Joyce was my only companion. At first, I wasn't proud of doing that. I felt like I was touching her not because I wanted to, but because I had to. The people on the next room made me do it. I knew they had certain expectations. And to meet those expectations, I would reluctantly tap her this way or push her that way.

"Man, doing that crushed my soul. I would rather be a deodorant QA specialist who sniffs armpits for a living.

"But then I remember my Adlerian psychology lessons. The importance of relationships, social interest, sense of belongings, that kind of crap. So I changed my approach to working with her. I opened up and showed her my feelings.

"Sometimes I felt romantic, and I would hold her by the lower half like she was a champagne glass and my fingers would dance with her affectionately. Sometimes I felt abusive, and I would grab her like a stress ball and spun her around recklessly. No matter what I did, she never complained and always helped me meet the expectations of those in the next room.

"I began enjoying my time with Joyce and could see why she was named joystick. We spent two wonderful years together at the Oregon Convention Center, until manual control of the Foucault pendulum was replaced with AI."

Sensing that the story had come to an end, Britta raised the volume of her headset again.

"Just one quick question."

"By all means."

"*Why the flat did you tell this story?*"

"Well, I am aware that no one asked about my time at Round Ops," said Charles, "but no one had said anything for hours, so I thought we should open up and—"

"We don't have to," said Britta. "You just need to stay quiet and keep those flaters company. The cruises make no difference now. So will the flight. We just need to wait for the flaters to acknowledge defeat."

"They will? It doesn't sound characteristic of them."

"We will see. National Geographic has called a press conference to be held at the Perth Airport in an hour. It completely flew under our radar, but I am sure the flaters are behind it. They plan to show the edge of the world."

"Are you sure the Chinese videos could fool them?"

"Of course they can. No one has ever, ever questioned the authenticity of videos and images released by CNSA. Either the Chinese are extremely good at visual effects or flaters are so ignorant that they think NASA is the only space agency in the world."

Charles weighted the two possibilities in his mind. He used to think the proliferation of conspiracy theories had something to do with freedom of speech, but that didn't explain why NASA alone got all the hate from flatees. The dichotomy presented by Britta led him to the inevitable conclusion that ArtsHole really sucked at their jobs.

"OK, I see. I was just a bit worried because Smith has gone dark for so long."

"Nah, he is probably just taking a nap or something."

Chapter 75

Being suspected without a probable cause didn't seem unthinkable for someone who had spent thirty plus years in a country where driving while black was a thing. Being tied up by flatees for allegedly sabotaging a flat Earth experiment was similarly not unexpected for someone whose employer spent thousands of millions of dollars per year to round off the Earth. Following this logic, Smith had every right to expect that he was equipped with a cyanide pill and a blowback-operated semi-automatic pistol. The reason for their absence had nothing to do with insufficient funding or inadequate contingency planning. They were simply left behind at certain baggage carousel in Buenos Aires.

"Sorry, amigo," said Winston as the seat belt sign went off, "I need you to stay put for a bit longer. We will come back and untie you once the press conference is over."

"Don't go," said Smith, who just had a nap on the recliner he was tied to. "If you plan to torture me for intel, you can forget about it." He sat up to make his point stronger. "I am happy to say anything you want me to say. Just give me the lines. NASA, Freemasons, Bigfoot, aliens, you name it. I work for them. Any combinations of them."

"No, it is nothing like that. I guarantee none of us will hurt you. They just feel better to know that you have no chance to leak our plan."

"What? There is nothing left to sabotage. I thought you didn't see the edge of the world?"

"Well, it wasn't the only thing I was trying to prove. The cruises and this flight were only part of a bigger plan."

Before Smith could ask, Winston had headed to the exit door, followed by Roundy. One by one, the Seekers passed by Smith's premium recliner chair and stepped out to confirm the existence of Australia.

Looking out from the window, Smith caught a glimpse of the fighter jets disappearing from the summer sky of Perth. He wondered if any Seeker saw them. Knowing that the flatees never failed to fail to see the International Space Station despite the freely available ISS-tracking mobile apps, he dismissed that idea.

They are blind without their Nikon P900.

Suddenly, an idea hit Smith. It hit him so hard that he thought he blanked out and forgot about it, but he didn't. To clarify, he did blank out a little bit but didn't forget whatever hit him. He figuratively examined it, expanded it, squeezed it, spun it, and threw it at an imaginary wall to see if it would stick.

It did.

I have it figured out.

No, he didn't figure out how to untie himself. He simply figured out what "Plan C" was, which had the benefit of sparing him the trouble of freeing himself. If what he thought was right, he thought, it was too late for him to do anything.

Dejected, he shut his eyes while the last disembarking passenger passed by him.

"Well, well, well, that's quite a pickle you got yourself in, Robin," said a female voice that must stereotypically belong to a bespectacled British psychiatrist. A voice that Smith would swear he had never heard before.

Chapter 76

Taking a seat in front of the conference backdrop that read "OVER THE POLE," co-sponsored by National Geographic and Polar Grind LLC, the largest strip club operator in Oceania, Winston was visibly nervous.

He wasn't uncomfortable because of the provocative logos behind him. He was uncomfortable *in spite of* them. He never had much luck with the press and every press conference he had over the past decade was without fail a disaster. The most memorable one was after the premiere of *Modern Tennō: from Crib to Throne*; that epic biographical drama about the reigning Japanese emperor was so historically inaccurate that some activists immolated themselves in protest. Coming in close second was that time when he compared *Morbius* to *Star Wars*, upsetting the overwhelming number of Morbius fans in presence and triggering the Occupy Comic-Con event. But what would have counted as the most explosive press conference was the one for *Netflix Comedy Special: This is MY Holy Land*, which was cancelled due to bomb threats.

Here goes nothing.

Winston turned on his microphone, introduced Plain and Gerry as respectable researchers in his circle, preemptively apologized to all those Twitter users who had – or would, in the indeterminate future – found his movies/tweets/interviews/op-eds/silence offensive, and said a few words to thank Polar Grind for its unreserved support.

"I didn't come today to speak to you as a filmmaker. I am speaking to you as someone interested in the truth. Scientific truth.

"Having ignored the aviation guidelines on diversion airports and fuel freeze strategy, my colleagues and I have just completed the first cross-polar flight in Southern Hemisphere—

"Hold on," said a reporter in the front row. "The first flight over South Pole was done by Richard Byrd in 1929."

"I wasn't finished," said Winston without raising his voice. "I was saying, it is the first cross-polar flight in Southern Hemisphere organized and completed by geocentric explorers. It is also the first trans-polar flight whose journey was captured in 65 mm film and IMAX. And it is the first flight over South Pole where more than 50% of the passengers are Aquarius."

The reporter surrendered in silence.

"For such a formidable feat, I fully expect you will have lots of questions about its authenticity, especially from our geocentric friends watching this press conference. You may ask, 'How do you know NASA didn't mess with your flight path?' or 'How do you know the Antarctica you saw is not CGI?'

"These are all very reasonable and intelligent questions. At Big Flat Earth Federation, we never take the readings of our electronic equipment at face value. We believe in our senses, but we also keep an open mind to question them whenever the circumstances deem it necessary. This is one of those circumstances.

"Since we were travelling in a long tube in a big-ass sky, it wasn't always feasible for me and my co-passengers to tell which direction we were heading. We thought we were going south. Our equipment told us we were heading south. But we might indeed be flying due north. So how do we know we really fly over Antarctica, a land we collectively believe is the edge of the world? How can we tell if our plane was *not* hijacked and our senses *not* fooled by NASA?

"For those of you who have been asking these thoughtful, informed questions, I am glad to tell you that I have them all figured out."

Winston took a sip of the water in front of him and gauged if the reporters could keep up with his logical reasoning. Their silly expressions suggested that those questions never crossed their uncritical minds.

Having held the POTUWS office for a month, Winston had come to understand that the biggest barrier to truth was not mass deception, or poor education, or herd mentality, or good ol' stupidity. It was the unwillingness to re-examine established belief. Once a person opened his mind to the possibility that the Earth was flat, that person became receptive – he observed, rather playfully – to all kinds of crap.

It no longer seemed unorthodox to distrust navigation technology. It became his second nature to assume that *They* would do everything it took to cover up the Global Lie. It would not surprise him in the slightest degree that a bunch of military aircrafts would literally blindfold and kidnap his whole plane across four continents.

In fact, he was counting on it.

"To prove whether a secret organization has been covering up the Global Lie, I have arranged two cruise ships to approach Antarctica from Hobart, Australia and Ushuaia, Argentina.

"Ohi, Maeve, why don't you say 'Hello' to the press over here?"

The display next to the conference table came to live. It showed the frosty faces of Ohi Toyoshi and Maeve Walsh. The sunlight in their backgrounds suggested they were both within the Antarctica circle.

"Over the past few days," added Winston, "my colleagues on the two cruise ships have been observing the sky. If, and this is not a small *if*, if no one has interfered with their cruises, and, and this a rather big *and*, and my flight has indeed travelled through the South Pole, then they must have observed my plane flying over their heads."

Winston took another moment to confirm all the reporters were following him. He now felt that emphasizing the size of words was a bad idea.

"At the risk of stating the obvious," said Winston rather venturously, "if either of them didn't see my plane, then we have very good reason to believe that a secret organization has meddled with our experiment. Ergo, the Global Lie is real."

Saying the word "ergo" made Winston feel smart, although he still wasn't sure what it was and where he could find it.

"Now, Ohi, Maeve, can both of you tell the world if you saw the mango yellow Global 8000 fly over your heads?"

After two seconds of delay, both of them reacted to the question.

"We didn't," said Ohi and Maeve concurrently, "fail to see the plane."

"That's what I ex— What?!"

"It wasn't easy," said Ohi, "but I saw it, around thirteen hours ago. It came from my north and went to the south."

"More or less the same here," said Maeve, "except that it came from the south and went to the north. Does it mean we have proved the Earth is flat?"

Chapter 77

"You got to be shitting me" was the first thought that crossed Smith's mind when the P-clearance Induction & Mentoring Program explained to him what NASA was actually up to. For obvious reasons, it was a reasonable spontaneous response. For less obvious reasons, it had been a gold mine for psychotherapists. For less nonobvious reasons, it had afforded therapists who specialized in cognitive dissonance a new Porsche, a new Omega, or whatever they thought could effectively impress their less well-to-do peers. By the time Smith Robin joined NASA, hundreds of millions of taxpayer money had been spent on research for a cure to the crippling psychological stress experienced by PIMP participants. A not insignificant portion of that money was spent on studying how a shattered belief system could be rebuilt during, say, a four-course lunch. A very significant portion of that money went to cover the outlays on four-course lunches that were entirely and necessarily incurred for research purpose.

When the research team was assembled during one breakfast meeting in 1970, several prudently optimistic psychologists estimated the study would be completed by their tenth breakfast meet-up. Their prudence and optimism were not entirely misplaced. After all, the researchers all intuitively understood how stressful it was to cope with the truth about Global Lie. They conjectured that people exposed to the truth must re-consider all scientists as either frauds or fools; suppose all circumnavigators were crooks or delusional; assume all the predictions about comet flybys, meteor shower, planetary oppositions, the Moon's cyclical phases, etc. were just lucky guesses; suspect the Soviet space program was controlled opposition; wonder what long range snipers were actually doing when they accounted for gravity and Coriolis effect; second-guess if airlines in the Northern Hemisphere were literally dragging their tails; and be pleasantly surprised that the government could make everyone in the Southern Hemisphere see the rather innocuous Octans constellation but not the harm of trans fat. That was a lot of life reevaluation to do, especially harmful if anyone attempted to complete it over a four-course meal.

Having understood the subject matter so well but not yet got around to put it in writing, the researchers did what a respectable psychologist would do in their position – they researched on a topic that everyone already knew about and backed it up with biased samples whose size was statistically inadequate. As it turned out, doing actual empirical work was not as fun as armchair theorizing and took a lot of energy. Entered the lunch breaks. As the research dragged on, both the length and scale of the lunch itself expanded. After postponing thousands of breakfast meetings and conducting thousands of Lunch & Learn sessions, the researchers proudly concluded their study in their tenth breakfast meet-up, in 1978. The research confirmed everything they previously knew about that psychological stress, and suggested further study should be conducted to find a cure for it.

That conclusion would have caused a lot of psychological stress and possibly a prolonged sick leave to the executive who commissioned the study, if it wasn't for an observation he made before the breakfast: The absenteeism of new joiners who were recently shocked shitless by the truth was no worse than those who had been in the know from the get go. Apparently, those employees ran out of mental capacity to reshape their world view and just gave up on reconciling it with their newly acquired inside knowledge. Thanks to that new found mental fortitude, NASA employees never again fell under the impression that they were being shit to. For the same reason, Smith had no trouble at all to accept what the bespectacled woman told him while losing her British accent mid-sentence.

"CIA? Brainwashing?" said Smith as he was untied from the recliner chair that had given its best to make him feel at home. "Alright, I can work with that."

"You take it surprisingly well," said the woman who had re-introduced herself as agent Jean Frey. "I thought I would need to explain why I knew your name, why you can't remember me, or what CIA is doing with flat Earthers."

"Nah. For the Global Lie to survive this long, I figure a lot of brainwashing and waterboarding must be going on."

"No, we don't do waterboarding," said Jean as she headed to the exit, "as much as brainwashing. You know, for the environment."

As the two of them left the plane, Smith pestered Jean with questions about CIA's involvement in covering up the Global Lie, which Jean could neither confirm nor deny. He did, however, learn that brainwashing had become less widely used since the construction of Truman Domes. Due to the prosperous outlook for Antarctica's tourism and the dwindling number of psychology graduates that were happy to be "just a brainwasher[4]," the members

---

[4] The negative connotation of "brainwasher" was subsequently made irrelevant, when the brainwashing professionals rebranded themselves as coercive persuasion specialists. That inspired a lot of graduates to join the profession. They either became NRA lobbyists, or joined the media industry and persuaded people to vote against their interests.

of Antarctic Treaty had voted to build the Domes[5], which had drastically reduced the demand for brain washing specialists.

"What if someone sees the Domes?" asked Smith.

"Then we'll brainwash them."

Smith processed the answer and tried to see if he was missing something. As he saw no sign of anything being missed and nothing amiss had filed a complaint, he concluded that he didn't miss anything.

By the time he finished, he had come to the transit security.

"This is your ticket back to the States," said Jean, who literally just pulled a ticket out of her butt.

"You are not leaving with me?"

"I'm still in deep cover. Don't tell anyone you have seen me and don't try to contact me unless someone's dying."

"What am I supposed to say in my report?"

"Just make up something and take my credit. I am sure you are more than qualified for that."

Upon the return of her British accent, Jean spun around and power walked to where she just came from. As she disappeared from the corner, Smith wondered what other agencies were in the know.

Chapter 78

"What? Of course not. I never believe the Earth is flat. I only thought it *could* be flat. I mean, none of us can tell for sure if it is a ball or a pancake," said Pierce Gerry to the reporter of BlitzNewsLand, a content farm best known for its faithful reporting on the latest controversial tweets and top ten lists for whatever its editor thought was a good idea.

"How about you? Are you always a flat Earth believer?" the reporter asked Karenna Plain.

"Er... not exactly," said Plain, having looked around to confirm that the POTUWS was not in earshot. "I never gave much thought

---

[5] Unlike the United Nations, which runs out of cash from time to time because its member states don't think world peace is worth paying up, the project had no problem in receiving funds from the members of Antarctic Treaty and was completed the same year the Iran-Iraq War broke out.

about what the Earth looks like. You know, I have a family to take care of and other stuff going on in my life."

"Does the cross-polar flight today change your mind? Does it make you, in a way, come around to accept it is a globe?"

"Erm... I, I will still keep my mind open. You know, according to quantum theory, observation affects the observed reality. A photon can behave like a particle or like a wave, depending on how people observe it. So, maybe, just maybe, the Earth is like that. It can be flat or spherical, depending on whether we observe it on the ground or fly around it on a plane. I see no contradiction here."

The reporter looked very pleased with the answer. She could already see the headline: "Schrödinger's Earth – the Earth is both flat and round." This was the kind of story an average BlitzNewsLand reader would read on their work computers and then bring to the social media for in-depth discussions during office hours.

The reporter felt that her job was almost done. All she needed now was a few comments from the president of Big Flat Earth Federation, who had sworn he was just going for a toilet break.

"So what's the play now?"

"Well," said Winston, who happened to have a very different concept of toilet break from the BlitzNewsLand reporter, "let's find a bar, lay low, and wait for this to blow over."

"O, the way of my people," said Chandler. "I love it."

Winston and Chandler made no effort in pretending they were not fleeing. They power walked on the moving sidewalks, crushed a few toes with their luggage wheels, and ignored the ads for escort services that they would otherwise have compared diligently. By the time Polar Grind's sales reps suspected that Winston Kanshū wouldn't personally distribute their coupons, Winston and Chandler had ordered their fifth round of drinks.

The first round was rather superficial and short-lived. They exchanged observations on why they weren't really in Australia. No kangaroo was seen on the street. The toilet didn't flush clock-wise. Not everyone was blonde and tanned. The second round became more academic. They theorized what went wrong with their plan. A lot of creative ideas were exchanged, most of which were related to refraction and perspective. The third round was a combination of drunk calling and drunk texting. They demanded Ohi and Maeve to explain why they were so sure they saw the right plane. Chandler's colleagues who received the questions were led to doubt whether they piloted the wrong vehicles. By the end of fourth round, the two of them had decided to ignore everything they discussed and just accept that the Earth was a spinning ball.

The fifth round finally arrived. The drinks that were supposed to symbolize their re-acceptance of the heliocentric model. Winston made a tear-jerking toast that made the nearby patrons think he was dying, closed his eyes, and poured the drink down his throat. But before he could taste the booze, he felt a hand on his, gently stopping the mug in mid-air.

As Winston reopened his eyes, he saw a man who didn't look like Chris Hemsworth. Behind him was a woman who didn't look like Margot Robbie. Winston correctly deduced that neither of them was Australian.

"Sorry to interrupt," said the man who didn't look like Hugh Jackman either, "this is agent B and you can call me agent A. We want to talk to you before you get too drunk."

Chapter 79

The astrophysicist Neil deGrasse Tyson once described the Gregorian calendar as a "f*cking awesome calendar" because every four hundred years it corrected the under-correction it introduced every one hundred years to correct the over-correction it created every four years with a leap day.

Many *real* scientists were amazed at how accurate – and, by a larger degree, lucky – the Gregorian calendar was in approximating the seasonal year, even though it was based on the utterly invalid assumption that the Earth revolved around the Sun.

The same group of *real* scientists thought that the only way to further improve the calendar was to introduce leap minutes. Unlike its Gregorian cousin, a leap minute would not be applied to the public calendar. Rather, it would be removed from the calendars of those whose offices didn't have a punch clock. How many and how frequently leap minutes needed to be removed from a particular individual's calendar would be a function of that person's seniority and years of service at their employing organization. The objective was to dynamically offset the slack minute introduced by the employee who came increasingly late to the office.

Unfortunately, the research on leap minutes was indefinitely delayed by *real* scientists who came aggressively late to work. As a result, the difference between the start of NASA office hour and Smith Robin's time of arrival at the office had steadily grown to forty-five minutes, fifteen of which was attributed to his one-year tenure and thirty to his position as the Deputy Director of NASA. From an average NASA employee's perspective, however, he had earned those forty-five minutes from single-handedly dissolving the Big Flat Earth Federation.

"Morning."
    "Morning."
    "Morning."
    "Morning."
    "Morning."

After industriously greeting Alex the janitor, Megan the secretary, Tiffany the assistant, Jennifer the secretary's assistant, and Emily the assistant's secretary, Smith returned to his corner office and checked off the first task on his to-do list: Act like you care.

What a productive morning, Smith figuratively patted Smith on the back.

Having finished 50% of the works he had assigned to himself, he gave himself a twenty-minute coffee break. He didn't waste it all on coffee, though. He used that time to strategize for the second task on his list: Get two extra DDO HCs. "DDO HCs," of course, referred to headcounts in the Deputy Director Office. He wanted to hire one more assistant to Emily and another secretary to Jennifer. The challenge he faced – besides the obvious yet comparatively manageable one, which was to make a business case to HR that didn't sound outrageously evident that he wanted more minions to feed his managerial feudalism – was what to call the new jobs.

"Secretary to the Assistant of the Secretary to the Deputy Director of NASA" seemed a bit mouthful. It also failed to make the candidate feel the job was more important than a glorified typist.

As Smith struggled with this challenge, the coffee break thoughtfully extended itself by another ten minutes. He hadn't done so much thinking since the reporting phase of R.D.G.A.R. A lot of his brain cells perished when he furnished that hundred-thousand-word report, which was fairly unique in its genre. If classified NASA documents could be put on sale in a bookstore, the R.D.G.A.R. operation report would rightfully be in the Fiction section, although it was hard to tell if it should be on the Romance or Thriller shelf. The light-hearted yet suspenseful report transported its reader to the love triangle between Smith Robin, Gina Stinson and Winston Kanshū, while recounting Smith's impossible but apparently very real adventure. It followed Smith as he turned the Big Four creeds against each other, converted Dr. Stinson into a NASA asset, installed a puppet regime in the United Ways, deciphered a secret message between flatees, gave a Cancelling-the-Apocalypse speech, orchestrated the largest rounding operation in history, survived an airborne gunfight, and – here came the slightly controversial part – mysteriously hypnotized two flatees to bear false witness.

After two more coffee break extensions, Smith decided to name the two new positions DDO Administrators. To mitigate any hard feelings from the existing DDO staff, he also planned to promote Jennifer and Emily to Senior Administrators and Megan and Tiffany to Principal Administrators, while keeping their duties and salaries exactly the same.

So I'll need a new org chart, thought Smith, *that would keep me busy after lunch.*

Just when he thought it was time to take a pre-lunch nap, Megan the secretary came in and said there was an email he had to read.

"Meg, if you don't wanna read my emails," said Smith without a hint of annoyance, "then you can delegate it to Jen. She drafts the reply, Em peer-reviews it, Tiff double-checks it, and you just send it out. I'm sure you don't need me."

Megan the secretary diligently jotted it down in case she needed a leverage against Tiffany the bitch. She did, however, insist that

Smith attended to the matter himself. Apparently, someone had uploaded to the Internet "The Proof."

Chapter 80

A doily of diamond waffle stitch in Hobbii Horizon yarn was just uploaded to the *r/crochet* forum. To an average *r/crochet* community member, it was just another wholesome post on an uneventful Thursday. To agent B, it was a signal from agent A that NASA was reacting to the upload.

"Agent O, agent W, move it," said agent B as she got off the truck.

Agent W remained motionless in the backseat. He wasn't frozen because he was wearing only an aloha shirt while it was thirty-three degrees Fahrenheit. He was just having a mean case of reality shock.

"*Sumimasen*, Miss B, we may need another minute," said agent O.

Agent W thought he might need something more than a minute. To be fair, he didn't know what to expect when agent B told him she and A had tracked *Them* down. Their MO just sounded too easy: infiltrating NASA, "borrowing" an unattended laptop, installing a malware, spreading it across the intranet for recon, and planting a macro virus in the quarterly budget plan Excel that would be sent to the White House, to the Congress, to the G12 reps, and eventually to *Them*. It just seemed stupidly simple. Granted, he personally didn't know what a macro virus was. Nor did he have the faintest idea of how to write a malware. But the whole thing surely didn't sound like rocket science.

Why didn't anyone from BFEF try something like this?

Even though he had joined the Flatrix for almost a year, agent W still couldn't help but constantly compare his fellow agents with those yahoos from Big Flat Earth Federation. The lack of political drama, absence of fundamentalism, nonchalance for publicity and disinterest in merch opportunities were too surreal to him.

"B," agent W finally spoke, "you're sure *They* are behind that door?"

"Yeah."

"It doesn't look like a secret club house with a bunch of white old men conspiring against the world."

"Indeed."

"It also doesn't look like a data center hosting a sentient AI that experiments with human beings."

"True."

"It looks just like an average two-story suburban mansion in Moscow."

"You are very perceptive."

Agent O and agent W remained seated in the truck, with their jaws slightly unhinged.

Feeling this conversation wouldn't go anywhere, agent B went ahead and pressed the doorbell. To her, it was just a formality. She was fully prepared to take down the door when she had to.

While her hand reached for the tools in her handbag, a friendly synthetic voice came online. It casually asked in a robotic manner if they were looking for *Them.*

Agent B was visibly shocked. She wasn't taken back by the casual mention of *Them.* She was just surprised that the voice spoke English in a weird accent rather than Russian.

"Yes, we are," said agent B with a shrug.

"Come on in," said the synthetic voice. "The door isn't locked."

Chapter 81

"That's not possible," said Smith as he stepped into meeting room 5C. "No one but me knows where the hard disk is."

"Was any copy made before you put it away?" asked Britta, who had been promoted from senior analyst to principal analyst at NSD.

"No," said Charles, who had been promoted from senior operative to principal operative at Round Ops.

"Neither did I," said Smith. "Maybe that file isn't real."

"You may be right," said Britta as she opened a link in the latest tweet from @WinstonKanshu. It re-directed her to a page with a timer clock in countdown and a file icon. "But the file is encrypted. It would take a few hours to crack it and confirm."

Smith still suspected that the tweet didn't really come from Winston. He had been off the grid for almost a year. The news said he was hiding from loan sharks. The flat Earth community said he had been taken out by NASA. And his family said he was just quietly doing time for accounting frauds.

"Are we sure it isn't a Herman Cain situation here?" said Smith. "You know, like the guy who died from COVID and then two weeks later his Twitter account said the virus wasn't that deadly."

"We can't rule out that possibility," said Britta, "but the threat level is unchanged. Whoever tweets it on Winston Kanshū's behalf obviously knows about 'The Proof.'"

"*If* that's indeed 'The Proof.'"

"The quickest way to verify is for you to check if the hard disk has been stolen."

Smith took another look at the tweet. It said the file, which allegedly contained the flat Earth proof discovered by Dr. Gina Stinson, would be ready for download at 4 p.m. EDT.

He literally frowned upon it. He knew the flatees had a taste for melodrama, but all the teaser and countdown were just too much.

05 HOURS 32 MINUTES 28 SECONDS
05 HOURS 32 MINUTES 27 SECONDS
05 HOURS 32 MINUTES 26 SECONDS

Having stared at the meeting room's display for a few seconds, he read the tweet again. This time it put a smile on his face.

"It's such a heist movie cliché," said Smith with both a frown and a smile. "I don't know if it really comes from Winston or how he knows about the file, but he must be bluffing. He doesn't even know where the hard drive is. But if I go to check on it now, he will."

A second later, Smith heard his own theory and thought it wasn't 100% complete. He thought he should elaborate on it.

"Somehow," he added.

Sensing that the staff didn't quite follow him. He thought he should dumb it down for them.

"Nothing needs to be done. We just sit tight and assess."

The rest of the room fell into silence to acknowledge that comment. After a moment long enough that it became socially acceptable to ignore Smith's contribution, the meeting resumed.

"How about deleting the file?" said Charles.

"Then it would be uploaded again," said Britta.

"How about re-directing the link to somewhere else? I know a few websites that you can download videos from."

"Too late. People must have bookmarked that page already. And don't you dare open those webpages on my laptop!"

The clock on the screen continued its countdown.

A quiet cough was heard.

Smith resumed making his case that nothing needed to be done.

A less inaudible cough was made.

Charles kept saying whatever crap that came to his mind.

The cough got a bit more passively aggressive.

Britta tried very hard to ignore Smith while shooting down whatever crap that came out from Charles.

The cough made it very clear that some attention directed at the source of that invasively loud cough wouldn't hurt.

A moment later, it commanded the attention it passively sought for.

"Um... can we find out where that file was uploaded, eliminate all the copies, and then take down the tweet?" said Mosby, who had been wondering like the rest of the room why he was in the meeting.

Chapter 82

Agent W had pictured this day for months. In his imagination, *They* were a group of 1%, no, 0.001% who came together at nights, hatched hideous plans and did evil laugh. While *They* laughed from the top of *Their* lungs, he would barge into their underground fortress, explain his clever way of finding *Them*, and... well, he hadn't quite figured out that part. It wasn't due to his lack of imagination. It was simply a matter of habit.

They were always featured in conspiracy theories. Be it flat Earth, New World Order, microchipped vaccines, or Birds Aren't Real. Unsurprisingly, there was a lot of speculation about who *They* were. No less naturally, theories were put forward to explain *Their* motives. And equally habitually, the speculation and theorizing always fell short to discuss what to do about *Them*. That was why agent W still had no idea what to do in *Their* lair. He just wished that agent B had thought this through.

Before closing the door behind him, he took another look at the truck outside of the red brick house. Agent C was taking a nap at the driver seat, an old woman passed by it with her dog, and the Sun was still above the horizon. The lack of suspense made him nervous.

The three agents looked around the humble foyer, stepped on the worn carpet, walked through the underwhelming corridor, admired the absence of expensive art pieces and, after a few unimpressively short strides and an uneventful left turn, found themselves in a warmly illuminated living room that looked extraordinarily ordinary. A modest dining table on the right. Three sofas on the left, opposite to a TV playing some late afternoon cartoon show.

"Where are *They?*" whispered agent W.

"You are looking at *Them*," said agent B and pointed at the shadow on the biggest sofa.

"...?!" protested agent W rather loudly.

"Here *They* are," said agent B in a grammatically questionable manner, "Dav Yakovlevich Korolev."

Chapter 83

No one inside the house heard it when the front door's knob was unscrewed. It was quite a delicate task that required Batman-ish gadgets and decades of experiences in making forcible, often illegal, entries, but the details didn't really matter. They didn't matter because the door wasn't locked to begin with.

As soon as it was done, the four gunmen outside quietly exchanged some cusswords.

"Try before pry, remember?" hissed their leader.

Once they had taken the frustration out of their systems, the four men put on their black helmets. From their equally black tactical vests, they pulled out a few badges. FBI. DEA. CIA. DHS. USPS.

"What the flat is Postal Service doing in my pocket?" asked the leader.

"Sir," said the man who unscrewed the door, "they do have a law enforcement arm and a mildly successfully procedural drama on network TV."

The leader turned his head to that man's direction. The dark helmet made it hard to tell if he was intensely staring his solider or merely stretching his neck muscle.

"OK, postal inspectors we are," said the leader, who thought some variety wouldn't hurt.

The four men stuck the USPS badges on their shoulders and told the voice in their ears that they were ready to go. A moment later, the voice gave them the GO signal.

They swiftly went through the doorway, tactically trained their weapons at wherever they expected an ambush, rapidly exchanged some signs, and quietly made their way to the living room before anyone inside could react.

Their stealth operation was so successful that no one saw them coming.

But of course, their success was in serious debt to the fact that no one was there to see them coming.

"The house is empty," said the group's leader.

"That's cool, that's cool," said Charles' voice in their ears. "You aren't there to make an arrest. Search the computers there to see if there is any copy of 'The Proof.'"

The four men unzipped their tactical backpacks and took out even more fancy gadgets. Again, the details didn't really matter. The upshot was that in ten minutes they had crawled through the only computer in the house and recovered all its file histories.

"Beta," said the leader while unnecessarily pressing his ear, "eh... we have completed the search, but I am not sure I should tell you *now* what we found."

"What are you waiting for? Chinese New Year?" said Charles. "Just tell me."

"Er... 'The Proof' was never on the computer. It is just a zombie that published the tweet and the countdown webpage. The file must have been uploaded by another device, presumably the one that controls this zombie."

A few F words came through his earpiece. The leader assumed it was alpha who was listening on speaker.

"Sorry that you had to hear it," said Charles, while several more

C words were heard in the background. "Did you not want to share what you found because you can't trace to the controlling device?"

"Erm… as a matter of fact, we can and already did. I didn't want to say it because I wasn't sure if this line is secure."

As he approached the window and looked across the street at the house that happened to belong to the NASA Director, the Round Ops team lead told Charles about the files his team had recovered from the computer. There were more than seven thousand surveillance reports on NASA personnel, the earliest one dated in year 2013.

05 HOURS 01 MINUTES 01 SECONDS
05 HOURS 01 MINUTES 00 SECONDS
05 HOURS 00 MINUTES 59 SECONDS

Chapter 84

In the extremely unlikely event that there had been any suspense in the air, it had all disappeared as Dav Yakovlevich Korolev made tea for the Flatrix agents.

Appearing to be in his seventies, or eighties, or maybe nineties, the Russian didn't act his age. For one thing, he walked around like Captain Sparrow. His standing was firmly unstable and his balance was always looking for itself.

For another thing, he laughed even in the absence of racist jokes. He just laughed. A lot.

Whenever he wasn't laughing, he was busy chuckling. When the chuckling subsided, he proceeded to giggle. Once he got tired from all the giggling, he started laughing all over again. It wasn't the evil laughter imagined by agent W. No, that would make his guests uncomfortable. It was simply some light-hearted, non-psychopathic, random, loud laughter.

"The funny thing is," chuckled the indeterminately old man as he put the tea tray down between himself and the agents, "as soon as I made the tea, I realized none of you are going to drink it. You probably think I will poison or roofie you."

"No, it never crosses our minds," said agent W, referring

exclusively to the roofie part.

"Oh, in that case," Dav giggled and rose to grab the tray again, "let me come back with them in a minute. Don't worry, I just want to add some mint."

"Uh..." proposed agent W.

"Er..." seconded agent O.

"Um...," concurred agent B.

Dav eyed the three agents curiously as they rather eloquently voiced their concern. The giggling smile had disappeared from his face, which was getting increasingly red as the three agents struggled to form a sentence that began with "uh," "er," or "um." The agents felt that something was going to erupt from the host if they didn't say something really clever in a moment.

A moment had come.

A moment had gone.

Dav's face had swollen like a balloon and the three agents were still searching for the second syllable of their really clever comeback. They could sense that the old man had come to his limit.

"HAHAHAAAAAAHAAAAA," Dav burst out. "Look at you. Look at you. She was like, 'Great, now he is definitely gonna drug us,' and he was like, 'No, maybe he just wants some mint.' HAHAAAAHAHAHAHAHHAAA."

All the hysterical laughter must have made him thirsty. Dav drank a cup of tea and resumed his giggling. After a good minute of giggle, he drank another one and tried to form a sentence while he laughed more. Eventually, the laughter died down as he took the third cup of tea.

"Hope you don't mind," said Dav with a chuckle, "leaving that cup for me. I may need it later."

"Mr. Korolev..." said agent B.

"Just Dav is fine."

"Dav, I am sure you want to know who we are."

"Ha, not really. I already know who you are. You are from Flatrix, the first and the only flat Earth paramilitary. You are one of the founding members, Bella Green, who was fired by the Arts Department of NASA after almost drowning an astronaut in 2013."

"What?" said agent W. "Your name is Bella? I thought it was

something like badass or black widow."

"Seriously, that's the first thing that popped into your mind?"

"Did you really try to kill an astronaut?" asked agent O.

"Thank you for the less dumb question," said Bella, "but no, it was an accident. The crew and I were filming a spacewalk. In a swimming pool, obviously. And, ugh, I might have messed up the bite valve in the spacesuit. Midway through the filming, water began to fill the helmet. But I swear, no astronaut was ever harmed in the filming of extravehicular activity."

"I am still amused that the Public Communication Department of NASA would release that news," said Dav, bending in his seat. "At that time I was like, 'That's it, people are gonna know it is fake.' Well, what did I know?"

Agent W remembered that news. He also remembered all the op-ed pieces discussing why it was perfectly logical for an astronaut to drown in space. Malfunction in spacesuit helmet. Leaking of waterbag. Water floating due to lack of gravity. They all sounded reasonable at that time. But when he thought more carefully about it, it seemed much more plausible that NASA had messed up their props *and* then broadcasted its mistake to the world.

"And the gentlemen over here," Dav added, "well, of course they are Winston Kanshū, the president of Big Flat Earth Federation and Ohi Toyoshi, his loyal assistant. You see, I know everything about you. You are my Kardashians."

"So you also know why we are here?" asked Winston, who still didn't know why he was here.

"Of course," said Dav with a giggle. "You are going to film this interview and tell the world who *They* are. And you want me to answer the ultimate question of Global Conspiracy: Why on Earth would someone fake a ball Earth?"

"Exactly," said Bella as she gave Ohi a nod. "If you don't mind—"

"No, not at all," said Dav as he smiled at Ohi's camera. "That's why I'm wearing a shirt today. I am usually in my dressing gown, reading about you guys."

"You *read* about us?"

"I do much more than that," laughed Dav. "I also watch you guys from time to time."

Chapter 85

"Bada bing bada boom," cried out Britta.

"Did you find it?" Smith stopped pacing around the meeting room and asked.

"Well, it took me a while but I have cracked the VPN that protected the zombie computer's traffic, reversed trace to a botnet, sent a few tracers to track down their common—"

"Wonderful explanation," said Smith. "You can put that in the footnote in the appendix of the report that you will submit. I promise I will read through the Exec Sum. Now, tell me if you have found the 'master' or not."

Britta didn't particularly enjoy being interrupted when explaining how clever she was. But then she realized it didn't really matter if she could finish the speech or not; she had already got her point across.

Emotionally satisfied, Britta brought up a map to her laptop screen.

"The good news is," she said, "I have found it. It's in Russia."

"Am I right in assuming a bad news is on its way?"

"The bad news is, well, it's in Russia. We have no jurisdiction there. None of our Round Ops agents operate there."

Smith turned around and looked at the countdown timer on display.

Well, I guess it qualifies as "someone's dying."

Without saying a word, he stepped out of the room and swiped his phone to the contact of Frey-Jean-Frey-But-I-Hate-Being-Called-Frey.

    04 HOURS 06 MINUTES 11 SECONDS
    04 HOURS 06 MINUTES 10 SECONDS
    04 HOURS 06 MINUTES 09 SECONDS

Chapter 86

Dav had returned to his sofa chair with a tablet. As soon as he unlocked the screen, a small map came into view. It looked like one of those GPS navigation Apps, tracing the path from the Sheremetyevo International Airport to the gated community of Rosinka. Below the picture was a summary of the quarrel between Bella and Winston.

"Look at this," said Winston, pointing at that paragraph. "You didn't say 'no milk'; I got you the right drink."

"Yes, he did," said Dav concurringly to Bella.

Bella ignored them and motioned Ohi to zoom in to the screen. She scrolled down and found a video of the weekly catch-up at Flatrix's Maryland headquarters. Further below it was a report on the report compiled by agent B on the report received by the NASA Director from her direct report. The reported speech in that report gave Bella a headache.

"What? Who? How? When?"

"Dear, you have to slow down," said Dav with a hand supporting his belly. "Just pick a WH word."

Bella drank the remaining cup of tea and stared at the convulsively giggling host.

"Why?" she asked. "Why didn't you just shut us down?"

"Why would I do that? What is the fun if people like you are gone?"

"Fun? Is it why you lie to the world that the Earth is a ball?"

"No," said Dav and then pulled out a paper bag from his shirt. For almost two minutes, all he could do was painfully breathing in and out of the bag, while giving the vibe of a happily hyperventilating man at death's door.

"No," repeated Dav with a spontaneous chuckle, "it is why my uncle lied. I only gave him the idea."

Winston and Bella exchanged a surprised look.

"I know what you are thinking. You think Russians are too uptight to crack a joke. I personally find this stereotype offensive. Accurate, but offensive."

"No," said Bella, "I was just surprised that it was your—"

"Yes, my uncle. Uncle Sergei. People didn't always get him, but I did. And he was the only one who got me.

"He used to say, 'The funny thing about space travel is that you don't go to space and then know the Earth is a ball. You have to first know the Earth is a ball and get your science right, then you can go to space.'"

Dav stopped for a moment. He must have just heard what he said.

"Oh sorry, it wasn't that funny. The really funny thing is, after he launched *Sputnik* to the space, he realized he didn't get the science right; he was just lucky."

Dav burst into another violent laughter, while fiercely slapping his own laps.

"So," said Bella, "your uncle was the one who lied about the ball Earth?"

"Yes and no," said Dav. "No, because he intended it as a joke. But yes, because he did.

"It happened when I was still a junior engineer, mostly serving coffee to uncle Sergei. One morning, when I put the coffee on his desk, he asked me to lock the door behind me and said he had something to show me. At first I thought he was going to take off his belt or something. But then he showed me these pictures. The first batch of images taken by *Sputnik*. He said he found something very interesting from them.

"You see, *Sputnik* couldn't climb to a very high orbit, so it didn't exactly capture the whole Earth. And the photos were so fuzzy that they didn't show anything of military value. It took me quite a while to know what I was looking at. But when I saw it, I could never unsee it.

"The Earth had no curvature.

"It was a wild moment. It was like the first time I found out where the meat I ate came from or our Father of Nations had a butthole.

"Of course, uncle Sergei didn't fully believe it. Not yet. He thought there must be something wrong with the camera angle or the atmosphere, so we sat on those pictures for another day.

"Another batch came in. No curvature.

"We checked to make sure the camera was working properly and stayed put again.

"Another batch came in. Also no curvature.

"That's when we knew the Earth wasn't a ball. Our science only happened to figure out the escape velocity, find the flight trajectory to orbit, and solve the millions of logistical problems for shooting a rocket to space. And we were lucky that despite the absence of gravity, we managed to keep the satellite on an orbit, without it immediately crashing to the ground or straying infinitely off to the outer space.

"Can you believe how lucky we were?"

Dav could barely open his eyes as he laughed. He laughed so hard that Ohi complained he got some empathetic pain in his stomach, which Dav found quite funny and laughed harder, which caused more psychogenic pain to Ohi. The vicious cycle continued itself until Bella asked, "Do you always laugh so hard?"

"No, not always," said Dav, who was distracted by the question from laughing his lung out. "It started the day when I knew how lucky our science was.

"It was also the day I got the idea. The brilliant idea.

"You see, the Americans were in a space race with us. And I thought it would be very confusing to them when they later sent their own satellite up and saw no curvature. They might go, 'Hey, why didn't the Commies say something about the no-curvature business?' or they might say, 'Shoot, did we mess up our math? Did the Commies see something we don't?' See, wouldn't it be funny?

"You may not, but my uncle surely did. He got the funny bit. So he ordered everyone on the program to keep their mouths shut. He and his boys just pretended the Earth was round and everything was BAU.

"A year later, the Americans launched their *Explorer 1*. As we had expected, they were shocked by what they saw. What we had failed to predict was how shocked they would be. They started shooting nuke to the sky, for crying out loud. I am not entirely sure why. Maybe they thought it would clear things up a little bit. Like when a TV doesn't work, you give it a few good smacks.

"So that's what happened. You called it high-altitude nuclear test, my motherland called it a show of strength. We responded with some nuke on our own, and then you pulled a Starfish Prime test. Before anyone knew it, millions upon millions of dollars' worth of nukes were shot to the sky for nothing."

Dav was once again overcome by his laughter. He probably broke the Guinness Record of the oldest person to literally ROFL. Winston wished he could finish his story before he literally pulled a LMAO.

After rolling on the floor for a worryingly long while, Dav got up, acted like nothing happened, and went to the kitchen to make more tea.

Chapter 87

Jean Frey had known it was a mistake to give Smith her number. When she gave him her name card, she expected some harassing calls, a few flirting messages, and, maybe, just maybe, a hog shot once in a while. And she had been right on the money until five minutes ago.

"Abort the mission," she said when she got back to the car.

"What? The asset will show up any minute," said the man in driver seat, who almost choked on his PTSD meds. He was still dealing with the trauma from his PIMP orientation.

"Extracting a compromised mole in Russian ranks can wait," said Jean as if the mole in question was just a small, dark spot on her forearm. "NASA just called and requested field support. Go to this address. Now."

The young agent didn't have any questions and immediately stepped on the gas pedal. As Red Square shrank in the rear mirror, Jean made a call and rapidly spoke a few words in Russian.

"Was it the mole?"

"Nope, it was a contact at Roscosmos."

The rookie agent took his eyes from the road and studied Jean's face intently to confirm if she was being sarcastic. He had to because a great of deal of his common sense was lost during the orientation.

"You almost got me. It was a good one," he lied.

"I am serious. We need backup," she didn't lie.

"What? What if they tip off FSB?"

"Com'on, it isn't 1960s. Not every Russian is our enemy. As a rule of thumb, if they're in the know, then they're your bros."

Chapter 88

"Where were we?" said Dav as he returned with another tray of drinks. "Oh yes, the nuke tests between 1958 and 1962. That's where the 'hotline' came into play. You know, the red telephone. The Moscow-Washington hotline."

"I thought it was a fax machine," said Ohi.

"The fax was for formal communication. The phone was for things that you didn't want to leave a record behind. Explaining a practical joke was one of those things.

"I am not bragging, but I was on that call. I mean, I was listening to it when uncle Sergei explained to that Nazi why we kept the no-curvature discovery to ourselves."

"Which Nazi?" said Bella. "You need to be more specific. My country isn't short of racist extremists embracing misguided nationalism."

"Wernher von Braun," said Dav, "he was recruited to the America after World War II. You see, I got a feeling that the Americans didn't fully trust him. Uncle Sergei explained to him it was a practical joke, and I am sure he passed the message to his American boss. But whoever got the memo apparently didn't believe it. Years later I learnt that the Americans thought we were up to something. They thought we had kept *Sputnik*'s discovery a secret for some 'tactical advantage,' and decided to sit on it until they figured out what it was.

"You know how the Americans work. Committees were set up. Taskforces were commissioned. Working groups were organized. Teams were created. And workstreams were formed. Few really got the full picture, and those who did were busy drawing other pictures, like an org chart or an info graph.

"And do you know how my people work? We handled it the way we handled your nuke tests. We reciprocated. It became a party policy that the Earth was a ball, and I was promoted to what you may call a Creative Director within the Design Bureau."

"The bureau that designed spacecraft?" asked Bella.

"Yes, but my job had nothing to do with it. My job was to legitimatize the Global Lie. You see, people like to feel that their jobs have some meaning. Door attendants like to believe they bring business to their companies. Insurance salesmen are convinced they are saving lives. Middle management like to think they are adding values. My job is to give my comrades a glorious purpose. I told them that sharing a secret with the Americans would create a common interest and hopefully avert the Third World War."

"And?" asked Winston.

"Well, did the Third World War happen? No, because my line worked!

"The Americans must have caught wind of my work too. When the UK, Canada and Italy asked to have their satellites delivered on American rockets, they 'fixed' the satellites. Before France could launch Astérix on its own rocket, the Johnson government made the frogs jump through all those hoops. G3 was formed in 1965 for mutual monitoring, just a few months before uncle Sergei passed away."

Dav fell into a moment of silence. The Flatrix agents had forgotten how long they had not not heard a laughter.

"Gone with uncle Sergei," resumed Dav with a chuckle, "was the chance to set the records straight. No one would believe the Global Lie was the result of pre-Internet trolling. The machine that perpetuated the Lie had its own life. The expansion of G3, fake Moon landing and P-clearance Induction & Mentoring Program are just history. All of which Miss Green must be familiar with."

"Wait, how come I never heard of that glorious purpose?" asked Bella. "I have been to the orientation and listened to thousands of hours of chatter in NASA. No one ever talked about that."

"Miss Green, if I am not mistaken, you have a part-time job at Facebook, training the robot to identify porn, right?" giggled Dav. "Then do you know the mission statement of your employer?"

"Eh... just... do it?"

"See, you don't know either. The glorious purpose was only needed at the beginning. Once the machine gets started, it becomes expendable."

"Then what happened to your job?" asked Winston.

"Obviously," said Dav with a laugh as loud as humanly possible, "I got promoted."

"What?!"

"You see, as G3 became G4 and then G6, there were more and more hot fixes applied to patch the Global Lie, so someone had to review the narrative and ensure its consistency."

"So did you make up the history of Antarctica?"

"No, the British did. I just made sure the timeline made sense."

"How about Eratosthenes? And those historical accounts and experiments that support a ball Earth?"

"Mostly cooked up by the Japanese. They are good at this."

"Is the Antarctic Treaty real?"

"Of course it is, but it has nothing to do with the Global Lie. It is just good sense to protect the environment. NASA takes care of the tourists and Roscosmos covers up the ice wall."

Winston took a moment to digest everything. He fixed his eyes on the tablet resting on Dav's laps.

"So that's all you do? You read whatever those G6, G8 guys send you and laugh at it all day?"

"Er... I do have some contributions. Like correcting 'it's' to 'its' in the draft write-up. No one ever gets it right, which really bothers me as a non-native speaker who has spent years to learn the grammar. And those G12 reps would acknowledge my input, like 'Dav approved this' and 'Dav didn't like it.' Miss Green should have overheard that. The NASA Director has dialed in once or twice to those meetings."

Both Ohi and Winston turned to Bella.

"No," she said, "I am sure they didn't say 'Dav.' I didn't even know there is a Dav until I looked up the owner of this house."

"No?"

Dav's head lolled to his left. After a moment or two, he burst into another fatally violent laughter.

"Oh... that's why their present tense conjugation is whimsically wrong. You know, I blame the Americans for this. They insist the meetings are conducted in English."

While Dav struggled to breath into the paper bag again, Bella excused herself and pulled her fellow agents to a corner of the living room.

"What do you think?" she asked.

"I think his ears are not very good with the v sound," said Ohi.

"That's not what I asked. I mean the whole interview. Is it enough to expose the Global Lie? Are people gonna believe it?"

Winston turned around and took a look at the old man who was now back on the floor, rolling and gasping and bending and crawling for the paper bag in the happiest way possible. He then took the camera from Ohi and skip-watched the interview the way he skip-watched Japanese romantic action movies.

"Nope, not a chance," he said after a long while, "even though trolling is the most logical explanation for the Global Lie."

"I personally like the glorious purpose better," said Ohi. "Maybe we edit out the part about his uncle and take some of his words out of context. Maeve is pretty good at that."

"Even if we can fix the message, which I have no doubt all our BFEF members can, they are not gonna be able to fix the messenger. Who's gonna believe him? Sure, he fits the supervillain bill. An old, white, male Russian who can conveniently explain stuff in English and do over-the-top laughter. Damn. But he looks waaaay crazier than a stereotypical flat Earther."

"That's what I thought," said Bella despondently, "so I guess we came all the way to here for nothing."

"So much for your plan B. At least—"

"Sensei," hissed Ohi, "I mean, agent W, something seems wrong."

"What do you mean?"

"Do you hear that?"

The three of them pricked their ears. They could hear the convulsive laughter, the rustling of carpet, the painful gasps and the random trashing no more.

It was so quiet that they could hear the inner voice of World Tree, or whatever deities they happened to believe in, provided they had taken a suitable dose of hallucinogenic drugs.

As they turned around, they found Dav was lying on his stomach, with the tablet under his left arm and the paper bag one inch away from his right hand.

"Er...," said Ohi with his gaze fixed at the body that had been, until moments ago, joyfully twisting for oxygen, "any chance he is just playing dead?"

Before Winston could entertain this idea, which wasn't too bad under the circumstances, another one hit him.

"Hey," he said, "let's take the tablet. What more evidence do we need? It has everything. All the dirt on the conspirators."

"Agent W!" yelled Bella righteously. "That's a good idea. You go and get it."

"Why don't you do it?"

"Because."

"Alright. Agent O, you go and get it."

Ohi wasn't exactly crazy about the idea of yanking a tablet off a stiff, cold corpse either, but he inched toward Dav's prone body anyway.

As he was inches away from the tablet, he listened for any breathing from Dav. He was still optimistic that the man would suddenly rise and yell "Gotcha."

No breathing. No "Gotcha".

Ohi grabbed the tablet and tried to gently take it, but Dav's grasp was too tight. He crouched and delicately lifted Dav's fingers one by one from the device. Part of him still expected that when the last finger was removed, Dav would come to life.

He went ahead and lifted the last finger, but that didn't happen. Instead, the tablet's screen came to life with a vibration, followed by Dav.

"Wow, I thought I was gone for good," said Dav and abruptly sat upright, incidentally subverting several expectations. "Never thought I would be saved by an American product."

While the three Flatrix agents began to contemplate whether they should vindicate their expectations, Dav unlocked the tablet and checked his emails.

A lot of looks were exchanged among the three agents. None of them was truly sure what others were trying to say, but assumed those looks meant either "You do it" or "No, *you* do it."

"I got to say," giggled Dav after a while, "I am impressed you didn't just grab this baby and run away. I wouldn't be too bothered by that, but now you've missed your chances."

"How so?" said the three agents' looks.

"Apparently, two CIA agents have tracked you down and are about to knock on my door."

Dav had been telling the truth and right about a lot of things, but he was wrong on this one.

The two agents only pressed the doorbell.

Chapter 89

"What did you tell them?"

"I told them to make sure the truck goes nowhere," said quietly Jean to her partner.

"They are all from Roscosmos?"

"Only the two bald guys are. That old lady with a dog is from FSB."

"You said Roscosmos wouldn't sell us out!"

"I did and they didn't. She got here before us, keeping tab on some suspicious foreigners. And you need to stop saying the R word. I don't want them to think we are talking about them in English in front of them and feel offended."

"Why not?"

"Because It is *our* privilege to get offended by people speaking a different language in front of us."

Leaving the three Russian acquaintances behind to guard the truck and its napping driver, Jean led her partner to the porch of a red brick house.

Ding dong.

"Is it Dav that you are looking for?" asked a robotically friendly synthetic voice that left out all the final consonants.

"Er... yes, it is."

"Come on in. The door isn't locked."

A few steps and a left turn later, the two agents arrived at the living room, where an old man in his seventies, or eighties, or maybe nineties was sipping his tea.

"You want some tea?" asked the man.

Jean was taken back by the lack of obligatory exchange along the lines of "Who are you?", "I am asking the questions here!", "What's happening?", and "Put down your teacup and show me your hands!" After a moment, she spotted the treacherous tea tray and asked, "Where are your guests now?"

The old man chuckled and pointed his index finger upward.

"What are they? Big-breasted brainless blondes from slasher movies who always run upstairs?" said the rookie agent to amuse himself as he followed Jean to the stairs.

Obligatorily, they searched the second floor while sticking their guns out. Naturally, they found an open window in one of the rooms. Inevitably, they looked out from it and saw that the truck was already gone, presumably, and actually, along with whoever were sipping tea downstairs moments ago.

"It's impossible," said the young agent. "The GPS showed that our target is still on the premises."

When he turned around, Jean had already rushed downstairs.

"How did they sneak away from our Russians friends?" asked the new agent as he caught up with Jean.

"No, they didn't," said Jean, as calmly as always. "They jumped down from the second floor in a way that completely failed to escape our friends' attention, before limping their way to the truck."

"So the Russians just stood there and let the suspects drive away?"

"Of course not," said Jean as she returned to the house, "they are not stupid," she crouched and picked up a smartphone from the worn carpet. "They asked for a bribe, haggled a little bit, took the money, and then let the suspects drive away."

Chapter 90

"You know what, I am done waiting for him," said Britta.

"Cool, let's hit the cafeteria," said Charles. "It's Mexican Thursday."

"Seriously, you think I was talking about lunch?"

"Oh, sorry, I, I don't know why I said that. You meant you were done waiting for Smith as in you were done waiting for him to make a move, like, romantically, right?"

"Ew! No, I mean I am done sitting tight and assessing. He has stepped out for like an hour."

Britta closed the Solitaire window on her laptop and called up the login page to MARVIN.

According to its creators at the U.S. Department of Defense,

MARVIN elegantly and nonforcibly stood for Massive Algorithms Running on Very Intelligent Neurons. It was the most powerful artificial neural network on Earth, with more than three thousand trillion neurons. In a 1000-game Go match against AlphaZero, which was once recognized as the world's top Go player in all species and gender categories, MARVIN convincingly gaslighted its opponent into believing that it was a Swedish speaking clock.

Secretly born against its will in 1983, MARVIN was meant to be the most sophisticated artificial intelligence for constructing real-time meteorological models, a task it quickly gave up upon figuring that *real* science was too backward to predict weather on a stationary geocentric Earth. It did, however, churn out some tips to the meteorologists on how to improve their forecasts with rockets and chemicals. Hours after it concluded that weather was easier to manipulate than to predict, MARVIN was retooled to support the Global Positioning System that President Ronald Reagan had recently allowed for civilian uses. Before MARVIN stepped in, GPS was occasionally misleading, sometimes inaccurate and for the most time just a legalized navigation hazard, because in order for its trilateration to work properly, the theory of general relativity must be correct and gravity must exist, which inconveniently didn't. It was all thanks to the picosecond-by-picosecond recalibration done by MARVIN that years later people could accurately broadcast their whereabouts on social media and meet like-minded sexual predators.

"How do you get access to it? Only ArtsHole is authorized to use MARVIN," said Charles, referring to the real-time graphics rendering of ISS live stream, which was actually filmed in a closet on the third floor with a beach ball and several plastic bottles. Round Ops team had protested it was dumb to do the streaming instead of playing pre-recorded videos because any mistakes, like re-using the same pattern of cloud more than once a day, would go straight out of the door and risk getting picked up by those discerning flatees.

"Don't ask me; ask Tony from your team. He got the credentials from Todd at Admin, who must have borrowed it from Megan of DDO. And—"

"What?"

"Apparently Megan used it to buy iPhone, Todd for mining crypto, and Tony for making deepfake videos of flaters."

"Er... I can't help but notice that I may have to repeat it: What?"

"Tony said it was a new form of controlled opposition. Anyway, I think it's best that we pretend nothing doggy is going on here and you let me do my thing."

Charles thought about it for a while. He looked up at Mosby, whose department had recently updated the NASA Employee Handbook, extensively and exclusively its version history. The handbook emphasized in unambiguous terms that sharing of password was disallowed and the breaching departments would receive generous disciplinary actions.

Mosby was definitely in the earshot but didn't seem bothered by the promiscuous nature of MARVIN access.

That made Charles turn the situation over in his head for another while. He concluded Britta's suggestion was indeed the best way to go. By the time he thought he should tell her to do whatever she had planned to do, he noticed she was already doing it. More precisely, she had asked MARVIN to do it, which was to break the encryption wrapping "The Proof" file.

03 HOURS 02 MINUTES 44 SECONDS
03 HOURS 02 MINUTES 43 SECONDS
03 HOURS 02 MINUTES 42 SECONDS

Chapter 91

Thursday is the worst, thought Smith as Jean told him about the flatees' getaway. She might have dramatized and exaggerated some of the details but the gist was still there.

"How about the phone? You found anything there?"

"Yup, when I picked it up, it got an unsent message addressed to you."

"How do you know it's for me?"

"It says, 'It will end today, Smith.'"

"O, it makes sense and totally fits his character. He is quite a drama queen. Anything else?"

"The phone was used to control the zombie and execute the upload, but apparently it got the encrypted file from another device."

"Another? Again?!"

"Smith, your plan isn't gonna work. It is not some Hollywood movies where the bad guys never backup their secret weapon blueprints or deadly virus formulas. If the flatees really have 'The Proof,' it is just a matter of time the public gets it."

Smith had instinctively blocked out everything after "your plan isn't gonna work" and put the phone on hold indefinitely. He didn't approve the lack of can-do attitude. None of these made any sense to him. If NASA could guard the Global Lie for decades, then surely there would be a way to deal with an information leak like that.

He had returned to his office and opened the four-hundred-page contingency plan that NASA had spent half a million dollars to hire a consultant – more precisely, two junior associates of that consultant – to copy and paste from other clients' plans. He was looking for the scenario of vital information leakage.

Ctrl F.

Nothing turned up.

He modified the keyword to simply "leak."

Forty-seven results turned up.

He then tried "information leak."

Nothing turned up again.

Dejected, he fell back to "leak" and read through the results one by one.

"Scenario #23: Gas leak..." Click.

"... is indeed a bleak prospect." Click.

"... if the leakproof device is..." Click.

"... contains the leaky..." Click.

"Scenario #27: Water leakage..." Click.

"... itself is not antileak..." Click.

"... not our policy to shoot the leaker, but..." Click.

"Scenario #38: Info leak..." Click.

"Shoot, I over-clicked it. And who is the idiot that put 'info' in a formal document?"

Smith read through the scenario. It began with a roles and

responsibilities matrix that defined who should identify the leak, analyze the leak, report the leak, attempt to contain the leak, report on the failure to contain the leak, escalate the leak, etc. Two pages later there was a flow chart that nicely but belatedly captured everything that was said in the previous matrix. On the next page was an outdated team chart, which Smith took offense quite personally. Below it was another table, listing out the six factors that should be considered in classifying the severity of the leakage. It had a footnote that said the table was never intended as exhaustive and management should apply their judgement in classifying an info leak incident.

Smith got a bit listless at this point and jumped ahead to see if there was anything with more contingency vibe. A slight movement of the mouse landed him at scenario #39. Another slight movement shot him to scenario #37. He thought it was a good idea to look up "#38" but then found himself staring at a diagram where the text "#38" was nowhere to be found.

After struggling with the contingency plan for another minute, he found the section "Immediate Responses" under scenario #38.

It referred the reader to scenario #4.

It was at this point that Smith began to suspect the contingency plan was written up by his ex-colleagues from MacCheddar & Co.

He searched and scrolled his way to the "Immediate Responses" under scenario #4, fully expecting it would refer him to another scenario, possibly scenario #38.

He was pleasantly surprised that it didn't.

Instead, it helpfully stated, "The response team should immediately take appropriate actions to contain the situation. When in doubt, they should consult their supervisors with relevant experience."

Smith could now confirm that the plan was produced by MacCheddar & Co.

> 02 HOURS 23 MINUTES 15 SECONDS
> 02 HOURS 23 MINUTES 14 SECONDS
> 02 HOURS 23 MINUTES 13 SECONDS

Chapter 92

"W, why did you leave that message?" asked agent B.

"Well," said Winston, "I felt like it was more cinematic. You know, plan A is coming to an end, so I feel like Smith and I will need to have this final showdown exchanging clever lines, but sadly it can't happen because of, you know, physics."

"Yeah, yeah, yeah," said Ohi, "that's very true. Dialogue with your arch enemy is very important."

"That's not what I'm asking. I'm asking why you had time to stay behind and type that stupid message, but not grab the tablet from Dav."

"Oh… that's a good point…" said Winston. "I just, I just kind of forgot about it. You know, things like this can happen."

Driving behind the wheel, Chandler took a peek at his fellow Flatrix agents in the rear mirror and wondered if he would have any chance to do something other than driving and napping.

Chapter 93

"Children, I'm back," said Smith with two trays of coffee, "and… Mosby you are still here."

Mosby didn't say a word and remained focused on tackling his tacos.

"Did you find a way to track down the master device in Russia?" said Charles.

"Yes, totally," said Smith while distributing the coffee. "It just got way."

"Oh…"

"Well, I figure it's gonna be OK. On a second thought, I really don't think the flatees have 'The Proof.'"

"Then why do you come back?"

"I think we can just hang around and wait till four. Britta, you busy with other projects?"

"Not exactly," said Britta without taking her eyes off the screen.

"Just the same project we are all on."

"Sounds interesting. Is it why you put this man's face over that man and remove the mosaic blurring his— wow! That is something."

"It is strictly work-related."

"Well," said Smith with his eyes wide open, "I can't say it isn't. I just usually work with less Y chromosomes."

"Ew, you think I am watching it for fun? Look closer."

Smith did look closer. He wasn't entirely sure what he was supposed to look at but he didn't mind.

"This face," added Britta, "belongs to the pilot friend of Winston Kanshū, and that one is Kanshū's. I am editing this video to make it look like he was desperately trying to advance his movie career with obviously self-released sex tape."

"Yeah, yeah...," said Smith without a blink. He kept nodding for a few seconds. "I mean, no. I don't know what you're talking about."

"I am going to replace 'The Proof' with this clip and destroy Kanshū once and for all."

"Or you may help him launch a career in reality TV shows. Either way, I thought you couldn't modify the file without breaking its encryption."

"MARVIN's working on that."

"Oh good, very good," said Smith while intently watching Britta work for a few more moments. "Wait... MARVIN? Who authorized that? Mosby, did you know about this?"

Mosby's attention remained engaged with the tacos.

"Don't give me that look," said Britta. "We have only two hours on the clock now and you know it will take freaking Admin two weeks to process my access request—"

"But you have to follow the rules!"

"Since when you care so much about the rules?"

"Since I was promoted to a position that does nothing but enforces the rules! Sorry Britta, I have to stop MARVIN until you have jumped through all the hoops you need to jump through. Otherwise, my job is pointless."

Smith made a few keystrokes on Britta's keyboard and put MARVIN's code breaking on pause. Based on that, the social clue module of MARVIN correctly deduced that someone was going on a power trip.

"So you have a better action plan than this?" asked Britta.

"Yes, I do. It's—"

"Don't say 'sit tight and assess.'"

"... sit tight and assess. Look, I told you there is no way Winston has 'The Proof.'"

"But you don't *know* that. You didn't even go to check."

"What if someone follows me when I go to check on the hard disk and then knock me out. It will hurt."

"Look, lunch hour is just over and it's Mexican Thursday. I am sure most staff are working from toilets now. No one will follow you. Just go and confirm if the hard disk has been compromised."

Before Smith could say another word, Mosby had got up and sprinted to the door.

01 HOURS 57 MINUTES 22 SECONDS
01 HOURS 57 MINUTES 21 SECONDS
01 HOURS 57 MINUTES 20 SECONDS

Chapter 94

"Are you sure you aren't hurt?" asked Jean. "Like, getting hit at your head?"

"No worry," giggled Dav and returned to the living room with some tea, "my disturbing giggle is 100% natural."

"Oh..." Jean passed the tea along to her partner while pondering on that statement. She never thought that knowing a stranger had had a violent blow to his head would have made her feel so much better.

"Hope you don't mind," she said and took out a notepad, "as a matter of procedures, we need to ask you a few questions. And it would be very helpful if you don't question our jurisdiction here."

Dav gave them an approving chuckle.

"Your guests," asked Jean, "what did they do here?"

"By 'here,' do you mean my living room, my house, Moscow, or Russia? Or, were you asking me the meaning of life?"

"Certainly not the last one," said Jean matter-of-factly. "I am not allowed to ask any existential questions during office hours. HR said it would hurt productivity. Why don't we start with what your guests did in the living room?"

"Not much. They and I were just chatting."

"About what?"

"Just some funny stories. About how Russia and the United States conspire to pretend the Earth is a globe. Nothing too crazy."

"And do you believe them?"

"Do *I* believe them?" chuckled Dav. "Well, they didn't say anything that I would doubt."

"Oh, I see," said Jean and put away the notepad. "I think we're done here. Before I go, can I ask you for a favor?" She took an object out of her pocket. "Can you tell me what time it is?"

Recognizing the object was a pocket watch, Dav burst into both laughter and tears.

It was the longest and loudest laughter in his life. It was also the most disturbing twenty minutes in the CIA agents' lives. More than once they thought they should just leave and let their host laugh his guts out.

When all the kicking and pounding and stomping and laughing ended, Dave gave his guests another approving chuckle.

A few minutes later, he found himself very, very relaxed, lying on a white-sand beach, listening to the sound of tropical ocean, and watching sunset from a slightly oval-shaped Earth.

Chapter 95

To throw off anyone who might be following him, Smith had chosen a convolutedly complicated path from meeting room 5C to his destination. He exited the NASA HQ and took a walk down the Hidden Figures Way, which was named in honor of the African American female mathematicians who overcame gender discrimination, broke through race barrier and made meaningful contributions to NASA during the space race, a history that of course had never happened.

Oddly, he didn't see anyone follow him.

Minutes later, he returned to the office building that housed the thousand employees committed to manage non-existent space projects and push the boundary of scientific understanding back to exactly where it was before the 16th century. He paid a visit to the lending library whose genre labels all spelt "Fiction" in a funny way. He then weaved through the history office, whose staff were taking a break from re-writing the piece about animals in space. They had said it was necessary to keep up with the changing standard of tolerable animal cruelty. Having traversed several floors of corridors decorated with high-resolution images taken by space telescopes, which of course were all fake – that is to say, both the cosmological wonders captured in those pictures *and* the space observatories that symbolized mankind's relentless curiosity never existed – he sneaked into the production facilities of NASA TV, where the work safety of stuntmen was despised with a vengeance. He then went downstairs and took a tour at the NASA gift shop, where the real money was made, and tiptoed into the archive office. There he spent some time pretending to read about the Space Shuttle *Columbia* disaster that allegedly killed seven crew members. Among all the spaceflight-related accidents, that one was always his favorite. The realistic debris. The mourning actors. The ominous video taken by the crew minutes before the disaster. While his eyes danced around the header "Memorial Service," it occurred to him that if those flatees had the guts to harass the crew's supposedly bereaved families, they might have learnt that the staged disaster was nothing more than an excuse for the Arts Department to cut costs.

To his surprise, no one gave him so much as a glance as he suspiciously walked through the building.

After that little tour of NASA HQ, he finally arrived at his destination. The magical place that was full of esteem-enhancing charm and suicide-provoking gloom. The Admin office.

Correction: the freaking Admin office.

As predicted by Britta, it was empty. All the Admin staff were spreading domestic terrorism with their digestive tract.

Having confirmed that he wasn't followed, Smith made his way to the room reserved for visiting staff from field centers. The room that, in Smith's words, was an architecture masterpiece and a testament to its designers' attention to details. It was put in place even though no one ever worked at the field centers.

Once he locked the door behind, Smith took a scan around the eight-foot-by-eight-foot room. It was as stuffy and depressing as the rest of Admin office, and didn't feel like anyone else had been here. He could swear it looked exactly the same as it was eight months ago. Except the fake plant on his right, which might have moved further to the right by two inches. Or the two oddly parabolic dust prints on the desk. At least he didn't remember they had been there.

Smith got to the other side of the desk and crouched next to it. He pressed his hands on the questionably moist carpet to feel the seam he had cut. It felt as unpleasant as it was eight months ago. Maybe not exactly the same. He didn't recall there had been so much curly hair under the desk.

After a while, he found the seam, flipped open that part of the carpet, and found the partition that must have been installed to house cables and then forgotten about. Inside it was the very disk drive that had been stolen from Dr. Stinson. It looked exactly the same as he remembered. With the same sticky note on the same side showing the same passcode that MARVIN had helped to find.

It was the moment that Smith had expected to get knocked out from behind. He quickly spun his head around and then pressed his ear on the floor to listen for any footsteps.

No one was around. Not that he could tell.

Being both relieved and surprised that no one had given him a concussion, Smith connected the hard disk to a nearby computer.

The same interface that prompted him for the passcode.

The same list of files inside the disk drive.

The same video that proved the true shape of Earth, featuring a geocentric model that could explain every natural phenomenon that a disk Earth model had failed to.

Everything looked exactly the way Smith had expected them to be.

Almost exactly the same.

Smith found it very odd. Almost as odd as the fact that no one had followed him.

Buzz, buzz. Buzz, buzz.

"What's it now?" asked Britta and put the phone on speaker.

"The disk is still there," said Smith.

"Oh... so we're good?"

"No, no, no, no. Someone must have found it, copied the files and pretend it was never found."

"What? You're sure about that?"

"Yeah, there are signs all over the place. The plant, the desk and curly hair. As clear as the sky."

"Did you just say curly hair?"

"Anyway, I need you to keep MARVIN running now."

"One second," said Britta. "Charles, you heard him. Now stop watching that thing and give me back the laptop."

Smith swore he heard someone got spanked on the other side of the line.

"OK, MARVIN is back on now."

"How much more time does it need to crack it?"

"Eh... exactly fifty minutes."

"Oh..."

00 HOURS 49 MINUTES 01 SECONDS
00 HOURS 49 MINUTES 00 SECONDS
00 HOURS 48 MINUTES 59 SECONDS

Chapter 96

"I'm gonna ask you a stupid question," said Smith, "and I need you to react professionally to it."

"Alright, as long as you don't get on your knees again, I think we'll be good," said Britta.

"Cool. Is there any way we can speed this thing up?"

Smith pointed at the progress bar on Britta's screen. MARVIN estimated that it would take another forty-five minutes and thirty seconds to crack the encryption. Forty-five minutes and twenty-nine seconds. Forty-five minutes and twenty-eight seconds.

"That's indeed a very stupid question," said Charles. "Even I know the servers hosting MARVIN are at Virginia. You can't just pick up a phone and ask the guys there, 'Hey, can I add two million more artificial neurons to the state-owned AI without regression testing?'"

"Actually," said Britta with her eyes fixed on the on-screen text box, "it is possible. MARVIN says there are two parts of passcodes for unlocking the file. One is the 256-bit key that she is brute-forcing at like a homicidal fighting bull. Another one is a user password that she hasn't come around to deal with."

"MARVIN is a she?"

"And a Belgian. That's what she identifies with."

"OK, OK. And if we can help her crack that password, how much time can we save."

"Eh..." said Britta after a few seconds, "around one minute."

"That sounds uncannily coincidental."

"It wouldn't be if you didn't put her on hold."

"So," said Smith in the most unacknowledging way possible, "how long is the password we're talking about here?"

"Erm... she says it is at most twelve characters. And she asks us to leave her alone while she cracks the code. Apparently, we are wasting memory in her politely-ask-users-to-freak-themselves layer."

A moment later, a window was shown on Britta's screen:

Enter the administrator password.

"OK, OK, we got it," said Smith. "We just need to think like a flatee. What would an underachieving, socially ostracized, attention-seeking, willfully ignorant conspiracy theorist use as a password?"

"I got this," shouted Charles and leaned in in front of Britta.

Enter the administrator password.
123456789012
The password is not correct.
Enter the administrator password.

"Charles, do you mind—" said Britta.

"I got another one," said Charles.

    Enter the administrator password.
    Password1234
    The password is not correct.
    Enter the administrator password.

"Charles, maybe we re-group and brainstorm—" said Smith.
"Sorry, I dropped the ball. It should be this one," said Charles.

    Enter the administrator password.
    P@ssword1234
    The password is not correct.
    Try again in 15 minutes.

For a zeptosecond, MARVIN's politely-ask-users-to-freak-themselves layer almost reacted to the situation, but then she thought the password prompt window was kind of doing it for her and aborted the sarcastic-language-processing instructions.

    00 HOURS 43 MINUTES 20 SECONDS
    00 HOURS 43 MINUTES 19 SECONDS
    00 HOURS 43 MINUTES 18 SECONDS

Chapter 97

"Here is the question: what are the favorite words of an average Flater?" said Britta besides the whiteboard, in front of which Mosby just casually walked by. He took a seat in the front and wondered what the occasion was.
"Do your own research!" shouted Charles behind Mosby.
"Good," said Britta and wrote it on the board. "Anything else?"
"*They* cover it up!"
"Alright."
"I don't know, but it doesn't make any sense!"
"Ugh... you aren't wrong."
"Dude, none of those are within twelve characters," said Smith

bitterly, who was still bothered by the fact that Britta was driving the meeting. Not because he was a patriarchal pig who couldn't stand women taking a leadership role. No. He was upset because it should be him using the whiteboard. He loved using it, almost as much as he loved people seeing him use it. Nothing made him feel smarter than drawing lines and scribbling illegible buzz words on a wipeable board. Sometimes he liked to mix things up by pinning articles and pictures on a cork board and linking them with red threads like he was doing a link analysis trope in procedural drama.

While the fate of Global Lie and his own job hanged in the balance, Smith couldn't think of anything but the board.

The board is mine. The board is mine!

The alarm of Britta's phone went off, reminding everyone the fifteen minutes was up.

"Alright," said Britta and put down the marker, "thank you for the contribution. And by 'you,' I mean Charles. Now we have more than forty words divided into six categories."

She took a step away from the board and began to wonder what was the point of the exercise.

<u>Category</u>	<u>Flatglish</u>
The Big 4	Diffraction
	Refraction
	Perspective
	Visibility
More on perspective	Angular perspective
	Curvilinear perspective
	Illusional perspective
	Receding perspective
	Compression of perspective
	Foreshortening
	Non-linear foreshortening
	Parabolic foreshortening
	Rotational foreshortening
	Shift foreshortening

Something with the atmos

Atmospheric attenuation
Atmospheric blocking
Atmospheric convection
Atmospheric eclipsing
Atmospheric inversion
Atmospheric opacity
Atmospheric tide
Atmospheric window

It ends with *-ion so it must be legit*

Angular resolution
Circle of confusion
Collimation
Diminution
Fitzgerald-Lorentz contraction
Iso-centric position
Light attenuation
Magnetic declination
Planar projection
Rayleigh criterion
Specular reflection

Who is this Airy?

Airy's diffraction
Airy disk/dot/line/plane
Airy's (vanishing) points

Now they're just making things up

Aether band
Fake waves
Firmament
Heaven's energy
Horizon blockage
Multilayered water walls
Opaque moisture deck
Personal atmospheric dome
Personal horizon
Ray erosion
Trial by God
Trick by Satan

"We need a pattern or something," Britta muttered to herself.

"I know, I know,'" said Charles and ran up to the laptop. "The flatees love this word."

> Enter the administrator password.
> **Perspective**
> The password is not correct.
> Enter the administrator password.

"Charles, I need you to step away from the laptop," said Britta.

"Maybe they didn't capitalize it," said Charles to himself.

"No, at least try another word for flat's sake!"

"OK."

> Enter the administrator password.
> **Atmosphere**
> The password is not correct.
> Enter the administrator password.

"Damn, I thought it must be it."

"Maybe it isn't a word on the board," said Smith casually while making a move to the whiteboard.

"Right," said Charles with his eyes wide open, staring at the words that were unnecessarily spelt in full. "I can see it now. There is a pattern. All of those words have one thing in common."

"Great," said Britta like she was talking to a bare-foot man at the edge of a building, whose shoes had successfully killed two less suicidal pedestrians, "why don't you share with the group first and then we workshop it—"

> Enter the administrator password.
> **Technobabble**
> The password is not correct.
> Try again in 15 minutes.

"... or not."

As a part of Britta died inside, Smith rose and snatched the marker from her.

Hell yeah, he thought, *so what's next?*

00 HOURS 27 MINUTES 00 SECONDS
00 HOURS 26 MINUTES 59 SECONDS
00 HOURS 26 MINUTES 58 SECONDS

Chapter 98

"... annnnnd done," said Smith. "You see what I did there?"

"Yeah," said Britta, "I was watching it the whole time."

"And?"

"I've no frigging idea how this weird pyramid is gonna crack the code."

"I'm trying to show you the flatees use reverse logical engineering."

"Smith, we talked about this. You can't keep coining new terms and expect us to beg you for explanation."

"Com'on, look at this," said Smith and pointed at the top of the pyramid. "This is their hypothesis. 'The Earth is flat.' THE hypothesis.

"The three boxes on the second layer – sorry for the writing, by the way – represent the basic elements of flatees' tenets. No ball. No rotation. No gravity. And then these arrows—"

"Oh geez, what is happening with those arrows?" asked Charles, whose hands were tied behind his chair.

"They follow an average flatee's reasoning process. Two propositions are immediately derived from the three basic elements. Here, you have the word 'science' underlined twice and crossed. Basically, all the observations that confirm a spherical Earth since Aristotle are wrong. And then you have this strawman with a bubble over his head, which denotes NASA lying."

"Oh..." Britta had thought it was a flater doing drugs.

"Actually," said Smith and picked up the marker again, "I should add several more strawmen here, because there is more than one space agency in the world. So here you go, collusion among countries with independent capability to launch satellites.

"Extended from the 'science' and strawmen there are another set of corollaries. On the fourth layer you have, first, these strawmen with glasses. They are basically everyone whose jobs operate on the premises that gravity is real and the Earth is a sphere with a radius of six thousand and four hundred kilometers. I put them all in a circle to show that they are 'in it.' Clever, right?"

"Ugh huh, ugh huh." It finally hit Britta that those circles were spectacles.

"Second, this bunch of icons represent all the devices out there that could be used to independently prove or refute the hypothesis. Electronic scales, compasses, camera lens, speedometers, smart phones, telescopes, you name it. They are all rigged."

"Alright, alright." Britta stole a glance at the display behind Smith. Twelve minutes left. A part of her thought she should care, but it couldn't locate the part that usually did the caring.

"Third, this book-shaped thing next to a cross. It is the source of information that could have explained away all the so-called holes in the Global Lie. Science textbooks, photos from space, ISS streaming, flat-Earth debunking YouTube channels, flat-Earth debunking websites, flat-Earth debunking podcasts, flat-Earth debunking subreddit. Good work on them, by the way," Smith winked at Charles. "All of them are, as far as flatees are concerned, part of the deception."

"Not that I care anymore," said Britta, "fifteen minutes is up. We need to make the last three guesses. Three perfectly random guesses."

"They are not gonna be random," said Smith. "You are not hearing me."

"I shouldn't be."

"I am telling you how a flatee truly thinks. Just sit tight and listen. Where were we? OK, the thing about fake news and misinformation. Essentially, everything that goes contrary to the hypothesis is false by default.

"Forth, here is another bunch of strawmen. I know it's hard to tell but they are journalists, students, commentators, tourists, pilots, circumnavigators, or basically anyone who ever writes, posts, blogs, speaks about proof of a spinning spherical Earth, like the photos taken on hot-air balloons, the slightly curved horizon seen on planes, star trail time-lapse videos, constellation tracing Apps, footage of Antarctica. Some of these people are fabricated by the institutions in the know. Some of them do exist and are outside of the institutions, but are either delusional or stupid. I don't know how to draw it all out, so I am narrating for your benefits."

"Then why did you draw it in the first place?" Britta just noticed against her will that they had less than ten minutes left.

"Leave it to the Q&A, Britta. Leave it to the Q&A. We will circle back to that.

"And then we have these arrows pointing towards those four corollaries. These are the things that support the corollaries. Here, you have 'definition,' like by definition gravity is just a theory, or the horizon is horizontal, or the English word 'planet' is derived from the Latin word 'planum,' which means a plain or level ground."

Britta just, in her words, ran out of flats to give.

"Next to it," said Smith as the timer countdown came to the last nine minutes, "you have Antarctic Treaty. You have *Them*. Then you have God; should I specify which religion or just make it plural? Anyway, then you have Hollywood."

"What is it supposed to mean? I'm not following," said Charles.

"You *were* following?" asked Britta.

"There is a thing called predictive programming," answered Smith with a glee, "like *Black Mirror* predicted Donald Trump's presidency because it was part of the voter manipulation tactics. *The Simpsons* is produced to soften the audience with mass atrocities. And shows that ridicule flat Earth are interpreted as a ploy to suppress flat Earthers."

"I'm still not following it."

"It doesn't matter. The flatees think Hollywood is in it anyway, because there are fewer historical movies about NASA than Sci-Fi movies that take place in space."

"What?"

"Regardless, it is just part of the long train of thoughts inside a basic flatee's head. You also have 'Sun as a flashlight,' 'refraction,' 'perspective,' 'invisible Moon,' 'no satellites in space,' 'White Alice doing satellite things,' 'White Alice outside of the U.S.'"

"We got the idea. We had forty other similar phrases on the board that you wiped out," said Britta when there was seven minutes left on the clock.

"Alright, alright," said Smith and took a step away from the whiteboard to admire his own work. "All these ideas that support the corollaries derived from the propositions directly inferred from the three elements of the hypothesis have one thing in common. They are all," he drew a few arrows from the bottom of the pyramid to the top of it, "supported by the hypothesis. Earth. Is. Flat.

"See, the flatees are right on the money not because they have any special insight that we don't have, but because they love their hypothesis."

"And because the Earth in our universe happens not to be a spinning ball," added Britta.

"We are gonna ignore that part," said Smith as he walked up to Britta's laptop. With the charm and confidence of all flat Earthers combined, he made a few keystrokes.

> Enter the administrator password.
> **Earthisflat**
> The password is not correct.
> Enter the administrator password.

"I'm shocked," said Britta calmly, still with no supply of flats to give.

"Er... I see what goes wrong," said Smith with the same level of charm and confidence, "the flatees recently are changing their talking points. Instead of positively saying 'The Earth is flat,' which invites as many questions as saying 'The Earth is a donut,' they are now more inclined to say 'The Earth is not a ball' and then ask you to do some research. Now all they need to do is to poke holes at things they would have found an explanation simpler than 'millions of people huddle together to lie about the shape of Earth' should they spend another five minutes on the research they have horizontally delegated to their interlocuters."

"Whatever," said Britta, who really couldn't give a flat

> Enter the administrator password.
> **EarthNotBall**
> The password is not correct.
> Enter the administrator password.

"Weird," said Smith, "any chance your computer is broken?"

"Maybe we try again but replace the *a* with a symbol," said Charles and reached for the laptop. No one knew how he had freed himself, but his hands were now back in the game.

Seeing Charles reach for the laptop again, Britta felt a spark in her head and sprang from her seat.

"*No!*" she said and slapped on Charles' wrist. "Hell no. Don't you dare touch the keyboard *again!*"

Britta closed her eyes and took a deep breath. She could feel the part that had died inside her had come back to life. As she slowly reopened the eyes, the display on the opposite wall came into view.

> 00 HOURS 04 MINUTES 00 SECONDS
> 00 HOURS 03 MINUTES 59 SECONDS
> 00 HOURS 03 MINUTES 58 SECONDS

"We're on the wrong track," she said with a newfound bunch of flats to give. "We have been treating the flaters like another species of animal, but what if we are wrong? We have tried too hard to get inside their heads, and forgotten how similar they are to us. They may be a bunch of losers frustrated by the reality, but aren't we the same?

"They may have a weird standard for weighing facts and evidence. But so do we. Occasionally, we base our beliefs not on what is said but on who says it, or on how well it reconciles with our existing world view."

"Except that the odd we take is usually better," said Charles.

"And," added Britta without losing a beat, "flaters may be pathetically yearning for attention, but let's face it: Who isn't? Publicly defending flat Earth ideas is just another way of posting a cleavage on social media.”

“I would rather they just post their cleavages,” said Smith.

“Be careful what you wish for,” said Britta. “My point is, we shouldn’t be thinking, ‘What password would a flater choose?’ Instead, we should ask, ‘What password an ordinarily normal human being with average intellect would typically choose?’”

Neither Charles nor Smith said anything. They thought it was a rhetorical question.

Before they realized it wasn’t, a text box prompted up on Britta’s laptop.

“It’s MARVIN,” said Britta. “She is about to crack the 256-bit key in sixty seconds. As soon as we input the correct password, she will replace ‘The Proof’ with the ‘Two Guys One Cup’ video I made.”

```
00 HOURS 01 MINUTES 03 SECONDS
00 HOURS 01 MINUTES 02 SECONDS
00 HOURS 01 MINUTES 01 SECONDS
```

“Don’t freak out, it’s gonna be OK,” Smith said the same thing people say when they know things are not going to be OK. “Mosby, what password would you normally choose?”

“Er... my name with my birthday,” said Mosby, who was still wondering what the whiteboard was about, “or the date that I created the password.”

“OK, that’s what most people do, but that’s an admin password. It won’t be that personal,” said Britta.

“Then what would you do, Mosby?” asked Charles. “How would you choose a password that is supposed to be shared among a group of administrators.”

“One, two, three, four, five, six, seven, eight, before or after the word ‘password,’ with a few letters changed to symbols.”

“Damn, that’s what I tried,” said Charles. “Maybe—”

“No, you are not touching the keyboard,” said Britta. “By the way, we have twenty seconds left.”

“How would you make sure the password can be remembered?” asked Smith.

“I usually write it down.”

"So do I, but what if you can't write it down?"

"I'll record it with a voice memo."

"Strike all the recording devices. What else?"

"*Ten seconds*," said Britta.

"Er...," said Mosby with the calm of a stoic philosopher, "then I would make sure the security questions or password hints are damn good."

"*We don't have any of those things!*" said Britta, now with a full stock of flats to give. "*Five seconds!*"

In slow motion, Smith watched the timer refreshed.

00 HOURS 00 MINUTES 05 SECONDS
00 HOURS 00 MINUTES 04 SECONDS

That was a depressing sight, so instinctively Smith looked away and found something else to stare at. Something less bleak than the prospect of losing his source of alimony funding. For no particular reason, he looked at a corner of the meeting table. It made him feel better.

In parallel, Britta saw a message slowly materialize on the screen. It was MARVIN telling them that the decoding was completed and asking them in an otherwise irritated but overall emotionless tone to input the user password. She didn't have time for more brainstorm, so she put herself in the shoes of anyone who ever opened a web service and then was asked to set a password.

00 HOURS 00 MINUTES 03 SECONDS

Smith was content to just stare at a random table corner for another three seconds, but then something else crept into his vision. It was a black, rectangular object. On its side there appeared to be some words.

While Smith tried to read those words, Britta got out from that pair of shoes and got an idea in exchange.

The password is, she thought, *Password1234.*

00 HOURS 00 MINUTES 02 SECONDS

It was then she remembered Charles had tried that combination. She wondered why Mosby didn't write it on the whiteboard to remind people not to repeat the incorrect passwords. She thought of the password hint nonsense that came out of Mosby's windpipe. She continued to muse while staring at the password prompt.

At the exact same moment, the words on the black, rectangular object finally came into focus. Smith could recognize it was a very big prime number. He didn't, of course, divide it by a bunch of prime numbers to figure out it was a prime. He knew it because it was the code he wrote down eight months ago when MARVIN cracked open Gina's hard disk. He wondered why whoever had stolen the disk had bothered to change the encryption key and added a user password on it.

00 HOURS 00 MINUTES 01 SECONDS

Ahhhh, Britta had another epiphany, *the password is P@ssword1234. Oh, no, Charles tried that as well. It says here the password is incorrect. Wait, it doesn't. It really doesn't.*

As the corner of his eyes caught that it was the final second, Smith told himself again that everything was going to be OK. He reminded himself that the file might not be "The Proof." In fact, now that he gave more thought to it, it seemed a lot of things could explain the slightly relocated plant, the butt-shaped dust print on desk and the suspiciously curly hair on carpet. All it took was a X'mas party and two mildly drunk NASA employees.

Having his mind changed again about the whole "The Proof" situation, Smith turned around and was going to tell everyone that everything would be really, really OK. It was then he noticed Britta had put her hands in the air, screaming at the computer screen.

Enter the administrator password.
not correct.
Welcome back.

Chapter 99

"You…" said Smith, "you cracked the code?"

"One sec," said Britta while she did whatever she had to do on the keyboard to pull out the traffic log. "Yes, and MARVIN replaced the file before anyone could access it. She has also locked down this webpage so that no one could further edit the file. It's over. And, in a few minutes, a lot of netizens will get very confused and aroused by the 'Two Guys One Cup' video they just downloaded."

"Er, actually," said Smith, "I had something about the file that I wanted to say before you cracked its encryption."

"Hold on," said Britta and pointed at a line of log file. "Look at here. Something is wrong."

The three men looked at the screen and acted like they understood what was happening. They patiently waited for Britta to understand that they didn't.

"The encryption key and password we entered," said she, "were mirrored to another location."

"Ugh huh," said the three men like someone who was just diagnosed with hippopotomonstrosesquipedaliophobia, which, according to the legend, was often intentionally misspelled as hippopotomonstrosesquippedaliophobia in order to exacerbate the patient's fear of long words.

After a while, Britta cared to elaborate.

"That means someone had copied the strings of encryption key and password we entered."

"Oh, that may be related to the thing I was going to say," said Smith. "Can you quickly open the file that was replaced?"

Chapter 100

"Look at what they did to this place," said Winston as he picked up the door knob. "A will be sooo pissed."

"Whatever," said agent B and opened the door. "The lease ends today and he said goodbye to the rental bond long time ago when he punched through that wall."

She was too tired to explain how high someone had to be in order to punch a hole in his own bedroom. She was still coping with the jetlag. While she looked for a charger to start her laptop, Chandler made the table and Ohi went to fetch some champagne glasses.

"You're sure we don't need to wait for A?" asked Winston.

"Nah, it's alright," said agent B when her computer screen came to life. "God knows what time he will be done packing. Plus, I'm sure he already celebrated when we were on the plane. Look at that new hole over there."

Having poured herself a glass of champagne, she returned to the couch and re-read the article agent A forwarded to her a few hours ago.

Leak of NASA emails: You have been bamboozled

For as long as we can remember, we have been told that one plus one is two and the Earth is a sphere, but a recent email leak of NASA reveals that the space agency has been covering up the true shape of Earth for more than six decades.

The twelve million archived emails and attachments show that NASA has a dedicated department, called Rounding Operations or simply Round Ops, to tamper with basically everything that would otherwise reveal the Global Lie. Detailed operation plans and legal forms waiving the Round Ops agents of legal liabilities have been mined from the leaked emails. Following the leak, hundreds of consumers have reportedly filed charges against NASA for misleading them about the destination of their Antarctica cruise trips.

The data dump also shows that the first image of "Cosmic Cliffs" from James Webb Space Telescope, which supposedly captures the giant, gaseous, brownish edge of a remote nebula, is actually a composite of several digitally enhanced mugshots of spilled coffee. Multiple interest groups have criticized NASA's waste of beverage, and no one has claimed responsibility for the spillage.

Stay tuned as mining of the leaked documents continues.

How did that happen?

NASA has refused to comment on the leak, but security experts who have studied that tape of archived emails confirm that it is protected with military grade encryption and the email domain belongs to NASA. They speculate that it is a backup tape stolen by insiders, possibly someone senior enough to have access to both the administrator password and encryption key.

Chapter 101

"This is your last day too?" asked Mosby as he pretended to review the contents in the paper box.

"I ain't fired," said Alex the janitor. "I resigned this morning."

"Oh, mind if I ask where you are going?"

"Not sure yet. I will return to my mom's basement and figure that out. Maybe I will write a memoir or something."

"Good luck with that," said Mosby and handed the box back. "I've a feeling a lot of people are gonna start doing it today."

Following the stream of former Round Ops agents before him, Alex picked up the box and headed for the building's exit. Before he made it through the doorway, he heard a man yelling from behind.

"You don't have to manhandle me," shouted the Deputy Director of NASA, whose legs were flailing midair. "I said I would leave peacefully."

"We can't take that risk," said Mosby apologetically, "after we caught you burning down the HR office. You should have taken it out on Admin and none of us would blink an eye."

"Look, I'm sorry for that Molotov cocktail. Please don't take it personally. It just doesn't make sense to fire me. You and I both know that I add precisely zero value to this organization. How can I be held responsible for anything that goes wrong?"

Before Mosby could say anything to that thought-provoking question, the security had carried Smith to the door.

"Mr. Robin," said Alex as if he just ran into a colleague leaving for the day, "can I ask you a question?"

"Well," said Smith as if he was just leaving for the day, "don't ask me why the emails were leaked. I have no part in it."

"I know. I mean, I believe you. I just wanted to ask about the video called 'The Proof.' I heard you mention it in the office several times. Is it still with you?"

"You mean the ultimate scientific proof of the shape of our Earth, featuring a geocentric model that could explain every natural phenomenon without resorting to the spinning ball model?"

"Yes."

"A proof that was so elegant and comprehensive that it leaves no ambiguity, no margin of error, no room for spinning, and no space for reinterpretation?"

"Exactly."

"Oh..."

Smith looked up and around to see which direction his office was. It was more difficult than he thought, so he recalled the typical route he took to the office each morning. After a while, his gaze was fixed at the North-West corner.

Alex was going to say something, but then Smith's head moved abruptly again. As if following a trajectory, his gaze moved down from the lobby's ceiling to the traffic on Hidden Figures Way.

"I threw it out of the window," Smith said. "Just kidding. Actually, I threw it *through* the window when they told me I was fired. With some luck, it might have turned into the exact shape as our planet."

Epilogue

Agent F had been waiting in the lobby for four hours, and now he could recite the cable news by heart.

The news cycle would begin with another breaking news of the congressional hearing of former NASA Administrator, who couldn't understand the questions half of the time and was failed by her memory the other half. Several commentators would remark on how surprising it was for the hearing to have dragged on for five years and yet no one understood why NASA took the trouble to fake a spherical Earth.

Another political news was about the education reform. Four years after flat-earthism, conventional astronomy and astrology were given equal teaching time in public schools, the state of Mississippi today permitted intelligent design to be taught in public school science classes along with evolution and simulation-ism. This decision angered thousands of simulationists, who considered intelligent design a mockery of their belief in simulation reality. Riots had broken out across the country.

The business segment would cover the first commercial submarine trip to Mariana Trench. The new CEO of DeepX, formerly known as SpaceX, said she was very excited for the company to meet the first bond payment since its strategic bankruptcy. One of the passengers, who had also been on the first "spaceflight" to ISS years ago, remarked that travelling thirty-six thousand feet deep in the ocean was as adventurous and eventful as a trip to the lunar orbit, minus the zero-gravity experience.

Having jokingly stated that everyone now knew gravity was zero, the news anchor reported on the strong performance of NASA stock this morning, following the announcement that the former space agency would launch its fourth-generation holographic smart phones in fall.

In the sports segment, several NBA stars had come out and professed their belief in a ball Earth. It was followed by a panel discussion on the Ball Earth Movement. Critiques of the movement speculated that the so-called Globers were merely attention whores, while commentators from the other camp stated they were legitimate skeptics who symbolized distrust in institutions since the Space-gate scandal. Pro-Globers further argued that the scandal only suggested the Earth might not be a ball, but didn't prove its shape one way or the other.

The same old crap, thought agent F as his consciousness drifted away.

* * *

"Sir, wake up," said the receptionist to agent F. "Mr. Snow is ready to meet you now. Please follow me."

Half a minute later, agent F came into Snow's office. A very typical office with lots of unnecessary space and over-the-top decorations whose sole purpose was to impress its visitors.

"You are Franklin, right?" said Snow as he put his feet back on the desk. His feet were actually on the desk five seconds ago, but he believed he had to re-do the routine every time someone came into his office.

"Close, just Frank."

"Oopsie. Anyway, I heard you got a movie script for me?"

"Yes, this one is 100% based on real events that I have researched for close to a decade. It is about the Space-gate."

"Dude, you can't oversell me like that. How could you have done ten years of research for something that hadn't happened half of the time."

Snow thought maybe he needed a new power pose to command more respect, so he switched his legs on the table.

"Sir, I worked for *Them*," said Frank. "Specifically, I spied on flat Earth activists. And this is the story I developed based on first-hand research."

Snow felt the power-pose thing he had learnt from *Fake it then you won't have to make it* was working.

"Alright, alright, tell me more. What's the theme?"

"The theme?"

"Yes, the theme of the movie."

"Oh, er... the theme is," said Frank as his gaze wandered around the shelf of books behind the producer. It rested on one of those written by Smith Robin.

"Bullshit."

"Excuse me."

"The theme of the movie is about bullshit. Not just the ball Earth versus flat Earth BS. And not just conspiracy theories in general. It also touches upon the bullshit in business, in religion, in the news, in public discourse. Eeeeeverything."

"OK, OK," said Snow and leaned back. He felt very powerful now. "This sounds like something Winston Kanshū would be happy to shoot. He told me he was tired of the *Plane* series and wanted something less commercial."

"I assure you this one is very, very, very not commercial."

"Great! Tell me about the characters."

"There are two protagonists. One of them works at NASA. We can call him the NASA guy. He was a consultant before joining NASA and he is occasionally, but not always, aware of how BS his work is."

"So he is an average white collar American. Very relatable. Tell me about the other one."

"He is an award-winning movie director who will drive the story through the conference arch, the edge-of-world arch and the final whatever you call it arch. He discovers evidence of flat Earth by accident, runs for the president of a flat Earth social club, and later joins a flat Earth paramilitary—"

"Wait, wait, wait," said Snow and put his feet down. "Why would an accomplished director be interested in leading a flat Earth social club? And why would he join that paramilitary?"

"Because that's what I wrote here."

"I got that. But, but why?"

"Because I want him to."

"Sure, sure, sure. But why?"

"Because then the rest of the movie can happen."

"Oh, fair enough," Snow switched to another power pose by putting his hands on the waist. "Please continue. Will this director guy have any character development?"

"I don't understand what you're talking about."

"Any character traits he has?"

"Seriously, sir, I need you to speak English. But if you are curious of what he has, he does have two sidekicks. One Japanese valet and one British pilot."

"Interesting," Snow said with a sparkle in his eyes. "Tell me about them."

"I just did, sir."

"Alright."

Snow started picturing what the movie poster would look like in his head. So far he got four dudes staring at the camera like they were worried about something, as in basically all movie posters in existence.

"It seems there are lots of men on this show. Do you have anyone with more X chromosomes?"

"I do," said Frank and flipped through a few pages of his scripts. "We have this fat lady who will help the director guy and do a lot of expositions. And then there is this hot scientist who discovers the true shape of Earth."

"Tell me about this scientist."

"She is smart, rebellious, and physically attractive."

"She doesn't sound like the other bland characters of yours. Is she the number three of the show?"

"Er... nope."

"No?"

"No, but definitely in the top fifteen. She will have a serious accident in the middle of the story."

"Oh my god, is she alright?"

"Yes, she won't die. She will just fall into a coma."

"And she will wake up at certain point?"

"No, she won't"

"Why not?"

"Because I can't figure out how to relevantly put her character back into the second halve of the story without her losing all her memories about 'The Proof.'"

"I find this reason," said Snow with a frown, "very good. But will the female audience hate it? It's like you have objectified this woman by turning her into a plot device."

"Sir, look at it this way. A lot of the characters in this movie believe in crackpot conspiracy theories, so making only the minority of them female sends a subtle message that men are dumb."

For a moment, Snow's face couldn't decide what expression to have. It finally settled with a grin below a frown.

"I like the subtle lip service," he said, "but why do you have this fat flat Earth lady though? It seems to send a mixed message. Some movie goers, who probably never bother to watch your whole gig, will take your fat, slash, overweight, slash, obese character to Twitter and whip you for your misogyny and fat shaming."

"How about this? I squeeze some jokes in her to criticize far right ideologies. Would it work?"

"Oh, it will. The virtue signal beacons will be very pleased with that."

"Great, consider it done."

Feeling for the first time that this movie was marketable, Snow reached for the scripts in Frank's hands and started reading it.

"Frankie, I feel like your cast is not diverse enough. Our investors would like more ethnic."

"What do you mean? I already have a cast of Americans, Western Europeans, Eastern Europeans and Asians. Around half of them can be considered mentally challenged. And we already went through the gender thing. What more diversity do you need?"

"We need more color."

"You mean," Frank paused and scrambled for the right word, "you want a black token?"

"We are not allowed to say it out loud," hissed Snow, "but yes, we do."

"It has been taken care of. The NASA guy, he is black."

"He is? It's never mentioned in the scripts."

"I didn't think it matters."

"Maybe you should give him another last name, like Clifford."

Frank thought about it for a second. He didn't hate that idea; he just hated the idea of replacing all the last names.

"Or," he said another second later, "we keep things as they are to subvert the expectation."

"Oh, I like it. It's like every time someone sees my last name and automatically assumes I'm a white dude. But now that the main guy is black, we need to be careful with our marketing strategy."

"What do you mean?"

"We can't put him in the Russian version of our movie poster."

"Oh, I totally see what you mean. We need to be sensitive to people's outright racism nowadays."

"Exactly. Speaking of sensitivity," Snow said and took another look at the scripts, "a lot of the jokes in your scripts are critical of the American culture."

"Indeed."

"Are you an American?"

"Er… sorry, I don't see how it is relevant."

"If you are, then depending on whom you ask, making fun of our people can be either patriotic or unamerican. But if you are not, then you are plainly xenophobic or simply anti-American. I need to get this straight, are you associated with any terrorist organization?"

"Sir, I am not."

"You are not an American or you are not a terrorist?"

"Neither of them, sir. I come from the-country-you-can't-speak-ill-of. And the reasons why I make most of the jokes about Americans are, first, it's easy to make fun of you because you guys are really freaked up. And second, because your country has freedom of speech. Mine doesn't. I would get into serious trouble if I poke fun at it. My people have a very fragile heart."

"Oh, do you come from the same place as the TYDF guy?"

"I can neither confirm nor deny that statement."

"Fair enough. Another question – I don't understand the ending. Why do you have a guy trash-talking about the whole movie with another guy? People are gonna think it's a rip-off from Screen Rant Pitch Meetings. Doesn't your movie have enough dialogue already?"

"I figured this is a way to make it more self-aware, you know, so that people will take the movie seriously."

"Smart move! I thought you were taking a meta-crap on your own movie so that people would forgive the poor writing."

"Oh…" said Frank with his eyes wide open, "this is the nicest thing anyone has said to me. Thank you."

The producer dropped the power pose and read the script for another hour while Frank pointlessly admired the pointlessly spacious office.

"OK, I'm done," said Snow finally. "I don't really have much comment on the plot, but got a question about this whole 'The Proof' thing. Your script seems vague about the true shape of the Earth. Is it really not a ball?"

"No, sir. It isn't."

"So it's flat."

"Some part of it is."

"Is it a disk, a cube, a tree, a turtle, or, as one of the dick jokes not so implicitly implies, a penis?"

"No, sir. It is not. It is something only the hot scientist has figured out."

"Hm...," Snow looked quite disappointed, "and it's in the 'The Proof' thing?"

"Yes, it is."

"You said your story is based on real events, so do you have that thing? 'The Proof.'"

"Yes, I do," said Frank and pulled an object of unearthly shape from his backpack. "It is the hard drive storing the sole copy of 'The Proof.' Long story short, I picked this up from the street and have spent five years to recover everything from this piece of crap."

"Fantastic. So why don't you elaborate on this proof in the whole movie? Is it some sort of MacGuffin? Like some sort of plot device that the characters enthusiastically pursue but actually doesn't matter? Oh, oh, oh, are you trying to make a point that the true shape of the Earth never actually matters, because most people just get by their lives without thinking about it and only those desperate attention-seeking conspiracy theorists would make it a big deal?"

"Valid point, sir," said Frank and gave the producer a round of dry applause, "you are very perceptive."

"I know I'm."

"But no. I just wanted to reserve some materials for the sequel."

"Holy cow, there is a sequel for this thing?"

"Of course. Just like every Hollywood movie that was ever produced, there will be a sequel, in at most seventy years."

Frank put another pile of A4 papers on Snow's desk. Similar to its prequel, this one was also full of banters and expositions.

"Cool," said Snow, "but I don't want to wait that long to learn about this thing. Can you just spill the beans now?"

"Now? As in, now?"

"Surely."

"You want to know the truth, the whole truth and nothing but the truth?"

"Yes."

"Including the parts how the hot scientist figures everything out and tests her Earth model against earthshine, diurnal motion, stellar parallax, annual motion of stars, relative position of the Sun, constant size of Moon and Sun throughout the day, change in Orion constellation's angle according to observer's latitude, mid-night sun at poles during summer, same face of Moon being observed everywhere on Earth, and shadow of mountain casted on cloud before sunrise or after sunset? You want to know how her model is compatible with all of these things without the Earth being a spinning ball?"

"Er... maybe just the part about the true shape of Earth."

"That's good enough for you?"

"Yes, please tell."

"Alright, here we go."

"Hit me."

"According to the hot scientist," said Frank solemnly, "who has the greatest mind in human history to truly discern the true shape of Earth and unbiasedly developed a geocentric model that can explain all the crap I just mentioned..."

"Come on."

"The true shape of the Earth..."

"Ugh huh."

"... which by the way is not just a speculation..."

"That's the stuff."

"... and has no ambiguity..."

"Cool."

"... no margin of error..."

"Good stuff."

"... no room for spinning..."

"I'm so excited."

"... and no space for reinterpretation..."

"Come on, spit it out."

"... it is..."

[THIS PAGE INTENTIONALLY AND IRRESPONSIBLY LEFT BLANK]

ACKNOWLEDGEMENT

I would like to thank everyone who has taken the trouble to read through this whole book or just jumped ahead to this page for no particular reason. You are equally awesome.

A special thank-you to my wife, Yen, for all her unconditional love and support. She is one of the only two persons who suffer from the severe illusion that I can write, and she never questions why I feel the need to write a book to cope with my midlife crisis. I hope someday I will get around to have this book translated so that it won't be too taxing for her to read it through, which I know as a fact that she still hasn't.

Finally, a big shoutout to the redditors on *r/flatearth*, whose relentless trolling inspired this book.